Winslow Anderson

Mineral Springs and Health Resorts of California

with a complete chemical analysis of every important mineral water in the world - a

prize essay - annual prize of the Medical Society of the State of California, awarded

April 20, 1889

Winslow Anderson

Mineral Springs and Health Resorts of California
*with a complete chemical analysis of every important mineral water in the world - a prize
essay - annual prize of the Medical Society of the State of California, awarded April 20, 1889*

ISBN/EAN: 9783337401153

Printed in Europe, USA, Canada, Australia, Japan

Cover: Foto ©Andreas Hilbeck / pixelio.de

More available books at **www.hansebooks.com**

MINERAL SPRINGS

AND

HEALTH RESORTS OF CALIFORNIA

WITH A

COMPLETE CHEMICAL ANALYSIS

OF

EVERY IMPORTANT MINERAL WATER
IN THE WORLD

— ——

𝕴𝖑𝖑𝖚𝖘𝖙𝖗𝖆𝖙𝖊𝖉

A PRIZE ESSAY

ANNUAL PRIZE OF THE MEDICAL SOCIETY OF THE STATE OF
CALIFORNIA, AWARDED APRIL 20, 1889

BY

WINSLOW ANDERSON, M. D.

Joint Editor and Publisher of the PACIFIC MEDICAL JOURNAL

Asst. Chair Medical Chemistry and Materia Medica, and Teacher of Chemistry in the Laboratories of the University of
California in the Medical and Dental Departments.
Active Member of the American Medical Association, and of the Medical Society of the State of California.
Active Member of the San Francisco County Medical Society, and of the College of Pharmacy and Pharmaceutical Society.
Secretary and Member of the Alumni Association of the Medical Department of the University of California.
Member of the Board of Medical Examiners for the State of California.
Member of the National Educational Association.
Analytical Chemist to the Coroner of the city of San Francisco.
Author of
"Desiccated Human Remains;" "Adulterations in Food Products;" "Western Mummies;"
"Mortality in Diphtheria;" Morphio-Mania, Etc., Etc."

SAN FRANCISCO
THE BANCROFT COMPANY
1890

———

PRICE $1.50
Special rates to Spring owners

TO THE

Faculty

OF THE

MEDICAL DEPARTMENT

OF THE

University of California

THIS LITTLE VOLUME IS RESPECTFULLY INSCRIBED

AS A SINCERE, THOUGH INADEQUATE, TOKEN OF ESTEEM FOR THEIR EMINENCE AS

Teachers and Professional

GENTLEMEN, AND AS AN ACKNOWLEDGMENT OF GRATITUDE FOR

THEIR FRIENDSHIP DURING MY EARLY PROFESSIONAL

CAREER, BY THEIR FRIEND

The Author

The author desires to acknowledge his obligations to the following authorities:

HOMER, PLINY, TACITUS	PROF. LE CONTE
PROF. WM. IRELAND, JR.	PROF. J. D. WHITNEY
PROF. EDW. EVERETT HALE	PROF. H. G. HANKS
PROF. W. F. McNUTT	U. S. DISPENASORY, 1880
PROF. WOOD	PROF. BARTHOLOW
PROF. HATCH	DR. BENNETT
DR. McCALL ANDERSON	DR. ROBERTS
PROF. LAVOISIER	PROF. SEGUIN
DR. RABATEAU	PROF. DA COSTA
PROF. FLINT	DR. SAPPEY
DR. TASSE	DR. SCHARLING
DR. SADTLER	DR. POKROWSKY
PROF. VUPIAN	DR. MOREAU
DR. SIGISMUND SUTRO	DR. BRUNTON
MR. E. McD. JOHNSTONE	DR. BEINSWANGER
MAJ. BEN C. TRUMAN	MR. EDWARD E. EITEL
	DR. WALTON

And many daily, weekly and monthly journals.

THE GOLDEN WEST

CALIFORNIA

The old Pacific harshly calls to Mendocino's shore,
But sighs at Santa Barbara's feet his love-song evermore;
The giant redwoods greeting send to orange, fig and lime,
And Siskiyou holds out a cup for wine of Anaheim.

Proud Shasta's snow-crowned head looks out to St. Helena's base,
Where Napa's vine-wrouth glory smiles in fair Sonoma's face,
Mt. Hamilton reads reverently the mysteries of the skies,
Where San Jose's wide valley-sweep in fruited richness lies.

Across the San Joaquin's broad reach of vines and waving wheat
The old Sierras pour their gold to San Diego's feet;
And northern pine and southern palm woo sea-winds from the west,
While over all a spirit broods of romance and unrest.

The rose entwines the orange tree, the sea-winds rock the pines,
And wheat sheaves lift their golden heads amid the clustering vines;
The latest glow of sunset still unfolds them evermore,
While strength and beauty stand hand-clasped upon the Western
                                                    [shore.

Carrie Stevens Walter.

PREFACE

Several years ago while visiting some of the prominent mineral springs and health resorts in this State the author satisfied himself that California possessed as valuable mineral springs as could be found anywhere in the world, and all that is needed to make them as serviceable in the restoration and maintenance of health as their famous sister springs in the East and in Europe is their further development, their chemical analysis, and the scientific administration and application of their waters.

In Europe Balneotherapy and the scientific internal administration of mineral waters have been investigated for centuries, and have proved of great benefit in the alleviation and eradication of many of the most chronic and almost intractable diseases, such as—The many chronic articular disorders, rheumatism, rheumatic arthritis, synovitis, gout, indigestion, dyspepsia, torpidity of the liver, and intestinal tract, glandular enlargement, renal affections, Bright's disease, etc., irritation and inflammation in the bladder, brickdust deposit, calculus or stone in the bladder, diabetes, blood glandular diseases, scrofulous, syphilitic and cutaneous contaminations, etc., etc.

Having obtained analyses of every European and American spring of any note, the author commenced the task of analyzing the California waters and comparing the results. For several years he has been carying on his investigations, making a great many original analyses and several supplementary ones, and he presents in the following pages the results of his labors.

It will be observed by referring to the analytical tables that the California waters compare favorably with those of the European and Eastern States, in fact many of them are almost identical in composition.

The springs of California have been alphabetically arranged, with a sketch of their surroundings, route of travel, etc., to facilitate ready reference. The analyses of the foreign and several of our local springs have been obtained from every available source that was authentic, and with each analysis has been appended the analyst's name whenever obtainable.

The article containing the mineral springs proper was read before the Medical Society of the State of California, April 20, 1889 and awarded the annual prize of the Society.

Short articles on the ancient uses of mineral springs, their classification and theory of origin, with the therapeutics or medicinal uses of the different waters have been added.

The medicinal virtues of the mineral waters and Moor baths have been dilated upon, for it is believed that they are among the most efficient auxiliaries in the treatment of these chronic disorders, providing the baths are properly and intelligently used.

The work contains the names of over two hundred California springs, with about one hundred analyses, and two hundred analyses of all the famous springs in America and abroad.

Short sketches have been introduced on the fertility and natural productions of California; its historical account; climate; comparative thermometric tables; rainfall, etc., from which it will be seen that our golden shores on the Pacific compare favorably with all the most noted health resorts, whether they be found in the Old or in the New World.

Should the author succeed in directing attention to our fountains of health and to their scientific utilization in the treatment of disease, he feels certain of their beneficial effects, and should any of the springs through his efforts prove a boon to suffering humanity, as an auxiliary remedy, an adjuvant to regular scientific medicine, then shall his labors have been amply repaid.

WINSLOW ANDERSON,

829 Broadway, San Francisco, Cal.

March, 1890.

TABLE OF CONTENTS

ILLUSTRATIONS

INDEX TO SPRINGS

CALIFORNIA SPRINGS

XV

OTHER SPRINGS—DOMESTIC AND FOREIGN

GENERAL AND THERAPEUTICAL INDEX

" There is a beautiful valley afar in the west,
    Where orange and fig trees are grown,
Where dawnlight like Eden is flooding its breast,
And the spirit of peace is ever its guest,
    Where storm and discord are unknown.

" And the stars shine down on that glen in the west
    When the light of the daytime has flown;
They mirror their gleam in the river's clear breast,
While the night zephyrs whisper each blossom to rest
    In the tenderest of loverlike tone."

INTRODUCTORY

MINERAL SPRINGS

ROM TIME IMMEMORIAL MINERAL WATERS
have been highly valued as medicinal agents. The
earliest Greek and Roman physicians admitted and
advocated their efficacy in the treatment of many
diseases, as may be seen from the writings of Hip-
pocrates, Aristotle and Herodotus. Temples were
erected in close proximity to mineral springs and
dedicated to their healing god, Æsculapius. The
ancients had recourse to the sulphurous thermal
springs of Tiberias (now Tabareah), which are also
extensively used at the present day by patients from all parts of Syria,
for the healing of painful tumors, rheumatism and skin diseases.
Josephus mentions the thermal baths of Calirrhoe, near the Dead
Sea, made famous by Herod, who used them during his sickness.

The Egyptians, Arabians and Mohammedans have used mineral
waters for the healing of the sick from a very early period down to the
present time. Homer frequently speaks of bathing and using the natural waters in the preparation of the sacrifice, in the reception of
oracles and the holy marriages. Pliny, in his natural history, mentions
a large number of mineral and thermal springs in different parts of
Europe and speaks highly of their curative properties. For five centuries mineral waters were almost the only medicines employed in Rome,
and the *aquæ calientes* have been in active use for drinking and bathing
purposes for over two thousand years. The hot springs from which
was derived the name Thermopylæ, immortalized by the heroic Spar-
tans, have also been used for over twenty centuries for the alleviation
of human sufferings. The popularity of these living health-giving

fountains has not decreased with the modern discoveries of medical science, but, on the contrary, mineral waters have become more useful and their application more extended, inasmuch as they have been reduced to scientific exactness in their mode of administration. During these two thousand years, and particularly during the last five hundred years, it has been fully demonstrated that the greatest beneficial results obtainable at these springs, for the various maladies to which they are applicable, have accrued from the scientific use of the waters and the exhibition of *judicious internal medication* at the same time, together with an adoption of the carefully prepared régime observed at the different spas, or mineral watering-places. Many of the ablest physicians of our day show their confidence in this plan of treating many of the intractable or chronic diseases, not only by going to the springs themselves when they fall victims to these disorders, as well as sending many of their patients to them, but by the fact that qualified European professors have been appointed to take charge of the mineral springs and chairs have been instituted in the medical colleges and universities, which these professors fill, by which means Balneotherapy and the use of mineral waters have become recognized branches of medical education. Students and medical men are taught the virtues of mineral waters and the practical results obtained through centuries of research at the springs in many of the German, French, Italian and English universities at the present day.

In America, and particularly in California, we cannot boast of twenty or even five centuries of continuous use of any of our mineral or thermal springs; but with this exception our mineral waters on the Atlantic Coast, in the Mississippi Valley and on the Pacific Coast can truthfully be said to be as valuable as, and in many cases, as may be seen from the analyses, almost identical with, the famous spas of Europe.

In California we have over two hundred cold and hot mineral springs, ranging from the cool, delicious, effervescent soda and sparkling vichy to the ferruginous, saline, alkaline and sulphurous wells, ever ready and overflowing, to be utilized for the healing of the "many ills to which the flesh is heir."

When our California springs become more generally known, and their similarity to the famous European spas is better understood, our invalids may not find it necessary to undertake the long, tedious, expensive, and in many instances hazardous journey, when they can find right here in California, at their very doors, as it were, almost the identical waters, with all the conveniences and luxurious accommodations found abroad, and with the additions of a variety of food products and a pure, dry and balmy atmosphere, and an invigorating and stimulating climate unequaled in any other country in the world.

GENERAL VIEW OF YOSEMITE VALLEY

MINERAL SPRINGS

AND

HEALTH RESORTS OF CALIFORNIA

Beyond the Rockies' grand expanse
Land of eternal Summer smiles ;
Stern Winter's rude and hoary King
Retreats before her magic wiles,
And when in olden days agone
He came snow-laden from afar,
And scattered crystals in his train,
And touched with frost each gleaming star,
Until he came where Summer dwells—
What plea she made I do not know,
But this the King was vanquished here,
And on the mountains left his snow.

Callie L. Bonney.

ORIGIN OF MINERAL SPRINGS.

The chemical and physical phenomena of natural
waters have been long and carefully studied by the ablest
chemists and physicists of the times. Yet the phenomena
are so complex and varied, that many problems connected
with this subject still await investigation. The subject is
such an extensive and intricate one that we shall content
ourselves with giving a brief explanation of a few of the
more important topics.

In a general way a mineral spring may be defined as
one yielding water impregnated to a greater or less extent
with subs.ances rendering it suitable for medicinal purposes. The quantity and the kind of these dissolved substances vary greatly in different springs. To find the

3

cause of this variance we must look to different circumstances, such as the strata passed through by the water, and the temperature and pressure at which it exerted its solvent action upon the various mineral ingredients.

Water may almost be said to be the universal solvent. Careful experiments show that water is capable of dissolving minute quantities of those minerals most difficult of solution; even glass is soluble to an appreciable extent, as careful experiment proves. Absolutely pure water is never found in nature; even the rain from the pure skies, the purest water known, contains small amounts of dissolved oxygen, nitrogen, carbonic acid gas, ammonia, and nitrous compounds, besides small quantities of solid matter, organic and inorganic, previously suspended in the atmosphere as dust.

FORMATION OF MINERAL SPRINGS.

A large proportion of the water that falls on the earth runs off in the streams and rivers; the rest sinks into the ground, percolating through porous places and crevices wherever it can find a way, finally reappearing at the surface in the form of springs. As water passes through the soil it comes in contact with decaying vegetable matter, which takes from it part of its oxygen, and gives up to it small quantities of organic acids and carbonic acid. Such acids, especially carbonic, increase very greatly the solvent powers of water, enabling it to attack slowly, but still effectually, otherwise practically indecomposible and insoluble substances. The carbonates of calcium and magnesium are readily dissolved; even silica and refractory silicates are slowly acted on, and their elements carried off in the water. Thus from the decomposition of igneous and metamorphic rocks, waters derive all the soluble compounds of their constituent minerals. Waters passing through sedimentary strata dissolve out many previously deposited salts. It is from such sources that salt springs derive their salt.

In volcanic regions, where secondary volcanic agencies are still at work, large quanties of free carbonic acid gas are often given off beneath the surface—its formation being in most cases probably due to the action of hot silicious solutions upon limestone, or other carbonates. Water coming in contact with this gas rapidly absorbs it, the amount varying in proportion to the pressure and inversely as the temperature. Thus at 60° F. and a pressure of one atmosphere (about 15 pounds to the square inch) water absorbs its own volume of the CO_2 gas ; at 32°F. and the same pressure, nearly two volumes. And the amount absorbed is increased directly as the pressure, so that at ten or twenty atmospheres (at 60°), ten or twenty volumes of gas may be taken up ; and with this increase in the gas absorbed, there is also an increase in the amounts of carbonates of lime, magnesia, iron and other salts dissolved.

When the excess of gas escapes, on the water standing long exposed to the air, the excess of salts is also deposited. In carbonated springs we often find large amounts of minerals deposited in beautiful and fantastic forms. In rare cases waters, especially in volcanic regions, contain free acids, sulphuric, hydrochloric, or nitric. Such waters, of course, exert a most powerful solvent chemical action upon minerals, and usually soon find bases to combine with the acids.

THERMAL WATERS.

Water in its subterranean courses, sometimes from various causes, becomes heated to a very high temperature ; often, if at considerable depths, where it is under pressure, to a point far above 212° F., the ordinary boiling point of water. Heated or superheated waters exert a powerful chemical action, being capable of dissolving many times more solid matter than when cold. When such water cools, the ingredients, which are held in solution by heat alone, are usually deposited. Such deposits may be seen at the mouths of geysers and are often quite beautiful.

Stalactites, curious and grotesque figures hanging like pendants from the roofs of caves, and stalagmites, from their drippings on the floors of caves, are formed in the same way from cold water charged with carbonate of lime.

CAUSES OF SUBTERRANEAN HEAT.

There are three causes principally effective in raising the temperature of the water of thermal or hot springs. These are (1), Secondary volcanic action ; (2) Chemical action ; and (3) The interior heat of the earth.

VOLCANIC ACTION.

By far the greatest number of hot springs are located either in regions of active volcanic action or in regions where, although active eruptions have not occurred for hundreds or even thousands of years, the evidences of former eruptions, such as old craters and beds of volcanic rocks, may still be seen. In such regions feeble secondary phenomena, such as geysers, fumaroles and hot springs, linger on for ages to attest to the slumbering fires within. Water, percolating through the crevices of the slowly cooling rocks beneath the surface, is often heated to a very high temperature. The interesting phenomenon of hot and cold springs existing side by side is common in such regions. The waters of such springs have evidently come from different strata of the rocks or from different depths where temperatures are different. (See cold springs.)

CHEMICAL ACTION.

Another source of heat of certain mineral springs is chemical action. It is well known that while some chemical reactions have the effect of producing cold, there are many that produce great quantities of heat. There are many such that may take place in mineral waters, For instance sulphur maybe oxidized to sulphur dioxide (SO, SO_2), thereby producing considerable heat ; this substance dissolves in water, forming sulphurous acid (H_2SO_3) which is capable of still further oxidation and the formation of sulphuric acid, (H_2SO_4) heat being again produced. And sulphuric acid, if it comes in contact with suitable substances, limestone for instance, or other carbonates, acts upon them with still further liberation of heat, forming sulphates.

Competent authorities estimate that under favorable circumstances and in waters highly charged with certain substances chemical action may raise the temperature of water as high as even 212° F. But it is usually not a predominant cause of the heat of thermal springs, but only a subordinate one, often operating in conjunction with other causes, especially in volcanic regions.

HEAT OF THE EARTH.

Occasionally warm and hot springs are found in regions free from evidences of volcanic action. Where the elevation of temperature is not due to chemical action we must look to another cause, the universal interior heat of the earth. In the boring of artesian wells it has been demonstrated that in non-volcanic regions there is a rise in temperature of 1° F. for about every fifty-five feet of descent. Thus a spring having a temperature of 120° issuing in a locality where the mean temperature is 50° should have come from a depth of about 3,850 feet. But such estimates are not always reliable, as in many places, even where there are no signs of volcanic activity, the rise in temperature is more rapid than that mentioned, owing, probably, to the inequalities of the earth's crust.

As so many of the mineral springs of California are found in the Coast Range, it may be interesting to compare their geological history with that of the Sierra Nevada

NOTE.—Warm and hot springs frequently become cool for a considerable period, varying from a few days to several weeks. Recently this phenomenon has been observed in the hot springs of Salt Lake City, Utah. These springs have temperatures of 122° F. ordinarily, but for one month, in June to July of 1889, and preceding years, at irregular times, the springs became as cold as 50° F.

CALIFORNIA PALMS

range. The Sierras were upheaved at the end of the Jurassic period, at the same time as the Wasatch range four hundred miles eastward. The Coast Range was not upheaved from the ocean until long after, toward the end of the Miocene Tertiary. On this subject Professor Le Conte says:

"The Coast chain of California is a very complex system of ranges with narrow valleys between, contrasting strongly in this respect with the grand simplicity of structure characteristic of the Sierra Nevada. The Cretaceous and Tertiary strata of which it is composed are strongly folded into repeated anticlines and synclines by the lateral pressure which produced the ranges. As shown by the age of the newest crumpled strata which enter into its composition, its birth-time was the end of the Miocene. In some places the strata are unchanged and full of fossils, but in others they are intersected by dikes and overflowed by lava, and are therefore highly metamorphic. This is especially true of the region to the north of the bay of San Francisco."

THEORY OF COLD SPRINGS.

Cold springs, such as carbonated waters, are formed without the aid of subterranean heat. In the mountains and on the hillsides water percolates through the soil during the precipitating season, filling up all the underground reservoirs until it reaches a clay bottom or impervious stratum upon which to rest or flow. Following the declivities the water passes through the many crevices and fissures and finds an outlet at a lower level, perhaps several miles away. During its passage through the different stratifications of the mineral constituents of the earth's crust, the water dissolves, first, some organic or vegetable matter, liberating gases, oxygen, carbonic acid gas, etc.; it next attacks the carbonates—limestone, etc.—in the rocks and becomes charged with gases and mineral ingredients from the chemical metamorphosis caused by the action of the various acidulous radicals on the baselous compounds. Hence the composition of a spring depends entirely on the rocks and minerals through which its water permeates. Passing through large salt deposits, the spring contains quantities of sodium chloride. Filtering through iron ores, we have a ferruginous spring. Permeating limestone or marble, we have water rich in calcium salts, and so on. Rain water, as we have remarked, contains enough gaseous impurities alone to act and react on the earth's crust. To these are added the organic acids and gases from the animal and the vegetable kingdoms, and when the action has once commenced chemical evolution or reaction continues. Through these agencies the rocks and minerals are acted upon and greater or less quantities of the different mineral ingredients are held in suspension and in solution in the mineral waters.

It has been stated that certain spring waters in this State, subjected to chemical analyses, have shown larger amounts of mineral ingredients than the water could possibly hold in solution, as the saturating point of such and such an ingredient was so much, hence the analysis has been deemed incorrect. It is not the writer's desire to champion inaccurate analyses, but to call attention to the fact that as carbonic acid gas (CO_2), the great solvent power in mineral springs, is held in solution in the water *directly* as the pressure and *inversely* as the temperature, so does it increase the solvent action of the water, *pari passu* on the mineral constituents to such an extent that many thousand grains of solids may be held in solution in a gallon of water as long as the gases also remain.

NEVADA FALLS

CASCADE FALLS

" To suffering man from Nature's genial breast
    A boon transcendant ever mayst thou flow ;
    Blest holy fount, still bid old age to know
Reviving vigor ; and if health repressed
    Fade in the virgin's cheek, renew its glow
For love and joy ; and they that in thy wave
Confiding trust and thankful lave,
Propitious aid, and speed the stranger band,
With health and life renewed, unto their native land."

Medicinal Uses
Of the Various Mineral Waters.

The internal administration and the external application of the natural mineral waters having been reduced to a scientific basis, it is quite important that the rules regulating their administration should be followed.

Thousands of invalids, ill-advised or perhaps wholly unadvised, seek the different springs and health resorts annually. During the author's travels among the springs of California he frequently found people whose cases were actually aggravated and the fatal termination hastened by the use of the wrong mineral waters.

Mineral springs are not "cure-alls." As a rule, too much is claimed for them. The many marvelous cures cited and the many improbable and ridiculous statements seen on printed circulars do more harm than good. Sensible people are not going to believe that a " magnetic" mineral water is going to cure a bad case of consumption, or that any " mineral water" cures heart disease, etc.

On the other hand, it would be quite as flagrant an error to suppose that all the reputed beneficial effects of mineral waters were only the result of extravagant or interested imaginings.

To obtain the greatest possible benefit from springs it is absolutely essential that the patient first consults his regular physician. A careful diagnosis should be made of his case, and then if a change of scene and a course of treatment at some spring be truly advantageous, let the physician, who is certainly the most competent to advise in such matters, recommend the resort best suited to the case. If the mineral waters and hygienic régime be used as an auxiliary to the regular internal treatment, the best results may be hoped for. Once at the springs the patient should implicitly follow the directions of the resident physician, who, if armed with a personal letter from the patient's regular physician, can prescribe wisely at once.

The indiscriminate use of mineral waters, either for drinking or bathing purposes, cannot be too strongly condemned, for while they look bland and harmless, they are potent therapeutic agents which may accomplish much good if judiciously employed, but may also do much harm and may be followed by serious if not fatal results in careless hands.

The climate here in California is conducive to the highest excellence in mental activity and physical strength. When an individual contracts a disease—rheumatism, for instance—which requires several weeks for a complete cure, he becomes restless and eager to follow his vocation. The result is that as soon as the patient is able to walk at all he commences the continuous rush of business, and neglects his disease, which gradually lapses into a sub-acute or chronic state. In this condition, perhaps, he goes to the springs. Here the same restlessness characterizes the average Californian, and, indeed, the majority of American patients. He will "rush" the treatment. If one glass of water be prescribed three times daily he will take half a dozen glasses as many times a day. If one sulphur water or mud bath be prescribed once in three or once in two days he will want to take it two or three times daily in order to hurry up the treatment.

This is not an overdrawn or an individual instance. Resident physicians have repeatedly informed the writer of the difficulty experienced in keeping patients within due bounds, and in more than one case this rushing and unauthorized self-treatment has resulted fatally in less than one week's time. And as to quick recoveries, in the majority of obstinate cases, repose, pure and simple, is the most potent remedial agent that can be employed; whilst heroic treatment only hastens the fatal moment of utter collapse. Business cares may be pressing, and of vital importance, but it is of far more importance that the fast wearing out machine be saved while there is yet time so that it may not run the risk of becoming a helpless encumbrance on the already overburdened shoulders of relatives and friends.

Therefore, let suffering humanity first seek medical advice, be thoroughly examined and carefully diagnosticated. Let the intelligent physician send the patient to the springs best suited to the individual case, and whilst there drink the waters and use the baths, and follow the regime directed by the resident or supervising physician. This plan, with judicious internal medication promises the best results.

All we need at American health resorts and mineral watering-places is to follow the natural scientific regime which has been worked out for centuries in Europe. There every patient confides in his physician, and medical men abroad value the mineral springs more, apparently, than we do in America. The patient is ordered to this or that spring for one, two or three months. He places himself entirely under the care of his family physician and the resident physician at the springs. Patients who are able to walk get up at 6 A. M. and walk to the springs, drink the prescribed amount of water and walk from one to two miles before breakfast. They take their meals regularly. Their diet is carefully regulated for each disease. They retire early, exercise freely, use the baths or drink the waters regularly and improve twice as rapidly in Germany, France and England for the same class of diseases, and with the same—almost the identical—mineral water treatment as we use in America, simply because they follow a regular scientific system. This we hope will be done in California.

Is it not well to follow in the footsteps of the sages who have gone before ? Is it not well to adopt anything we find abroad where the experience has been extended over centuries, when we know it is philosophic and conducive to our own health and welfare? A moment's reflection will convince any one how much better the European plan is than our own. We sleep until breakfast is nearly over, use the mineral water when we feel like it, exercise as little as possible, and recognize no superior in this free and independent country. A medical man is not allowed to tell one of these sovereigns that he must get up at 6 A. M. and drink the prescribed amount of mineral water and walk the necessary number of miles before breakfast ; eat the regulation diet and strictly follow the *regime* best calculated to improve his disease ; it would jar too much on his sensitive republican feelings. Yet this is just what American watering-places and sanitariums need. *It is the only thing our California mineral springs need* to make them as successful in this treatment of the many chronic diseases as the spas of Europe are. In the writer's travels among the different springs of California he frequently found spring owners who advised their patients to throw away all their pills, powders and potions and rely entirely on the natural product from Nature's laboratory. This is not the wisest course to pursue. Many of our local springs could be made to assist the regular scientific medical treatment. The two combined (mineral waters and medicine) will effect a cure in many of the obstinate and intractable diseases, when either taken alone may not benefit the patient so much. Mineral waters hasten the cure by assisting in the absorption of appropriate remedies as well as by their eliminating powers. Comparatively larger doses, for instance, of many blood purifying remedies can be tolerated when taken in conjunction with mineral waters, because the medicine acts more rapidly on the disease, and is in turn more rapidly discharged from the body, carrying with it the poison from the disease under treatment.

This is the explanation of the great secret in rapidly curing chronic diseases at the springs. At the Arkansas springs, at Virginia, at New York, and at the European spas, this is their successful plan--medicine and mineral waters combined. Many a poor suffering mortal has had occasion to thank the intelligence of the medical man who first combined nature and art, and made it possible to rid the system of those serious and almost worse than fatal chronic, lingering, painful diseases by combining generous medication with natural mineral waters.

The following extract is from an editorial in the *Journal of Balneology and Medical Clippings*, A. L. A. Toboldt, M. D., and J. A. Beebe, M. D., editors, New York, June, 1889:

SANITARIUMS AND HEALTH RESORTS

It is a fact greatly to be deplored that more time and study is not devoted to the subject of mineral springs in this country, as they seem best suited to the treatment of so vast a number of cases, especially when properly directed by some physician who is thoroughly conversant, not only with the disease to be treated, but also with the mineral spring at his disposal.

It would be a grand thing for this country, and we may say for the undertakers of the enterprise as well, to build a few large hotels in a location specially suited for the purpose, on account of its healthfulness, salubrious climate, hygienic surroundings, etc., to thoroughly equip these with all the latest appliances for the various kinds of baths, not excepting the moor, or, as they are sometimes styled in the country, "mud baths." Let the place be thoroughly stocked with all the leading brands of imported as well as domestic mineral spring waters. Then let a physician be placed in charge who is thoroughly familiar with this branch of medicine, and we have no doubt but what the enterprise will receive the indorsement and support of all the more enlightened and intelligent physicians of this country. Such an institution has become a necessity, and we have little doubt but what, if not this year, the next few years will see such an enterprise, not alone started, but flourishing. There is that so little understood disease, "diabetes." Let any patient, among the better class, be suffering from this disease and his physician at once orders him to Carlsbad. And why? Because experience has demonstrated the fact over and over again that diabetic patients get well at Carlsbad. The reason why they get well there quicker than when drinking the imported waters at home is no great secret to the profession. They know that in Carlsbad the patient at once places himself under the care of an intelligent physician who has mastered every detail of the treatment of this disease, a regular bill of fare is made out for the patient, which he adheres to as strictly as to the drinking of the Carlsbad waters. Then the fact of the patient being away from home comes in here as a very great factor, never to be overlooked. He is, by leaving home, at once removed from the probable *cause* of the disease, let this be mental overwork, worry, anxiety, grief or what not, he is placed under entirely different surroundings, and in addition to this there come the factors of a salubrious climate, systematic out-of-door exercise, regular habits, and the diet specially adapted to his disease. It is, no doubt, largely owing to these factors that the patients improve so rapidly at Carlsbad. But all these additions to the drinking of Carlsbad water can be had here as well as the Carlsbad water itself; in fact, whereas the water must be imported we already have all the necessary adjuncts, we have the climate, the hygiene, etc., the only thing we lack as yet is the sanitarium or health resort under proper management. Diabetes is only one of the many diseases that can best be reached and conquered in this way. The many diseases of the female generative organs, let them be induced by inflammations in the pelvis, severe child-bed or other causes, may also be mentioned here; that they are better treated away from home, from the cares and trials of a household or from the annoyance of officious and over-sympathetic friends, no one will question.

Then there is that host of diseases due to nervous breakdown, from overwork, anxiety, worry, grief, dissipation, etc. To attempt to treat these at home is generally a long, tedious and wearisome task, and when convalescence has but fairly started, the physician, having regard for the other members of the family, hastens to suggest travel, the sea-shore, mountains, etc., generally, however, not before some other member of the family is thoroughly broken down with the nursing. What a boon a properly located and equipped sanitarium would be to those patients; a place they could go to, knowing they would receive the best treatment, care and attention, instead as it is at present in this country, stay at home, wear out all the rest of the family, and either finally succumb to the disease, or else, what seems still worse, become an invalid for life, only a fit subject for the numerous institutions for invalids.

In this category let us also mention the old liver diseases, chronic constipation, obesity, etc. The taking of these patients away from their daily tasks, their sedentary habits, compelling them to live out of doors, take properly regulated exercise, diet, etc., etc., and if their stay at such a sanitarium be ever so short, they will return home to their accustomed duties with a vim, activity and vigor they hardly deemed possible.

But enough of these examples; let us hope that at no distant day this country, so rich in every kind of institution, will not have to send her sick to Europe to be treated at Carlsbad, Franzensbad, etc., but will have as good institutions here at home, and, if Carlsbad water must be drunk, let it be drunk *here*, no necessity of having to go to Europe to get that which is already imported and at hand, and surely no one will say that we need import a salubrious atmosphere, or healthy climate ; our climate is surely as good as any to be found in Europe.

SCENE IN THE SIERRAS

The Therapeutic Action of Mineral Waters on the Human Economy.

The specific action of any mineral spring must of course depend upon the chemical ingredients found in its waters. In the following classification of the various distinct mineral waters, short notes on their therapeutic action have been added. Generally speaking, mineral waters are well received and well borne by the stomach.

The following extract is from a description of Dr. Moorman, resident physician at the White Sulphur Springs in Virginia for over thirty years. He is probably the best qualified medical man in America on the special subject of mineral waters. He says, in speaking of the action of the mineral waters generally :

" Mineral waters are evidently absorbed; they enter into the circulation and change the consistency as well as the composition of the fluids ; they course through the system and apply the medicinal materials which they hold in solution, in the most minute form of subdivision that can be conceived, to the diseased surfaces and tissues; they reach and search the most minute ramifications of the capillaries, and remove the morbid condition of those vessels which are so frequently the primary seats of disease. It is thus that they relieve chronic disordered action, and impart natural energy and elasticity to vessels that have been distended either by inflammation or congestion, while they communicate an energy to the muscular fibre and to the animal tissues generally, which is not witnessed from the administration of ordinary remedies. Mineral waters also dissolve many pathological and morbific materials which are more readily eliminated from the body. They also act on the nervous system, regulating and stimulating important blood forming centers whose abnormal action is often the primary cause of deleterious changes in the blood itself. The waters are also serviceable as simple diluents, washing out the gastro-intestinal tract, diluting the different fluids of the body, and serving as vehicles of waste products, besides having their own tonic action.

"Carbonic acid gas, although a poisonous, effete, worn out substance when eliminated from the integumentary system and pulmonary mucous membranes, laden as it is, with noxious materials, when taken in the natural mineral waters, which nearly always contain more or less of this gas, not only dissolves the one substance without disuniting the combinations of the others, but it enters the system charged with mineral particles, and presents them to the mouths of the absorbent vessels in this highly diluted condition, while at the same time it promotes their direct absorption by naturally creating a stimulating power on the vascular and nervous system. Thus you may understand why six-tenths of a grain of iron imbibed into the duodenal lacteals with abundance of the gaseous acid may exercise a greater influence on the circulating system than three or four times the quantity of pharmaceutic carbonate of iron, which has to be dissolved in the gastric juice previous to absorption."

The foregoing extract is from Dr. Sigismund Sutro of London, who is an expert on mineral waters, and whose able lectures delivered in London before the Hunterian School of Medicine, show that he has studied his subject thoroughly. Chemical experience teaches us that although a chalybeate water contains only a few grains of iron salt to each gallon, yet its tonic effect is greater than larger quantities given without the aid of the mineral water.

From the foregoing it will be observed that mineral waters act beneficially on the economy from the fact that they are easily borne by the stomach and are pleasant to drink; besides their specific action depending on the preponderance of any one or more special ingredients, the waters acts as stimulants, not only to the digestive organs, but also to the absorbing organs. By these means the fractional part of a grain of iron may become more powerful than vastly larger quantities otherwise administered. Mineral waters also dissolve and remove morbific products and prevent their further development and deposit in the human economy.

1. ACID MINERAL SPRINGS.

There are mineral springs containing some natural mineral acid—notably sulphuric. The Oak Orchard Spring in Genesee County, N. Y., contains over 133 grains of sulphuric acid to each gallon, having only 211 grains of solid ingredients. This is perhaps the strongest acid spring in America. The Thermal Acid Springs in California contain 78 parts in 1,000 of sulphuric acid. Several other springs contain appreciable amounts of sulphuric, hydrochloric (muriatic), and nitric acids. Nearly all the cold and many of the hot springs contain carbonic acid gas. This in solution in the water forms carbonic acid. When drank at the springs, or immediately after opening, that which is bottled, it is found to be acid, but allowing the water free exposure, the gas evaporates and the water becomes alkaline and loses much of its medicinal effect (see (8), carbonated waters).

THERAPEUTICS OF ACID MINERAL WATERS.

These waters are highly useful in many conditions of the digestive apparatus. In atonic dyspepsia, the acids, especially hydrochloric, should be taken after meals to assist in the digestion of nitrogenous food in the stomach. Taken in conjunction with the usual concomitant mineral constituents found in spring waters, acids are important tonics in these cases taken after the meals.

In the many cases of excessive formation of acid in the stomach from the faulty digestion or fermentation of saccharine and starchy foods with the troublesome symptoms of acid eructation (pyrosis) or "heartburn," the mineral acids and waters are beneficial, but in these cases they must be taken before meals, otherwise the waters would be increasing instead of decreasing the trouble. These acid waters are useful in the treatment of colliquative or night sweats, acting as astringents; for this purpose they should be taken before retiring. In chronic serous diarrhœa, congestion of the liver, so called " bilious attacks," jaundice, with portal torpidity, early stages of cirrhosis and chronic hepatitis, the acid waters are recommended—taken two hours after meals three times daily.

For chronic lead poisoning the sulphuric acid waters are valuable, forming insoluble and inert sulphates of lead which pass from the system.

Certain urinary disorders are much benefited by these waters, for example, the phosphate diathesis, oxaluria, alkalinity of the urine with a feeling of general *malaise* and a loss of ambition, etc.

Mineral and acid waters are also useful in chronic catarrhal affections of the stomach and bladder, in biliary or cystic calculi (phosphatic), in fevers and certain skin diseases.

Acid baths or topical applications of the acid waters are also recommended in chronic liver and skin troubles.

2. ALKALINE MINERAL WATERS.

The alkaline waters may be divided into three classes, viz: (a) alkalo-carbonated.   (b) alkalo-chalybeate.   (c) alkalo-saline.

(a) The alkalo-carbonated variety comprises a long list of cold mineral springs having carbonates and bicarbonates of sodium, potassium, etc., with a small amount of carbonic anhydride. Upon standing in the air a short time a small amount of gas evaporates. These waters are alkaline.

(b) The alkalo-chalybeate waters contain besides the carbonates of sodium and potassium, etc., carbonates (usually) or some other salt of iron.

(c) Alkalo-saline mineral waters have in addition to the alkaline carbonates, sulphates of magnesia (Epsom salts) and sulphate of sodium (Glauber's salt).

THERAPEUTICS OF ALKALINE WATERS.

The medicinal uses of the alkaline mineral waters are quite considerable as well as beneficial if judiciously administered as to time, quantity and quality.

THE ALKALO-CARBONATED WATERS.

These are advised in dyspepsia with excessive acidity of the gastric secretions, with sour and disagreeable eructations and regurgitations, with flatulent distention of the abdomen. For these purposes the waters are taken after meals.

In atonic dyspepsia an acid is exhibited after meals to assist in the chymification of the nitrogenous elements of food in the stomach. Alkaline waters taken before meals will also stimulate the peptic glands into activity and thereby assist in stomach digestion. In this way these waters act as a tonic. For this purpose they are taken in moderate quantities fifteen to thirty minutes before meals.

The alkalo-carbonated waters are usually diuretic and correct any acid tendency of the urinary secretions, hence they are of great utility in fevers and rheumatism, gout, chronic arthritis, congestion and irritation of kidneys and bladder, etc.

The lithontriptic value of alkalo-carbonated waters has been established in the most conclusive way, by carefully conducted experiments at many of the celebrated spas in Europe. Many of the greatest masters of clinical medicine thoroughly indorse these waters in the treatment of calculi, gravel and gout. The waters are of special value in the cystic and nephretic calculi (urinary stones), which are made up of inorganic molecules united by crystallization or by mucous debris. Indeed, many of these little granules

are composed of a little mucous epithelium or some acci-
dental foreign body for a nucleus, around which uric acid,
carbonate of lime, phosphates of magnesia, ammonia and
soda or oxalate of lime crystallize. The active determining
cause appears to be urinary fermentation which produces
the crystallization. In uric acid gravel the alkalo-carbonated mineral waters assist in diluting the urine and rendering it alkaline, thereby preventing the formation of calculi.

It is also claimed that these carbonated waters dissolve
the uric acid calculi, transforming them into urate of soda,
which is more readily soluble in the alkaline waters.

In vesical catarrh, with all the concomitant symptoms
of irritation, pain, etc., the alkalo-carbonated waters have a
pleasant effect.

For metritis, leucorrhœa and sterility these waters have
long been in use in Europe.

M. M. Petrequin and Socquet, in their " Trait des Eaux
Minerales," write as follows : " In women, alkaline waters
have a complex physiological action on the uterine systems.
They tend to diminish the catarrhal secretions, and the
same result is observed in cases of leucorrhœa.

"As for derangement of menstruation, resulting either
from chlorosis or from obstruction of the womb, they also
may be combated by the same springs.

" Their influence favors conception. This is doubtless
attributable to the above combination of circumstances and
it is for this reason they can be prescribed in cases of sterility." (See also article on uterine douche.)

In gout these waters are highly extolled. The excessive acid condition of the blood is modified and the uric acid
is rapidly eliminated.

The use of alkaline mineral waters forms the only
treatment used for rheumatism in many cases and the
patients recover rapidly.

In diabetes (sugar in the urine) European springs,
especially the alkaline waters, have been much used. The

eminent chemist, Pelouze, expresses himself in the following emphatic way in writing to his friend, Prof. Mialhe:

"I shall not take upon myself to decide whether the
theory which you sustain respecting the destruction of
sugar in the system be true or false; but I can affirm that I
myself have witnessed, as a result of appropriate alkaline
treatment, the disappearance of sugar from the urine of
many diabetic patients subjected to its action, and, more-
over, in many of these cases it had not reappeared several
months after the treatment was stopped, the system having,
so to speak, laid in a stock of health." The salines which
frequently become alkalo-salines are of much value in
catarrhal conditions of the gastro-intestinal tract with chlyo-
poietic engorgements.

For obesity it is necessary to use large quantities of the
alkalo-carbonated and alkalo-saline waters to keep the intestinal circulation well depleted. The water should be taken
an hour before meals and again two or three hours afterwards, using several quarts daily. The hot alkaline baths
may also be taken daily (under the immediate supervision
of the medical attendant) with perfect safety and with much
benefit. The diet must be carefully regulated. Nothing
should be eaten that grows underneath the ground, and the
starchy and saccharine foods which assist in the accumula-
tion of adipose tissue should be sedulously avoided. Lean
meats may be eaten and hot alkaline waters drank. Systematic exercise should be observed. In this way the author
succeeded in reducing one female patient from 255 pounds
to 180 pounds in five months, the patient at the same time
enjoying perfect health.

For rheumatism and gout the alkaline springs have
long had a deservedly high reputation. The water is taken
in moderate quantities, six to twelve glasses daily, with its
external application in the form of hot baths. In rheumatism the blood is surcharged with acids, and the alkaline
waters seem to neutralize this condition.

The alkalo-chalybeate waters are especially serviceable in anæmia and lithiæmia, or the lithic acid diathesis, in "gravel" or "sand" in the urine; also in diabetes mellitus, especially when it is hepatic in origin or when it occurs in obese people. The chalybeate waters are of great service in the many diseases superinduced by a paucity of red blood corpuscles or depending on toxæmia which deteriorated the quality of the blood.

3. ALUM MINERAL SPRINGS.

Several springs in California contain considerable quantities of alum.

Therapeutically, as far as the alum itself is concerned, those springs are not of any special value. The waters have been used for hemorrhages and for uterine douches.

4. ARSENICAL MINERAL SPRINGS.

In many localities up and down the coast we find distinct traces of arsenic in combination with other elements among the mineral ingredients of springs.

THERAPEUTICS.

Arsenical waters have proved highly beneficial in irritative dyspepsia, chronic gastric catarrh, gastralgia and enteralgia. For this purpose small draughts should be taken half an hour before meals. In chronic diarrhœa and dysentery it should be taken an hour before meals or two hours after meals. Jaundice with catarrh of the bile ducts and chronic cirrhosis of the liver are improved by these waters. The waters are also highly extolled in chlorosis and anæmia, chronic malarial toxæmia, hemicrania and malarial neuralgia, and in cutaneous diseases, scrofulous sores and syphilitic contaminations. The skin diseases most benefited are the chronic scaly variety—especially psoriasis, eczema, pemphigus and old cases of acne (pimples). For these diseases the waters containing both iron

LAKE IN THE SIERRAS

and arsenic are especially serviceable, taken one hour after meals. Menorrhagia and functional impotence are also improved by a course at these arsenical and chalybeate springs, with wholesome food and free outdoor exercise.

5. BORAX MINERAL SPRINGS.

Springs containing borates and borax are plentiful in California.

THERAPEUTICS.

The waters are useful for catamenial irregularities, and for cystic and nephretic calculi depending on a uric acid diathesis. In these latter cases the borax probably acts by liberating the alkali sodium, which then neutralizes the uric acid, setting free the boric acid.

The borax mineral waters have also been found very beneficial in clergymen's sorethroat, alleviating the hoarseness and curing the chronic or sub-acute inflammation of the mucous membranes and strengthening the larynx and vocal chords.

Borax waters may be drank four to six times daily between meals. Gargles may be used.

Borax forms quite an article of commerce. California produced during the last twenty years over $5,000,000 worth.

6. BROMINE AND BROMIDE SPRINGS.

The bromides of sodium, potassium, etc., are found in considerable quantities in several of the mineral springs on the coast.

THERAPEUTICS.

Bromine mineral waters are valuable adjuncts in the treatment of rheumatism, gout, blood-glandular diseases, goitre, synovites, etc. In obesity they hasten retrograde tissue metamorphosis and lessen the bodily weight. Chronic mercurial and saturnine poisoning are greatly benefited by a course of these waters. The bromides combine with the mercury or with the lead forming soluble compounds, which are readily eliminated from the system. In many cases of wakefulness from mental worry and fatigue, unrest of the peripheral nerves, over-brainwork, etc., the bromine waters have proved of great benefit. Asthma and chronic bronchitis also improve under the waters.

The bromine waters act as alteratives, and stimulants to the lymphatic system, promoting absorption and the elimination of morbific material; hence they are of special value in scrufulous tumors and ulcerations, syphilitic swellings and nodes, and chronic cutaneous diseases.

7. Calcareous or Earthy Mineral Waters.

The solid ingredients of these waters predominate with calcium, carbonate and sulphate, producing the "temporary" and "permanently" hard water.

Therapeutically, the waters are not much used. They may prove useful in rickets and softening of the bones when the lime salts are deficient.

8. Carbonated Mineral Springs.

This class of mineral waters is rich in carbonates and bicarbonates of many of the mineral compounds, such as soda, lime, potash, magnesia, etc., and has an excess of carbonic acid gas. The waters are all acid when first drawn, owing to the excess of the carbonic acid in the water. The carbonated waters resemble the alkaline waters in this, that they have carbonates and bicarbonates of the alkaline elements—alkalo carbonated, alkalo chalybeate and alkalo saline—with the addition of an excess of carbonic acid gas, making the waters alkalo acidulous, alkalo-chalybeate acidulous and alkalo-salino acidulous. Most cold mineral springs contain free carbonic anhydride; hence become carbonated waters, unless some other ingredients predominate.

THERAPEUTICS.

The carbonated waters are used much the same as the alkaline (*quo vide*), as we have simple alkaline waters; so have we also simple carbonated waters, such as seltzer, soda, apollinaris, etc. Most of the simple carbonated or soda waters are manufactured artificially and sold on an extensive scale as "soda" and "seltzer."

The natural carbonated-acidulous mineral waters are much to be preferred on account of the several ferruginous and alkaline ingredients they contain.

These waters are very grateful to the stomach of febrile patients, lessening nausea and gastric irritability, rendering the fluids in the body alkaline, and promoting a more copious secretion of the urinary organs.

The carbonated waters are pleasant vehicles in which to administer medicines, lemonades, etc., etc.

Frequently these waters are better borne by the stomach than anything else. The carbonated waters are antacid, tonic and diuretic, very useful in dyspepsia, to be taken before or after the meal, according to the form of the malady.

In biliary calculi the carbonated waters have been found very beneficial. An acid which dissolves feldspathic and micaceous rock must also have some action on urate of lime and biliary salts.

Vesical calculi are also influenced by these waters. As in catarrhal affections of the bladder, chronic cystitis, etc.

Carbonated waters are also extensively used in Europe for albumenurea (Bright's disease of the kidneys). The chalybeate carbonated waters would be even more beneficial than the simple alkalo-carbonated.

In the sick-room the waters may be taken in wine-glassful doses *pro re nata.*

9.   CHALYBEATE OR FERRUGINOUS MINERAL WATER.

These are waters impregnated with the salts of iron as well as with the other mineral constituents, in varying proportions.   The (*a*) simple-acidulous-chalybeate waters are the carbonated waters with iron.   The (*b*) salino-acidulous chalybeate are the alkalo-salino-carbonated impregnated with ferruginous salts as well.

THERAPEUTICS.

Chalybeate mineral waters are of great benefit in the treatment of anæmia—a condition of the blood in which there is a paucity of red blood corpuscles, hæmato-globulin in the blood.   The ferruginous waters produce a constructive metamorphosis creating more red blood corpuscles, thereby increasing the specific gravity of the blood and of the bodily weight, reproducing a healthy glow and the rosy cheek on the faded and bleached out face.

It appears to be a well-established fact that one of the functions of the red blood corpuscles, besides taking up oxygen and eliminating carbonic anhydride is to convert oxygen into ozone, in which form the oxygen becomes so efficient in the system.   After a course of iron water the bodily temperature rises, the cold feet and chilly nights are changed into warmth and comfort.   The elimination of urea increases.

The ferruginous waters are recommended in debility consequent upon chronic discharges, anæmia, chlorosis, fluor-albus, scrofula, rickets, passive hemorrhages, dyspepsia, when depending on deficient energy of the digestive function, neuralgia, chronic malarial fevers, all of which destroy the health giving properties in the blood—the red globules—as well as the functions of the reproductive organs ; in all these wasting diseases the chalybeate waters are of undoubted value.   Pure air, pleasant and healthy surroundings and plain, wholesome food, are important adjuncts in the restoration of the vital powers.

The iron waters are best taken after meals after a lapse of from a half to one hour, in wineglassful to tumblerful doses. The stomach, gastric and intestinal juices are then in the best condition for absorption. Taken for passive hemorrhages, the hemorrhagic diathesis, ammenorrhœa, hysteria and the many pelvic disorders frequently depending on anæmia, and in the paludal cachexia, leucocythemic exophthalmic goitre, etc., the waters may be taken every three hours in wineglassful doses.

The ferruginous waters, more or less charged with the salines, are recommended in the treatment of hepatic engorgement, hæmorrhoidal affections, chronic diarrhœa, strumous diseases, albuminurea (Bright's disease), etc. To reap the fullest benefit of a course at the chalybeate springs, it is necessary to pursue the treatment faithfully, and under the guidance of competent medical advice. Under such conditions the author does not hesitate to say that these ferruginous waters are invaluable in the treatment of the many diseases above named.

10. Chlorinated or Muriated Mineral Waters.

This class of springs contains chlorides of sodium (common salt), potassium, lime, etc., and conveniently may be divided into: *a*. Simple chlorinated. *b*. Chlorino-lithiated. *c*. Brines.

The (*a*) simple chlorinated springs are such as we find at the foot of the Salt Mountains.

The (*b*) chlorino-lithiated contain in addition some salt of lithium, and the (*c*)brines are the stronger chlorinated waters.

Therapeutics.

The chlorinated waters are strongly diuretic and antacid, useful in rheumatism, gout, scrofula and abdominal plethora. Chronic catarrh of the mucous membranes is also much benefited by these springs. As many of these salt springs are hot, bathing for rheumatics is found to be a beneficial mode of treatment.

(II). Iodine Mineral Springs

The existence of iodine, bromine and arsenical natural mineral waters has been doubted for a long time, but the author has now personal knowledge of their existence on this coast. (See analysis.)

As iodine, bromine and chlorine exist in the sea-water and submarine vegetable life, a fact demonstratable at any time, it is not at all wonderful that a country for ages submerged in the briny deep, and in which we find mountains of salt, should also have iodides and bromides from the submarine deposits. Well-known spas on the continent contain them, and so do many of our springs in California.

The principal salts of iodine found are: *a*. Iodo-bromine. *b*. Iodo-sodic. *c*. Iodo-potassic. *d*. Iodo-magnesic, etc.

THERAPEUTICS

The utility of iodine or any of its salts is most conspicuous in the treatment of constitutional states, such as enlargements of the lymphatic glands, glandular swellings, enlargements of any of the internal organs, spleen, from chronic malarial poisoning, goitre, scrofulous tumors, syphilitic enlargements, etc. Iodine salts and waters are also found to be of great benefit in chronic bronchitis, catarrhs, asthma, chronic pleurisy, rheumatism, gout, and chronic Bright's disease, scrofulous and syphilitic contaminations producing cutaneous or internal tumefaction or ulcerations are successfully treated by this class of waters. Aneurisms have also been benefited.

Springs containing iodides have usually salines enough to act gently on the gastro-intestinal tract, ferruginous salts to act on the blood, chlorides and carbonates to act as diuretics, besides the iodides to act specifically on the constitutional state, counteracting, as they do, many pathological (abnormal) conditions, strumous or glandular enlargements, and producing disintegration of the morbific proliferation, by causing its absorption, removal and elimination.

The iodine mineral waters are contra-indicated in stomachic irritation and acute inflammation. The waters may usually be taken freely one or two hours after meals.

(12) MAGNESIAN MINERAL SPRINGS (BITTER WATERS)

These springs contain Epsom salts (sulphate of magnesia) in varying proportions, and may be divided into: *a.* Laxative mineral waters. *b.* Purgative mineral waters. *c.* Saline mineral waters. *d.* Salino-alkaline waters. *e.* Salino-sulphureted waters.

The (*a*) laxative waters contain less and the (*b*) purgative more sulphates of magnesia and sodium. The (*c*) salines are more or less aperient according to the dose, and the (*d*) salino-alkaline contain alkaline chlorides and carbonates, while the (*e*) salino-sulphureted have also sulphur or sulphureted hydrogen besides the magnesia salts.

THERAPEUTICS

As a rule these magnesian waters are carbonated and pleasantly laxative and purgative according to the dose. They are well received by the stomach. The action is due to an increased intestinal secretion superinduced by the active endosmotic and exosmotic action of the magnesian and saline salts, hence the easy watery evacuations produced. This exosmotic or outward flow takes place chiefly from the blood-vessels and is not so much from the glandular appendages of the intestinal mucous membrane. The magnesian laxative, purgative and salines are of especial efficacy in acute inflammatory diseases. They are important remedies in the treatment of renal and cardiac anasarca (dropsy), and in acites from obstruction of the portal circulation.

There is probably not a better treatment for cachexia from saturnine poisoning or painters' palsy, etc., than these magnesian waters. Bitter-salz is also an important remedy in mercurial and copper poisoning, forming inert

Yosemite Falls.

Yosemite Falls.

and insoluble sulphates of mercury, lead or copper, and as such is eliminated from the economy.

For dysenteries, sick headaches, flatulence, colic, and acidity, magnesia waters are of great value. The engorgement of the liver, superinduced by congestion of the pelvic viscera, sub-involution, chronic metritis, etc., and in hæmorrhoidal difficulties these waters have proved highly beneficial. The best time to take aperient or laxative waters is about half an hour to an hour before breakfast a gobletful or two according to circumstances. For chronic constipation nothing is better. For obesity the waters may be taken several times during the day in large doses with marked loss of weight in a week or two.

The pendulous abdomen of middle life may be largely removed by a course of the magnesian waters. For chronic eczema and other skin diseases the salines are serviceable.

The saline-sulphureted waters will be noted under the head of "sulphureted waters."

13. Siliceous Mineral Waters

These waters contain alkaline silicates and salines. They are not used in medicine.

The springs are famous for their petrifying qualities. Many are so strong in silicates that a piece of bark or wood may be petrified in a few days. The wood is not "turned to stone," but each atom and molecule of the woody fibre is dissolved by the silicates, and silicon oxide molecules and atoms occupy the identical spots, reproducing the fine lines and traces so admirably that the kind of wood can easily be determined by the grain of the petrification.

14. Sulphureted (Sulphurous) Mineral Springs.

These waters are usually surcharged with sulphureted hydrogen, characterized by the ancient-egg smell familiar to all who have visited sulphurous regions. The springs are usually hot or warm, and contain sulphates of many elements, sulphides and frequently sulphuric acid.

The *a.* sulphides are rare, the *b.* sulphates and *c.* salino-sulphur are quite common, while the sulphureted hydrogen is more frequent in sulphurous waters. There are also cold or white sulphur springs, which do not have much sulphureted hydrogen, but are frequently mixed with carbonates and carbonic acid gas.

THERAPEUTICS

The great reputation which sulphureted waters have acquired is the best proof of their efficacy as adjuncts to other treatment. Especially is this the case in rheumatism, gout and skin diseases. The waters being usually saline as well as sulphurous are valued in congestion of the liver, abdominal plethora, chronic malarial fever with enlarged spleen, etc., engorgements of the pelvic viscera, metritis and hæmorrhoidal diseases. Uterine tumors are said to have been improved by using these waters.

Syphilitic and strumous diseases are markedly benefited by the sulphur waters. Bright's disease also has been improved while using the mineral waters. Tuberculosis during its incipiency is benefited by the inhalation of the sulphureted hydrogen and by drinking a moderate amount of the water. Acute and chronic rheumatism and gouty arthritis, synovitis, white swelling, chronic joint injuries, and the many chronic cutaneous diseases, are certainly immeasurably benefited by a course at these springs, especially by the hot sulphurous water and mud bathing. (See baths.) The sulphureted waters are taken internally in six to eight ounce doses several times daily, according to the disease. It is best to take the water before breakfast and between meals. For chronic laryngeal, pharyngeal and nasal catarrhs the waters are used as a douche with much benefit. Likewise in the chronic uterine catarrhs and disorders the hot sulphurous mineral water douche, using several gallons two or three times daily, has proved very successful in the author's experience.

THERMAL SPRINGS

Most thermal mineral waters are sulphurous, varying in temperature from 85° F. to 214° F. Thermal waters also contain salines, chlorides, carbonates, etc., etc. Occasionally thermal springs are not sulphurous, but calcic or alkaline.

THERAPEUTICS

The thermal waters are extensively used for bathing purposes, especially those that are sulphureted. For chronic cutaneous diseases, and cases requiring the absorption of chronic exudations in swellings of the joints, old gunshot wounds, chronic gout and articular affections, etc., etc., the treatment is very popular, and certainly aids materially judicious internal medication in alleviating and curing these obstinate and troublesome diseases.

All over the State the thermal and mineral springs, of which there are about three hundred, are being rapidly developed. Extensive improvements are being pushed; elegant and commodious hotels and cottages are being built, with all the modern conveniences and luxuries; gardens and parks, with shady walks and commanding outlooks, are growing; and California, with her excellent climatic advantages, may confidently be expected to rank first in the Union, if not in the world, as a health resort and mineral water sanitarium.

THE BATH

Bathing dates back to the earliest existence of the human race. It was practiced for the treatment of diseases as well as for the preservation of health, and for luxurious enjoyment. The most ancient historical accounts, and the primeval mythologies speak of the bath as being of divine origin.

The Egyptians practiced bathing as a religious rite; and throughout antiquity purification of the body was supposed to be conducive to moral purity. Man was taught to present himself pure in body and in soul when he engaged in the service of his God.

Thus we find that Moses made the bath a religious duty, partly, no doubt to prevent the many cutaneous diseases so prevalent among his people, from spreading. The Mosaic law prescribes in special cases the use of running water, which has probably given rise to the deleterious cellar bathing, at one time extensively practiced by the Jews.

In the cities of the East, particularly Palestine, the wealthier people indulge in costly and extravagant bathing facilities and luxurious baths. Bathing conveniences were established in their houses and in their gardens, where considerable time was spent each day in the enjoyment of the warm bath. The same arrangements still prevail in most of the civilized parts of the East.

Homer frequently speaks about bathing among the early Greeks. It was indispensable in the religious preparations for the sacrifice, for the reception of oracles, and for the holy sacrament of marriage.

Most ancient civilized nations observed the practice of bathing as a religious rite. Public and private bathing establishments existed in the larger cities throughout Greece, some being exclusively for men, some others for women, and others again were for men and women promiscuously.

Rome, at the zenith of her power, possessed some of the finest edifices for bathing that the world has ever seen. The accommodations were perfect, and are scarcely equaled by those of to-day. The baths were taken warm or hot. After one of these luxurious baths the Romans had their bodies anointed with perfumed oils; the bathers then indulged in gentle exercise, such as games, etc., and lastly the body was washed, rubbed, dried and perfumed with costly essence. The ancient Germans used medicated baths, but to a less extent than the Romans. In England bathing was first instituted by the Romans.

When Roman luxury was driven out by German thrift, those splendid bathing edifices, the finest the world has ever seen, fell into disuse and ruin, and were it not for Christianity, by its institution of baptism preserving the religious signification of the bath, the dark ages would possibly have wiped out its existence in the West for some considerable time.

The Arabians and Mohammedans adopted bathing early. Islam enjoined on the faithful corporal purity and prescribed daily ablutions. The rich erected costly baths, and in every city in which there was a mosque the public bath was also instituted.

Imitations of those costly oriental bathing establishments are found to-day in the structures in Constantinople and other European cities. The bathing process is described as follows—not a bad one, by the way, for many diseases of the present day :

The bather undresses in a warm, comfortable room, wraps a blanket around himself, puts on wooden slippers to protect his feet from the hot floor, and then enters the bathroom proper. Here are plunges of hot and cold water, douches of hot and cold water and hot steam. After spending a few minutes in the steaming-room the bather soon breaks into a general perspiration. This lasts from five to fifteen minutes. The next step is a plunge into the cold water or the use of the cold douche; immediately after which the body is rubbed with woolen cloths and anointed with a salve which softens and whitens the skin. This is generally accompanied by "kneading" the body. The bath attendant stretches the bather on a table, pours warm water and salve over him and begins to press, squeeze and twist his whole body with wonderful dexterity. Every limb is straightened and stretched. The attendant kneels upon the bather, seizes him by the shoulders and makes his back crack till the vertebræ quivers. The bather is next treated to soft blows all over the fleshy parts of the body. After this he is rubbed with hair cloths. The hard and calloused skin on the feet is next rubbed with pumice-stone. The whole body is next rubbed with soft soap and the bather plunges into the hot water. Here he remains a few minutes and is taken out and thoroughly rubbed dry. The body is now anointed with perfumes, the hair and beard are trimmed and the bath proper is completed for one day. The bath lasts about two hours and makes one feel as if he were born anew. An inexpressibly delightful sensation of comfort pervades the entire body, and as the bather stretches himself in one of the cooler rooms the sense of luxurious contentment soon wafts him off into a sweet and refreshing sleep. At the end of an hour or two he is awakened and partakes of coffee, sherbet or lemonade, and the bath is completed.

The healing of the sick by means of bathing in mineral and thermal springs became a recognized plan of treatment among the earliest fathers of medicine. The god of medicine, Æsculapius, was invoked and temples were erected to his honor.

Over the thermal baths of Antoninus was engraved on a large marble slab a Latin sentence imparting instruction and warning to the bathers and invalids that, if they wished to be relieved and cured of their diseases, they must first leave all cares behind them, otherwise the waters would be inoperative.

During the Crusades the Europeans first felt the great necessity for frequent ablutions in medicated baths. The wanderers brought home leprosy and other skin diseases, which spread rapidly by contact; hence bathing became universal, and the mineral springs were sought out and used extensively.

In Russia the hot steam and medicated and mineral baths are much used. The bathing facilities are not so extensive as they are farther south. Many of the poorer bathing establishments consist of a small apartment built of wood, with benches all around a central pit. In this pit water is thrown on red hot pebbles. Immediately dense hot fumes are produced, which envelope the bather, who lies undressed on one of the benches. The steam often rises to a temperature of 112° F. After sweating for some time cold water is dashed over the bather, who is then rubbed and anointed and dressed.

Frequently a bather will run from the heated steam chamber out into the snowbanks, in which he rolls for some minutes before he is rubbed and dressed.

Our American aborigines used the hot sulphur springs faithfully for nearly all their ills. They have been known to travel hundreds of miles to reach a special thermal spring. When, however, no mineral spring is within reach they use an appliance very similar to that of the Russians. It consists of a hole in the ground, or a hut whose floor is covered with stones. These are made hot by burning logs of wood over them. When sufficiently heated water is thrown upon the fire and heated stones, and the patient is shut up in the hut or covered in the hole for a specific time, lasting from a few minutes to half an hour, and in some instances as long as three hours. This is the "sweat bath" so much in vogue by many tribes in California.

CLASSIFICATION OF BATHS.

The bath may be classified according to the medium in which a part or the whole body is immersed or surrounded, and according to the temperature, etc., employed. Thus we have the hand and foot bath, the eye bath, the sitz bath and the half or the whole bath. We may take a sea bath, a river bath, a slipper bath, a plunge, shower, dripping or douche bath. The temperature may be cold, tepid, warm or hot. The medium may be pure water, mineral water, saline, sea or sulphurous water, or composed of sand, earth, mud or moor, or of animal excretions. (This latter is used to a considerable extent in California, and sometimes is mixed with mineral waters for bathing purposes.) In Mexico, Central America and among the Indians of California this method of applying animal egesta in the form of poultices to sores and inflamed limbs, etc., is much in vogue.

Then we have vapor baths, cold, warm or hot. These may be simple or medicated, natural or artificial. Compressed air baths have also been instituted. The animal and vegetable baths are not used to any extent at present. The vegetable medicated baths, in which the body is soaked, may be composed of wine, vinegar, solutions of essential oils, infusions of thyme, rosemary, lavender, wormwood, willow, oak or Peruvian bark, etc., etc.

Animal medicated baths are made up of milk, blood, bouillon, oils or fat.

Then there is the medicated vapor bath, in which aromatics, incense, myrrh, benzoin, amber, sulphur, calomel, etc., may be used for a part or the whole of the body. These baths are usually administered in vapor boxes, in which the body is incased and the head is free.

Suitable rooms are also arranged for vapor baths, where the patient walks about naked for a specific time each day. Compressed air chambers and medicated heated air chambers for pulmonary diseases have also been introduced with some success.

The animal bath, much used by the ancients and highly extolled by them for many cutaneous and joint diseases, consisted in wrapping the whole or a part of the patient's body in the warm skin of a recently killed animal. In the case of lameness the patient's limb would be incased in freshly drawn blood. Frequently the smaller animals were killed, split open and applied directly to the affected part. In some instances a patient's limb would be introduced into the breast or abdomen of one of the larger animals while it was yet alive. This practice is now all but obsolete.

The vegetable and animal medicated baths, in which the patient's body is surrounded by wine, milk or both, etc., for some considerable time, can be safely recommended in many cases of inanition, or where the stomach or digestive apparatus is out of order and starvation is imminent. The skin will absorb enough to keep the patient alive for a considerable time.

THE TEMPERATURE IN BATHING

The cold bath has a temperature of 40° to 60° F.; the tepid bath is from 60° to 95° F., and the warm bath from 95° to 100°, and the hot bath from 106° to 110° to 140° F.

Bathing is recognized to-day as a very important agent in the preservation and restoration of health. Besides promoting the healthy and regular exudation and secretion of the sudoriferous and cutaneous glands, bathing assists very materially in absorbing and removing pathological products, particularly in the skin or in and around the joints.

The virtues of water bathing, especially those of the natural mineral waters, have long been established and are daily receiving a more extended application.

Since the modern developments of Balneotherapeutics a new school or class of people have styled themselves "hydropaths," "water-curers," etc., and, with the exaggeration which is incident to everything new, the promoters have promised a panacea for "all the ills to which the flesh is heir," which, of course, is as absurd as it is ill-founded. Now that these quackish pretensions are all but universally ignored or buried in oblivion, it is generally admitted by scientific and medical experimenters that mineral waters are capable of a large range of effects. Taken internally the action, of course, depends upon the mineral ingredients. Used externally in the bath the action depends upon the temperature at which it is employed, as well as upon its chemical composition, the duration of bathing, the reaction which follows, etc.

The Skin

An average-sized individual has from 200 to 240 square inches of cutaneous surface—sixteen to twenty square feet—containing from 2,300,000 to 7,000,000 pores or orifices, through which the normal healthy secretion and excretion of the sudoriferous ducts, sudoriferous and cutaneous glands, pass. The skin also exhales gases besides the solids and liquids. If these 7,000,000 little outlets, each one of which measures one millimeter or more in length (about half a line or one-twenty-fifth of an inch), were joined together in as straight line or tube we should have a canal or pipe over twenty-eight miles long!

Many experimenters have carefully weighed the transpiration passing through the skin. The most notable experimenter—Sanctorious—carried on for thirty years a most careful analysis. He daily weighed all his food and drink and the natural excretions from his person. By careful computation extending over more than a quarter of a century he determined that more than one-half of all foods and drinks were eliminated by means of the skin and pulmonary exhalations. The skin carries on one-fortieth to one-fiftieth of the entire respiratory act; that is to say, through the cutaneous surface we exhale carbonic acid gas and inhale oxygen.

The skin throws off many poisonous substances from the body, such as urea, uric acid, lactic acid, biliary acids, poisons from malaria, cutaneous diseases, and blood diseases and water, fatty matters and epidermic debris. The activity of this eliminative process is hastened and kept in perfect order by the use of mineral baths, thus ridding the system of these morbific agencies. This supplementary action of the organs of the skin may be seen in the "yellow jaundice." Here the normal secretion of the biliary pigments and the natural flow of bile are interfered with through disease. Almost immediately the skin attempts to throw off the bile and pigments. The perspiration will be found to be tinged yellowish, and react to bile acids.

In many diseases the skin is made to act as an adjunct to the organ or organs affected. Thus, in kidney disease, the skin and lungs are made to eliminate the effete materials which should pass through the diseased organ. In lung troubles, the skin and kidneys work off what the lungs normally do, and so on. Indeed the skin can be made to do more. We can keep a person alive for a considerable time by frequent bathing in milk, broths and soups, etc., the whole nourishment passing through the cutaneous openings. Medicaments may be applied to the skin and be completely absorbed. The skin can even be made to inhale oxygen and exhale the poisonous waste product, carbonic acid gas, from the system. Hence we see that the function of the skin is far more important than we imagined, in the preservation and maintenance of health and in restoring the body in disease. As a rule too little attention is given to the subject of bathing and cutaneous medication in America. We have no time, "business, energy and push" absorbs us wholly.

From the foregoing it will be seen that should these 3,000,000 to 7,000,000 little pores be stopped up by decayed scales from the skin—epidermis, by oil, grease, or any waste product from the body, or by dust or dirt from without the body all or a part of this normal exudation or transpiration of solids, liquids and gases must of necessity be repressed and retained in the system to the detriment of health and strength. If half of all our ingesta were naturally eliminated from the cutaneous surface and lungs, the suppression of any of the outlets must throw an extra amount of labor on the remaining pores, or the effete materials must find their way out of the body by some other channel or produce immediately serious results. Fortunately the economy is so admirably constructed that if one organ gets out of order another steps in and takes its place - at least for a time. But this doing double duty, working without sleep or rest cannot be endured for any length of time. In this way, from any partial suppression of cutaneous exhalation and excretion the lungs, and more especially the kidneys, are obliged to dispose of any work the skin is incapacitated from doing, thereby throwing an extra amount of strain on these organs, which it is impossible for them to endure long without showing signs of overwork. This frequently ends in kidney (Bright's) disease, and the long train of symptoms with which only too many have had personal experience. It is a *sine qua non*, that if the skin does not act, the organs of egestion must dispose of the morbific material, and most of the work, as before remarked, falls to the kidneys, producing irritation, inflammation and the many diseases which follow.

The author does not doubt that many cases of Bright's disease in California can be traced to an impaired function of the skin, because the hygroscopic state of the atmosphere prevents the rapid evaporation of perspired fluids and interferes with a perfect function of the cutaneous surface. (This at least is the case on the sea-coast.) Hence we see the necessity of keeping the skin in prime condition. Any impervious coating applied to the entire cutaneous surface of a person would produce death in a short time, as we know from the instance of the child who was once gilded to take a part in a great Roman festival.

NATURAL MINERAL WATER BATHS.

The external application of several of our mineral waters is more efficacious in the treatment of many diseases than the internal administration. This is particularly noticeable in the rheumatic, gouty, strumous joint affections and in several varieties of skin diseases.

The most beneficial bath in the world may, however, do great harm if injudiciously used. Indeed, fatal effects have been repeatedly observed. It is, therefore, urged that a careful diagnosis be made of the case and that medical surveillance be kept up constantly during a course of bathing, and that self-treatment and indiscriminate bathing be discountenanced. Not only will the spring waters do more good if intelligently used, but the many fatal results occurring every year will be prevented.

To follow medical advice in the matter of bathing and using mineral waters becomes all the more necessary and important, when it is borne in mind that each thermal and mineral spring differs materially in composition and temperature from any that may have been used before. Hence it follows that when one water may be used in more than one way, to derive any benefit, or the greatest benefit, from

CAP OF LIBERTY

it, it must be applied discriminately. Place yourself, therefore, under the management of the competent keepers of the baths and the attendant physician, and do not use your own judgment about a matter which you but imperfectly understand.

With these precautions there can be no doubt about the beneficial results accruing from a systematic course of mineral water or mud bathing, instituted as an auxiliary measure, in the treatment of these chronic diseases. The beneficial results obtainable by the warm (95° to 100° F.) and hot (100° to 140° F.) mineral water and mud bathing are perfectly logical and susceptible of actual demonstration.

The sensations experienced on entering a warm mineral bath are exceedingly pleasant. A feeling of comfort and enjoyment steals over one immediately following immersion. This continues during the bath, imparting to the system generally a genial sensation productive of luxurious contentment. If in pain the patient is much relieved, and if moderately well he feels at ease with the world and only wishes this paradise of enjoyment and physical well-doing could endure forever.

The warmth with which the body is surrounded is communicated to its surface and rapidly permeates the entire system, internal as well as external, until it reaches the central nervous system, from which reaction supervenes.

The first noticeable phenomena after the pleasurable sensations are a slight redness, and considerable swelling and expansion of the integument. These effects are produced by the dilatation of the smaller blood-vessels under the relaxant influence of the heat. As the bath continues this relaxant action is not confined to the skin alone, but is also felt in the structures which lie beneath it, as well as in the organs within the body. The fascia, muscles, tendons, and particularly the products of inflammation and tumefaction in and around the joints, seem to soften and exhibit less tension. This influence of softening and expansion of the cutaneous surface observed after immersion in the warm bath is not an apparent but a real swelling and distension, as may be demonstrated by the wearing apparel, such as the finger rings, etc , becoming too small. Now this increased circumference of a foot, hand or finger, and the enlargement of the cutaneous surface generally, is not altogether due to the dilation of the blood-vessels and relaxant action of the warmth and moisture, but to the fact that part of the mineral waters, gases and mineral ingredients have actually been absorbed into the integumentary system and circulation throughout the body, through the millions of little pores and absorbent orifices, and even through the skin by the well-known law of osmosis. This absorption is further found to be in direct ratio to the specific gravity of the bathing medium. The blood has a specific gravity of 1,050 to 1,070, pure water being 1,000. An ordinary warm, fresh water bath has a specific gravity of 1,005 to 1,010. Applying the law of endosmosis and exosmosis, the bath abstracts vitality instead of imparting vigor. This we know is actually a fact. A hot bath always leaves one weaker. Now the mineral saline and sulphureted, and the mud waters used for bathing at many of our spring resorts, have specific gravities of from 1,100 to 1,250, therefore it will be seen that the greater specific gravity medium may pass through the animal membrane—the skin—into the blood, which has a less specific gravity. This actually occurs. The mineral constituents—crystalline—readily penetrate the integument and enter the circulation, as may be demonstrated by a chemical examination of the blood and urine before and after bathing. Not only have the salts of minerals—sodium, potassium, iodine, sulphur, etc.—been tested and verified, but the gases in the bath themselves have been observed in minute traces in the blood.

It was not until recently that this question of the power of the skin to absorb water, mineral ingredients and gases assumed anything like definite proportions, as authorities and experimenters were at variance. The mooted point may, however, be regarded as satisfactorily settled now by the many carefully conducted observations of Maden and Collard de Martigue, confirmed by the excellent experiments of Barthold, Williams and Edwards, who unhesitatingly affirm that salines and mineral ingredients are absorbed into the system and may as such exert their specific influence and be tested chemically in the blood and secretions.

THE EFFECTS OF MINERAL-WATER BATHING ON THE CIRCULATION AND RESPIRATION

The temperature of the bath determines the relative force and frequency of the heart's action.

Both pulsation and respiration are increased in frequency on first entering the bath. If the heat be moderate, however, say from 95° to 100° F., the normal pulsation is restored as soon as the body and the organs are thoroughly warmed. After that the only observable phenomenon is a greater fullness of the pulse, due in part to the absorption of the bathing fluid into the circulation and a relaxation of the arterial tension.

With every additional degree of heat beyond 98.5 ° F. (blood heat) to which the bath is raised, the rapidity of the pulse *pari passu* is increased. The bodily temperature also rises. This cardiac exhilaration often continues for a considerable time after the bath. It may run so high at the time of bathing as to be extremely dangerous where there is any heart disease at all, and may require prompt attention.

The pulmonary and the cutaneous transpiration are also increased by the warm and the hot bath, rapid disintegration of tissue ensues. The same is accomplished by prolonged bathing at a temperature of 105° F. The waste products of the body or of disease escape through the skin and pulmonary mucous membrane. Prolonged bathing of a high temperature in a water of low specific gravity can be advantageously and safely employed among the obese.

With the general dilation of the capillaries and the concomitant relaxation of the integumentary, nervous, muscular and articular systems, and with the osmotic absorption of some of the salts and bathing fluids into the general circulation, there certainly seems to be a greater volume to the pulsations after a generous bath; capillaries, small veins and arteries, and the absorbents apparently sluggish in the performance of their duties from the tumefaction or inflamed condition of the surrounding tissues about a joint, take up renewed activity under the relaxant influence of the warm bath, and this is probably one of the explanations of the *modus operandi* by which a swollen joint or an arthritic affection improves so considerably under the use of thermal baths. The blood-vessels and absorbents dilate, their capacity thereby allowing freer movement of the circulation. The inflammatory products, usually partially organized tissue, also seem to soften and become absorbed.

Certain it is that these warm baths relieve the engorged condition of blood-vessels and inflamed tumefied joints, equalizing the circulation, as it were, and causing the swelling and stiffness to disappear gradually, especially when these means are combined with proper internal treatment. This can readily be demonstrated.

The nervous system is also benefited. We are all familiar with the soothing result of the delightful warm bath. The hot bath (110° F.) is stimulating and exciting to the nervous system, but a bath at 98° to 100° F. produces a sedative effect, allays irritability and alleviates the pain in over-sensitive nerves. This is exemplified by the soothing effect of a poultice in local pains or the immersion of a hand or a foot in warm water when it is painful or inflamed. After a tedious railroad journey or a prolonged mental strain nothing so allays the nervous irritability and calms the over-sensitive nerves as a warm bath. This sedative action is probably due to the general equalization of the arterial circulation removing local congestions or internal inflammations. Try a warm mineral bath after a tiresome journey and see how it refreshes you.

How to Bathe.

The palliative or curative effects of mineral-water bathing depend largely upon the composition of the water, the temperature of the bath, duration of bathing, and the diseases for which the treatment is taken.

Mineral baths are tonic, sedative, diaphoratic, derivative and alterative, according to their composition and mode of administration.

Rules for Bathing.

Time of day.—It is almost impossible to lay down a hard and fast rule of universal application relative to the hour of bathing for invalids, as there may be many subjective and objective circumstances which demand considerable latitude.

The best time for the usual warm 95° to 100°F. mineral

spring bath is about two or three hours after breakfast and one or two hours before luncheon, about 10 or 11 A. M. for those who dine early, and about the same number of hours after luncheon for those who dine late. In any event the preceding meal must be digested prior to the bath and the system must be beginning to feel the effects of the conversion of the food-fuel into force and vital energy. The system is then placed in the most advantageous condition for deriving benefit from the bath, which is then both agreeable and safe.

Caution.—Never take a warm, hot or cold bath immediately preceding nor directly succeeding a meal. The reason is obvious. During the process of digestion a relatively larger proportion of blood is invited to the digestive organs to assist in the chymification and chylification and absorption of the blood in order that the process may be more efficiently performed. Any unusual stimulation, such as would be superinduced by the application of warm or hot water to the entire cutaneous surface of the body, would be sure to abstract a large quantity of blood from the organs of digestion to the integumentary capillaries, and, in the case of bathing after meals, produce sudden interruption of the digestive process, checking the proper secretion of the digestive fluids, retarding assimilation and not infrequently producing congestive headaches, pre-cordial oppression, fainting and possibly cramps in the stomach and intestines from the undigested food. In the case of bathing just before dinner the same results are induced, with the exception that the internal anæmia and the cutaneous engorgement are produced before food is taken, instead of afterward, which militates against digestion fully as much, for besides not having much appetite immediately after the bath the food that is introduced into the stomach finds no juices to digest it and remains for hours in an undigested condition, thus laying the foundation for dyspepsia and all the evil effects of retained, undigestive food.

Bathing before breakfast, especially in cold (40° to

60° F.) water, is not recommended for invalids. Early morning ablutions can only be advantageously employed by one who is robust and vigorous in constitution, who has reactive power enough to render the bath beneficial or at least not injurious.

The author knew of a case—a gentleman of fine physique, who used to go down to the San Francisco bay every morning about six o'clock, winter and summer, and take a cold plunge and a swim. It did him good, or at least it did him no harm, for he was well and full of vitality. One day a sickly friend of his remarked how well he looked. "Yes," said the bather, "that is the result of my plunge in the bay every morning before breakfast. Why don't you come down to-morrow morning and try it?" "I believe I will," was the reply. The next day, a bright January morning, the two friends plunged into the bay. Alas! it was his last plunge, poor fellow, for the sickly friend did not have vitality enough to establish a reaction, although he walked home, a distance of about one mile. In the afternoon he was taken with a congestive chill, and in three days he died.

In perfect health it is considered highly beneficial to take a cold plunge, a slipper or a sponge bath before the morning meal, inducing complete and thorough reaction by rubbing, exercise, etc. It certainly seems to prevent a susceptible patient from taking cold as readily as without them, but one ought to be guarded about establishing the reaction.

Occasionally circumstances might render it expedient, or the personal habits and conveniences of the patient might require a warm mineral bath at night. Let it always be taken sufficiently long after dinner to insure more or less complete digestion. After the bath take care of the night air, for it is never as pleasant nor as safe for bathing as the morning atmosphere between the hours of ten and twelve o'clock.

The hot saline or alkalino-sulphureted waters, which are

principally used for bathing, open the pores of the skin, dissolve and cut away the oils and debris from the little outlets and induce more or less perspiration ; hence, while the liability to catching cold is not nearly so great as when using plain water, it is nevertheless wise to guard against such a possibility.

TEMPERATURE OF BATHING

The cold bath is from 40° to 60° F.

The tepid bath is from 60° to 95° F.

The warm bath is from 95° to 100° F.

And the hot bath ranges from 100° to 110°, 120° and 140° F.

Steam baths range in temperature from 96° to 140° F. The temperature of every mineral bath should be ascertained by a thermometer *in the bathtub* all the time.

The remarks on temperature will apply principally to warm and hot mineral water bathing, as cold or tepid baths are seldom used by, or recommended to, invalids seeking relief at mineral springs.

Individual idiosyncracies require consideration in the matter of warm bathing. A temperature soothing and onic to one person might prove too exciting and too stimulating for another having a highly sensitive and nervous organization.

As a general rule, a bath at 96° to 98° F. is found to produce an agreeable, soothing and tonic effect. It is the temperature most generally recommended for entering the water. Should it be desired to produce severe diaphoresis or a strong tonic effect the bath may be entered at 100° F. to 105° or 110° F., but the conditions requiring such a bath are not often met with. Enter the bath at blood heat 98.5°F., and then gradually increase it to any desired temperature for the specific purpose of the bath. This will be found the most agreeable, as well as the safest and best plan. It will add much to the comfort of the patient and not a little to the

efficacy of the treatment if the dressing-rooms be sufficiently warmed to be agreeable, say from 75° F. to 80° F.
This is quite important in the after-treatment (*quod vide*),
and decidedly pleasant before the bath.

Whatever degree of temperature is desired it should
be reached gradually, if above 100° F., and then steadily
maintained throughout the duration of the bath, having a
thermometer in each bathtub or plunge.

Caution: Persons of weak constitutions and invalids
reduced by disease, as well as delicate and convalescent
patients, should on no account venture into the warm or
hot mineral bath without medical advice.

Hot baths should never be used by patients suffering
with organic disease of the heart, nor by those who are
subject to hemorrhages of the lungs. A plethoric condition of the body, with a tendency to cerebral congestion,
indicated by vertigo, or swimming in the head, also contra-
indicates hot bathing. Consumptives, especially the more
advanced cases, do not receive much benefit from mineral
waters, and the baths may, and often do, hasten the
unhappy end if persistently used.

DURATION OF THE BATH

The time during which complete immersion is observed
requires considerable attention. The mineral bath is a
potent agent for good or for evil, and not by any means
devoid of danger, if the temperature and the duration are
not carefully watched and considered. The bather must
be governed by the requirements and peculiarities of his
individual case. For this purpose medical advice should
be sought from time to time.

As a rule, the bath at a temperature of 98° to 100° F.
for ten minutes acts as a stimulant and a tonic to the general system, and especially to the cutaneous surface.

Immersion from 15 to 30 minutes in the same temperature (98° to 100° F.) produces a decidedly relaxant effect,

opening the twenty-eight miles of tubing and the 7,000,000 pores of the skin, dilating the capillaries, softening the muscles and tendons and inflammatory products surrounding a swollen joint, assisting in the excretion of the effete materials, and allowing the absorption of many of the saline and mineral ingredients found in the mineral waters. This is the bath for joint affections—keeping the temperature at the desired point by allowing more hot water to flow in when necessary.

The patient must be watched. If faintness or giddiness, or præcordial or pulmonary oppression occurs, the bath must be instantly discontinued and reaction brought on as rapidly as possible. (See treatment after bathing). Should it be deemed advisable or necessary to continue the bath for a longer period in order to produce more pronounced effects, then greater care must also be exercised; when a prolonged bath is used, such as may be beneficial in many cases of cutaneous diseases and in scrofulous and syphilitic contaminations, then the temperature ought not to be above 100° F. Bloodheat 98.5° F. will always be agreeable and just as beneficial. In prolonged bathing always watch the heart's action.

One cause of faintness and præcordial oppression and labored breathing is the amount of water on *top* of the chest. It is not necessary to fill the bathtub so as to have six or twelve inches of water on your body. One or two inches above you is all that is necessary, and the weight is much less.

The lower the temperature the longer must be the immersion to produce the same results, and vice versa.

For a soothing and tonic effect, a bath lasting from five to fifteen minutes at a temperature of about 100° F. will prove most beneficial. For complete relaxation and profuse perspiration, this may be extended to thirty minutes.

In the case of a decided tonic and stimulant action, the hot bath may be used at a temperature of 106°-10°F., for a period of two to five minutes.

For the slow and continuous effect (used principally for skin diseases), a bath of 98°-99° F. for one, two or three hours, will be most serviceable.

TREATMENT AFTER THE BATH

It is important to establish complete reaction after bathing, be the temperature cold, warm or hot. The dressing-rooms and sweating-rooms should be comfortably warmed. Much additional comfort and benefit will accrue from having towels thoroughly warmed before using them for drying the patient. These are small matters, but of considerable importance in preventing bathers from becoming suddenly chilled by coming in contact with cold air and cold towels.

Immediately after leaving the bath the cutaneous surface should be briskly rubbed and thoroughly dried with rough Turkish towels. Should reaction be feeble the flesh-rubber, or flesh-brush, or flesh-strap may be advantageously used to stimulate the integumentary circulation.

In cases of retarded reaction, recourse may also be had to hot beef-tea or soup containing cayenne pepper, hot coffee, etc. In extreme cases Hoffman's anodyne (Spiritus Aetheris Compositus U. S. P.) fifteen to thirty drops in a hot whisky or brandy punch may be of great value. Let the bather observe the recumbent position, keeping him warm and continuing the rubbing process, and if the bath has not been indiscreetly used, reaction will soon follow.

In many cases it may be desirable to promote profuse perspiration. Such patients are briskly rubbed and dried, and then wrapped in warmed woolen blankets and placed in a comfortable cot or couch in a warm room for an hour or two. After which the body is again thoroughly rubbed and dried and the patient is then dressed. It is also recommended in certain cases to use the cold douche after a hot bath. Weakly patients, or those suffering with acute inflammation in the joints or in the skin should not resort to its use unless advised by the attendant physician, as the shock may be too great.

After a warm or hot bath great care must be exercised to prevent the possibility of taking cold. Take a gentle walk or exercise slowly in the open air, providing the season permits. If this can not be done, then quietly remain in your own apartments for an hour or two after each bath.

It has been observed that in mineral water and saline water bathing much more tonic and stimulating effects are produced if reaction be thoroughly established than after bathing in ordinary water. Mineral baths are much more strengthening and more derivative to the surface and the entire system and can be taken consecutively for a much longer period than with the use of ordinary water. The liability to take cold is also much less. It is an excellent plan to gently rub a stiff or sore joint with some stimulating and anodyne lotion after each hot bath. This seems to assist in the absorption of the inflammatory proliferation around the joint.

FREQUENCY OF BATHING.

The frequency of bathing must necessarily depend upon the disease for which the patient is being treated, the condition of the individual's strength, the duration of each bath, the reaction that follows and the temperature employed.

At first the most benefit will probably accrue from the use of one or two baths per week. Then take a bath every other day, and, if necessary, one every day. It is a matter of great importance, and as each case is an individual one the best advice can only be given by your physician.

CAUTION.—Do not commence a course of treatment at the springs by bathing once or twice daily. The American fashion, as noted elsewhere, of hastening and rushing through everything may do well enough for business, but where the life of an individual or the treatment of an obstinate disease is at issue this plan is not only deleterious, but may prove fatal to the life of the patient.

BRIDAL VAIL FALLS

"Upreared within the azure sky,
Like temples leaf-crowned, vast and high
        They firmly stand ;
No breeze can sway their massive strength,
Or shake their mighty breadth and length,
        By tempests fanned :
Their first of life what man shall know,
That sprung two thousand years ago ?

"Two thousand years ! two thousand years !
Of human sufferings, joys and tears,
        In ceaseless chase ;
When these great structures had their birth
Our Saviour had not walked the earth
        To save our race :
Yet then, amid their boughs on high,
Time's diapasons swept them by."

Minor Ablutions.

Occasionally, in the treatment of young children, delicate women and persons of feeble constitutions, it may be deemed unadvisable to immerse the whole body in any kind of water. For such as these we can recommend the partial bath.

The writer has repeatedly treated subacute and chronic rheumatic affections with marked benefit by the partial bath, immersing only the affected member, hand or foot, in the hot water or mud bath. At the springs the hands, elbows, knees and hips may be similarly treated, with good results.

In most partial ablutions the duration of the time may be longer, the water hotter, and the bath taken more frequently if thought advisable.

HOT SITZ BATH

The sitz bath is of great value in many pelvic disorders peculiar to females. The sitz bath may also prove serviceable in rheumatic and joint troubles in the hips and gluteal region when a general bath cannot be taken.

THE DOUCHE

This is a powerful agent and must be used with due consideration. It consists of a jet of water, usually cold, which is discharged with considerable force against the body for a few seconds to a few minutes' duration. If the patient be strong enough to stand it, the cold douche taken after a hot bath produces a marked stimulating effect, providing complete reaction is brought about.

A capital use can be made of the douche by employing hot mineral water and allowing it to strike a swollen joint such as the knee. Considerable force may be employed and the douche applied one or more times daily.

The douche, be it hot or cold, ought never to strike the head or the abdomen.

THE SENTINEL.

THE UTERINE DOUCHE

Several of the mineral waters used very hot (110-120° F.) by means of the douche have been found efficacious in the treatment of female disorders and uterine troubles, such as leucorrhœa, congestion, inflammation, menstrual irregularities, etc., etc. For this purpose the patient observes a horizontal position and allows a gentle stream of hot mineral water to be directed into the vaginal cavity. The uterine douche may be applied twice daily for from five to ten minutes in duration, using several gallons of the hot sulphurous or mineral water at each operation. This has proved a most valuable and admirable plan in these chronic disorders, and is well worth trying.

THE SPINAL BATH

This consists in having a jet of cold, warm or hot water gently strike up and down the spinal column—a douche, in other words, applied to the spine. A pail or pitcher may be used for pouring the water on the spine instead of the pipe, although the latter, being continuous, is much more efficacious.

The spinal bath is recommended in the nervous disorders of females, especially that form of nervo-hysterical troubles frequently observed in the young ladies who are fond of late evening parties, theatres, balls, etc., and who spend most of the following day in bed or in the house reading exciting novels.

The bath can be advantageously used from three to five minutes every morning, according to the conditions of the patient. It should be followed by brisk rubbing and exercise in the open air.

The shallow or slipper bath, dripping bath, sheet bath, or wet pack, etc., etc., are not used at mineral springs, and will not be dilated upon in this place.

THE MUD OR MOOR BATH

These mud baths have been in use on this coast for many years. The aborigines used them long before the pale-faced stranger arrived. Wonderful and miraculous cures are handed down in the traditions of the red men. Crude huts were erected over these mud springs, and many an Indian has traveled hundreds of miles to bathe in a certain spring.

These ancient Indian moor baths have been extensively utilized at several of the mineral springs in California. Modern bathing facilities have been constructed, and mud bathing has been reduced to a practical and scientific basis. A mud bath can be borne at a much higher temperature than one of water, on account of its low conducting power of heat. This aids in the absorption of the saline and mineral constituents and volatile gases and acids. The baths are stimulating to the skin, promoting secretion and excretion, and are much extolled in the treatment of obstinate joint affections of rheumatic, gouty, syphilitic or strumous origin. In chronic hypertrophy of the liver and the spleen, inflammation of the pelvic organs, kidney and bladder troubles, and in old, indolent skin diseases the writer has witnessed decided improvements. The temperature may be taken from 100° to 120° F., with the same precautions and observations noted under the head of water bathing. For a partial bath for hand, foot or knee the mud promises every advantage. For chronic rheumatism there is no better treatment instituted anywhere than these hot sulphurous and saline mud baths, together with the proper internal treatment.

VAPOR AND GAS BATHS

In many localities on this coast hot vapors and gases arise from the earth in conjunction with the mineral springs. The fumes are principally sulphurous, with a certain amount of steam from the water.

Suitable apartments are arranged for bathing purposes. The rooms are so arranged that the heated steam and sulphurous fumes can be regulated to any desired temperature. A hot and a cold plunge bath also adjoin it. The temperature of the vapor may range from 100° F. to 140° F., and the duration of a bath from a few seconds to several minutes. Care should be taken that no sulphurous (SO_2) or sulphuric (SO_3) anhydride is present in the inhaled vapors, as these gases are poisonous. It is also necessary to watch the heart's action and the respiratory process lest the gases be too oppressive and produce serious results.

After a sweating vapor bath the plunge may be prescribed, after which the usual rubbing to establish reaction should be resorted to. If prolonged diaphoresis be desirable, wrap up the patient in a warm blanket and place him in the sweating-room for one or two hours.

These natural vapor baths are very useful in catarrhal affections of the nose, pharynx, larynx and bronchial tubes. Chronic bronchitis and incipient phthisis improve by inhaling dry sulphurous vapors and mineral water steam. For inaction of the integument in chronic skin diseases the vapors have also proven beneficial.

Partial vapor baths may also be taken; and a limb, hand or foot can be encased in the hot steam.

The mineral water and mud baths, and, indeed, the mineral springs themselves, are not held out as "cure-alls." The author merely desires to call attention to their utility and the proper method of their application. Thousands— yes, millions—are using mineral waters and bathing in mineral springs yearly with more or less benefit. Used intelligently, carefully and persistently as auxiliaries to the recognized internal treatment, there can be no doubt that natural mineral waters do assist in the alleviation of human suffering and in the cure of many of the obstinately chronic diseases which unfortunately attack our fellow-men.

NOTE.—In making analyses of mineral waters and presenting them to the profession and public generally, it has been deemed expedient to employ the universal method of computing the mineral ingredients by the *grains* to the gallon. The more exact and scientific system of using *grammes* to the litre or parts per hundred or thousand, although superior, is not as universally adopted, and hence more imperfectly understood. Most of the analytical tables of foreign and domestic springs have, therefore, been reduced to conform to the analyses made by the author according to the old system of *grains* in each *gallon* of water. It will also be observed that all the *salts* of the same element are placed together, invariably beginning with those of sodium and following with those of potassium, magnesium, calcium, etc. The object in view has been to facilitate ready reference, which is accomplished by this arrangement, and, as sodium chloride is nearly always present in mineral springs on this coast, it has been thought proper to begin each analytical table with the most universal mineral ingredient.

—*The Author.*

OCEAN SCULPTURE NEAR SANTA MONICA

"*Imprimis*, my darling, they drink
　　The waters so sparkling and clear ;
Though the flavor is none of the best,
　　And the odor exceedingly queer ;
But the fluid is mingled, you know,
　　With wholesome *medicinal things*,
So they drink, and they drink, and they drink,
　　And that's what they do at the springs.

　　　＊　　　＊　　＊　　＊

"In short—as it goes in the world—
　　They eat, and they drink, and they sleep ;
They talk, and they walk, and they woo ;
　　They sigh, and they laugh, and they weep ;
They read, and they ride, and they dance,
　　(With other unspeakable things);
They pray, and they play, and they pay,
　　And that's what they do at the springs."

I. ADAMS SPRINGS

These picturesque springs are in Lake county, two miles from Cobb's Valley, eight miles south of Clear Lake, and five miles from Glenbrook. They may be reached by the train which goes by way of Oakland Pier, Vallejo and Calistoga. From the last point a stage is taken which carries one along a pleasant mountain road hedged in on either side by manzanita copses, scrub oaks, and towards the summit fragrant redwood trees.

The resort itself lies among rolling hills which are thickly shrouded in verdant loveliness a greater part of the year. Beyond these hills lie the larger mountains of the Coast Range, banked to the summits with their heavy growths of redwood and pine. Fogs are rare in Lake county, and the air is uniformly dry, pure and balmy; more like Nice in the south of France than one would suppose from the difference in latitude.

The springs lie at an elevation of 3,300 feet above the sea level. Commodious quarters have been prepared for guests, and every effort is made to make every one feel at home. Hunting and fishing are excellent. Deer is rather scarce, but quail and rabbit are plenty; and the Clear Lake fish bite rapidly.

ADAMS SPRINGS
MAIN SPRING—ALKALO-CARBONATED WATER
Dr. Winslow Anderson, Analyst, 1888

U. S. gal. contains

Mineral Ingredients	Grains	Mineral Ingredients	Grains
Sodium Chloride	4.64	Calcium Carbonate	27.95
Sodium Carbonate	50.70	Calcium Sulphate	1.36
Sodium Bicarbonate	8.07	Ferrous Carbonate	.55
Potassium Salts	traces	Silica	7.42
Magnesium Carbonate	97.90	Alumina	traces
Magnesium Sulphate	traces	Organic Matter	2.60

Total Solids, 201.19

Gases	Cubic inches
Free Carbonic Acid Gas,	265.76

The water is cool and sparkling, and belongs to the alkaline-carbonated class. It is highly recruitive to persons suffering from chronic dyspepsia and portal congestion. It is also used for rheumatism. In cases of chronic Bright's disease it is reported to have especial efficacy. Chronic metritis has also been benefited. Facilities for hot and cold bathing have been provided, and the springs have acquired a high reputation, and are much frequented by visitors and invalids.

ADAMS SPRINGS
MAIN SPRING—ALKALO-CARBONATED WATER
PROF. PRICE AND MR. HEWSTON

Mineral Ingredients	U. S. gal contains Grains	Mineral Ingredients	U. S. gal. contains Grains
Sodium Chloride	4.112	Calcium Sulphate	——
Sodium Carbonate	57.036	Ferrous Carbonate	.517
Sodium Bicarbonate	——	Silica	7.218
Potassium Salts	trace	Alumina	——
Magnesium Carbonate	99.022	Organic Matter	2.811
Magnesium Sulphate	——	Nitric Acid	trace
Calcium Carbonate	28.714		

Total Solids, 199.430

Gases	Cubic Inches
Free Carbonated Acid Gas,	304.

2. ÆTNA SPRINGS

Ætna Springs are located at the upper end of Pope Valley, at an altitude of 1,000 feet, in Napa County, sixteen miles northeast from the town of St. Helena. They are of easy access by rail via Napa to St. Helena and then by stage or carriage over a well-graded road. The drive is pleasant and full of interest; winding around and over Mt. Howell, along the cañon with its picturesque tangle of shrubbery, over brooks and mountain streams until the springs are reached. They are pleasantly situated in the midst of wild mountain surroundings. The atmosphere is delightfully dry and bracing, making one feel as though our primitive forefathers manifested their common sense when they scorned shelter of confining dwellings and lived out in the open air. The humidity is very low, consequently the heat of the middle of the day is not felt. The exhilarating, balmy breezes of the afternoon give way to pleasantly cool evenings and perfect nights, insuring refreshing rest and sleep. In climate and natural surroundings Ætna springs are admirably located for a health as well as for a pleasure resort. There are ample accommodations for guests at the hotel and several handsome cottages for private use. The grounds are particularly well adapted for camping parties. The mountains in the vicinity of the resort are well stocked with wild game and the streams afford good fishing.

The temperature of the two principal mineral springs used for drinking purposes is about 98° F. The waters are sparkling, invigorating and tonic and slightly aperient. There are also springs having a temperature of 106° F., which are largely used for bathing, ample facilities having been provided for that purpose. Several other springs whose waters have not been analyzed are similar in composition, with the addition of more iron. These are known as the "Iron-soda" springs and are much used for anæmic and wasting diseases, producing constructive metamorphosis.

Ætna soda springs are rapidly gaining in public favor, and from the large number of visitors who go there yearly it is certain that decidedly beneficial results accrue from the use of the waters. Especially is this the case in the renal affections so frequent on this coast. Beneficial results are reported in rheumatism and neuralgia; also in dyspepsia, torpidity of the bowels, hepatic and uterine engorgement.

There is considerable similarity between the noted Ems water of European fame and our California Ætna soda, as may be observed by the following analyses. The Ems analyst is Professor Fresenius of Wiesbaden and the Ætna analyst is J. A. Bauer of San Francisco, made several years ago. My own analysis was made in 1888:

ÆTNA SODA
ALKALINE WATER
DR. WINSLOW ANDERSON, Analyst, 1858

U. S. Gal. contains		U. S. Gal. contains	
Mineral Ingredients	Grains	Mineral Ingredients	Grains
Sodium Chloride	28.75	Magnesium Sulphate	.45
Sodium Carbonate	73.06	Calcium Carbonate	8.94
Sodium Sulphate	8.92	Ferrous Carbonate	.05
Potassium Sulphate	.56	Silica	.09
Potassium Carbonate	13.23	Organic Matter	trace

Total Solids, 134.17

Gases	Cubic Inches
Carbonic Acid Gas,	63.

This analysis, made ten years after the preceding one, shows some little change in the composition of the water, Therapeutically, the change is probably for the better.

There are several important mineral springs not yet named and but slightly developed, which will doubtless be as important remedial agents (and about which pleasure resorts will spring up when they are developed), as we find their improved sister springs to be.

ÆTNA SPRINGS
ALKALINE WATER
J. A. BAUER, Analyst
Temperature 98° F.
ÆTNA, 1878

U. S. Gal. contains		U. S. Gal. contains	
Mineral Ingredients	Grains	Mineral Ingredients	Grains
Sodium Chloride	29.	Magnesium Carbonate	14.
Sodium Carbonate	75.	Calcium Carbonate	10.
Sodium Sulphate	08.	Ferrous Carbonate	trace
Potassium Sulphate	trace	Silica	trace

Total Solids, 136

Gases	Cubic Inches
Carbonic Acid Gas,	58.

EMS
ALKALINE WATER
Prof. Fresenius, Analyst, Ems, 1871

Temperature 115° F.

Mineral Ingredients	U. S. gal. contains Grains	Mineral Ingredients	U. S. gal. contains Grains
Sodium Chloride	62.	Magnesium Carbonate	7.
Sodium Carbonate	84.	Calcium Carbonate	10.
Sodium Sulphate	trace	Ferrous Carbonates	trace
Potassium Sulphate	3.	Silica	3.

Total Solids, 169.

Gases	Cubic Inches
Carbonic Acid Gas,	59.

PALM VALLEY

3. AGUAS CALIENTES

In the southern portion of the State are located a number of important mineral springs. Several of these in different parts have been known as " Agua Caliente." Those situated in the Coahuila or Cabezon Valley, some ten miles south of White River, on Warner's ranch, fifty miles from San Diego city, in San Diego County, having acquired considerable celebrity especially among the native population. They are believed to be infallible remedies in syphilis and in cutaneous affections. These springs are situated on the slope of one of the ridges at the most easterly part of Warner's ranch. They are thermal, varying in temperature from 58° F. to 142° F.

The water boils up from a granite ledge through a number of openings or cleavage-fissures. It flows copiously, giving a volume of about a two inch pipe under two foot pressure. Bubbles of sulphureted hydrogen and steam issue forth with considerable force, producing the characteristic smell of sulphur and clouds of vapor. At one place a small geyser has developed, emitting steam and water with a hissing sound. Incrustations of crystallized sulphur are deposited on the surrounding rock. (Blake.)

The waters possess a sulphurous and a not unpleasant acid taste, and are much used for drinking and bathing purposes. Formerly several Indian families were in charge of the springs and gave visitors the best accommodations they had in their crude huts. Latterly, since the springs have become generally known, better accommodations and facilities have been provided.

These hot sulphurous waters are highly recommended by many persons who have been there and used the baths and taken the waters. The diseases treated most frequently are rheumatism, sub-acute and chronic, syphilitic contaminations and strumous diseases, cutaneous affections, and renal and hepatic engorgement.

ANALYSIS

ANALYZED BY MR. OSCAR LOEW

Mineral Ingredients	U. S. gal. contains Grains	Mineral Ingredients	U. S. gal. contains Grains
Sodium Carbonate	8.3	Lithia	trace
Sodium Sulphate	trace	Silica	trace
Sodium Chloride	31.	Sulph-hydric acid	trace
Lime	trace	Organic Matter	trace
Magnesia	trace		

Total Solids, 39.3
Gases not given.

4. AGUA CALIENTE

Another Agua Caliente of some repute is located some thirty miles from Caliente station, on the Southern Pacific Railroad line in Kern county.

These waters are also thermal and sulphureted. The temperature varies from 80° F. to 100° F.

There is a small resort at the springs.

I have not been able to obtain water for analysis.

5.   AGUA DE VIDA SPRINGS.

The springs are on the Arroyo Mucho, among the foothills of Cedar Mountain, southeast of Livermore, and at an elevation of 1,700 feet.   There are a number of mineral waters on the place, both carbonated and sulphureted. The lower drinking spring is of light carbonated water, which is clear, sparkling and extremely palatable. In action it is tonic, antacid, diuretic and aperient. The upper or larger spring is mildly sulphurous, saline and laxative. These mineral springs were used many years ago, not only by the early settlers, but by the natives who dwelt in the valley before them.

Extensive improvements are being made on the grounds, consisting of a magnificent hotel surrounded by commodious family cottages. The grounds, which are naturally picturesque, will be still further enhanced by the construction of broad driveways, rustic bridges, cool arbors, in fact everything that can add in any way to the luxurious comfort of the guests.

Being only three hours' ride from San Francisco by rail, and possessing in the highest degree delightful climatic advantages, this ought to become a favored resort for health as well as pleasure seekers.

We find a number of springs here, most of them being carbonated.   The principal drinking spring is found on analysis to yield as follows:

AGUA DE VIDA SPRINGS
"LOWER SPRING"—LIGHT CARBONATED WATER
Dr. Winslow Anderson, Analyst, 1888

Mineral Ingredients	U. S. gal. contains Grains	Mineral Ingredients	U. S. gal. contains Grains
Sodium Chloride	4.02	Calcium Carbonate	13.75
Sodium Carbonate	3.65	Calcium Sulphate	.10
Sodium Sulphate	14.73	Alumina	.37
Potassium Carbonate	.55	Silica	.42
Magnesium Carbonate	7.95	Organic Matter	trace
Magnesium Sulphate	.46		

Total Solids, 46.00

Gases	Cubic Inches
Carbonic Acid Gas	19.25

This comes under the head of light carbonated water, gently aperient and diuretic, an excellent antacid in many cases of dyspepsia. In several cases of cystitis, congestion of kidneys, etc., etc., I have found it of great benefit. There are other springs said to contain iron, and still others are lightly sulphurous. These latter are used for anæmia, chronic malarial toxæmia, chlorosis and rheumatic troubles. Further analyses will be made in the near future.

AGUA DE VIDA SPRINGS
"LOWER SPRING"—LIGHT CARBONATED WATER
(Unknown Analyst.)

Mineral Ingredients	U. S. gal. contains Grains	Mineral Ingredients	U. S. gal. contains Grains
Sodium Chloride	3.08	Magnesium	8.89
Sodium Carbonate	.25	Calcium Carbonate	15.50
Sodium Sulphate	12.45	Silica	.42

Total Solids, 41.19

Gases	Cubic Inches
Carbonic Acid Gas	Not determined

This spring is one of the light carbonated mineral waters, gently laxative and diuretic, and excellent in certain forms of dyspepsia, liver and kidney troubles, etc. The writer has used it in a number of cases of cystitis with marked success. The springs have only lately been developed. A good hotel is built, and several cottages are nearing completion for summer occupation. Bathing facilities are also being constructed. The route of travel is to Livermore on the Central Pacific Railroad, and thence by carriage a few miles to the springs.

AGUA DE VIDA SPRINGS
"UPPER" OR LARGER SPRING—LIGHT SALINO-SULPHURETED WATER
DR. WINSLOW ANDERSON, Analyst, '89
Temperature 57.5° F.

Mineral Ingredients	U. S. gal. contains Grains	Mineral Ingredients	U. S. gal. contains Grains
Sodium Chloride	5.07	Calcium Carbonate	11.92
Sodium Carbonate	2.25	Calcium Sulphate	4.35
Sodium Sulphate	17.50	Manganese Carbonate	traces
Potassium Carbonate	traces	Alumina	.40
Magnesium Carbonate	3.19	Silica	.55
Magnesium Sulphate	8.70	Organic Matter	traces

Total Solids, 53.93

Gases	Cubic Inches
Sulphureted Hydrogen,	2.74
Carbonic Acid Gas	9.25

This mineral water is of service in dyspepsia, torpidity of the liver and bowels, rheumatism, glandular affections, renal troubles and skin diseases. It would also be an excellent bathing water.

6. ALABASTER CAVE SPRING

Located in El Dorado county.

7. ALAMEDA WARM SPRINGS

Near San Jose, in Alameda county. These are all alkaline and carbonated.

8. ALDER GLEN SPRING

Situated two and a half miles from Cloverdale, in Sonoma county, which is now being developed.

9. ALKALI SPRINGS

Several alkali springs are situated in the northern end of Mono county. There are no analyses and no improvements.

Alkali springs, eight miles northwest of Quincy. No analysis.

Alkali springs, one mile above the mouth of Spanish creek. No analysis has reached us.

11. ALKALINE LAKES

Several large sheets of alkaline waters, fed by springs, are found in Modoc county about fifteen miles southeast of Alturas. No analysis.

There is also a small alkaline lake in Lake county, near Clear Lake. Not analyzed.

12. ALLEN SPRINGS

These valuable mineral springs are situated in the Coast Range of mountains in Lake county. They lie in a cañon near the head of Cache creek, some forty miles

west of the town of Williams, and three miles east of Bartlett Springs. The altitude is 1,800 feet above tide water.
The resort and springs are beautifully situated in the
cañon recess, shaded by huge oaks and towering pines, and
surrounded by evergreen hills. The climate is delightful
and salubrious, the atmosphere bracing and invigorating,
and the evening air cool and pleasant. Out-of-door living
is charming for a large portion of each year. There is
good hunting and fishing near by, quite a consideration
for overworked brains and underworked bodies reared in
the cities like hot-house plants.

There are three alkaline and two ferruginous springs
on the place. All are cool and pleasantly aërated with
carbonic anhydride. The "Soda" spring, cool and sparkling, makes a delicious drink, which may be improved
by adding a little syrup. The waters are all gently aperient, and have gained considerable reputation in chronic
hepatic and renal affections associated with dropsy. Dyspepsia, chronic constipation, chronic malarial disorders,
etc., are reported alleviated and cured by using the
waters. The resort has ample accommodations and sets a
good table.

Hot and cold bathing conveniences have been erected.
There is also a hot steam bath, the water being artificially
heated for this purpose. The grounds afford good camping
facilities.

The following qualitative analysis is reported by Prof.
W. T. Wenzell:

ALLEN SPRINGS

Mineral Ingredients	Mineral Ingredients
Sodium Chloride	Magnesium Bicarbonate
Sodium Bicarbonate	Calcium Bicarbonate
Sodium Sulphate	Ferrous Phosphate
Potassium Chloride	Silica
Magnesium Chloride	

The water is strongly charged with carbonic acid gas.
The salts of sodium and magnesium predominate, while the

relative amount of calcium salt is small; therefore, the medicinal value of these waters is superior.

On analysis I find the water to yield:

ALLEN SPRINGS
ALKALO-SALINE
DR. WINSLOW ANDERSON, Analyst, 1888

Temperature 58° F.

Mineral Ingredients	U. S. gal. contains Grains	Mineral Ingredients	U. S. gal. contains Grains
Sodium Chloride	23.16	Magnesium Chloride	.03
Sodium Bicarbonate	4.25	Calcium Bicarbonate	20.14
Sodium Sulphate	.78	Calcium Phosphate	.55
Potassium Chloride	1.90	Ferrous Carbonate	.93
Magnesium Bicarbonate	27.40	Organic Matter	trace
Potassium Bicarbonate	.75		

Total Solids, 84.20

Gases		Cubic Inches
Carbonic Acid Gas		36.

Samples of other springs were also analyzed and found to differ in some important particulars, viz.: in containing larger amounts of iron and less of magnesia and soda, and being less strongly aërated, rendering these springs more tonic and strengthening, and the former more antacid, diuretic and laxative.

13.   ALUM ROCK SPRINGS

These springs are located in a romantic cañon with an unromantic name—"Penitentiary Cañon"—on the western slope of the Coast Range, about seven miles northeast of San José, in Santa Clara County. The cañon is so named in consequence of the habit among the early Jesuits on this coast of assembling there to perform penance.

The drive to San José is one of unusual grandeur, especially during the last two miles of the road, presenting an ever varying scene of ruggedness and natural beauty. Much of the roadbed is hewn out of the solid rock on the mountain side. The cañon is densely wooded, and the almost perpendicular cliffs shade the carriage drive, making it delightfully cool and pleasant even in the hottest part of the day. The nearness of these springs to San José, and the splendid accommodations offered at the hotel, with the many natural advantages in consequence of the glorious Garden City climate, to say nothing of the health-giving constituents of the mineral waters, make Alum Rock Springs a favorite resort for tourists, Summer visitors and invalids. The temperature in Summer is rarely above 90° F., and in Winter never too low for comfort. Trout and mountain quail abound, affording good sport for the rod and gun.

There are several springs in activity at Alum Rock. The principal "soda" or drinking water is found on quantitative analysis to contain:

ALUM ROCK SPRINGS
ALKALINE WATER
Dr. Winslow Anderson, Analyst, 1888

Mineral Ingredients	U. S. Gal. contains Grains	Mineral Ingredients	U. S. Gal. contains Grains
Sodium Chloride	10.21	Calcium Carbonate	19.05
Sodium Carbonate	7.14	Manganese Carbonate	trace
Potassium Carbonate	.76	Ferrous Carbonate	trace
Magnesium Carbonate	8.92	Alumina	6.45
Magnesium Sulphate	7.16	Silica	2.52

Total Solids, 62.21

Free Carbonic Acid Gas, Excess

CHALYBEATE SPRINGS
ALUM ROCK SPRINGS—CHALYBEATE AND ALKALINE
Prof. Hatch, Analyst

Mineral Ingredients	U. S. Gal. contains Grains	Mineral Ingredients	U. S. Gal. contains Grains
Ferrous Oxide	.30	Potassa	.20
Alumina	.15	Chlorine	1.60
Manganese	.70	Sulphydric Acid	3.30
Soda	3.40		

Total Solids (anhydrous), 9.65

It is well to mention that in this analysis the salts and elements are reduced to an anhydrous state. The same analysis with the water of crystallization would probably weigh several times more.

There are also two sulphur springs at a temperature of 85° F. These are used for bathing purposes. Alum Rock Springs have gained considerable reputation in the treatment of anæmia, chlorosis, chronic malaria, nervous prostration and debility. They ought to be of especial value in the hæmorrhagic diathesis, menorrhagia, etc., on account of the iron, alum and acids the waters contain.

THROUGH LAKE COUNTY

A lake that seems a silver mirror, swung
    Up near the clear blue sky,
Around whose loveliness the guardian hills
    In circling beauty lie.

Mountains that hide within their silent breasts
    Ashes of fires spent,
Whose torches lighted through the night of Time
    Chaos' black firmament.

Cedars and pines that strike their piercing roots
    In cold volcanoes' hearts,
That throbbed their lives out in some dead world grief
    As human pain departs.

Valleys whose curves are like the carved designs
    The hand of genius makes,
Inheritors of all the riches left
    By long departed lakes.

Unnumbered springs and rills that from the Earth
    Leap forth in melody
And take, down mountain side and valley sweep,
    Their graceful, sinuous way.

This lake, that lonely watched through untold years
    Orion his pathway trace
Now takes, in Beauty's western wonderland,
    A proud and honored place.

CLEAR LAKE AND UNCLE SAM IN THE DISTANCE

Above the tombs of countless ages dead—
  Nature's mute battle-fields—
Beauty and Strength have wrought their mysteries,
  Order his scepter wields.

The burned-out passion of a dead world's pain
  This granite dust of Time
Is re-incarnated in the lovely forms
  Of flower, and tree, and vine.

The Spirit of the Past that wrought its work
  And seemed to pass away,
Through loam and vine and grape is born again
  The rich wine of to-day.

The old-world trees whose lavishness of leaf
  Formed this rich valley soil,
Yielded their lives in travel, to the fruits
  That now reward our toil.

Thus ceaselessly the mystic whirl of Life
  Makes its eternal round,
No link is lost, no hurry mars its sweep—
  One perfect Whole is found.

—*Carrie Stevens Walter.*

ANDERSON MINERAL SPRINGS

These valuable mineral springs are situated in Lake County, nineteen miles from Calistoga, five miles from Middletown, and ten miles from the Great Geysers. They are of easy access by stage from the termini of the railroads, Calistoga and Cloverdale. The mountain roads are well kept, and the stage ride is one of the most picturesque in the State. The ever changing scene of hill and dale, forest and shrubbery, brooks with ferns and mosses, all combine to produce one of those pleasing scenes which one loves to mentally recall and review with realistic vividness.

The springs and health resort are themselves romantically located in a cozy nook in a small cañon, surrounded by forests and picturesque waterfalls.

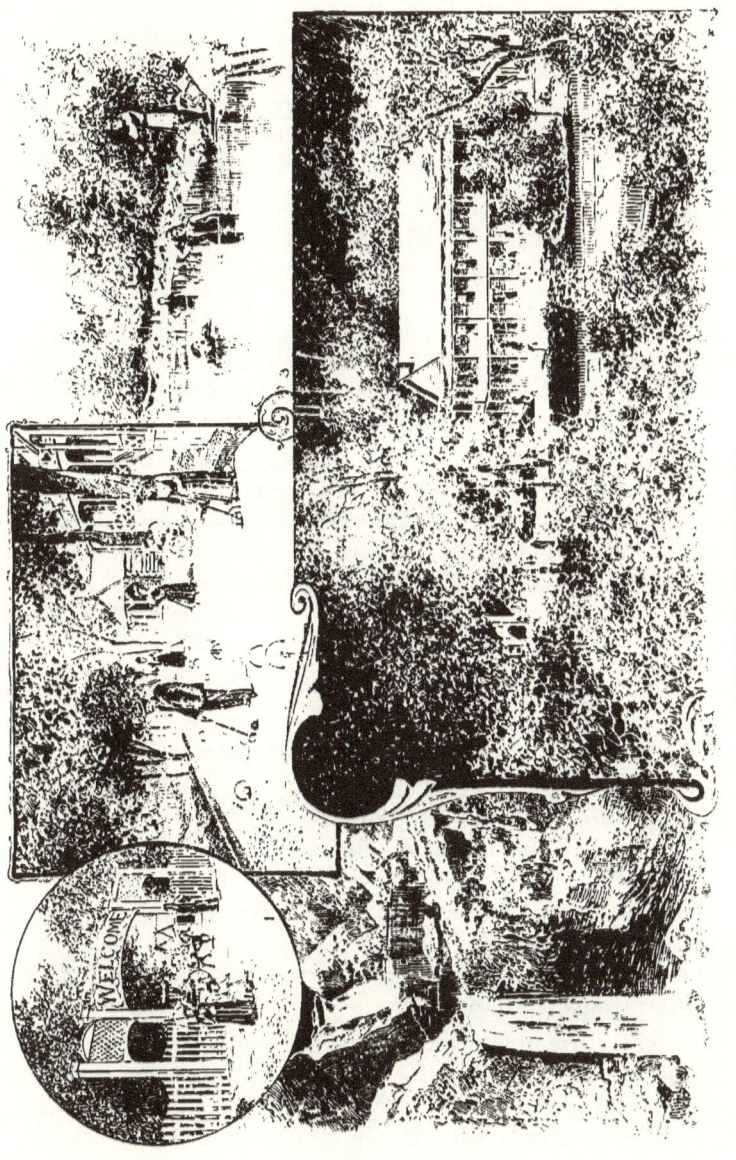

ANDERSON SPRINGS

The climate is famous in Lake County; and in and around the springs, in the pine groves, the climate is unrivaled. The atmosphere is balmy and exhilarating, and free from humidity. One could live out-of-doors for six months in the year.

The worshiper at Nature's shrine, the lover of grand and varied scenery, will find all that can be desired at the Anderson Springs. The perennial mountain streams that softly murmur past the cottages, the bright water sliding over mossy banks and beds of pebbles, breaking into showers of sparkling diamonds; the caves, cascades and waterfalls; the cool, leafy dells; the cozy nooks and commanding outlooks; the conical shaped hills, covered with evergreen trees; the profound silence and solitude of the forest, where one can commune with one's inmost self, and where one might almost expect to surprise Pan and his pipes—all, in the glistening moonlight or brighter rays of old *Sol*—make a picture that only the pen of a Thoreau could describe or the pencil of a Bierstadt display.

Hunting and fishing are found in abundance all the year round.

During the season invalids and pleasure seekers come to Anderson Springs by the thousands and enjoy the invigorating mineral waters and the bracing mountain air.

The hotel and cottages afford ample accommodations, with every facility for comfort. The table is superior. For camping and outdoor life the grounds around the springs are well adapted. Miss Joey Anderson, the proprietress. is untiring in her efforts to please her guests and make them comfortable.

There are nine principal mineral springs. The main drinking spring is the "Cold Sulphur;" it is located about one hundred and fifty yards from the hotel. It is a saline and mildly sulphureted water, very useful in chronic skin diseases of strumous and syphilitic origin. In liver and bowel troubles, glandular congestion, uterine and ovarian engorgement the water has been found of special value. It is aperient, diuretic and alterative in its action.

"ANDERSON SULPHUR SPRINGS"—ANALYSIS
MILD ALKALO-SULPHURETED WATER
DR. WINSLOW ANDERSON, Analyst, 1888
Temperature 63° F.

Mineral Ingredients	U. S. gal. contains Grains	Mineral Ingredients	U. S. gal. contains Grains
Sodium Chloride	1.00	Calcium Carbonate	20.40
Sodium Carbonate	9.27	Calcium Sulphate	9.10
Sodium Sulphate	6.18	Ferrous Carbonate	.46
Potassium Salts	traces	Arsenious Salts	traces
Magnesium Carbonate	11.73	Silica	2.45
Magnesium Sulphate	16.05	Organic Matter	traces

Total Solids, 77.63

Gases	Cubic Inches
Carbonic Acid Gas	243.50
Sulphureted Hydrogen	4.20

Another valuable water is the "Iron Spring." Its action is tonic, laxative and restorative, of value in anæmia, chlorosis and diseases requiring recuperative agents. It is clear and sparkling, and palatable to the taste.

ANALYSIS ANDERSON SPRINGS "IRON SPRING"
MILD CHALYBEATE WATER
GEO. E. COLBY, Analyst, July, 1889
Temperature 124° F.

Mineral Ingredients	U. S. gal. contains Grains	Mineral Ingredients	U. S. gal. contains Grains
Sodium Chloride	.183	Alumina	.093
Sodium Bicarbonate	.196	Boracic Acid (with spectroscope)	Strong test
Sodium Sulphate	3.421	Lithium (with spectroscope)	Well marked test
Potassium Sulphate	1.168	Manganous Carbonate	1.772
Magnesium Sulphate	7.359	Silica	4.217
Calcium Sulphate	10.884	Organic Matter	Small
Calcium Phosphate	.154		
Ferrous Carbonate	1.184		

Total Solids, 30.631.

Gases	Cubic Inches
Free Carbonic Acid Gas	25.8

THE "SOUR" SPRING

This is one of the few mineral springs in California containing free sulphuric acid. Its sour taste was supposed to be due to alum, but from the following analysis, made for me by Mr. George E. Colby of the university, it will be seen that there is no alum present. The sour spring waters have proved very beneficial in hæmorrhages of lungs, menorrhagia, dyspepsia, etc. The water is tonic, astringent and gently laxative, pleasant to drink and of value in malarial poisoning and blood-glandular diseases.

ANDERSON SPRINGS—"SOUR SPRING"

SALINO-ACIDULOUS WATER

GEORGE E. COLBY, Analyst

Temperature 64.3° F.

JULY, 1889

Mineral Ingredients	U. S. Gal. contains Grains	Mineral Ingredients	U. S. Gal. contains Grains
Sodium Chloride	.082	*Aluminium Sulphate	7.112
Sodium Sulphate	.492	Boracic Acid (with specro-	
Potassium Sulphate	.866	scope)	strong test
Magnesium Sulphate	4.766	Lithium (with spec.)..well marked test	
Calcium Sulphate	2.073	Ammonia (manganous Sul)	.326
Ferric Sulphate	.634	Silica	3.943
		Organic Matter	traces

Total Solids, 20.294

Gases	Cubic Inches
Free Sulphuric Acid	1.225

Total Mineral Ingredients, 21.519

*A *microscopical examination* of the residue obtained by slow evaporation does not show any characteristic crystals of alum.

The "Bellmer" spring, so named after Mr. Bellmer of San Francisco, who used it for several years during the Summer season with marked benefit in rheumatism, torpidity of the liver and irritation of the kidneys.

The water is salino-sulphurous, laxative and antacid in its action.

ANDERSON SPRINGS—"BELLMER SPRING"

LIGHT SALINO-SULPHUROUS

DR. WINSLOW ANDERSON, Analyst, 1889

Temperature 71° F.

Mineral Ingredients	U. S. gal. contains Grains	Mineral Ingredients	U. S. gal. contains Grains
Sodium Chloride	.04	Ferrous Carbonate	.12
Sodium Bicarbonate	1.32	Arsenic	traces
Sodium Sulphate	7.91	Alumina	traces
Potassium Carbonate	traces	Borates	strong traces
Magnesium Carbonate	2.74	Lithium	traces
Magnesium Sulphate	8.40	Silica	4.20
Calcium Carbonate	12.63	Organic Matter	traces
Calcium Sulphate	0.17		

Total Solids, 47.13

Gases	Cubic Inches
Free Carbonic Acid Gas,	149.6
Free Sulphureted Hydrogen,	9.47

The "Magnesia" or "Father Joseph" spring is an active laxative, rich in Epsom and Glauber's salt.

Another spring, known as the "Caro," is carbonated, and much used in kidney and bladder irritation.

Dr. Woolsey, of Oakland, has named one of these springs the "Cosmopolitan," because he considers it generally applicable for tourists and pleasure seekers.

It is a pleasant drinking water, gently laxative in its action, and of universal use.

One of the most valuable springs at the Anderson resort is the "hot sulphurous" or "bathing spring." These waters have a temperature of 145.5° F., and are very beneficial in rheumatism and chronic joint swellings, and skin diseases. Excellent facilities for bathing have been constructed, and the baths are extensively patronized. There is an abundance of hot sulphurous steam highly extolled in the treatment of weak lungs, chronic bronchitis and incipient phthisis, and catarrhal affections of the nose and throat. Many persons have experienced much relief from the inhalation of these vapors.

ANDERSON SPRINGS—"HOT SPRING"
THERMAL-SULPHUROUS
GEO. E. COLBY, Analyst, July, 1889
Temperature 115.5° F.

U. S. gal. contains

Mineral Ingredients	Grains	Mineral Ingredients	Grains
Sodium Chloride	.443	Arsenic	traces
Sodium Bicarbonate	.320	Alumina	traces
Sodium Sulphate	5.518	Boracic Acid (with spectroscope)	strong test
Potassium Sulphate	1.360		
Magnesium Carbonate	1.893	Lithium (with spectroscope)	well-marked test
Magnesium Sulphate	6.010		
Calcium Carbonate	10.397	Manganus Carbonate	.636
Calcium Sulphate	3.908	Silica	6.600
Calcium Phosphate	.164	Organic Matter	small
Ferrous Carbonate	.133		

Total Solids, 37.382

Gases	Cubic Inches
Free Carbonic Acid Gas,	70.20
Free Sulphureted Hydrogen Gas,	3.34

THE CATARRH SNUFF OR POWDER

On the rocks over the hot sulphurous and vapor springs are deposited incrustations of the vaporized minerals. This is carefully collected and powdered, and used as snuff in cases of chronic catarrhal troubles. The snuff has already gained quite a name, and is said to afford almost instant relief. Even in acute coryza or colds in the throat it produces an agreeable effect, and shortens the attack.

The following analysis is made from the dried powder:

ANDERSON SPRINGS—ANALYSIS "CATARRH POWDER"
INCRUSTATIONS ON ROCKS
DR. WINSLOW ANDERSON, Analyst, 1889

Mineral Ingredients	Parts in 100	Mineral Ingredients	Parts in 100
Sodium Chloride	2.16	Arsenious Salts	traces
Sodium Carbonate	3.73	Alumina	traces
Sodium Sulphate	6.67	Lithium	traces
Potassium Salts	1.10	Borates	.43
Magnesium Carbonate	5.18	Manganesium Salts	.74
Magnesium Sulphate	8.70	Silica	8.55
Calcium Carbonate	36.45	Organic Matter	1.44
Calcium Sulphate	9.13	Water and Loss	14.53
Ferrous Oxide	1.19.		

Total, 100.00

Thousands of people are benefited at Anderson Springs every year. The waters, as will be seen from the foregoing complete analysis, are among the finest in the State, and the pine forests, elevation and climate are of unquestionable value in many sub-acute and chronic diseases. As a pleasure resort it is one of the loveliest spots on the coast.

ANTI-FAT SPRINGS

These springs are located in San Bernardino County, twelve miles from Temescal. The waters are alkalo-saline in character. A glassful taken three or four times daily relieves the portal and intestinal circulation, producing gentle purgation and thereby a lessening in bodily weight, hence the name.

There is a small resort at the springs. I have been unable to obtain water enough for a careful chemical analysis in time for this work.

14. ARROWHEAD HOT SPRINGS

These springs are located ten miles from Colton, in the San Bernardino Mountains, San Bernardino County. They are at an elevation of 1,600 feet above the sea. The Arrowhead Springs number twenty or more, and the combined volume of hot water issuing from the granite and limestone formation is very large. It has been likened to a good-sized millstream (Blake). The water is very hot, several springs having a temperature of 172° F. to 210° F.; others range from 166° F. to 108° F. The springs form one of the tributaries of the Santa Ana River. The springs are largely calcic or earthy, and contain:

Calcium Carbonate.
Magnesium Carbonate.
Alumina.
Ferrous Carbonate.
Silica.
Phosphoric Acid.

The Arrowhead Springs are so named from being at the foot of what is known as "Arrowhead" Mountain, which has a large spot on the side facing the springs that is comparatively free from brush and shaped just like an Indian's arrow. The length is 1,320 feet, and the breadth from shoulder to shoulder 350 feet. This space forms a conspicuous landmark for miles around. When the Mormons first settled there they used it for part of their religious ceremony, and it was known as the "Lord's mighty arrowhead" for the wicked.

These springs first came into general notice in 1858. Prior to that time the natives used to bring their sick and camp around the springs. They have gained favorable notice of late years in the treatment of cutaneous affections and rheumatism.

A large artificial pond has been erected for bathing purposes, the dimensions of which are 100 by 75 feet (Prof. McNutt). There are also a number of hot soft mud baths, which the Indians used extensively in former years and which had the reputation of being a certain cure for syphilis.

A large resort ought to be built at Arrowhead Mountain in the near future, as the springs are of undoubted value.

15.   ARROYO GRANDE SPRINGS

These springs are located in San Luis Obispo County, fourteen miles north of the city. The waters are alkaline and carbonated and much used locally in bladder and urethral irritation and inflammation.

There is a small resort at the springs.

16.   AZULE SPRINGS

These are located twelve miles west of San Jose, in Santa Clara County. The name is derived from the Spanish word *azule*, meaning blue. As the mountains in which

these valuable springs are situated have a bluish tint
when viewed from a distance, so the springs came to be
known as the blue springs in early days. The mineral
water flows pure and sparkling from the subterranean
chemical laboratory at an elevation of one thousand feet
above the sea level. The grounds are owned by Hon. J.
W. Ryland of San Jose, and while there is no resort on the
place, the waters are bottled and shipped in large quantities
to all parts of the State. The mean temperature of the air
is 62° F. and the mean rainfall not excessive, being only
31 inches. The temperature of the spring water is 59.6°
F. It is carbonated and pungent and is very similar to
the famous seltzer of Nassau in Germany. Its action is
antacid, aperient, diuretic and tonic, and it is of great
value in dyspepsia, torpidity of the liver and the intestinal
tract, increasing the process of secretion and excretion, and
eliminating the morbific waste materials in the visceral and
cutaneous systems. It is highly useful in habitual constipation, alcoholic dyspepsia, Bright's disease, uric and lithic
acids in the urine, etc. On analysis one gallon of the
water from the principal spring is found to contain:

AZULE SPRINGS
HEAVY CARBONATED (LAXATIVE) WATER
Dr Winslow Anderson, Analyst, 1888
Temperature 59.6°

Mineral Ingredients	U. S. Gal. contains Grains	Mineral Ingredients	U. S. Gal. contains Grains
Sodium Chloride	86.73	Magnesium Chloride	17.42
Sodium Carbonate	52.19	Calcium Carbonate	10.05
Potassium Chloride	10.90	Silica	3.20
Potassium Carbonate	2.85	Organic Matter	.18
Magnesium Carbonate	78.16		

Total Solids, 261.60

Gases	Grains
Free Carbonic Acid Gas	153.77

17. BARTLETT SPRINGS

These famous springs are situated on the western
slope of the mountain ranges near the head of Cache

Creek, in the northeastern portion of Lake County. They are reached via Oakland, Vallejo and Calistoga and thence by easy stage, or by Sacramento and Williams, or by way of Cloverdale.

LATEST ROUTE

"Formerly there were 35 miles of staging from the Sacramento Valley via Bites, and 55 to 60 miles via either Calistoga and Lower Lake, or Cloverdale and Lakeport. Now, the San Francisco passengers will stop at Hopland, and, after a stage-ride of 16¼ miles over an easy grade, will reach Lakeport to enjoy the steamer-ride of ten miles across the lake, while 14 miles more of staging brings them to Bartlett; so that passengers leaving San Francisco at 7:15 A. M. will get to Hopland about noon, Lakeport between 3 and 4 P. M., and Bartlett's in time for supper at 7 o'clock on the same day, and at an expense of about $2 less than by the old routes."

The distance is about 150 miles from San Francisco. The springs are located at an altitude of 2,325 feet above the sea. They are near the pine forests of the summits, in perfectly pure atmosphere. At this elevation the temperature is 10° F. cooler in Summer than in the valley 1,000 feet below. It averages 85° F. for Summer months. Humidity and fogs are seldom noticed.

THE DISCOVERY OF BARTLETT SPRINGS

Mr. Green Bartlett of Kentucky, having early suffered with rheumatism, came to this coast in 1856 in the hopes of being benefited by the climate. During one of his camping trips in Lake County Mr. Bartlett was taken ill with his rheumatism and happened to camp near the present springs. In the course of his disease he drank freely from the sparkling waters and rapidly convalesced. The springs were then taken up and a resort established. The springs are picturesquely located, with huge oaks and pines to shade the now cultivated grounds. The hotel and cottages are excellently kept and offer facilities for about one thousand persons.

The main Bartlett spring is quite a curiosity. It is walled with artificial stone and surrounding it is laid pavement of the same material. A jar-shaped chamber about two feet in diameter and three feet in height is constructed directly over the spring, having outlets similar to those of a public fountain. It is estimated that the spring flows about 110 gallons per hour. One outlet flows in pipes to the bottling house and another leads into the hotel for the use of guests. There are also a number of other springs at the resort. One of these, some little distance away, is known as the "gas well." It is continually bubbling up with great force, resembling a boiling spring, yet the temperature was found in 1888 to be 54° F. This remarkable gas spring emits a large quantity of carbonic acid gas. It is asserted that if birds or animals remain at the spring for a few seconds they are sure to die from asphyxiation. The water is strongly carbonated and said by many persons who have tried it to be a sure cure for corns. South of the hotel are the "soda" spring, the "iron" spring and the "magnesia" spring. There are also several cold sulphur springs. The springs are all charged with carbonic anhydride and are pleasant, sparkling carbonated waters. Thousands of persons visit Bartlett every year and much benefit has accrued from the use of the waters in chronic malarial and rheumatic affections, chronic uterine diseases, etc. The waters are diuretic, laxative and alterative in their effects. Bathing facilities have also been added. The mineral and sulphurous waters are artificially heated for this purpose. The following analysis was made by Geo. E. Colby some years ago:

BARTLETT SPRINGS

CARBONATED WATER

Geo. E. Colby, Analyst

Mineral Ingredients	U. S. gal. contains Grains	Mineral Ingredients	U. S. gal. contains Grains
Sodium Chloride	.500	Iron Compounds	traces
Sodium Bicarbonate	1.050	Silica	3.409
Potassium Bicarbonate	.390	Lithium	traces
Magnesium Carbonate	6.620	Barium Carbonate	.054
Calcium Carbonate	30.141	Stontium	none
Calcium Phosphate	.494	Boracic Acid	traces
Calcium Sulphate	.626	Organic Matter	traces

Total Solids, 43.349

Gases	Cubic Inches
Free Carbonic Acid Gas	242.1

Ammonia, .03 parts per million

BARTLETT MINERAL SPRINGS

LIGHT CARBONATED WATER

Dr. Winslow Anderson, Analyst, 1888

Mineral Ingredients	U. S. gal. contains Grains	Mineral Ingredients	U. S. gal. contains Grains
Sodium Chloride	.54	Calcium Sulphate	.63
Sodium Bicarbonate	1.21	Ferrous Carbonate	.51
Potassium Bicarbonate	.36	Barium Carbonate	traces
Magnesium Carbonate	7.74	Silica	3.73
Magnesium Sulphate	1.62	Lithium	traces
Calcium Carbonate	29.07	Borates	traces
Calcium Phosphate	.50	Organic Matter	trace

Total Solids, 45.91

Free Gases	Cubic Inches
Carbonic Anhydride	224.56

It is worthy of remark that in a number of instances I have found these superficial springs to change in composition in the course of years, or suddenly in the case of earthquakes. They are always changed by the surface waters and during rainy seasons, so that an analysis made in the spring of the year would necessarily be a little differed from one made in the fall, even though carefully performed under the same conditions and by the same analyst.

18. BEAR VALLEY HOT SPRINGS

In San Bernardino County, near Bear Lake and north of San Bernardino Peak, are situated a number of hot springs. The waters are saline and calcic. The inhabitants in the vicinity use the water for kidney and bladder affections.

Water for analysis has not been obtainable.

19. BENTON HOT SPRINGS

Near Benton, in Mono County, is a very hot spring. It has a diameter of eighteen feet, and flows 2,700 cubic feet per hour. The temperature is 135° F. The waters are slightly alkaline, and much used for bathing purposes. It is claimed that an agreeable softness of the skin is obtained by its external use. The water is also used internally for rheumatism, gravel, etc. On evaporation it leaves very little residue, which is found to contain carbonates of sodium, magnesium and calcium.

20. BERKELEY SODA SPRINGS

These excellent soda springs are located about ten miles south of Summit Station, on the C. P. R. R, in Placer County. They are the same as those we describe later on as the " Summit Soda Springs," by which name they are generally known.

21. BIG HOT SPRINGS

In Lassen County, some three miles north of Honey Lake, we find a large hot saline spring several feet in diameter. The water is constantly boiling up in a large stream, and forms one of the wonders of that section of the country. It has a temperature of 200° F., and flows 2,700 cubic inches per hour. There is no resort, and the water is not utilized.

22.   BIG SULPHUR SPRING

In section 36, township 32 s. and range 21 east, Mount Diablo meridian, is located a large sulphur spring. It is not improved.

SIERRA SCENE.

23. BITTER SPRING

This unique spring is situated in San Bernardino County, about eighteen miles north of Camp Cody. It is a cold saline spring. The water is not used commercially, nor is there any resort at the place. The water is rich in magnesium sulphate (Epsom salt), hence its name. It is much used locally for "bilious" attacks.

24. BLACK LAKE

This is quite a sheet of water, fed by several springs. It is located in Mono County, one mile west of Benton. The water is sulphurous and saline. Not used.

25. BLACK SULPHUR SPRINGS

A number of these black sulphurous iron springs are located in section 4, township 32 s., range 18 e. No resort.

26. BLANK'S HOT SULPHUR SPRINGS

These hot sulphur springs are located in Colusa County, and are the private property of Mrs. Lottie Blank. The waters are used locally for purposes of bathing and drinking, and have acquired considerable fame in the treatment of chronic skin diseases and rheumatic troubles, etc. There is only a local resort.

27. BLODGETT'S SPRING

These excellent mineral springs are picturesquely located in the Coast Range of mountains, about eight miles west of Gilroy. They are of easy access by the Southern Pacific Railway to Gilroy, and from there by daily stage to the springs.

The springs are under the personal supervision of Mr. Blodgett, who has erected a hotel and several comfortable cottages. The surroundings are beautiful. The atmosphere is pure, balmy and invigorating, and the mineral waters and mineral baths are of great therapeutic value.

One of the principal waters on the premises is the "Soda Spring." Its waters are found on analysis to be antacid, diuretic, aperient and tonic, and of great value in acid dyspepsia and catarrh of the stomach, constipation, kidney and bladder troubles.

The analysis shows that the spring is alkalo-carbonated and lightly sulphureted.

BLODGETT SPRINGS—"SODA SPRING"
ALKALO-CARBONATED AND SULPHURETED
Dr. WINSLOW ANDERSON, Analyst, 1889

Mineral Ingredients	U. S. gal. contains Grains	Mineral Ingredients	U. S. gal. contains Grains
Sodium Chloride	8.20	Calcium Carbonate	7.31
Sodium Carbonate	9.02	Calcium Sulphate	2.19
Sodium Sulphate	trace	Ferrous Carbonate	trace
Potassium Chloride	trace	Alumina	4.13
Potassium Iodide	trace	Borates	trace
Potassium Carbonate	.47	Silica	4.11
Magesium Carbonate	6.65	Organic Matter	trace
Magnesium Sulphate	1.15		

Total Solids, 44.13

Gases	Cubic Inches
Carbonic Acid Gas	9.25
Sulphureted Hydrogen	trace

The next most important spring is the "Sulphur." It also is antacid, laxative, tonic and diuretic, besides acting on the liver, kidneys and blood-glandular system. This water is good for rheumatism and sciatica, swelling of the joints and skin diseases. Excellent bathing facilities have been constructed, and Blodgett's Springs are rapidly gaining in reputation as a health and pleasure resort.

BLODGETT SPRINGS—"SULPHUR SPRING"

ALKALO-CARBONATED AND SULPHURETED

DR. WINSLOW ANDERSON, Analyst, 1889

Mineral Ingredients	U. S. gal. contains Grains	Mineral Ingredients	U. S. gal. contains Grains
Sodium Chloride	10.75	Calcium Carbonate	.74
Sodium Carbonate	3.14	Calcium Sulphate	4.90
Sodium Sulphate	2.78	Ferrous Carbonate	trace
Potassium Chloride	traces	Alumina	trace
Potassium Iodide	traces	Borates	traces
Potassium Carbonate	3.55	Silica	5.42
Magnesium Carbonate	7.10	Organic Matter	.70
Magnesium Sulphate	9.63		

Total Solids, 48.71

Gases	Cubic Inches
Carbonic Acid Gas	3.75
Sulphureted Hydrogen	7.25

28. BOILING LAKES

In Plumas County, seven miles south of Lassen's Peak, are a number of hot bubbling and boiling springs. They are located quite close together, and several of them coalesce, forming lakes. The waters are alkaline. No resort.

29. BOILING SPRINGS

On the east side of Dry Salt Lake, and on the west side of Resting Mountain, in Inyo County, are several hot and boiling springs. The waters are reported alkaline.

30. BOILING SULPHUR SPRINGS

Several of these boiling sulphur springs are very picturesquely located on the south branch of Owen's River, northwest of Long Valley, in Mono County. They could be made valuable as a resort. The waters are alkalo-sulphureted and well calculated for the treatment of many diseases for which these sulphur waters are frequently used. There are no improvements.

31. BONANZA HOT AND COLD SPRINGS

These springs are located in a sequestered spot on the side of the mountain, among the pines and old oaks. It is one of the coolest and pleasantest places in Lake County during the heated summer season. The springs are two miles from Seigler's, six miles from Glenbrook and eight miles from Lower Lake. The elevation is about 2,500 feet. There are several pleasant carbonated waters on the place. One of these—the "Cold Soda," is a sparkling antacid water, containing diuretic and aperient properties. On qualitative analysis the Soda Spring is found to contain :

Sodium Carbonate,
Potassium Carbonate,
Magnesium Carbonate,
Magnesium Sulphate,
Calcium Carbonate,
Silica,
And Free Carbonic Acid Gas.

Another spring close by is found to be sulphureted and has a temperature of 84.2° F. This is used principally for bathing. It yields on analysis :

Sodium Sulphate,
Sodium Chloride,
Magnesium Sulphate,
Calcium Carbonate,
Calcium Sulphate,
Silica,
And Free Sulphureted Hydrogen Gas.

This is found beneficial in gouty and strumous joint affections.

The chalybeate spring has found a large use by the anæmic and pale-faced overworked city people who go to the resort. There is good gunning and fishing all the year round.

32. BORAX POND

This remarkable pond is situated about half a mile east of the lower end of Clear Lake in Lake County. The water is highly charged with biborate of soda (borax). During the dry season this water largely evaporates, and the borax, crystallizing out, is found around the margin of the pond.

Twenty-five to thirty years ago large quantities of this salt was manufactured here, supposedly the first made in the State, but latterly there has been no work done here, owing no doubt to the extensive borax discoveries in the southern portion of California.

33. BORAX FLAT

is situated in San Bernardino County, near the intersections of 117° 15' and 35° 45'. They are all cold. Large crusts of borates are seen on the surface as the water evaporates during the Summer months.

Another borax spring is known as

34. BORAX MARSH

and is located some eight miles southeast of Hawley's Station in San Bernardino County. Then we have

35. BORAX PATCH

near Black's ranch on the S. P. R. R. line in San Bernardino County. The supply of borax seems inexhaustible, and all we need to make this a large industry is a little experimentation. I do not see why the sun's rays could not be utilized in the evaporating process.

36. BORAX SPRINGS

On the edge of Clear Lake, in Lake County, are several borax springs. The salt exists in considerable quantities as a biborate of soda. These waters are used locally.

During the last twenty years California has produced $5,000,000 worth of borax. (Report of State Mineralogist, Prof. Wm. Ireland, Jr., 1888.)

BORAX SPRINGS

There are extensive borax springs in the southern portion of the State—large shallow marshes, through which flow the mineral waters richly laden with borates.

37. BOYD'S HOT SPRINGS

By the side of Upper Alkaline Lake, in Modoc County, are located these springs. They are in Surprise Valley. The waters are alkaline and heavily charged with carbonic acid gas. Qualitatively the waters are found to contain:

> Bicarbonate of Soda and Potash.
> Carbonates of Soda.
> Lime and Magnesia.

A resort will probably be established at the springs in the near future.

38. BRANBECK'S BOILING SPRINGS

These springs are situated on the east side of Honey Lake, in Lassen County. There is one large boiling alkaline spring. No resort and no analysis. Water used locally.

> " Soon did the portals of the east unclose,
> 　Then all the waterfalls and mountain floods
> Shouted with joy, and up the mountains rose
> 　A solemn anthem from the bowing woods,
> And morning's misty curtains rolled away ;
> 　The clouds in their superb apparel shone
> As o'er the mountain tops the lord of day
> 　Rose like a gorgeous monarch from his throne,
> 　And shed refulgence on the lake below."

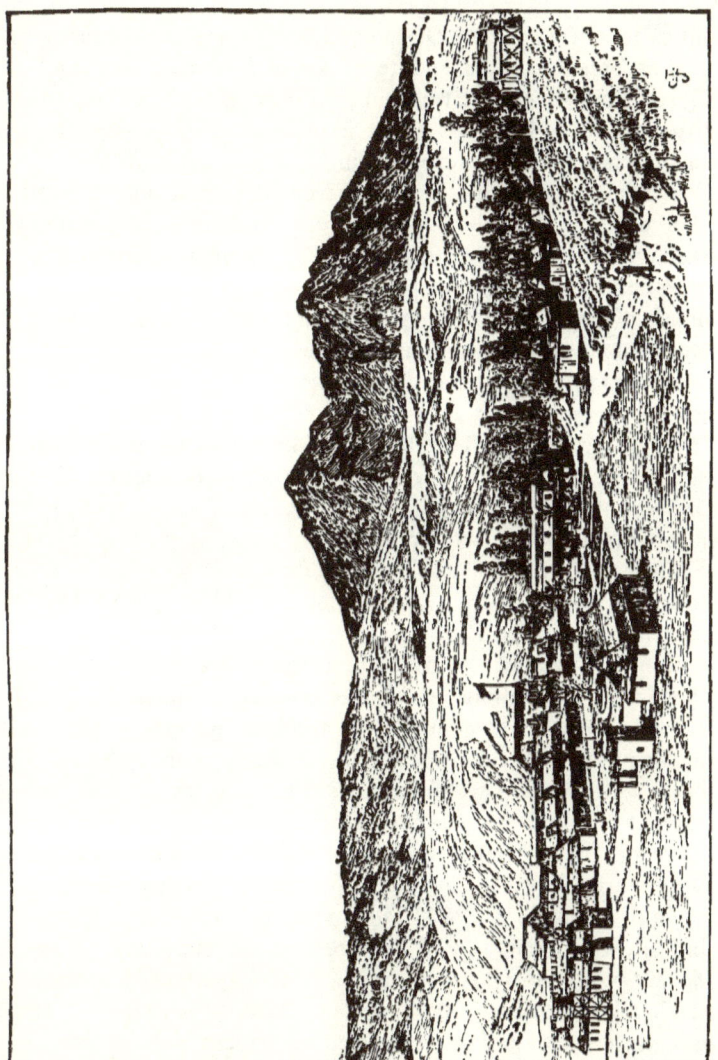

39. BYRON SPRINGS

These excellent and already famous springs are pleasantly situated near the foothills in a spur of the Coast
Range of mountains in Contra Costa County, about sixteen

miles southeast of Mt. Diablo and sixty-eight miles northeast of San Francisco, and about one and a half miles from
Byron Station, on the railroad line from San Francisco to
Stockton and Sacramento via Martinez. The springs lie
in a small valley leading from the San Joaquin plains.
The surrounding hills are composed of calcareous shales;
the valley is covered with adobe clay and fine white sand,
through which the springs bubble. About a quarter of a
mile eastward from the springs a well has been sunk to a
depth of 125 feet. The strata penetrated are coarse sand
stone on the surface, and a conglomerate gravel, all bearing
evidences of volcanic action. The gravel has been subjected to great heat and permeated with steaming gases
from nature's laboratory below. The well contains about
sixty feet of good water. The springs are among the
many natural wonders in the State, and being centrally
located and within easy access—only three hours from San
Francisco—they are much visited by tourists. As a sanitarium, however, Byron ranks among the first in the State;
invalids go to the Byron springs from all over the coast
and many remarkable cures are ascribed to the waters. A
large and commodious hotel has been constructed for the
accommodation of about two hundred guests. Several
handsome cottages for private and family use have recently
been added. The architecture is after the fashion of the
ancient and middle ages, inclosing between the building a
large square laid out in parks and walks. Two sides of the
square are formed by the hotel proper, a third side by the
several bathhouses, and a fourth side by the cottages, forming quite a village, with picturesque surroundings. The
cuisine is elegantly appointed, with an experienced *chef* at
its head. A new dining-hall has recently been added. It
is handsomely finished in paneled primavera and furnished
with polished oak. Nourishing and appetizing viands are
supplied in abundance and invalids are well cared for. The
climate is mild and pleasant. Cool, balmy breezes spring

up from the tule lands every afternoon, making it pleasant even in the hottest day. The elevation is about one hundred feet above high tide.

Admirable as are the location and appointments, the chief excellence lies in the mineral springs. These became renowned many years before the Spanish invasion. Our Indians and Mexicans hand down traditions of the cures effected by the waters. The Indian used to travel many miles to bathe in the mud and drink the waters.

The springs and resort are now visited by thousands every year. Nothing succeeds like success, and these mineral waters have certainly achieved success.

During my visit to the sanitarium, in 1889, I counted more than fifty springs or outlets from the subterranean passages. Some are cold and others are hot, ranging from 52° F. to 140° F. Within a few feet of each other there will be a cold carbonated spring and a hot sulphureted spring. The whole basin has the appearance of being an extinct volcanic crater. The cold soda springs come from the surface water, but the hot water—sulphurous—must come from a considerable distance down in the earth's crust. Chemical metamorphosis could probably not produce the amount of heat found at Byron.

There are also several inflammable gas-wells or springs, two of which have been developed by sinking about thirty feet and erecting small receivers over them. I burned the gas for fifteen or more minutes and found it to consist largely of carbureted hydrogen (CH_4). The supply seems inexhaustible, amply sufficient to heat and light the entire resort. Special gas receivers, etc., for the utilization of this valuable natural product will shortly be erected and then Byron will be illuminated with natural gas.

Of the fifty or more mineral springs only seven or eight are in active use. One of the most important of these is the "liver and kidney" spring. It is so named on account of the action of the water on these organs. This spring was used by many people prior to the occupancy of the place as a resort. For miles around they used to come and carry away the water in bottles and barrels and use it medicinally.

The following analyses were made in the early part of 1889:

BYRON SPRINGS—"LIVER AND KIDNEY SPRING"
HEAVY SALINE WATER
Dr. WINSLOW ANDERSON, Analyst, 1889

Temperature 66° F.

Mineral Ingredients	U. S. gal. contains Grains	Mineral Ingredients	U. S. gal. contains Grains
Sodium Chloride	622.07	Calcium Sulphate	1.12
Potassium Chloride	33.74	Calcium Carbonate	.59
Potassium Iodide	.79	Barium Carbonate	.93
Potassium Bromide	trace	Ferrous Carbonate	.72
Magnesium Chloride	3.92	Ammonium Chloride	3.05
Magnesium Carbonate	15.75	Silica	1.00
Calcium Chloride	85.37	Organic Matter	trace

Total Solids, 769.05

Gases	Cubic Inches
Free Carbolic Acid Gas	7.82

This has proved a most valuable water in dyspepsia, chronic hepatic diseases, obstruction to the gall ducts, and what is known as "gin livers." The action also extends to torpidity of the bowels. It is exceedingly diuretic, and has a record of curing several cases of albumenurea (Bright's disease). Its action also extends to the mucous membranes of the nose, throat and lungs. A glassful taken before breakfast acts agreeably on the stomach, liver and kidneys and intestinal tract, assisting the process of elimination, secretion and excretion of morbific

BYRON SPRINGS

and waste material in the visceral and cutaneous systems. In alcoholic dyspepsia it is very beneficial. Gentlemen whose acquaintance with, and long, assiduous devotion to Bacchus, which has at last, as must of necessity follow such friendships, resulted in a worn-out gastric mucous membrane, with atonic or catarrhal dyspepsia and shattered health, will find wonderful improvement in a month's sojourn at Byron by using the "Liver and Kidney" water.

Long before my chemical analysis had been made of this "Liver and Kidney Spring" water it was extensively used by alcoholics whose stomachs, livers and kidneys were diseased. Several people in Sacramento who had albumen in their urine from this cause were entirely relieved by the use of the water. Thus practice stepped in and demonstrated a fact before science had had a chance to announce it.

Quite a contrast to this heavy saline water is the spring known as the

BYRON SPRINGS—"WHITE SULPHUR SPRING"

LIGHT ALKALO-SULPHUROUS WATER

Dr. WINSLOW ANDERSON, Analyst, 1889

Temperature 76° F.

Mineral Ingredients	U. S. gal. contains Grains	Mineral Ingredients	U. S. gal. contains Grains
Sodium Chloride	12.01	Magnesium Carbonate	2.50
Sodium Bicarbonate	12.94	Calcium Carbonate	1.13
Sodium Sulphate	1.34	Calcium Sulphate	.51
Potassium Chloride	trace	Ferrous Carbonate	3.00
Potassium Carbonate	2.37	Silica	.26
Potassium Sulphate	trace	Organic Matter	trace
Magnesium Chloride	trace		

Total Solids, 36.06

Gases	Cubic Inches
Carbonic Acid Gas	21.17
Sulphureted Hydrogen	5.80

This light alkalo-sulphurous water is palatable and invigorating, containing a large quantity of ferruginous salt, so necessary in strumous diathesis, rheumatism, gout, chronic malarial poisons, cutaneous diseases, etc., etc. Its action is tonic, diuretic, alterative, aperient and antacid. Its use is indicated in acid blood or acid urine, or diseases having or depending upon these pathological conditions, such as rheumatism, chronic joint diseases, glandular enlargements and many forms of skin diseases. It should be taken between meals in six to eight ounce doses.

BYRON SPRINGS—"BLACK SULPHUR"

HEAVY CHLORINATED SULPHUROUS WATER

Dr. Winslow Anderson, Analyst, 1889

Temperature 90.3° F.

Mineral Ingredients	U. S. gal. contains Grains	Mineral Ingredients	U. S. gal. contains Grains
Sodium Chloride	395.00	Calcium Chloride	9.00
Sodium Sulphate.	trace	Calcium Sulphate	3.20
Sodium Bicarbonate	trace	Calcium Carbonate	5.95
Potassium Chloride	35.62	Ferrous Carbonate	.70
Potassium Sulphate	trace	Barium Carbonate	trace
Potassium Iodide	.74	Ammonium Chloride	trace
Potassium Bromide	.16	Silica	1.10
Maguesium Chloride	1.00	Organic Matter	trace
Magnesium Carbonate	9.50		

Total Solids, 461.97

Gases	Cubic Inches
Carbonic Acid Gas,	25.00
Sulphureted Hydrogen,	8.00

Lovers Lane.

The action of the water is largely diuretic, as it contains considerable quantity of the chlorides and carbonates and a large amount of carbonic acid gas. It is indicated in catarrhal irritation and inflammation of the genito-urinary tract, and has proved of service in Bright's disease, cystitis, acid dyspepsia and constipation.

The water is largely used for bathing purposes. Used internally, it should be taken one hour before meals.

The "Black Sulphur" water is an excellent alterative, containing potassium salts so valuable in scrofulous and blood glandular diseases. This water is much used for bathing purposes.

BYRON SPRINGS—" IRON SPRING."

ALKALINE AND CHALYBEATE WATER

Dr. Winslow Anderson, Analyst, 1889

Temperature 79.5° F.

Mineral Ingredients	U. S. gal. contains Grains	Mineral Ingredients	U. S. gal. contains Grains
Sodium Chloride	670.43	Calcium Chloride	9.75
Sodium Sulphate	trace	Calcium Sulphate	10.80
Sodium Carbonate	trace	Calcium Carbonate	6.03
Potassium Chloride	48.05	Ferrum Peroxide	.43
Potassium Sulphate	trace	Barium Carbonate	trace
Potassium Bromide	trace	Ammonium Chloride	trace
Potassium Iodide	.04	Silica	2.29
Maguesium Chloride	1.82	Organic Matter	.06
Maguesium Carbonate	15.94		

Total Solids, 765.64

Gases	Cubic Inches
Carbonic Acid Gas,	25.00
Sulphureted Hydrogen,	12.95

This spring has been in extensive use for many years. When the Indians bathed in the hot sulphurous mud springs centuries ago they are also supposed to have drank the iron water. For years invalids have used this water as a cure for fever and ague and malarial chills. Its action is tonic, diuretic, antacid and laxative, and is used with success in anæmia, chlorosis, loss of appetite, want of strength, malarial toxæmia and allied diseases tending to destroy the vitality of the red-blood corpuscles and the organs presiding over their manufacture. It is a significant fact that although this spring contains considerably less than many other springs on the premises, yet the "Iron Spring" water is more tonic and invigorating. The secret lies in the kind of iron in the spring. Here it will be observed to be a *peroxide*. As the noted authority on mineral springs, Dr. Sigismund Sutro, of London, remarks (see therapeutics of mineral waters in front part of this book), you may understand why six-tenths of a grain of iron imbibed into the duodenal lacteals (absorbent vessels in the intestines just beyond the stomach), with the abundance of the gaseous (carbonic) acid, may exercise a greater influence on the circulating system than three or four times the quantity

of pharmaceutical carbonate of iron, which has to be dissolved in the gastric juice previous to absorption, hence it
is that this spring has been so valuable and so extensively
used long before any chemical analysis had been made of it.

BYRON SPRINGS—" HOT SALT "
ALKALO-CHLORINATED
Dr. Winslow Anderson, Analyst, 1889
Temperature 122.3° F.

Mineral Ingredients	U. S. gal. contains Grains	Mineral Ingredients	U. S. gal. contains Grains
Sodium Chloride	555.26	Calcium Carbonate	.68
Sodium Carbonate	0.21	Calcium Sulphate	.85
Potassium Chloride	36.02	Ferrous Carbonate	.86
Potassium Bromide	trace	Ammonium Chloride	.09
Potassium Iodide	0.03	Barium Carbonate	.17
Maguesium Chloride	2.06	Silica	2.00
Magnesium Carbonate	12.11	Organic Matter	.06
Calcium Chloride	96.54		

Total Solids, 706.94

Gases	Cubic Inches
Free Carbonic Acid Gas	3.00

The "Hot Salt" water is used for bathing. It has a
temperature of 122.3° F. The water is alkalo-chlorinated,
of a good specific gravity to be readily absorbed into the
cutaneous system (see article on bath). The potassium
salts and other mineral ingredients, principally chlorides,
make the water diuretic, detergent and alterative. It has
been drank and bathed in with marked success in rheumatism, gout and joint diseases, cutaneous affections, etc., etc.

BYRON SPRINGS—"IRON PIPE "
ALKALO-CHLORINATED
Dr. Winslow Anderson, Analyst, 1889
Temperature 76° F.

Mineral Ingredients	U. S. Gal. contains Grains	Mineral Ingredients	U. S. Gal. contains Grains
Sodium Chloride	594.10	Calcium Carbonate	.29
Sodium Carbonate	trace	Calcium Sulphate	.02
Potassium Chloride	40.75	Ferrous Carbonate	.90
Potassium Bromide	0.07	Ammonium Chloride	trace
Potassium Iodide	0.13	Barium Carbonate	trace
Magnesium Chloride	3.25	Silica	0.05
Magnesium Carbonate	10.78	Organic Matter	0.10
Calcium Chloride	16.35		

Total Solids, 668.14

Gases	Cubic Inches
Free Carbonic Acid Gas	10.24

The "Iron Pipe" spring lies to the east of the hotel and is not much used.

BYRON SPRINGS—"SURPRISE"
HEAVY CHLORINATED
DR. WINSLOW ANDERSON, Analyst, 1889
Temperature 74° F.

Mineral Ingredients	U. S. Gal. contains Grains	Mineral Ingredients	U. S. Gal. contains Grains
Sodium Chloride	15,417.03	Calcium Carbonate	5.42
Sodium Carbonate	....	Calcium Sulphate.	66.14
Potassium Chloride	142,00	Ferrous Carbonate.	2.72
Potassium Bromide	0.06	Ammonium Chloride	trace
Potassium Iodide	.13	Barium Carbonate	trace
Magnesium Chloride..	622.56	Barium Chloride	0.13
Magnesium Carbonate	151.92	Silica	0.85
Calcium Chloride	2,364.77	Organic Matter	trace

Total Solids, 18,773.73

Gases
Free Carbonic Acid Gas................trace

The "Surprise" water is indeed a wonderful spring. The most careful analysis yields over 15,000 grains of common salt to each gallon of 231 cubic inches of water, and has over 18,000 grains—about 40 ounces, or 33 per cent.—of solid mineral ingredients in solution in the water. Comparative analyses of heavy waters show the "Surprise" to be the most remarkable.

Total Solids	U. S. Gal. contains Grains	Total Solids	U. S. Gal. contains Grains
Sea Water	2,138.91	Salt Lake (Utah)about	11,000.00
Mono Lake (Cal.)	2,915.16	Michigan Salt Wells	11,665.00
Castalian Min. Sp. (Cal)	4,422.25	Dead Sea (Holy Land)	13,488.10
Owens Lake (Cal.)	7,000.60	Byron Surprise Spring	18,773.73
Syracuse (N. Y.) Salt W	9,221.00		

For bathing purposes this "Surprise" water ought to be one of the most valuable on the coast, as the absorption is in direct ratio to the specific gravity of the bath. (See article on the bath at the beginning of the volume.)

The water is highly diuretic and laxative when taken internally.

The bathing facilities at Byron are a special feature. Two large bathhouses have been built, and baths, either sulphurous, steam, vapor or water, in tub or plunge, can be taken at all temperatures.

The hot saline and sulphur waters are used with considerable success. But the most noted of all the baths are those of moor or mud. They are so constructed that complete immersion can be secured and the temperature regulated to suit each case. The baths can also be partial if desired. These baths are all taken in individual bathtubs, and the mud is changed after each bath. This hot sulphurous saline mud has become famous in the treatment of rheumatism, gout, swollen joints, chronic arthritis, scrofula, skin diseases, etc., etc. In several cases of chronic rheu-

On the way to Sulphur Spring.

matism the writer can attest to its beneficial effects. The "Hot Salt" water has proved superior to almost any other uterine douche in the treatment of leucorrhœa and inflammation of the pelvic organs. (See uterine douche.) The following is an analysis of the sulphurous mud and water used for bathing:

BYRON SPRINGS—"BLACK SULPHUROUS MUD"
SALINO-SULPHUROUS MUD WATER
Dr. Winslow Anderson, Analyst, 1889

Temperature 110° F.

Mineral Ingredients	U. S. gal contains Grains	Mineral Ingredients	U. S. gal. contains Grains
Sodium Chloride	274.93	Calcium Chloride	7.50
Sodium Sulphate	42.16	Calcium Sulphate	36.05
Potassium Chloride	26.40	Calcium Carbonate	3.09
Potassium Iodide	0.32	Ferrous Sulphate	0.76
Potassium Bromide	trace	Ammonium Chloride	trace
Magnesium Chloride	2.06	Silica	5.62
Magnesium Sulphate	19.60	Organic Matter	7.34

Total Solids, 425.83

Gases	Cubic Inches
Free Carbonic Acid Gas	17.75
Free Sulphureted Hydrogen	14.50

This mud is used for bathing purposes by thousands of rheumatics every year, and it certainly has considerable therapeutic value as an auxiliary in the treatment of many of these cases.

40. CALIFORNIA SELTZER

These springs are pleasantly located in the Coast Range of mountains, twelve miles from Cloverdale, in Mendocino County. The surroundings are picturesque, and the climate is good. There is a comfortable resort at the springs.

The waters are sparkling and carbonated and of especial benefit in dyspepsia with acid eructations, constipation, acid conditions of the urine, cystitis, etc. The waters are diuretic and aperient, and highly charged with carbonic anhydride. They are quite palatable.

On analysis the seltzer is found to contain:

CALIFORNIA SELTZER
ALKALINE CARBONATED
Dr. WINSLOW ANDERSON, Analyst, 1889

Temperature 57° F.

Mineral Ingredients	U. S. Gal. contains Grains	Mineral Ingredients	U. S. Gal. contains Grains
Sodium Chloride	17.15	Ferrous Carbonate	trace
Sodium Bicarbonate	53.00	Calcium Carbonate	72.40
Sodium Carbonate	trace	Organic Matter	trace
Magnesium Carbonate	44.60	Silica	trace

Total Solids, 187.15

Gases	Cubic Inches
Free Carbonic Acid Gas	18.

41. CALISTOGA MINERAL SPRINGS

These valuable mineral springs are situated in Napa County, nine miles south of Mt. St. Helena. There are two sets of springs—one set in the city of Calistoga and another set just outside the town. They are about the same in composition, so that one description will do for both.

In 1858 Mr. Samuel Brannan purchased the springs and a large tract of land. He expended about $100,000 on the place, built an elegant hotel and twenty fine cottages, erected handsome and excellent bathing facilities, and had in the course of a few years one of the finest resorts on the coast. In 1868, ten years later, the hotel and several of the cottages burned down, and since that time the place has changed hands many times. We learned during our visit to the springs last year that Senator Stanford now owns the premises, and contemplates restoring the once handsome resort. The mineral springs number some twenty or more. They range in temperature from 75° F. to 186° F. The waters are used for drinking and bathing purposes, and have acquired considerable reputation. Dr. Alden M. Gardiner, one of the leading physicians in Calistoga, informed the writer that he had used the waters with considerable efficacy in many obstinate cases of syphilitic contamination, rheumatism, etc. From what I saw of the place I should judge that it could be made a first-class sanitarium for chronic cutaneous diseases, rheumatism, scrofula and constitutional taints.

CALISTOGA SPRINGS—AT MAGNOLIA HOTEL

LIGHT SULPHURETED WATER

DR. WINSLOW ANDERSON, Analyst, 1888

Temperature 95° F.

Mineral Ingredients	U. S. Gal. contains Grains	Mineral Ingredients	U. S. Gal. contains Grains
Sodium Chloride	20.76	Calcium Chloride	5.57
Sodium Carbonate	5.10	Calcium Sulphate	.63
Sodium Sulphate	1.75	Alumina	.47
Sodium Iodide	.16	Silica	4.55
Potassium Iodide	trace	Organic Matter	trace
Magnesium Sulphate	2.90		

Total Solids, 41.89

Gases	Cubic Inches
Free Sulphureted Hydrogen	4.74

CALISTOGA HOT SPRINGS

(On Senator Stanford's Grounds)

HOT SWIMMING POOL

Temperature 121.6° F.

HOT SPRING BY CREEK

Temperature 106.3° F.

Mineral Ingredients	U. S. gal. contains Grains
Sodium Chloride...	23.07
Sodium Carbonate	2.19
Sodium Sulphate	6.92
Sodium Iodide	.73
Potassium Iodide	.21
Potassium Carbonate	.76
Magnesium Sulphate	1.16
Magnesium Chloride	.40
Calcium Chloride	.96
Calcium Sulphate	1.25
Ferrous Protoxide	.45
Manganese	trace
Alumina	.27
Silica	3.61
Organic Matter	traces
Total Solids, 41.98	

Gases	Cubic Inches
Sulphureted Hydrogen,	6.30

Mineral Ingredients	U. S. gal. contains Grains
Sodium Chloride	17.46
Sodium Carbonate	3.70
Sodium Sulphate	5.14
Sodium Iodide	.08
Potassium Iodide	trace
Potassium Carbonate	trace
Magnesium Sulphate	.62
Magnesium Chloride	.21
Calcium Chloride	.37
Calcium Sulphate	trace
Ferrous Protoxide	.10
Manganese	trace
Alumina	.46
Silica	1.75
Organic Matter	.63
Total Solids, 30.52	

Gases	Cubic Inches
Sulphureted Hydrogen,	4.23

42. CAMETA WARM SPRINGS

Lie in township 29 S., range 17, Mt. Diablo M. Unimproved.

43. CAMPBELL'S HOT SPRINGS

These springs are located in Sierra County, one mile from the town of Sierraville. There are three principal springs, one of which is cold and the other two hot, having a temperature of 104° F. The surrounding scenery is grand and a first-class resort has been established there. The elevation is 5,025 feet; climate, during the summer season, is fine. There is good fishing and splendid hunting in the immediate neighborhood.

The waters are slightly saline and mildly sulphurous, and used for the same diseases that such mineral waters seem to help.

44. CAMPO'S CHALYBEATE SPRINGS

Not developed, and I have been unable to obtain water for analysis.

The Petrified Forest

Near Calistoga, situated in the adjacent mountains, and forming an interesting study for the tourist and scientist, is the petrified forest grotto, composed entirely of the trunks and limbs of trees. Much has been written concerning the origin of this wonderful forest, which may have been submerged in distant ages by the eruption of some volcano, discharging water and ashes, covering it and sealing it in an eternal tomb. Ages gradually exhumed it in the original form, but turned to stone. The area covered is about twenty acres, and is well worth a visit.

There are about one hundred trees and traces of trees, all lying in the same general direction, having been thrown down from north to south, the largest of which is called the "Pride of the Forest," and is sixty-seven feet in length and nearly twelve feet in diameter.

SCENE IN PETRIFIED FOREST, NEAR CALISTOGA, CALIFORNIA

45. CARBONATED SPRINGS

Located on Shovel Creek road, in the northern part of Siskiyou County. They are used locally and are said to have a very agreeable soda taste. Unimproved.

CARNELIAN, OR LAKE TAHOE HOT SPRINGS

See Lake Tahoe springs.

47. CASA DIABLO HOT SPRINGS

These hot springs lie about ten miles east of Mammoth, in Mono County. They are on the road to Burton. The waters are saline and sulphureted. Farther up the road are found a number of small steaming, boiling geysers, issuing from small crevices in the igneous rock. They spout up with considerable force. The temperature of these sulphurous springs is near the boiling point. Unimproved.

48. CASTALIAN MINERAL WATER SPRINGS

These are found near Owen's Lake, in Inyo County. They number thirteen, mostly cold. One or two are sulphurous and the others are alkaline and carbonated. A resort is building up about the springs. Some of the water is also used commercially for the curing of cutaneous affections.

The following analysis was made by Prof. Price in 1880:

CASTALIAN MINERAL WATER
THOMAS PRICE, Analyst, 1880

Mineral Ingredients	U. S. gal. contains Grains	Mineral Ingredients	U. S. gal. contains Grains
Sodium Carbonate	1724.11	Silica	14.28
Sodium Sulphate	651.02	Boracic Acid	trace
Sodium Sulphate	46.34	Phosphoric Acid	trace
Sodium Chloride	1840.72	Iodine	trace
Potassium Chloride	132.30	Bromine	trace
Lime	trace	Iron	trace
Magnesia	trace	Organic Matter	13.48

Total Solids, 4422.25
Gases not determined

This is one of the heaviest waters we have on the coast, and is much too dense to use medicinally, it could, however, be used very much diluted. We are informed that there are several other springs not so dense as this one, which are used medicinally.

49. CASTLE ROCK SPRINGS

On the Mt. Shasta scenic route are situated several sulphureted and carbonated soda springs, known as " Castle Rock." They lie near the foot of Mt. Shasta. They are used locally for rheumatic troubles.

50. CHALYBEATE MINERAL SPRINGS

Unnamed springs of iron, soda, magnesia, etc., are found in several portions of the State. Several of these are in Tehama County, about two miles from Tom's Head Mountain. They have gained a local reputation in chronic malaria, anæmia, etc., chlorosis, hemorrhages, etc. There are no improvements on the grounds yet, and no analysis has been made. Other Chalybeate springs are located in Shasta County, northwest of Fort Crook on Bear Creek, near the head of Falls River. These springs are reported to be highly ferruginous. The water is said to be pleasant to the taste, sparkling and carbonated. Unimproved.

COAL.—Extensive coal beds are found in various parts of the State.

COAL OIL SPRINGS.—See petroleum.

51. COAL VALLEY BOILING SPRINGS

These hot springs lie some eight miles west of Canby, in Modoc County. They are truly boiling, having a temperature of 214° F. An egg boils in the water in a few minutes. White incrustations of soda form about the margins of the springs. The property is unimproved.

52.   COLD SODA LAKE

This alkaline sheet of water is found near the head of Mill and Battle Creeks, south of Lassen's Peak, in Plumas County. The Lake is fed by many small springs bubbling up all over its bottom. The water is palatable and sparkling, and the location will no doubt develop into a resort before long. The water is found to contain:

> Sodium Chloride.
> Sodium Bicarbonate.
> Sodium Carbonate.
> Potassium Bicarbonate.
> Magnesium Carbonate.
> Calcium Carbonate.
> Free Carbonic Anhydride.

53.   COLD SODA SPRINGS

These delicious springs are located near the Yosemite Valley, in Tuolumne County. The springs, though unimproved, are much visited by tourists, who drink the water with decided relish. By adding sugar or syrup to these alkaline and carbonated waters a genuine soda may be prepared.

54.   COOK'S SPRINGS

Located in Indian Valley, Colusa County, some thirty-two miles from Williams. The waters are saline and sulphurous, acting pleasantly on the liver and bowels. They are used locally.

" The waves come crowding up on the shore like nymphs in silv'ry
> green ;
> Forward in line they trip to the time of orchestras unseen.
> They sport and leap by the rocky point, sparkling in gems and gold,
> Murmuring ever a liquid strain, like siren songs of old.
> With snowy plumes, which wreathe and curl and toss in wanton
> glee,
> Their riotous dance brings to the heart the gladness of the sea !
> Oh ! the sea seems in a happy mood—happy ! and so am I,
> With heart as light as the foamy crest of waves that jostle by!"

THE HOTEL DEL CORONADO   NORTH-WESTERN VIEW

55. CORONADO MINERAL SPRINGS

In San Diego County and on the Coronado Beach are located some excellent mineral waters. The springs are at an elevation of thirty feet above the ocean tide, and flow the enormous amount of 50,000 gallons per hour. The water is clear and sparkling, pleasing to the eye and pleasant to the taste, being soft, pure and wholesome.

On analysis it is found to compare favorably with the noted Waukesha Water of Wisconsin, the Betheseda Spring, as follows :

CORONADO SPRINGS
LIGHT ALKALO CARBONATED WATER
C. GILBERT WHEELER, Analyst

Mineral Ingredients	SAN DIEGO U. S. gal. contains Grains	BETHESDA, WIS. U. S. gal. contains Grains
Sodium Chloride	10.168	1.160
Sodium Carbonate	———	.872
Sodium Sulphate	———	.544
Potassium Chloride	.912	———
Potassium Sulphate	.552	.456
Magnesium	4.728	7.344
Calcium Carbonate	6.488	11.824
Calcium Sulphate	1.328	———
Ferros Sesquioxide	.040	.032
Alumina	———	.120
Silica	1.080	.728
Organic Matter	.992	1.984
Total Solids	26.288	25.064
Gases	Not determined	Not determined

The waters are gently aperient, diuretic and tonic, of value in dyspepsia, anæmia, renal and cystic disorders. The accommodations at the Coronado Hotel are among the finest in the world. The building is a magnificent structure, and the scenery on the beach, on the banks of the grand Pacific Ocean is never to be forgotten by one fortunate enough to have beheld it.

56.   CORRAL DE LUZ WARM SPRINGS

These noted springs are found in San Diego County, near Oceanside. They are pleasantly located in a valley about two miles in diameter, with mountains on all sides; about eight miles from the ocean. Sycamores, oaks and alders are scattered in wild profusion about the springs. There is only a small resort at these springs at present, owing, no doubt, to the fact that an old gentleman nearly eighty years of age, owns the place. The climate is delightful, having a temperature of 70° F. to 85° F. Winter and Summer.

The de Luz Springs—several in number—from their surroundings and natural advantages offer a sanitarium second to none in the State. The temperature of the water ranges from 85° F. to 135° F., and all the place needs is some live man with a little capital to develop the country and build up a first-class resort. The waters are highly charged with sulphur and sulphurous acid, sulphates of magnesia, soda and calcium.

Crude baths are arranged and several small cottages are for hire. The place is much frequented by Spaniards and Mexicans, and the usual number of diseases are treated by the baths and sulphur waters.

57.   CRYSTAL SPRINGS

Several carbonated-alkaline waters are found in Napa County and known as "Crystal Springs." The water is used by the people in the vicinity. No improvements.

In San Mateo County we find several more mineral springs named "crystal." The waters are reported to be

alkaline and saline, acting on the stomach, bowels and
kidneys. It is a favored remedy in the neighborhood for
"biliousness."

58. CUYANA HOT SPRINGS

These springs are also sulphurous, and located in the
cañon and valley of Cuyana in Santa Barbara County.
There is no analysis.

59. DESERT OR CAVE SPRINGS

These are located in Kern County, and consist of alkaline
carboneted waters with borates. Unimproved.

60. DR. SOUPAN'S HOT SPRINGS

We find these hot sulphur springs at the head of the
road on a branch of Battle Creek, in Plumas County. The
surroundings are picturesque, and we understand improvements are contemplated. No analysis.

DE LUZ SPRINGS

See Corral de Luz warm springs.

EL PASO DE ROBLES
HOT AND COLD SULPHUR SPRINGS

These valuable mineral springs are situated midway
between the mission of San Miguel Archangel and La Casa
del Paso de Robles. They lie in the beautiful valley of
the Salinas River about sixteen miles from the shores of the
Pacific and two hundred and sixteen miles from San Francisco. The springs are of easy access by the Southern
Pacific Railroad (northern division) via Soledad, through
trains daily. Also from San Luis Obispo by stage. The
name, El Paso de Robles (ail-parso day roh-blais) is derived
from the Spanish, meaning "in a pass of the oaks," from

PASO ROBLES

the fact that the main highway ran through this valley. For many miles this picturesque valley is covered with gigantic white oaks, live oaks and huge cottonwoods, and nestled in one of these cosy groves is Paso Robles retreat.

The once wild " pass in the oaks" is now transformed into a blooming resort, with cultivated grounds, and Paso Robles is a delightful little town of about one thousand inhabitants. It is situated in the center of a very rich agricultural section in San Luis Obispo County. The town is principally built of handsome brick buildings and is growing rapidly. When the Southern Pacific Railroad is completed Paso Robles will be of considerable commercial importance.

Near the springs, and overlooking the prosperous little town, there is in course of construction an elegant and commodious hotel, which is to be built of solid brick throughout. This building, when completed, will not only be an ornament to the town, but of great comfort and convenience to the many guests who go to the springs yearly for their health.

Under the umbrageous oaks in different parts of the extensive grounds are located some eighteen cosy cottages for private and family use. On each side of the resort and valley the evergreen hills, covered with forests of pine, oaks, manzanita groves and sweet-scented shrubbery, form a pleasant contrast to Paso Robles proper. The climate is remarkably mild and luxurious all the year round, and the atmosphere is pure, balmy and invigorating.

Few mineral springs in America have acquired such a favorable reputation for the treatment of constitutional contaminations, rheumatism, gout, joint, blood, glandular and cutaneous diseases as Paso Robles have, and thousands go there yearly to receive the joint benefit of the bathing and drinking waters, as well as the internal medical treatment.

The waters at Paso Robles are sulphurous and alkaline, ranging in temperature from 59° F. to 104° and 122° F., and comprise the "Main Hot Sulphur" spring, the "Mud or Moor" springs, the "Soda," "Sand," "Cold White Sulphur," "Iron" and "Garden" springs.

The great hot sulphureted spring is located about three hundred yards from the hotel in a southeasterly direction. Over it has been constructed one of the finest bathing establishments on the coast, consisting of sixty individual bathtubs, and a large vat fifteen by thirty feet for a swimming or a plunge bath. One side is used for women and the other side for men. Immediately over the source of the spring is

built a large dome-shaped receptacle twenty-five feet in diameter and about twenty feet high. This tank collects the hot water and gases as they issue from the subterranean laboratory, and, being constructed of solid masonry and hermetically sealed, all the vapors and mineral properties are kept saturated in the water. From this tank or reservoir lead several faucets, whereby the water may be drawn for drinking purposes. Most of the water, however, is used for bathing, for which purpose it is led into the several bathtubs.

The flow of this main spring is about 5,000 gallons per hour, and it has a temperature from 105° F. to 110° F.

EL PASO DE ROBLES—"MAIN SULPHUR WATER"

ALKALO-SULPHUROUS

Flows 5,000 gallons per hour

PROFS. PRICE and HEWSTON'S Analysis, several years ago. *Temperature 110° F.*		DR. WINSLOW ANDERSON, Analyst, 1889 *Temperature 107.6° F.*

Mineral Ingredients	Imp. gal. contains Grains	U. S. gal. contains Grains
Sodium Chloride	27.18	25.73
Sodium Bicarbonate	50.74	41.19
Sodium Carbonate	——	7.62
Sodium Sulphate	7.85	7.25
Sodium Iodide	——	trace
Sodium Bromide	——	trace
Potassium Chloride	——	1.57
Potassium Carbonate	——	2.05
Potassium Iodide	——	trace
Potassium Sulphate	.88	trace
Magnesium Bicarbonate	.92	——
Magnesium Carbonate	——	2.15
Magnesium Sulphate	——	5.11
Calcium Carbonate	——	1.23
Calcium Sulphate	3.21	2.94
Ferrum Peroxide	.36	.73
Borates	——	trace
Lithiates	——	trace
Alumina	.22	.25
Silica	.44	1.75
Iodides and Bromides	trace	——
Organic Matter	1.64	1.90
Total Solids	93.44	101.47
Gases	Grains	Cubic Inches
Free Sulphureted Hydrogen	4.45	3.75
Free Carbonated Acid Gas	10.50	8.90

These waters are found to be especially serviceable in acute and chronic rheumatism and articular affections, scrofula, blood, glandular and cutaneous diseases. In catarrh of the naso-pharynx the water, used as a hot douche, has proved highly beneficial, likewise in leucorrhœal discharges and engorgement of the pelvic organs, etc., etc.

It is important, as has been remarked when speaking of the therapeutic properties of mineral waters, to carefully follow the instructions of the resident physician, in order to fully and rapidly receive the benefits of the springs. Con-

nected with Paso Robles is an experienced physician, Dr.
David L. Deal, who has made a special study of the action
of these waters in health and in disease, and his instructions should be conscientiously followed.

The next most important water at Paso Robles is that
used for the mud or moor baths. This now famous spring
is situated about one mile and a half north of the hotel,
near the line of the Southern Pacific Railroad and on the
edge of the Salinas River.

The walk from the hotel to this spring is a pleasant
one under the shady oaks and along the well-kept road and
grassy lawns. Patients unable to walk, and others who
may desire it, can ride in the hotel carriage to and from the
mud baths twice daily.

These mud springs—for there are several—cover a
space of about twenty-five feet square, over which has been
constructed suitable bathing conveniences, consisting of
dressing-rooms, hot sulphurous water plunges and the mud
plunge. This latter is a compartment or vat four by eight
feet and nearly filled with prepared moor or mud, and so
arranged that the hot sulphurous water and gases rise
directly into it from the ground beneath.

The facilities are admirably arranged for both ladies
and gentlemen, and competent persons administer the baths
under directions of the resident physician.

During my visit to these springs, in 1889, I found the
temperature of the mud and sulphurous waters to vary
from 104° F. to 122° F. Baths are prescribed once, twice
or three times a week of different degrees of temperature
and of varying duration, to suit each individual case. The
mud springs flow collectively about 6,000 gallons per hour.

Moor bathing has been practised by the Indians for
generations, and of late years it has been extensively introduced among the white people all over the world. These
baths at Paso Robles have gained considerable celebrity,
and justly so. The writer has had occasion to note the
beneficial results in many cases subjected to this plan of

treatment and he does not hesitate in remarking that for rheumatism, arthritis, stiff joints, sprains, white swellings (synovitis), glandular enlargements, chronic cutaneous diseases, etc., much benefit will accrue, especially if the internal medication be kept up during the treatment.

EL PASO DE ROBLES—"MUD SPRINGS"

SULPHUROUS

Flows 6.000 gallons per hour

	PROFS. PRICE AND HEWSTON'S Analysis, several years ago Temperature 122° F.	DR. WINSLOW ANDERSON Analyst, 1889 Temperature 104 to 122° F.
Mineral Ingredients	One Imp. Gal. contains Grains	One U. S. Gal. contains Grains
Sodium Chloride	96.48	83.72
Sodium Carbonate	5.21	7.41
Sodium Sulphate	41.11	36.97
Sodium Iodide	——	trace
Potassium Chloride	——	3.19
Potassium Iodide	——	trace
Potassium Sulphate	trace	.82
Magnesium Carbonate	3.10	4.25
Magnesium Sulphate	——	1.13
Calcium Carbonate	——	2.10
Calcium Sulphate	17.90	15.75
Ferrous Sulphate	——	.23
Alumina	——	.80
Manganese Salts	——	trace
Silica	1.11	.251
Lithium Salts	——	trace
Organic Matter	3.47	7.14
Total Solids	168.38	166.02
Gases	Grains	Cubic Inches
Ammonia and Nitrogen	——	trace
Free Sulphureted Hydrogen	3.24	4.16
Free Carbonic Acid Gas	47.84	42.50

About two hundred yards north of the Mud Baths is the "Soda Spring." Its temperature is 77° F., and its flow is limited. The water is much used for drinking purposes. By allowing the small amount of sulphureted hydrogen to escape the water becomes very palatable.

EL PASO DE ROBLES—"SODA SPRING"

Dr. Winslow Anderson, Analyst, 1889

Temperature 77° F.

Mineral Ingredients	U. S. gal. contains Grains	Mineral Ingredients	U. S. gal. contains Grains
Sodium Chloride	25.10	Magnesium Sulphate	7.80
Sodium Carbonate	7.25	Calcium Carbonate	5.32
Sodium Bicarbonate	10.70	Calcium Sulphate	6.47
Sodium Sulphate	5.05	Ferrum Peroxide	trace
Potassium Carbonate	1.16	Silica	.92
Potassium Sulphate	.83	Alumina	.85
Magnesium Carbonate	3.17	Organic Matter	trace

Total Solids, 83.82

Free Gases	Cubic Inches
Carbonic Acid Gas	9.20
Sulphureted Hydrogen	1.60

About midway between the "Mud Springs" and the "Sand Spring" is found a carbonated spring, known as the "Garden." The water is palatable, and of value in Bright's disease, bladder troubles, etc., as an antacid and diuretic.

On analysis it yields:

EL PASO DE ROBLES SPRINGS—"GARDEN SPRING"

CARBONATED WATER

Dr. Winslow Anderson, Analyst, July, 1889

Mineral Ingredients	U. S. gal. contains Grains	Mineral Ingredients	U. S. gal. contains Grains
Sodium Chloride	20.76	Calcium Carbonate	6.23
Sodium Carbonate	1.16	Calcium Sulphate	12.35
Sodium Bicarbonate	25.17	Ferrous Carbonate	traces
Sodium Sulphate	traces	Manganese Carbonate	traces
Potassium Chloride	traces	Alumina	.47
Potassium Carbonate	.83	Silica	.22
Magnesium Carbonate	4.95	Organic Matter	traces
Magnesium Sulphate	3.47		

Total Solids, 75.61.

Free Gases	Cubic Inches
Carbonic Acid Gas	25.60
Sulphureted Hydrogen	traces

This soda water is found to be of special value in kidney and bladder irritation.

"SAND" SPRING

About one-quarter of a mile south of the mud springs we find a large "sand" spring. It is about twelve feet in diameter, and situated in the old bed of the Salinas River. The waters are carbonated and sulphureted and bubbling up with considerable force, carrying with it quantities of white silicon oxide, which sparkles in the water as it rises and falls.

The waters have a temperature of 79.1° F., and are not utilized to any extent at present.

EL PASO DE ROBLES "SAND" SPRINGS
ALKALO-SULPHUROUS
DR. WINSLOW ANDERSON, Analyst, 1889
Temperature 79.1 F.°

Mineral Ingredients	U. S. gal. contains Grains	Mineral Ingredients	U. S. gal. contain Grains
Sodium Chloride	92.20	Magnesium Sulphate	4.10
Sodium Carbonate	9.41	Calcium Carbonate	6.62
Sodium Sulphate	36.95	Calcium Sulphate	16.04
Sodium Iodide	trace	Ferrous Carbonate	.29
Sodium Bromide	trace	Manganese Carbonate	.13
Potassium Chloride	7.50	Alumina	1.17
Potassium Carbonate	5.03	Lithium Salts	trace
Potassium Iodide	trace	Barium Salts	trace
Potassium Bromide	trace	Silica	6.51
Magnesium Carbonate	3.72	Organic Matter	.87

Total Solids, 190.54

Gases	Cubic Inches
Free Carbonic Acid Gas,	11.76
Free Sulphureted Hydrogen	3.40
Nitrogen	trace

A quarter of a mile southeast of the hotel is located the large "White Sulphur" spring. It is inclosed in twenty feet square masonry walls. The waters are salino-sulphurous, and strongly charged with hydrogen sulphide. The waters are not extensively used.

EL PASO DE ROBLES "WHITE SULPHUR SPRING"
SALINO-SULPHUROUS
DR. WINSLOW ANDERSON, Analyst, 1889
Temperature 59° F.

Mineral Ingredients	U. S. gal. contains Grains	Mineral Ingredients	U. S. gal. contains Grains
Sodium Chloride	31.76	Magnesium Chloride	9.03
Sodium Carbonate	3.19	Calcium Sulphide	5.10
Sodium Sulphate	23.14	Manganese	trace
Potassium Chloride	10.73	Ferrous Sulphate	trace
Potassium Sulphate	13.23	Alumina	.84
Potassium Iodide	trace	Silica	1.05
Magnesium Sulphate	14.76	Organic Matter	trace

Total Solids, 112.85

Gases	Cubic Inches
Free Sulphureted Hydrogen,	9.40
Free Carbonic Acid Gas,	5.25

EL PASO ROBLES "IRON SPRING"

A little farther eastward and towards the bank of the river is located the "Iron" spring. It is a small spring incased in a box two by four feet, and has a moderate flow. Its temperature is 64.4° F. The waters are restorative, tonic, diuretic and aperient, and of value in the treatment of anæmia, chronic malarial toxæmia, chlorosis and the many diseases requiring recuperative ferruginous tonics.

EL PASO ROBLES "CHALYBEATE" SPRINGS
FERRUGINOUS AND CARBONATED
DR. WINSLOW ANDERSON, Analyst, 1889
Temperature 64.4° F.

Mineral Ingredients	U. S. gal. contains Grains	Mineral Ingredients	U. S. gal. contains Grains
Sodium Chloride	23.18	Calcium Sulphate	6.20
Sodium Carbonate	7.14	Ferrous Carbonate	1.40
Sodium Bicarbonate	20.87	Borates	trace
Sodium Sulphate	1.03	Alumina	.26
Potassium Carbonate	trace	Manganese Carbonate	trace
Magnesium Carbonate	6.23	Silica	.85
Magnesium Sulphate	10.06	Organic Matter	trace
Calcium Carbonate	2.11		

Total Solids, 79.42

Gases	Cubic Inches
Free Sulphureted Hydrogen	trace
Free Carbonic Acid Gas	trace

61. ELSINORE SPRINGS

Near Elsinore, in San Diego County, lies a little valley, which is teeming and steaming with mineral springs. Some are hot and others are cold. They number some two hundred. The temperature ranges from 57°F. to 212° F. The cold springs are carbonated, containing soda, magnesia and iron; the hot waters are sulphurous, with lime, magnesia and borax. There are also hot mud springs. The place is not developed. We predict a large resort for the valley in the course of a few years.

62. EUREKA SPRINGS

These springs are located in Humboldt County, near the town of Eureka, and they issue from the bank of the Bay. The waters belong to the chlorinated-sulphureted class, and were analyzed by Professor W. D. Johnston in 1885, as follows :

EUREKA SPRINGS
CHLORINATED—HEAVY
PROF. W D. JOHNSTON, Analyst, 1885

Mineral Ingredients	U. S. gal contains Grains	Mineral Ingredients	U. S. gal contains Grains
Sodium Chloride	1,403.00	Alumina	1.30
Sodium Carbonate	10.10	Silica	.95
Sodium Bromide	14.00	Ferrous Carbonate	.12
Potassium Sulphate	12.20	Manganese	trace
Magnesium Chloride	101.00	Boracic Acid	trace
Magnesium Sulphate	211.30	Iodine	trace
Calcium Carbonate	3.80	Lithium	trace
Calcium Sulphate	42.50		

Total Solids, 1,800.27

Gases

Carbonic Acid Gas..................small amount

Sulphureted Hydrogen..................saturated

This Eureka Spring water is now extensively used by the inhabitants. It is also shipped to San Francisco. The action of the water is laxative and diuretic, acting also on the glandular and lymphatic systems. It has also been used in skin diseases.

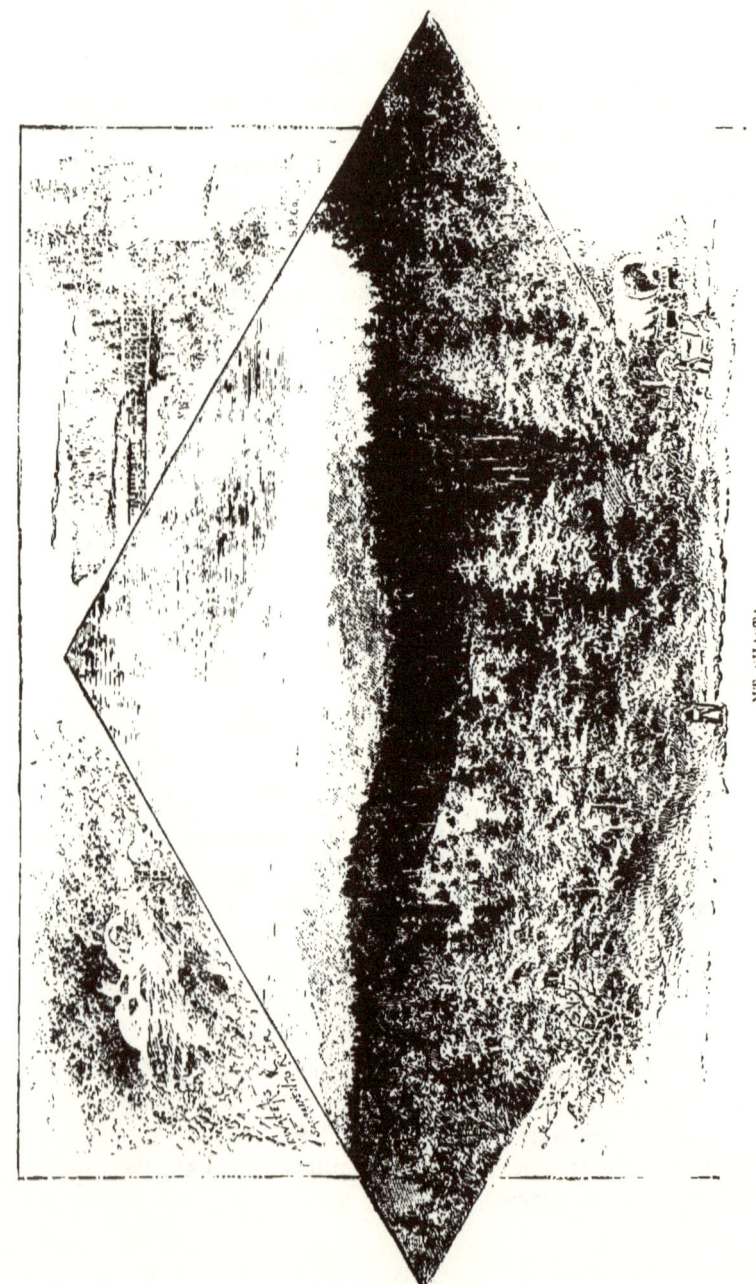

MT. SHASTA

FAIRMOUNT MINERAL SPRINGS

These recently developed springs are located in Sonoma Valley, about five miles from Cloverdale.

The water is alkaline and carbonated, very palatable and has a pleasant antacid effect on the stomach. The building of a resort is contemplated.

FELT'S MINERAL SPRINGS

These springs are located in Humboldt County, about twenty-five miles from Eureka, near the head of Strong's Valley. There are quite a number of springs on the place, the most important of which yields, on analysis:

Sodium Chloride.	Magnesium Chloride.
Sodium Carbonate.	Magnesium Carbonate.
Potassium Chloride	Calcium Carbonate.
Potassium Carbonate.	Manganese.
Potassium Sulphate.	Traces of Iron.
Silica.	Alumina.

The grounds are elegantly laid out, and commodious quarters have been erected for the accommodation of guests. The resort is illuminated by natural gas from the premises. The waters are said to be beneficial in dropsical tendencies depending on the liver or kidneys.

65. FRESNO HOT SPRINGS

Located near Warthan, in Fresno County. Unimproved.

66. FREY'S SODA SPRINGS

These springs lie near the line between Shasta and Siskiyou Counties. The waters are alkaline and carbonated. Temperature 52° F.

67. FULTON WELLS

This resort is located in Los Angeles County, about three miles north of Norwalk Station, on the Los Angeles Railroad, and thirteen miles from Los Angeles City. The wells were bored by Dr. Fulton, a very intelligent physician, who conducts the sanitarium himself. The two principal wells are 350 feet deep and flow copiously. The waters are carbonated and sulphurous, and contain:

FULTON WELLS—350 Feet Well
CARBONATED AND SULPHUROUS
Dr. WINSLOW ANDERSON, Analyst, 1888
Temperature, 64° F.

Mineral Ingredients	U. S. gal. contains Grains	Mineral Ingredients	U. S. gal. contains Grains
Sodium Chloride	9.60	Calcium Carbonate	12.62
Sodium Bicarbonate	2.90	Calcium Sulphate	23.41
Sodium Sulphate	.95	Silica	2.45
Magnesium Bicarbonate	17.45	Organic Matter	trace
Ferrous Carbonate	11.75		

Total Solids, 81.13

Gases
Free Carbonic Acid Gas................excess
Free Sulphureted Hydrogen..........excess

Comfortable cottages, a large hotel and excellent bathing facilities have been erected, and the resort enjoys considerable reputation in the treatment of anæmia, malarial troubles, atonic dyspepsia, congestion of the liver, etc. It will be observed that the waters contain a very large percentage of iron salts.

CALIFORNIA GEYSERS

This marvelous region—this branch of Hades, nestling among the umbrageous oaks and firs in the pine-clad mountains, rich in manzanita groves, sweet-scented shrubbery and wild flowers, and surrounded on all sides by his Satanic Majesty's prodigious laboratory—is located in the northeastern part of Sonoma County, about one hundred miles north of San Francisco, sixteen miles from Clover-

BIRDS EYE VIEW OF THE GEYSERS, SHOWING HOTEL & COTTAGES

dale, and twenty-six miles from Calistoga. This Plutonian realm was discovered in 1847 by Mr. William B. Elliot. One day while out hunting in that section of the country he scaled the northern mountain overlooking this partially extinct volcanic region, and came suddenly upon this wonderful scene. Imagine his fear and astonishment at beholding for the first time the Geysers! He remained awestruck for a few moments, and then hastened away to inform his companions that he had discoverd the very mouth of the infernal regions!

Since that time to the present these famous springs have been the objects of wonder and admiration to all the many thousands who visit them yearly.

Formerly tourists rode on horseback for many miles up the narrow mountain trails to visit this natural wonderland, which is situated about 1,700 feet above the sea level, but, thanks to the push and enterprise of western civilization, we now travel in comfortable six-horse stages from the termini of the Cloverdale and Calistoga railroads over excellent mountain roads to the geysers. It is a good plan to go by way of Cloverdale and return by way of Calistoga, as you then see all the grandeur and beauty of the surrounding country.

Leaving Cloverdale after luncheon, comfortably seated in your stage, with an experienced and accommodatingly communicative driver, who takes pleasure in pointing out the many objects of interest, you soon cross the Russian River and commence the ascent. The hills and mountains are robed in evergreen verdure of indigenous flora, gigantic oaks and towering pines. Here and there the huge boulders and rocky cliffs stand out in bold relief, and as you wind up and around the mountain sides, with the Pluton River many hundred feet below, basking and smiling in the afternoon sun and rippling along its moss-covered banks and bright-pebbled bottom, with here and there a miniature cascade and waterfall, you feel that words cannot describe the grandeur of the scenery. The elevated roads

on the mountain slopes frequently bring you to a sharp
curve, where the view is unobstructed, and where the stage-
driver is afforded an excellent opportunity of showing his
skill in handling the six-in-hand. Now and again the road
turns so sharply that the "leaders" are out of sight before
the curve is rounded.

CALIFORNIA GEYSERS

As you gain in altitude the view becomes more and
more extended until your eyes leap like live thunder from
peak to peak and valley to valley for miles around, feasting
upon the beauties of nature.

Some two or three miles down the cañon, before you
reach the Geysers, your attention is called to the large
white, or yellowish-white, banks across the cañon. They
are known as "sulphur" banks and consist of deposits of
sulphur and cinnabar with incrustations of salts of sodium,

potassium, magnesium, sulphur, etc. They are extinct craters, or the deposits of geysers and fumaroles which have died out, leaving evidences of volcanic action behind.

In the immediate vicinity of the Geysers several large deposits of sulphur and quicksilver have been mined and ores shipped to San Francisco.

Near these sulphur banks we found the famous "Indian Springs," at which the great Edwin Forest camped for one season and was completely restored to health. Tradition informs us that our aborigines traveled to these springs from far and near, and bathed in the extensive mud or moor springs close by and drank the water, which they found possessed miraculous curative powers.

On analysis this water is found to yield:

"INDIAN SPRING"
LIGHT SALINO-SULPHUROUS WATER
PROF. THOMAS PRICE, Analyst, 1888
Temperature 108° F.

Mineral Ingredients	U. S. gal. contains Grains	Mineral Ingredients	U. S. gal. contains Grains
Sodium Sulphate	3.29	Calcium Carbonate	7.35
Sodium Carbonate	1.40	Ferrous Carbonate	0.07
Potassium Sulphate	0.21	Alumina	0.18
Magnesium Carbonate	15.47	Silicic Acid	5.42

Total Solids, 33.39

Gases
Free Sulphureted Hydrogen.......saturated

This water has been found of considerable value as a tonic—diuretic, laxative and antacid—of great value in dyspepsia, torpidity of the liver and bowels, and in renal and cystic diseases.

Near by are the real "Indian Mud Springs," which are found to contain:

"INDIAN MUD SPRINGS"
ACIDULOUS-SALINO-ALUMINIC MUD
PROF. THOMAS PRICE, Analyst, 1888

Mineral Ingredients	U. S. gal. contains Grains	Mineral Ingredients	U. S. gal. contains Grains
Sodium Bisulphate	17.12	Alumina Sulphate	22.78
Magnesia Sulphate	59.33	Free Sulphuric Acid	32.30
Calcium Sulphate	6.42	Silicic Acid	12.25

Total Solids, 150.20

Gases

Free Sulphureted Hydrogen.........saturated

These mud baths will prove of great benefit in the
treatment of chronic rheumatism, gout, arthritis and synovites, and scrofulous and cutaneous contaminations.

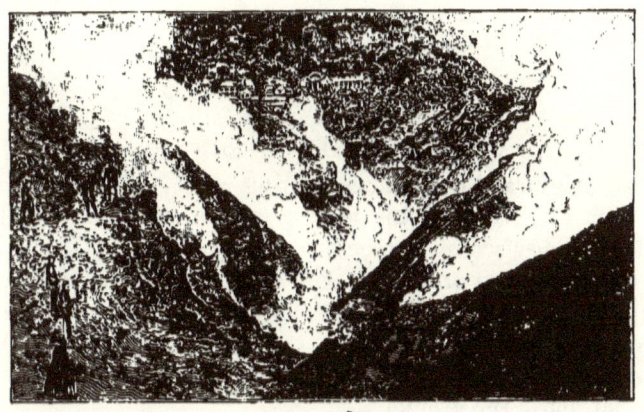

GEYSER CAÑON

As we drew nearer and nearer the sylvan resort our
ears were greeted with sounds like those of a steamboat or
locomotive—puff—puff—at regular intervals. These, we
were told, and as we ascertained afterwards, came from the
"steamboat" springs.

After a few more horseshoe curves have been passed,
and several more of those magnificent landscapes have
been mentally photographed on your brain, you reach the
Geyser resort.

The many cozy cottages, the hotel and grounds, are
situated in a leafy dell on the side of the mountain oppo-

site the Geyser cañon. The huge oaks and pines afford
pleasant shade to the commodious verandas as you sit and
enjoy the pure, dry, invigorating and exhilarating mountain atmosphere and picturesque scenery which surrounds
you on every side.

Having indulged in one of those splendid sulphur
Hammam baths, where the skin is rendered soft, white and
pliable owing to the medicinal effects of the mineral ingredients, you are ready for dinner, and a good one it was
during our visit to the Geysers in 1888.

The evenings are cool, clear and charming, insuring
sound and refreshing sleep.

A TRIP THROUGH GEYSER CAÑON

Bright and early next morning we set out for our trip
"over the river" to his majesty's Plutonian shores. In
the Summer season the best time to start out is from 4:30
to 5:00 A. M., in order that you may perceive the full volume of the steam and sulphurous vapors as they rise several hundred feet into the air. Later in the morning the
sun's rays condense the vapors so that they are not visible
as far above the ground.

You are now armed with a long staff, like the pilgrims
of old, and with your guide you set out to cross the Pluton
River—this time on a bridge. Before doing so, however,
your attention is called to a cool, clear spring, known as
the "iron" spring. It is located near the edge of the Pluton River, on the same side as the hotel. This iron spring,
on analysis, is found to contain valuable salino-chalybeate
mineral ingredients.

"IRON SPRING"

LIGHT SALINO CHALYBEATE WATER

DR. WINSLOW ANDERSON, Analyst, 1888

Temperature, 72° F.

Mineral Ingredients	U. S. Gal. contains Grains	Mineral Ingredients	U. S. Gal. contains Grains
Sodium Sulphate	traces	Barium Salts	traces
Potassium Sulphate	traces	Alumina	0.23
Magnesium Sulphate	2.75	Silica	1.44
Calcium Sulphate	3.96	Organic Matter	traces
Ferrous Sulphate	0.19		

Total Solids, 8.57

Gases	Cubic inches
Free Carbonic Acid Gas	traces
Free Sulphureted Hydrogen	4.26

This water belongs to the light chalybeate class; its action is tonic, aperient and detergent, of value in anæmia, chlorosis and wasting diseases, torpidity of the bowels and liver, etc., producing constructive tissue metamorphosis.

Immediately after crossing the Pluton River, a change in the atmosphere becomes noticeable. On the side where the hotel and resort with the many picturesque and cozy cottages are built, the air is pure, dry and invigorating, on the side where Geyser Cañon is located, the atmosphere is mixed with the perfumes from the interior realm.

Near the path on the bank of the river, as you proceed up the cañon is situated quite a remarkable spring, containing large quantities of aluminium, sulphate magnesia and silicic acid. It is known as the "Alum Spring." Its waters are really alumino-ferrugino-sulphurous. On analysis it is found to contain:

"ALUM" SPRING

ALUMINO-FERRUGINO SULPHUROUS WATER

DR. WINSLOW ANDERSON, Analyst, 1888

Temperature, 98° F.

Mineral Ingredients	U. S. Gal. contains Grains	Mineral Ingredients	U. S. Gal. contains Grains
Sodium Chloride	traces	Manganesium Salts	traces
Sodium Carbonate	0.72	Barium Salts	traces
Sodium Sulphate	6.24	Aluminium Sulphate	57.62
Potassium Sulphate	traces	Borates	1.20
Magnesium Sulphate	23.76	Free Sulphuric Acid	3.10
Calcium Sulphate	2.43	Silica	9.40
Ferrous Sulphate	6.25	Organic Matter	traces

Total Solids, 110.72

Gases	Cubic Inches
Free Sulphureted Hydrogen	6.35

This spring contains large quantities of ferruginous salts so essential in the treatment of malarial toxœmia and blood glandular diseases. The acid renders its action tonic and the magnesium gives it a pleasant laxative effect.

Following your guide, you soon realize that you are nearing the brink of eternity. You now cross the "Devil's," or Geyser, cañon and come to the "alum and sulphur" spring, having a temperature of 160° F. Proceeding farther on you next see the "black sulphur" springs, in which we find sulphide of iron. The ground is now getting warm under your feet, and the fumes from the "lower regions" make you think of the hereafter, and as you push on, a deep and steep ravine is entered, from which boiling hot steam and gases escape in every direction until you feel awestruck in this strange place! Passing along through the ravine, with the boiling water running at your feet, you enter "Proserpine's Grotto," in which is placed the "devil's arm-chair." This latter is a huge boulder which nature has hollowed out in the shape and form of a large parlor chair. In this you sit with great solemnity, to make sure of the benevolent friendship of his Satanic majesty.

The next point of interest is the "Devil's Kitchen," with warning signs of "danger" stuck up in every direction. The country rock is serpentine, sandstone and limestone, with igneous deposits and incrustations of sulphur, soda, cinnabar, etc., and as the fumaroles, cracks and fissures emit their boiling waters and vapors saturated with free sulphurous, sulphuric, hydrochloric acids and carbonic anhydride, all having strong disintegrating action on the formation, everything is, in consequence, soft and yielding. The banks and rocks are like clay and sand, easily dislodged upon the slightest touch—hence the signs of danger.

You are now fairly in the mouth of a boiling, seething, trembling and smoking Plutonian realm. The ground under your feet is becoming hotter and hotter, and the sulphurous fumes and vaporous steam are nearly suffocating. Early in the morning these vapors rise to a height of three hundred to five hundred feet. It is also observed that these wonderful subterranean forces exhibit more activity at or near the full moon.

In this *olla podrida* of Hadean liquids are several interesting points and springs to be observed. Near at hand is a hot "Epsom salt" spring, having a temperature of 150° F., and over 140 grains of magnesium sulphate to the gallon of water. Another boiling spring of "iron and sulphur" has a temperature of 208° F. On the right side of the path is a large, black, sulphurous spring continually boiling and rumbling as the black, inky fluid reaches the bright dawn of day at a temperature of 162° F. It is the "Devil's Inkstand," a hot sulphurous iron and alum sulphide and sulphate water which makes very fair writing fluid. For this purpose it is used at the Geyser hotel, where the visitor inscribes his name on the register with his majesty's ink.

You next come to the "hot alum" spring, containing, as will be seen from the following analysis, over sixty grains of aluminium sulphate to the gallon. It is an alumino-ferruginous sulphurous water.

GEYSERS—"HOT ALUM SPRING"

ALUMINO-FERRUGINO-SULPHUROUS WATER

Dr. Winslow Anderson, Analyst, 1888

Temperature 139° F.

Mineral Ingredients	U. S. gal. contains Grains	Mineral Ingredients	U. S. gal. contains Grains
Sodium Bisulphate	4.92	Magnesium Borate	traces
Sodium Sulphate	.46	Ferrous Sulphate	7.11
Potassium Sulphate	traces	Aluminium Sulphate	62.87
Magnesium Sulphate	36.14	Silica	16.43
Organic Matter	trace		

Total Solids, 127.93

Sulphuric Acid.............. ....7.02

Cases	Cubic Inches
Free Sulphureted Hydrogen	0.37

This spring water is an excellent hæmostatic in hemorrhages of the lungs, etc. It is also of service in dyspepsia and torpidity of the bowels and liver, its action being laxative, tonic and astringent, containing large quantities of sulphate of iron and aluminium, so valuable for medicinal purposes. (See therapeutical effects of mineral waters in preceding chapter.)

As you proceed along the not over "straight and narrow path," it is literally and practically important that you follow your guide and the "narrow path" here, lest one misstep hurl you into that "undiscovered country, from whose bourn no traveler returns." Innumerable springs and vents and subterranean outlets spurt and spout in every direction. "Pluto's Punch Bowl" is a large spring of hot lemonade, containing sulphuric acid and sulphates. The "Geyser Smokestack" is a large opening, from which issue volumes of sulphur-laden fumes, which rise into the air for several hundred feet, where it condenses and deposits again on the ground as water and sulphur, etc.

One of the most interesting springs in Geyser Cañon is the "Witch's Cauldron," a large, boiling, circular spring of over seven feet in diameter and of unfathomable depth. The water has a temperature of 212° F., and is unceasingly boiling and bubbling. The spring is a black, sulphurous fluid as black as the inky cloak of Hamlet. As the awestruck tourists "round about the cauldron go" they see, in their imagination, the solemn ghost of Banquo rising and materializing in the fumes of the "charmed pot," and with a small stretch of the imagination you once more see the three witches and hear their husky voices chanting the solemn incantation—

> " Round about the cauldron go ;
> In the poisoned entrails throw—
> Toad, that under coldest stone
> Days and nights has thirty-one.
> Swelter'd venom, sleeping got,
> Boil thou first i' the charmed pot !
> Double, double, toil and trouble ;
> Fire burn and cauldron bubble.

" Fillet of a fenny snake
In the cauldron boil and bake ;
Eye of mewt, and toe of frog ;
Wool of bat, and tongue of dog ;
Adder's fork and blind worm's sting ;
Lizard's leg and owlet's wing,
For a charm of powerful trouble,
Like a hell-broth boil and bubble.
Double, double, toil and trouble ;
Fire burn and cauldron bubble.''

On analysis this remarkable fumarole, having its source probably hundreds of feet below the surface, yields water rich in sodium, calcium and magnesium sulphates.

GEYSERS—"WITCH'S CAULDRON"

SALINO-SULPHUROUS WATER

PROF. THOS. PRICE, Analyst, 1888

Temperature 212° F.

Mineral Ingredients	U. S. gal. contains Grains	Mineral Ingredients	U. S. gal. contains Grains
Sodium Bisulphate	39.83	Alumina Sulphate	2.04
Potassium Bisulphate	0.42	Alumina	0.27
Magnesium Sulphate	9.62	Silicic Acid	4.37
Calcium Sulphate	6.98		

Total Solids, 63.53

Gases

Free Sulphureted Hydrogen.........saturated

Next comes the "Devil's Canopy" and the "Geyser Safety-valve," an intermitting, scalding spring, which ejects streams of boiling water to the height of fifteen feet; then the "Devil's Pulpit," a little elevation where his Satanic Majesty (presumably) goes to direct the workings of his laboratory.

A little farther up and to the left are the wonderful "Steamboat Geysers," which can be heard a mile or more away, blowing and snorting intermittently at high pressure. This is seemingly a true geyser. The steam is so hot that it does not begin to condense until it is ten or fifteen feet from the surface. Tourists are very apt to burn their fingers trying to find out what makes the noise, as the steam is not visible. The temperature here is 214° F.

Around these hundreds of springs are incrusted deposits of crystallized sulphur, magnesium, alum, etc., etc. In many places one can stick his alpenstock into the sides of the banks, and immediately hot steam and vapors will issue.

You then pass on to the "Devil's Gristmill," where a large column of steam escapes from a hole in a rock with so much force that stones and sticks placed at the orifice are blown away like bits of paper. Loud subterranean noises are heard within resembling those of a gristmill, hence its name.

Going still farther up, the ravine is found to bifurcate. The left fork is still active, having dozens of springs, with temperatures ranging from 100° F. to 210° F. The right fork is cool and pleasant, with several pure water springs. Ascending at the bifurcation some one hundred and sixty feet you come to an elevation—a plateau of smooth, plastic clay stained with iron and sulphur. This clay has a temperature of 170° F. A long pole is introduced into the yielding clay and forthwith issue hot, smoking vapors. The edge of this plateau is called "Lover's Leap." Here the view of the boiling, seething, roaring, steaming, groaning and bubbling springs below is one of unrivaled grandeur. One hundred and sixty feet below you and all along the "Devil's" Cañon is one mass of smoking fury, shrill whistles, regularly intermitting puffs and groans, issuing from the interior of the earth. This sight alone is worth the whole trip.

To the eastward is "Lover's Retreat," a pleasant oasis in this wilderness of sulphurous clouds. Here also is the "Temperance Spring,"—of clear cold water. Near it is a large fallen oak, which serves at once for a seat, and a knot hole in one of its huge branches is known as the "Post-office." Here we leave our cards in case civilization is never reached again.

Going along the usual route, we pass over the "Fire Mountain" with its hundreds of small orifices through which miniature geysers issue. The temperature of this ocherous clay is 175°F. A little east of this is located "Alkali Lake" and the "Lava Beds." Here the crust is so thin that stamping hard on it produces a hollow sound. This is evidently an extinct volcanic crater on a small scale. We now pass the "Indian sweat bath" and come to another remarkable spring known as the "Devil's Tea Kettle." This is one of the strongest vapor springs on the coast. The orifice is three feet in diameter, opening out of the side of the mountain with a huge boulder overhanging it. The "Tea Kettle" spring is about half a mile from the active springs in Geyser cañon. The vapor is emitted with such force that a large bunch of brush placed in front of it is instantly swept away for many feet. This steam is above the boiling point and is sulphurous in character, and contains a large quantity of free sulphuric acid. Formerly a huge cone with a steam whistle attached to it was constructed over the orifice, but it made such a noise as to keep the guests awake at night, and was therefore taken down.

GEYSERS—"DEVIL'S TEA KETTLE"

SALINO-ALUMINO-SULPHUROUS

PROF. THOMAS PRICE, Analyst, 1888

Temperature, 212° F.

Mineral Ingredients	U. S. gal. contains Grains	Mineral Ingredients	U. S. gal. contains Grains
Sodium Bi sulphate	98.16	Alumina Sulphate	31.16
Magnesium Sulphate	39.09	Silicic Acid	12.83
Calcium Sulphate	4.36	Free Sulphuric Acid	110.04

Total Solids, 296.24

Gases

Free Sulphureted Hydrogen.......... saturated

Your route now lies along the side of a mountain where a narrow path has been cut out of solid igneous rock. Below you is the Pluton River, and above you the snorting geysers. Issuing from the side of the solid glass mountain are two remarkable springs—the "Hot Acid" and the "Lemonade," whose waters are rich in the potassium salts so valuable in many conditions and diseases. The acid spring is remarkable for the fact of its having 154 grains of free sulphuric acid to the gallon, and the lemonade spring from the fact that it is one of the few springs in California which has free muriatic acid.

Analyzing these waters they are found to contain:

GEYSER SPRINGS
ACID WATERS
PROF. THOMAS PRICE, Analyst, 1888

	LEMONADE SPRING Temperature, 103° F.	HOT ACID SPRING Temperature, 130° F.
Mineral Ingredients	U. S. gal. contains Grains	U. S. gal. contains Grains
Sodium Bisulphate	53.91	9.02
Potassium Bisulphate	7.53	1.14
Magnesium Sulphate	40.73	91.29
Calcium Sulphate	—	4.44
Ferric Sulphate	12.25	16.63
Alumina Sulphate	32.02	20.62
Free Sulphuric Acid	31.82	154.37
Free Hydrochloric Acid	1.19	—
Silicic Acid	16.50	21.11
Boracic Acid	—	strong traces
Total	195.95	319.23

Gases
Free Sulphureted Hydrogen....... saturated

These waters are among the finest in the State for dyspepsia, torpidity of the liver and bowels, malaria, anæmia, and many blood, glandular and cutaneous affections.

They are pleasantly sour, and with sugar or syrup, make one of the nicest of lemonades.

The next place of interest is the "Devil's Oven," a large excavation in this silicon oxide mountain where in years gone by this igneous rock was at a white heat. All over this realm of subterranean outlets the crust of the earth is covered with the products of the Plutonean shores—sulphur, iron, magnesia, nitre, alum, etc., etc. On again reaching Pluton River, several more cold and hot springs are seen. Some are sulphureted and others are ferruginous, magnesic and aluminic.

Several hundred feet up the Pluton River has been constructed a large and commodious bathing establishment, which spans the river. Every facility for bathing has been arranged. The hot sulphurous vapor issues directly through the side of the mountain, and gains admission into suitable apartments where the bather can enjoy the medicinal effects of the sulphurous fumes and steam vapors at any desired temperature. Then there is the plunge and individual tubs and sweating chambers, and comfortable dressing-rooms. One half of the bathing facilities are for ladies and the other half for gentlemen.

This bathing fluid is remarkable on account of the large amount of borates it holds in solution.

One gallon contains as follows:

GEYSERS—BATHING WATER
LIGHT SALINO-BORIC-SULPHUROUS WATER
Dr. Winslow Anderson, Analyst, 1888
Temperature 137° F.

Mineral Ingredients	U. S. gal. contains Grains	Mineral Ingredients	U. S. gal. contains Grains
Sodium Sulphate	3.96	Maganesium Salts	traces
Potassium Sulphate	traces	Ferric Sulphate	0.25
Magnesium Sulphate	0.26	Aluminium Sulphate	1.87
Magnesium Borate	18.20	Boracic Acid	0.27
Calcium Sulphate	0.73	Silica	7.98
Calcium Borate	7.10	Organic Matter	traces

Total Solids, 40.62

Free Gases	Cubic Inches
Free Sulphureted Hydrogen	27.90

This is one of the best bathing waters on the coast. The borates and sulphates render the skin soft, white and pliable, cleansing the 7,000,000 little pores on the cutaneous surface of an average-sized man. (See article on bathing in front part of book.) This water has proved highly beneficial in the treatment of the many cutaneous, syphilitic and strumous contaminations, rheumatism and chronic joint troubles, white swellings (synovites), gout and articular diseases.

The water is also used for internal administration. Its action is laxative, diuretic and diaphoretic, effecting chylopoietic and intestinal tracts as well as the kidney and skin.

A large swimming pond has been constructed by damming the Pluton River. The water has a temperature of 75° F., and is a combination of all the mineral spring waters.

The Geyser Springs, hot and cold, flow daily about 100,000 gallons. The area covered is about four hundred acres. Most of the activity, however, is confined to the "Devil's" or Geyser Cañon, and comprises about sixty acres.

Many of the springs resemble *true* geysers, such as we have in the "wonderland of America"—Yellowstone Park—and in Iceland; but scientific authorities classify our California geysers as fumaroles or openings and outlets in a volcanic district.

From the following analyses, made by Prof. Price and the writer, it will be observed that at the Geysers can be found perhaps a greater variety of mineral waters than at any other place on the continent, or perhaps in the world. The waters are valuable for the many conditions noted under the head of "Therapeutics of Mineral Waters" in a preceding chapter, and they cannot fail to attract attention. Extensive Indian mud baths are found near the edge of the river, between the hotel and the sulphur banks.

Analyses of Waters From Several Springs at the California Geysers

Samples Taken and Analyzed by Thomas Price, M. D.

Contents per U. S. Gallon Expressed in Grains	From Spout of Devil's Teakettle. Temp. 212° Fahr.	Hot Sulphur Water in bed of Pluton River, little above bathhouse. Temp. 140° Fahr.	Spring little above Indian Spring. Tastes very acid. Temp. 105° Fahr.	Indian Spring near (Cloverdale Sulphur Bank). Supposed real Indian Mud Spring. Temp. 100° Fahr.	Indian Spring. Temp. water 108° Fahr.; temp. mud 110° Fahr.	Iron Spring (north of Hotel). Temp. 70° Fahr.	Spring on side of Hill (near Pluton River). Temp. 138° Fahr. Eye Water.	From Geyser Creek (below Alum Spring). Temp. 96° Fahr.	Alum Spring. Temp. 136° Fahr.	Acid Spring. Temp. 140° Fahr.	Witch's Cauldron. Temp. 212° Fahr.	Lemonade Spring. Temp. 103° Fahr.
Bisulphate of Potassa					0.21					1.14	0.42	7.53
Sulphate of Potassa	98.16			17.12					5.14			
Bisulphate of Soda		2.36			3.29		3.23	3.15		9.62	39.83	53.91
Sulphate of Soda	4.36	0.63			1.40		1.10		3.81	4.44	6.98	
Carbonate of Soda							10.18					
Sulphate of Lime			8.72	6.42	7.35	3.32		5.34				
Carbonate of Lime												
Silicate of Lime												
Borate of Lime												
Sulphate of Magnesia	39.09	6.62	41.12	59.33	15.47	2.52	15.46	16.66	34.49	91.29	9.62	40.73
Carbonate of Magnesia												
Silicate of Magnesia												
Borate of Magnesia												
Sulphate of Iron	31.16	17.31			0.07	0.12	0.11	0.08	7.34	16.63		12.25
Carbonate of Iron		0.16				0.17						
Sulphate of Alumina			28.81	22.78	0.18		0.20	0.89	63.82	20.62	2.04	32.02
Alumina						0.99			6.45		0.27	
Free Sulphuric Acid			118.78	32.30			17.25			154.37		31.82
Hydrochloric Acid		2.39	5.75						17.26			1.19
Silicic Acid	110.64	6.63	18.08	12.25	5.42			3.50		21.11	4.37	16.50
Sulphureted Hydrogen	Saturated	Saturated	Saturated	Saturated	Saturated		Saturated	Saturated	Saturated	Saturated	Saturated	Saturated
Boracic Acid	12.83	Str. traces								Str. traces	Str. traces	
	296.24	38.12	221.26	150.20	33.39	7.12	47.53	29.62	138.11	319.22	63.53	195.95

They are sulphurous and ferruginous, and of great therapeutic value as soon as suitable bathing facilities shall have been constructed.

As the first visitors at this California Hecla were at a loss for motive power to produce all these boiling, steaming and spouting Stygian sluices, they naturally turned to their early teachings for a solution of the phenomena. As they were all good people and had early been taught the power of his Satanic Majesty located—well he used to reside in the infernal regions, presumably in the center of the earth—why they most naturally gave him the credit and named the springs with their present euphonious names of "Devil's" this and "Devil's" that, a process of reasoning that has been applied to names given at a more recent date. In order to be true to nature we have described the springs with their names as we found them.

The owners of these valuable springs and health resort contemplate making extensive improvements in the near future. New hotels and cottages will be erected, new and complete bathing facilities will be constructed, and the springs will be placed in the hands of a competent, graduated physician, who will study the therapeutical effects of the different springs and administer the waters and prescribe the baths intelligently.

The Geysers are wonderful and picturesque exhibitions of the nearly extinct volcanic forces slumbering beneath the romantic " Devil's Cañon," and the resort is one of the pleasantest and most salubrious watering places we find on the coast, and destined to become one of the world's greatest sanitariums.

LITTLE GEYSERS

About four miles farther up the cañon we find the " Little Geysers." These are small sulphurous, steaming springs of no special importance.

69. OTHER GEYSERS

Near the mouth of Willow and Warner Creeks, in Plumas County, are found a number of small geyser springs. The temperature is near the boiling point, and sulphurous steam and vapors rise from twenty to fifty feet into the air. The property is unimproved.

70. GEYSER SPRINGS

Near Geyser's Station, in Sonoma County, are located several hot and cold springs. There is a growing resort established there. The waters are alkaline, and range in temperature from 55° F. to 212° F. Collectively the springs flow about 1,000 gallons per hour. The water is also used commercially.

71. GEYSERS IN LONG VALLEY

At the extreme western end of Long Valley lie a few spouting hot springs. They are on the south branch of Owen's River in Mono County. The property is unimproved at present.

72. GEYSER SPA OR SODA SPRINGS

These springs are located near Litton's Station in Sonoma County, some four miles from Geyserville. There is a pleasant resort on the grounds. The surrounding country is picturesque. The climate is mild and salubrious, and many people go to Geyser Spa every year. The waters are highly esteemed for their antacid, diuretic and aperient properties. The following analyses are made by Bauer or Price, I am not certain which, and the author shows that the water belongs to the light alkaline class:

GEYSER SPA
ALKALINE AND CHALYBEATE
Temperature not given

Mineral Ingredients	BAUER OR PRICE, Analyst. U S. gal. contains Grains	DR. WINSLOW ANDERSON, Analyst, 1888 U. S. gal. contains Grains
Sodium Chloride	9.96	8.93
Sodium Carbonate	——	4.97
Sodium Bicarbonate	23.48	21.16
Sodium Sulphate	3.40	2.00
Potassium Carbonate	——	trace
Magnesium Bicarbonate	9.80	9.03
Magnesium Sulphate	——	1.14
Calcium Carbonate	4.56	4.90
Ferrous Carbonate	3.80	2.09
Silica	1.80	3.75
Organic Matter	——	trace
Loss	.32	——
Total Solids	57.12	58.57

Gases
Carbonated Acid Gas................................not given   saturated

73. GILROY HOT SPRINGS

The Gilroy Hot Springs are located on the Coyote River, about nine miles northeast of the town of Gilroy, in the Santa Clara Mountains. They are reached by the Southern Pacific Railroad to Gilroy, and from thence by easy stage over a good mountainous road with picturesque surroundings. Nestled in among the mountains like a fortress of old lie the Gilroy Springs. The delicious atmosphere, rich in ozone, is daily brought from the fragrant spruce and pine forests by the gentle zephyrs, to insure health and vigor to all who breathe it.

Gilroy has one main spring which flows in great abundance. The temperature varies from 108° F. to 115° F.

This is a light alkalo-sulphurous water, and is used with considerable benefit in syphilis, rheumatism, scrofula and glandular swellings, chronic skin eruptions, etc., etc. It is taken internally in four to eight ounce doses and acts kindly on the liver and bowels. The water is also used for bathing, for which excellent facilities have been constructed.

GILROY SPRINGS

ALKALO-SULPHURETED

DR. WINSLOW ANDERSON, Analyst, 1888

Temperature 110° F.

Mineral Ingredients	U. S. gal. contains Grains	Mineral Ingredients	U. S. gal. contains Grains
Sodium Chloride	31.75	Calcium Chloride	8.50
Sodium Carbonate	1.42	Calcium Sulphate	2.70
Sodium Sulphate	.75	Ferrous Carbonate	.20
Potassium Iodide	trace	Ferrous Oxide	trace
Potassium Sulphate	2.16	Arsenic	trace
Magnesium Carbonate	2.45	Silica	3.31
Magnesium Sulphate	9.04	Organic Matter	.52

Total Solids, 62.86

Gases	Cubic Inches
Free Carbonic Acid Gas	12.17
Free Sulphureted Hydrogen	0.25

Near this hot sulphur spring are two cold sulphur springs flowing very much less. Some six miles along the mountain side is a delicious soda spring free from sulphur and highly carbonated.

The hotel is large and commodious. Every appointment is complete, and guests are well cared for. There are several handsome cottages on the sunny slope of the mountain for private and family use.

Hot sulphurous mud baths have recently been added, which are much used by the rheumatic, gouty, syphilitic and strumous, and those having joint troubles.

GILMORE'S GLEN ALPINE MINERAL SPRINGS AND HEALTH RESORT

Back in the mountain fastnesses, at a distance of seven miles from Lake Tahoe and with an elevation of 6,700 feet, are the Gilmore Glen Alpine Mineral Springs.

The wild, rugged gorge in which they are situated runs back from Tahoe a distance of some ten miles, filled throughout its entire length with varied scenes of beauty and grandeur, and terminating abruptly in a glacial amphitheater. The mighty glacier which originated here went grinding, crushing and cutting its way down, forming the beds in which now lie the beautiful lakes, in a chain of which Tahoe is the last link. The old glacier has written its record deep in the granite faces of the majestic mountains, which looked down in silence upon that work of the terrific forces of nature still revealed in the masses of giant boulders piled upon their sides, and in the scratched or polished surfaces of stone in the bed of the cañon below.

But there is no suggestion of the chaos and desolation of those days of their birth in the tranquil bosoms of the lakes, which now slumber or awake and sparkle in the depths of the cañon, where thick groves of pine, tamarack, spruce and silver fir cast deep, cool shadows. The region is rich in exquisite flowers and ferns.

SUSIE LAKE—Gilmore's "Glen Alpine"

These dimpling lakes, with the wild beauty of their surroundings, are sufficient to enthral the heart of him who visits them, but if he be devoted to the rod and reel he will find an additional charm in the swarms of speckled beauties which sport in the clear depths and rise to his glancing fly.

YOSEMITE SCENE

First in the chain of lakes is the Half-Moon, which lies with Lake Alta Morris in the amphitheater at the head of the cañon. Their outlet tumbles down its rocky bed into Lake Susie, a mile below, a picturesque, romantic spot. Near by is Heather Lake, which needs a Scott to sing its beauties. Quantities of heather hand their dainty bells, white, pink and purple, around its pebbly shores, and the

GLEN ALPINE FALLS

snowbanks lie very near. The stream continues from Lake Susie, making an abrupt leap at first, which forms the beautiful Glen Alpine Falls; then babbling on to feed Lake '84, less than a mile below.

Leaving that lake the bright stream dashes on, passing the Glen Alpine Springs, from which point it can be watched, as one drives down, making its way to another haunt of the trout. There it "glides under lily-pads" into a lake named Lily, from the abundance of its water-lilies.

Fallen Leaf Lake, the gem of the Sierras, is just a mile below Lily, and separated from Tahoe by a level strip one mile in width. The drive from Tahoe to the head of Fallen Leaf, winding around its shores, is very beautiful. The early morning reflection here is perfectly enchanting.

This region has been opened to the public with great labor and expense by the construction of a wagon road as far as Glen Alpine Springs, and mountain trails to all the lakes, including a trail for the ascent of Mt. Tallac, which rears its head 10,000 feet above the sea and commands a wide and magnificent view of the distant peaks and numerous lakes.

The lakes have been furnished with boats and stocked with the finest trout, and black bass have been added, making the Glen Alpine fly fishery one of the finest, nor do the finny tribes scorn a baited hook. Saddle horses are kept for use on any of the trails.

Accommodations for guests have been prepared at Glen Alpine Springs, where those in search of health or pleasure may remain almost with a certainty of gaining both. The air possesses the quality of purity and balminess in perfection, and the granite walls surrounding the Glen radiate in the evening the heat which they absorb during the day, making the evening air soft and dry; and frost is rarely seen from the first of June until the first of September.

GILMORE'S GLEN ALPINE SPRINGS
CARBONATED AND CHALYBEATE
DR. WINSLOW ANDERSON, Analyst, 1888

Temperature, 39.6 F.

Mineral Ingredients	U. S. Gal. contains Grains	Mineral Ingredients	U. S. Gal. contains Grains
Sodium Chloride	21.17	Ferrous Carbonate	1.80
Sodium Carbonate	32.75	Alumina	1.43
Potassium Carbonate	trace	Borates	trace
Magnesium Carbonate	9.96	Silica	2.50
Calcium Carbonate	45.09	Organic Matter	trace
Calcium Sulphate	4.10		

Total Solids, 118.80

Gases	Cubic Inches
Free Carbonic Acid Gas	138.36

The water is pleasant to the taste and highly charged with carbonic acid gas. Its action is gently aperient and diuretic, useful in dyspepsia, torpidity of the bowels and kidney and bladder irritation. It is also tonic and of value where iron is indicated.

75. GORDON'S MINERAL SPRINGS

About half way between Calistoga and Lakeport, in Cobb's Valley, Lake County, lie Gordon's Springs. They are romantically situated in the heart of a mountain and forest region. The climate, too, is beautiful. Invalids pronounce it mild and balmy. During Summer months the temperature ranges from 72° to 90° F.

The springs are at an elevation of about 3,000 feet. The principal spring flows about three hundred gallons per hour, having a temperature of 100° F. The waters are sparkling alkaline, having antacid and aperient properties. For chronic albumenurea and cystitis these springs have a high reputation. In acid dyspepsia the water is recommended before meals.

A pleasant resort has been established in this mountainous region, and it is worthy of remark that persons suffering with chronic bronchitis, catarrh, asthma, and early stages of consumption, do well at this altitude among the pines.

GORDON'S MINERAL SPRINGS
ALKALO SALINE
Temperature, 100° F.

DR WINSLOW ANDERSON, Analyst, 1888

U. S. gal. contains		U. S. gal. contains	
Mineral Ingredients	Grains	Mineral Ingredients	Grains
Sodium Chloride	20.75	Calcium Carbonate	11.16
Sodium Carbonate	3.19	Calcium Sulphate	23.46
Sodium Sulphate	8.62	Alumina	3.55
Potassium Carbonate	.73	Silica	2.27
Magnesium Carbonate	6.14	Organic Matter	trace
Magnesium Sulphate	10.93		

Total Solids, 90.80

Gases

Carbonic Acid Gas.........large excess

The circling hills that guard Clear Lake like lazy giants lie
Beneath the ardent sunshine, their faces to the sky;
Konocti sees across her waves Night's elfin shadows play,
And loves to catch and fling to her the first red lights of Day.

Back from the lake the pretty town goes dancing to the hills
That greet her with a gift of flowers and serenade of rills.
The wine of life is in the air that wafts the fragrance down
From resinous pines and odorous flowers to lake and shore and town.

Oh! fairest land beneath the sun, within whose border lies
The glory of an emerald earth o'erhung by sapphire skies,
And where, like threads of finest gold, the yellow sun-rays fall—
Where Beauty makes her dwelling-place, and Heaven is over all.
                              —*Carrie Stevens Walter.*

HARBIN HOT SULPHUROUS AND MINERAL SPRINGS

At an elevation of about 1,700 feet above tide-water, and
at the base of a spur of the Coast Range of mountains, in
Lake County, about twenty miles from Calistoga, are located
these excellent springs and resort. It would be difficult to
find a more delightful or picturesque spot so rich in scenery, mountains perpetually clad in evergreen garments and
hills with verdure bright forming the background of the
landscape. Then we have brooks and rills, now smoothly
gliding over moss-covered banks and now trickling down
silvered paths with pebbles bright, forming miniature cascades in their ever restless pace to join the broad Pacific.

The climate, too, is one of the most salubrious in the State, having a mean thermometric degree of about 70° F. Although the climate and surroundings are exceedingly favorable to the healthfulness and pleasure of visitors and invalids, the great virtue of Harbin lies in the intrinsic therapeutic value of the mineral springs.

The waters are sulphurous and saline, the principal spring flowing 1,500 gallons per hour. There is also a smaller chalybeate spring fount, yielding only sixty gallons per hour.

The Sulphur Spring has a temperature of 122° F. For this hot water excellent bathing facilities have been constructed, and much benefit accrues in the treatment of chronic rheumatism, gout, joint diseases and cutaneous affections by prolonged or frequent bathing in this water.

For internal administration the sulphur water, as well as the ferruginous waters, are used. In torpidity of the chylo-poietic and intestinal tissues, dyspepsia, kidney troubles, etc., and especially in glandular and skin diseases, on account of the arsenic present, the Harbin mineral waters have proven of great value.

HARBIN HOT SULPHUR SPRING
SALINO-SULPHURETED
DR. WINSLOW ANDERSON, Analyst, 1888

Temperature 122° F.

Flows 1,500 gallons per hour

Mineral Ingredients	U. S. gal. contains Grains	Mineral Ingredients	U. S. gal. contains Grains
Sodium Chloride	23.05	Calcium Sulphate	14.63
Sodium Carbonate	5.42	Ferrous Sulphate	1.75
Sodium Sulphate	10.19	Arsenious Salts	0.07
Potassium Carbonate	1.74	Alumina	1.60
Magnesium Carbonate	6.18	Silica	2.76
Magnesium Sulphate	11.94	Organic Matter	trace
Calcium Carbonate	9.10		

Total Solids, 88.63

Gases	Cubic Inches
Carbonic Acid Gas	4.26
Free Sulphureted Hydrogen	11.74

The chalybeate spring is clear and sparkling and has a pleasant taste. The waters are tonic, antacid, diuretic and aperient, valuable in dyspepsia, anæmia, chlorosis, chronic malarial poisoning and wasting diseases.

HARBIN SPRINGS—"IRON" SPRING
LIGHT CHALYBEATE-CARBONATED WATER
DR. WINSLOW ANDERSON, Analyst, 1889
Temperature 116° F.

Flows 60 gallons per hour

Mineral Ingredients	U. S. gal. contains Grains	Mineral Ingredients	U. S. gal. contains Grains
Sodium Chloride	7.50	Magnesium Sulphate	6.11
Sodium Carbonate	14.22	Calcium Carbonate	2.07
Sodium Bicarbonate	1.45	Calcium Sulphate	trace
Sodium Sulphate	5.25	Ferrous Carbonate	1.90
Potassium Chloride	trace	Alumina	.73
Potassium Carbonate	1.73	Silica	1.41
Magnesium Carbonate	4.16	Organic Matter	trace

Total Solids, 46.53

Gases	Cubic Inches
Carbonic Acid Gas	9.34

The salino-carbonated water, or soda, is a very pleasant and palatable table water. It is very gently laxative, and tonic. An excellent water for the dyspepsia superinduced by a too familiar friendship with Bacchus. It is good in morning vomiting and irritative indigestion. For Bright's disease and irritation of the kidneys and bladder, with acidity of the urine, it is highly recommended.

HARBIN SPRINGS—"MAGNESIA" SPRING
SALINO-CARBONATED
DR. WINSLOW ANDERSON, Analyst, 1889
Temperature 60° F.

Mineral Ingredients	U. S. gal. contains Grains	Mineral Ingredients	U. S. gal. contains Grains
Sodium Chloride	1.72	Ferrous Carbonate	.27
Sodium Carbonate	5.17	Arsenic	trace
Sodium Sulphate	4.32	Alumina	.68
Potassium Salts	1.05	Lithium	trace
Magnesium Carbonate	7.15	Borates	trace
Magnesium Sulphate	15.92	Silica	2.82
Calcium Carbonate	8.43	Organic Matter	trace
Calcium Sulphate	.93		

Total Solids, 48.46

Gases	Cubic Inches
Free Carbonic Acid Gas	17.25

The "arsenic" spring presents an excellent combination for blood-glandular disorders, cutaneous diseases, scrofula, gout and rheumatism. The potassium salts, iron and arsenic are valuable medicinal agents. It has carbonic anhydride enough to make it palatable. Its action is tonic and alterative, laxative and diuretic.

In syphilitic and skin diseases, goitre, swollen glands, etc., this water has become quite famous.

HARBIN SPRINGS—" ARSENIC " SPRING
SALINO-CARBONATED
DR. WINSLOW ANDERSON, Analyst, 1889
Temperature 90° F.

Flows only 15 gallons per hour

Mineral Ingredients	U. S. Gal. contains Grains	Mineral Ingredients	U. S. Gal. contains Grains
Sodium Chloride	9.70	Ferrous Carbonate	.92
Sodium Carbonate	7.35	Manganese Carbonate	trace
Sodium Sulphate	trace	Lithium	trace
Potassium Chloride	1.10	Arsenious Salts	.27
Potassium Carbonate	3.09	Borates	trace
Magnesium Carbonate	14.76	Alumina	2.20
Magnesium Sulphate	3.95	Silica	1.90
Calcium Carbonate	6.10	Organic Matter	trace
Calcium Sulphate	.76		

Total Solids, 52.16

Gases	Cubic Inches
Sulphureted Hydrogen	traces
Carbonic Acid Gas	6.22

At Harbin Springs we find first-class accommodations, a good table, fine fishing and hunting, with the excellent climatic advantages common throughout Lake County.

77. HATCHIN HAMA SPRINGS

This is a salino-alkalo lake fed by a number of springs. It was found four miles west of Borax Lake, southeast of Clear Lake, in Lake County.

78. HENSLEY'S SPRINGS

These are found in Tehama County, and are strongly impregnated with iron. They are much used locally.

79. HIBB'S SODA SPRINGS

These mineral springs are found sixty-two miles north of Redding, in Shasta County. They are reported as pleasant, sparkling soda waters, gently diuretic and aperient, and of value in kidney and bladder troubles. The waters are used for miles around.

80. HIGHLAND SPRINGS

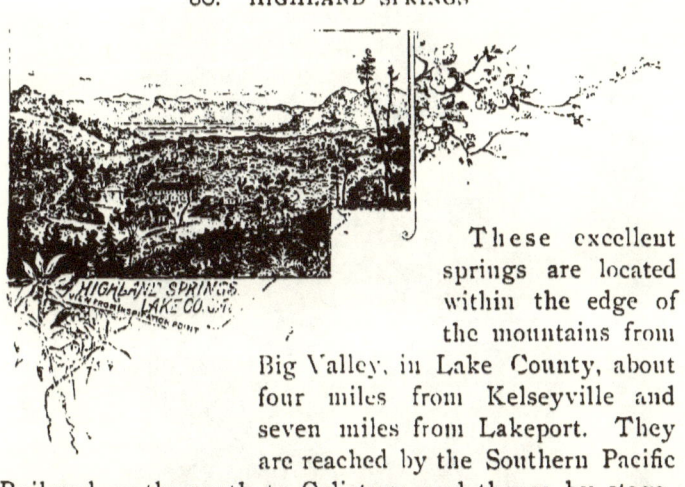

These excellent springs are located within the edge of the mountains from Big Valley, in Lake County, about four miles from Kelseyville and seven miles from Lakeport. They are reached by the Southern Pacific Railroad on the south to Calistoga, and thence by stage, by the Northern Pacific ("Donohue Road") on the southwest to Cloverdale, and thence by stage; by stage from Mendocino County on the north and Colusa County from the east. The drive by stage from Calistoga or Cloverdale to the springs is exceedingly picturesque. Every turn presents something new and interesting. Here and there are seen the mountains thickly covered with woods. Here and there are moss-covered banks and running brooks over which hang huge ferns and shrubbery. Now we are on the narrow road on the mountain side, several hundred feet above the river, and an almost precipitous descent over the banks. With a short turn we sweep around the curve in the road, and the dexterity with which the trained stage driver wheels his six-in-hand around these cuts and curves is something marvelous. At length the summit is gained. This is an elevation of 3,200 feet above

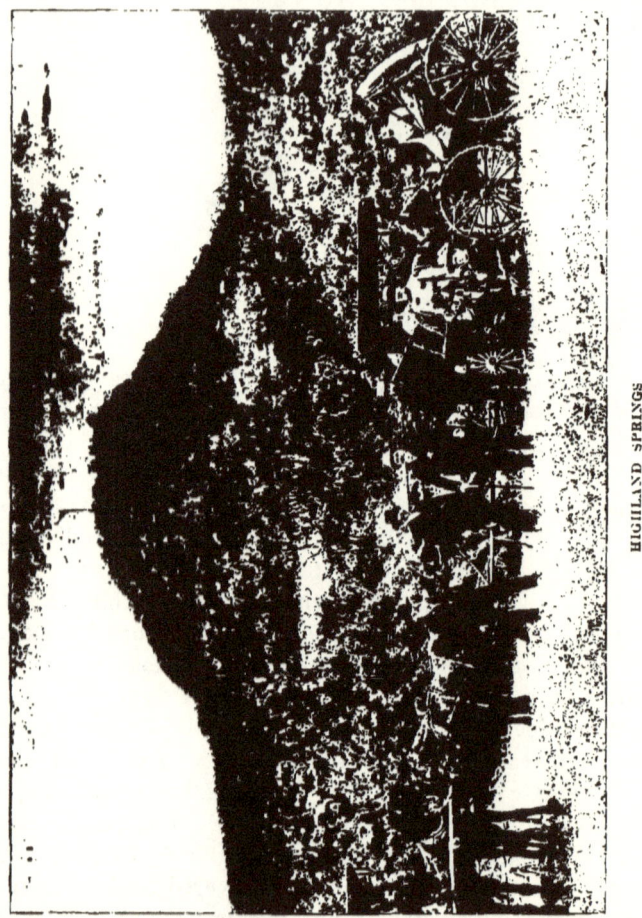

HIGHLAND SPRINGS

the sea level. Here one sees one of the grandest sights imaginable. As far as the eye can reach in every direction are mountains and valleys, peaks upon peaks, moun-

tain streams and brooks, forest and shrubbery. The most
picturesque of all is the view northward over Clear Lake
and Lake County. The lake itself, a magnificent sheet of
water, is twenty-five miles long and six to eight miles
wide. It has an altitude of 1,200 feet, and lies peacefully
smiling in the embrace of the mountains on all sides, with
"Uncle Sam's" head above them all. We see the bright
cultivated fields like a huge checkerboard in the valley
below. The gigantic oaks—the largest in the State—are
scattered here and there to complete the kaleidoscopic
panorama. Well might this be called the "Switzerland of
America," for a more magnificent picture can scarcely be
imagined. The descent to the springs is made in much
less than half the time that it takes to make the ascent,
and the springs are soon seen lying in a level sequestered
spot surrounded by hills, and by trees of many years'
growth.

At Highland's we find a commodious hotel and many
elegant cottages built with a view to health and beauty
combined. There is also a livery stable at which saddle
horses and carriages may be procured for the drives to
Lakeport, Soda Bay, Kelseyville, etc. A large pure mountain stream runs past the hotel, which is well supplied with
fish. The climate is mild and dry, and the air is pure and
filled with ozone and scents from the fragrant woods and
plants which abound on the grounds. The altitude is about
1,700 feet, and it is claimed to be an excellent place for
consumptives.

Mineral springs are usually abundant in Lake County,
and some of them are of considerable therapeutic value.
At Highland's there are some twenty springs, all of which
I examined in 1888. Five of the most important are subjected to careful analyses.

THE SELTZER SPRING

This valuable spring is situated about five hundred
yards from the hotel, eastward. It is conveniently cemented

and covered with a summer-house. The waters are alkalo-saline and chalybeate, and very efficacious in many diseases requiring antacid, laxative, diuretic and tonic properties. It has been used with much success in dyspepsia, neuralgia, kidney and bladder troubles, calculi, etc., and rheumatism, gout and skin diseases. This spring has changed but little in six years, as seen by the following analyses:

HIGHLAND SELTZER
ALKALO-SALINE AND CHALYBEATE

	Dr. Winslow Anderson's Analysis, 1888 Temperature 60.4° F.	Prof. Rising's Analysis, 1882 Temperature 64.8° F.
	U. S. gal. contains	U. S. gal. contains
Mineral Ingredients	Grains	Grains
Sodium Chloride	.67	.723
Sodium Carbonate	2.06	——
Sodium Bicarbonate	12.72	12.796
Potassium Bicarbonate	.50	.489
Magnesium Bicarbonate	33.95	34.872
Calcium Bicarbonate	52.25	52.046
Manganese Bicarbonate	trace	trace
Ferrous Carbonate	1.43	——
Ferrous Bicarbonate	-——	1.267
Silica	5.13	5.245
Alumina	1.75	1.565
Organic Matter	trace	trace
Total Solids	110.46	109.002
	Gases Grains	Grains
Free Carbonic Acid Gas	98.41	100.250

The "Dutch or Ems," " Neptune," "Diana" and "Magic" are located on a small bank across the little stream. The distance from the hotel westward is from one hundred to two hundred yards. The springs are all nicely cemented with artificial stone. They are kept clean and inviting. In most cases suitable houses or coverings have been constructed.

The Dutch or Ems Spring is more diuretic and laxative than the Seltzer. It has a larger amount of iron and less strongly carbonated. But little change is observable in six years.

HIGHLAND DUTCH OR EMS
ALKALO-SALINE
Total flow 63 gallons per hour

	DR. WINSLOW ANDERSON'S Analysis, 1888 *Temperature 77° F.*	PROF. RISING'S Analysis, 1882 *Temperature 70.5° F.*
Mineral Ingredients	U. S. gal. contains Grains	U. S. gal. contains Grains
Sodium Chloride	1.76	1.862
Sodium Bicarbonate	17.50	18.348
Sodium Carbonate	2.45	——
Potassium Bicarbonate	.78	.770
Magnesium Bicarbonate	66.55	67.634
Magnesium Carbonate	1.63	——
Calcium Bicarbonate	57.82	57.302
Manganese Bicarbonate	trace	trace
Ferrous Carbonate	1.53	——
Ferrous Bicarbonate	——	1.344
Silica	7.22	7.126
Alumina	.12	.117
Organic Matter	traces	trace
Total Solids	156.86	154.503
	Gases Grains	Grains
Free Carbonic Acid Gas	85.90	87.822

The Magic Spring is found to be slightly more saline and less carbonated. It is reported to act like "magic" on the liver, bowels and kidneys, hence the name.

HIGHLAND MAGIC SPRING
ALKALO-SALINE
Flow 165 gallons per hour

	DR. WINSLOW ANDERSON'S Analysis, 1888 *Temperature 79.3° F.*	PROF. RISING'S Analysis, 1882 *Temperature 82.4° F.*
Mineral Ingredients	U. S. Gal. contains Grains	U. S. Gal. contains Grains
Sodium Chloride	1.53	1.290
Sodium Bicarbonate	20.13	21.763
Sodium Carbonate	3.70	——
Potassium Bicarbonate	.51	.544
Potassium Carbonate	.21	——
Magnesium Bicarbonate	70.50	70.243
Magnesium Carbonate	.27	——
Calcium Bicarbonate	49.06	50.411
Calcium Carbonate	.73	——
Manganese Bicarbonate	trace	trace
Ferrous Bicarbonate	——	1.087
Ferrous Carbonate	1.22	——
Alumina	.14	.169
Barium Carbonate	.07	——
Borates	.28	——
Silica	6.40	7.398
Organic Matter	trace	trace
Total Solids	154.75	152.905
	Gases Grains	Grains
Free Carbonic Acid Gas	75.90	74.462

HIGHLAND NEPTUNE SPRING
HEAVY SALINE

Mineral Ingredients	Dr. Winslow Anderson's Analysis, 1888. Temperature 80.5° F. U. S. Gal. contains Grains	Prof. Rising's Analysis, 1882. Temperature 81.7° F. U. S. Gal. contains Grains
Sodium Chloride	1.65	1.080
Sodium Bicarbonate	21.12	22.100
Sodium Carbonate	.76	——
Potassium Bicarbonate	.78	.803
Potassium Carbonate	.35	——
Magnesium Bicarbonate	70.09	89.870
Magnesium Carbonate	20.52	——
Calcium Bicarbonate	37.80	77.770
Manganese Bicarbonate	trace	——
Ferrous Bicarbonate	——	1.370
Ferrous Carbonate	1.67	. ——
Barium Bicarbonate	——	1.75
Barium Carbonate	.22	———
Lithium Bicarbonate	——	trace
Borates	.53	———
Boracic Acid	——	.470
Alumina	1.20	1.370
Silica	7.90	8.420
Organic Matter	trace	trace
Total Solids	164.65	204.008
Gases Free Carbonic Acid Gas	Grains 93.06	Grains 94.120

In this analysis of Neptune Spring will be observed quite a change, especially in the calcium salts. Many of these cold carbonated or superficial springs are known to change from year to year, depending largely on the rainfall, etc.

HIGHLAND

Besides the springs herewith mentioned, there are several others on the premises not fully developed. Their names are: "Lime Kiln," "Ladies' Delight," "Small Diana," Nos. "1," "2," "3," "4," "5," "Minna," and others. On looking over partial analyses made by Mr. O'Neil, of the University of California, I find their composition is very similar to those already analyzed.

Highland Springs health resort, with its picturesque surroundings and excellent climatic advantages, bids fair to become one of our most popular watering places in the State.

HIGHLAND DIANA SPRING

HEAVY SALINE

Total flow 116 gallons per hour

	Dr. Winslow Anderson, Analyst, 1888 Temperature 82.7° F.	Prof. Rising, Analyst, 1882 Temperature 81.1° F.
Mineral Ingredients	U. S. Gal. contains Grains	U. S. Gal. contains Grains
Sodium Chloride	1.90	1.890
Sodium Bicarbonate	23.70	24.080
Sodium Carbonate	1.40	———
Potassium Bicarbonate	1.50	1.466
Potassium Carbonate	.18	———
Magnesium Bicarbonate	75.52	78.950
Magnesium Carbonate	3.17	———
Calcium Bicarbonate	69.83	73.270
Manganese Bicarbonate	trace	trace
Ferrous Bicarbonate	———	1.400
Ferrous Carbonate	1.56	———
Barium Bicarbonate	.24	.200
Lithium Bicarbonate	trace	trace
Alumina	.29	.230
Boracic Acid	———	undetermined
Borates	.56	
Silica	7.17	8.079
Organic Matter	trace	trace
Total Solids	189.02	189.574
Gases	Grains	Grains
Free Carbonic Acid Gas	70.02	71.850

HIGHLAND SPRINGS

The bathing water is artificially heated. It is found to be an alkalo-saline water, also containing iron.

The baths are invigorating, and have been used for rheumatism and joint affections.

HIGHLAND BATHING WATER

ARTIFICIALLY HEATED ALKALO-SALINE

Dr. Winslow Anderson, Analyst, 1888

Mineral Ingredients	U. S. Gal. contains Grains	Mineral Ingredients	U. S. Gal. contains Grains
Sodium Chloride	2.17	Calcium Bicarbonate	36.45
Sodium Bicarbonate	1.61	Manganese Bicarbonate	trace
Sodium Carbonate	trace	Ferrous Carbonate	1.75
Potassium Bicarbonate	.70	Alumina	1.25
Magnesium Bicarbonate	65.10	Silica	7.85
Magnesium Carbonate	7.04	Organic Matter	trace

Total Solids, 123.92

Gases	Grains
Free Carbonic Acid Gas	63.50

HIGH ROCK SPRING

Nine miles east of Honey Lake, in Lassen County, is found an alkaline spring having a temperature of 100° F. The property is unimproved.

HOOD'S SPRINGS

These springs are located ten miles northwest of Cloverdale. The waters are alkaline and carbonated. A resort is contemplated.

HOT BORATE SPRING

This remarkable spring is situated near the town of Lakeport, and on the edge of Clear Lake. The elevation is about 1,200 feet. The spring flows 18,000 gallons per hour, and has a temperature of 124° F. (July, 1888). On analysis Hot Borate Spring contains:

HOT BORATE SPRING
BORATE WATER
Flow 18,000 gallons per hour

	Dr. Winslow Anderson, Analyst, 1888 Temperature 124° F.	Mr. Moore, Analyst
	U. S. gal. contains	U. S. gal. contains
Mineral Ingredients	Grains	Grains
Sodium Chloride	86.42	84.62
Sodium Bicarbonate	75.40	76.96
Sodium Biborate	201.75	103.29
Potassium Iodide	.12	———
Potassium Chloride	trace	trace
Potassium Bromide	trace	———
Potassium Bicarbonate	4.26	———
Ammonium Bicarbonate	96.20	107.76
Magnesium Bicarbonate	.73	———
Magnesium Iodide	———	.09
Magnesium Bromide	———	trace
Calcium Sulphate	trace	trace
Alumina	2.04	1.26
Silica	7.96	———
Silicic Acid	———	8.23
Organic Matter	9.07	———
Matter Volatile at red heat	———	65.77
Total Solids	483.95	447.98
Gases	Grains	Grains
Free Carbonic Acid Gas	39.76	36.37

HOT BORAX SPRING

This spring is remarkable on account of its large value, the excessive amount of ammonium salts and the large quantity of borax present in the water. Prof. Whitney speaks of the changeableness of this spring, both in its flow and in its ingredients.

The water is used in Lakeport and surrounding country for inflammation of the kidneys and bladder. It is also claimed to have dissolved a stone in the bladder.

HOT MUD SPRINGS

Extensive hot mud beds and springs are found on the banks of Shovel Creek, in Siskiyou County. The locality is filled with sulphurous fumes and mud, and incrustations of native sulphur deposits on the cooler margins of the springs.

A small resort has sprung up at this place, and chronic rheumatic and crippled invalids are said to improve while bathing in the mud.

HOT SPRINGS

Thermal springs—sulphurous, calcic, saline and alkaline—abound all over the State. Many have not been even named as yet.

The following list comprises a number of the undeveloped hot springs in California:

HOT SODA SPRINGS

Near the head of Battle Creek, in Plumas County, are located several hot soda springs. They flow a large volume and the waters have a high temperature. No improvements.

HOT SPRINGS—ON PAOHA ISLAND IN MONO LAKE
F. M. CHATARD, Analyst

Mineral Ingredients	Grammes per Litre	Mineral Ingredients	Grammes per Litre
Sodium Carbonate	.0506	Sodium Chloride	.0104
Magnesium Bicarbonate	.0154	Potassium Chloride	.0169
Calcium Carbonate	.1035	Silica	.0178
Sodium Sulphate	.0799		

Total Solids (37 grains to gallon) 0.2945

This spring has a temperature of 110 F., and is in the middle of Mono Lake, which contains 3,000 grains of salt to the gallon, while this water has only 37.88 to the gallon.

HOT SPRINGS NOT NAMED

Three miles east of Canby, in Modoc County, sulphurous.

In Modoc County, on the east side of Middle Alkali Lake, seven miles southeast of Cedarville.

Southeast of Lassen's Peak, in Plumas County, at the head of Warner's Creek.

At the base of Warner's range in Modoc County, at the south end of Lower Alkali Lake.

In Santa Barbara County, five miles south of the city of Santa Barbara, are several hot springs having a temperature of 112° F. to 118° F. The water is sulphureted, and a resort is being built.

West Side of Lower Alkali Lake in Modoc County.

Between Upper and Lower Alkali Lakes, in Modoc County.

In Mono County, thirteen miles west of Bridgeport.

In Plumas County are several more springs. Some are sulphureted, others are alkaline.

In northwest part of San Diego County, at the bend of San Jacinto River.

In Kern County, near Kern River, seven miles below Kernville. These waters are highly charged with sulphureted hydrogen. Temperature 127° F.

Near Big Valley, in Lassen County, between Clear Creek and Pitt River are several springs—mostly sulphureted.

In Los Angeles County, about twelve miles northwest of San Juan Capistrano, are six alkalo-sulphurous springs. The temperature varies from 123° F. to 130° F.

Near the summit of Mt. Shasta are several hot alkaline springs.

In Ventura County, south of Rafael Peak. One of the many springs has a temperature of 195° F.

In Mono County, two miles southeast of Bridgeport.

Near Benton, in Mono County. Hot saline. Temperature 138° F.

In Kern County, seven miles southeast of Kernville and five miles northwest of Havilah.

In Long Valley, Mono County, five miles east of the Geysers. Temperature 140° F.

In Inyo County, west of Dry Salt Lake, on the Armagosa Creek.

On the east side of Hot Cove, on the Paoha Island, in Mono Lake, Mono County. Temperature 110° F.

In Amador County, in a small valley west of Markleeville.

West of Panamint, six miles, in Inyo County.

In Colusa County, four miles south of Bear Valley. Temperature 120° F. Saline.

In Inyo County, on both east and west side of Owen's River, in the valley south of Bishop's Creek. Temperature 132° F.

In Plumas County, south of Lake Cañon, near the head of Battle Creek. The waters are alkaline. Temperature 85° F.

In Modoc County, two miles north of Fort Bidwell.

In Surprise Valley, Modoc County, east side of Middle Alkali Lake and opposite Cedarville. Several springs have a temperature of 180° F., and are sulphurous.

A. 12.

HOT SODA SPRINGS

Located in Plumas County, on Battle Creek. Temperature 196° to 200° F. A large volume of hot alkaline water issues from the springs. The property is not improved.

HOUGH'S MINERAL SPRINGS

These springs are pleasantly located in Lake County, on the north fork of Cache Creek, about thirty-two miles from Williams. The altitude is 1,960 feet.

Route of travel: Take ferry and railroad from San Francisco to Williams, or via Calistoga, and thence by stage. The waters are all cold, having a temperature of about 60° F.

No. 1, the main spring, contains magnesia, soda, silica, alumina and ferruginous salts, with an excess of carbonic acid gas. The water is tonic, aperient and diuretic.

No. 2 flows from an artificial well dug about twenty-five feet deep. It contains a stronger impregnation of iron and more magnesia salts, producing free evacuations after each large draught.

No. 3, also a well, twenty-eight feet deep, contains some sulphur, and is much used for cutaneous and rheumatic diseases.

No. 4 is a carbonated water. The resort is a pleasant one, and gaining in public favor every year.

HOWARD SPRINGS

The Howard Springs, some fourteen in all, are located in Lake County, six miles from Lower Lake and thirty-two miles from Calistoga. They lie in a small basin, at an elevation of 2,220 feet, surrounded on all sides by hills covered with luxuriant vegetation, flowers and sweet woods. The resort is growing every year, and ample accommodations are found for invalids and pleasure-seekers. Hunting and fishing, the "California diamond fields," pine forests and good tonic alkalo-carbonated waters are among the attractions found at Howard Springs.

The springs consist principally of sparkling carbonated waters. Two or three also contain sulphur. These are used for bathing.

The carbonated waters contain sodium chloride, sodium bicarbonate, magnesia and calcium salts, with small quantities of potassa, silica, iron and alumina, and are heavily charged with carbonic acid gas. The springs are very useful for many conditions requiring this class of medication.

ANALYZED BY PROF. WM. T. WENZELL

	The Excelsior	The Twins	Eureka	Neptune	Soda
Temperature...........................	75° Fahr.	102°Fahr.	110°Fahr.	85° Fahr.	60° Fahr.
Free Carbonic Acid, per gal......	134.	77.5	150.	120.	117 cubic
Barometric Pressure................	27.87 in...	....	....	....	inches
Solids, per gal :					
Chloride of Sodium..................	101.67	30.96	35.70	29.61	9.38 gr.
Chloride of Potassium..............	1.13	19.71	25.65	14.61	12.81 gr.
Chloride of Lithium	8.35	.03	.09	.06	.... gr.
Bicarbonate of Soda.................	34.10	73.97	82.35	....	37.72 gr.
Bicarbonate of Magnesia..........	2.81	114.10	110.25	73.34	59.32 gr.
Bicarbonate of Lime.................	6.30	10.88	5.84	32.14	35.62 gr.
Bicarbonate of Iron.................	1.85	1.14	....	....	...... gr.
Alumina................................	.03	.15	.10	.19	.13 gr.
Oxide of Iron.........................	....	....	4.95	.20	.09 gr.
Silica...................................	34.10	9.24	3.40	8.34	6.95 gr.
Organic Matter......................	.14	.32	.20	.25	.20 gr.
Total	156.84	260.50	268.53	158.77	152.28 gr.

INFLAMMABLE NATURAL GAS

In many places all up and down the coast this product is found, and we are glad to see that it has already been utilized for heating and illuminating purposes. The gas is capable of lighting and heating many of the health resorts near which it is found.

One of the most remarkable of these natural inflammable gas springs is found at Byron hot springs (see Byron Springs).

Another at Kelseyville, the property of Mr. Young, and described under the head of "Young's Gas Well."

On the south side of Sulphur Creek, three hundred yards back from the original Wilbur springs, in Colusa County, is located a large natural gas spring, which has been burning for years. The flame reaches up about two feet from the ground, a foot or more in diameter, and burns with a pale-blue flame and yellow tips.

Near Upper Lake, in Lake County, is another gas spring, yielding large quantities of natural gas.

Valuable natural gas is found in Colusa, Los Angeles, Monterey, San Joaquin, San Mateo, Santa Barbara and other counties.

An extensive utilization of natural gas is being made at the Crown Mills, in the San Joaquin County. The main gas well is 1,330 feet deep and yields 15,000 cubic feet of gas in twenty-four hours. The gas is now used for heating the boilers in the mill, being burned with a small quantity of coal for that purpose. It has also been used for illuminating the mill, and a great saving in fuel and light is reported.

The most productive gas well is found near the southwestern edge of the city of Stockton. The well has a depth of over 2,000 feet and produces from 70,000 to 80,000 cubic feet of gas in twenty-four hours. As the gas issues from the well it burns with a slight empyreumatic odor, undoubtedly owing to the imperfect combustion of its carbon. When burned in a lamp—the "Lundgallon," specially constructed for the purpose—complete oxidation occurs and a good light is produced. On analysis this gas is found to contain:

Hydrogen (CH_4), marsh gas, the light carburetted, 83 per cent., and small quantities of hydrogen, oxygen, carbonic acid gas and carbonic oxide gas.

The owners purpose laying pipes into the city of Stockton in order to supply it with heat and light from nature's laboratory at greatly reduced rates.

IODINE SPRINGS

These remarkable springs are located in Grizzly Cañon, Lake County. The iodine is found in combination with sodium, potassium and magnesium in considerable quantities. The inhabitants in the neighborhood speak highly of the springs, and the water is used for miles around for consumption, glandular swellings, skin diseases, etc. The springs are in a wild, picturesque cañon, and are unimproved. These iodine springs were analyzed by Hanks and Falkenau several years ago and pronounced remarkable on account of the large amount of iodine present.

Iodine, with sodium, potassium and manganese, has been found in several parts of the State, as will be seen by the analyses.

IRON SPRINGS

Several unnamed ferruginous springs are located in Tehama County, some two miles north of Tom's Head Mountain. The waters are said to be strongly charged with iron salts and carbonic acid gas, as seen from the incrustations around the springs.

Another iron spring is located near the Huero-Huero Rancho. No analysis.

KLAMATH HOT SPRINGS

In the northern county of California, Siskiyou, some eighteen miles from Ager, and on the Shasta Division of the Southern Pacific Railroad, are located these famous springs and the sanitarium. Situated as they are in the wild and picturesque country of Mt. Shasta region, 2,700 feet above sea level, with snow-capped mountain peaks and hills clad in evergreen forest groves, the springs have become noted for the surrounding scenery as well as for the therapeutic properties of the mineral waters.

At Klamath we find ample accommodations for invalids and guests.

Excellent bathing facilities have been added, so that hot or cold sulphurous baths or hot steam baths may be had at the springs.

Gunning and fishing may be had in abundance in the immediate vicinity.

The waters are alkalo-saline and sulphurous. Some are carbonated, but most are sulphureted. The springs

KLAMATH HOT SPRINGS

have already gained considerable celebrity in the treatment of chronic rheumatism, gout, white swelling of the joints, glandular enlargements, and chronic cutaneous diseases. The saline and carbonated waters are used for liver and kidney troubles, dyspepsia, etc., and the sulphur waters and sulphurous water or steam baths for rheumatism and skin affections.

LAKE TAHOE OR CARNELIAN HOT SPRINGS

"O, lovely lake, while life remains,
　Will thy enchantment hold my heart!
And song rehearse in willing strains,
　Lake of the hills! how fair thou art!"

These hot and cold mineral springs are located on Carnelian Bay, at the northern end of Lake Tahoe, in Placer County. They form part of the attractions of this famous inland sea. They are reached by railroad to Truckee, and then by stage over a good mountain road for about two and a half hours' drive.

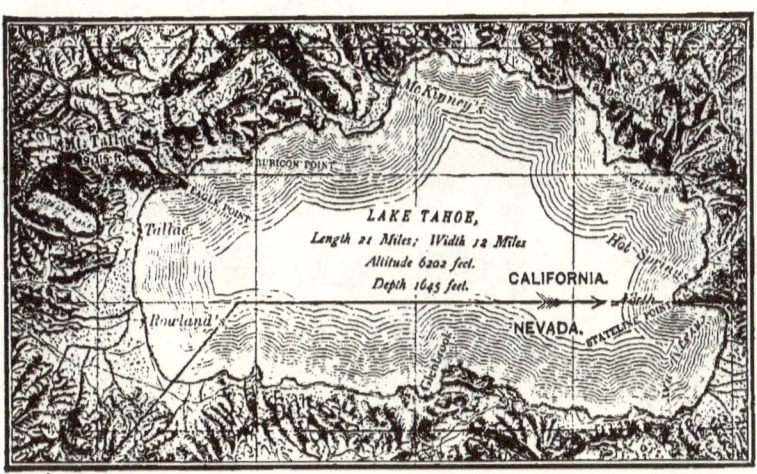

The scenery is grand. The Truckee River is crossed and recrossed. Mountain sides and heights are scaled. Fertile valleys, grazed by immense herds of cattle, are traversed. Forests of beautiful pines and cedar rear themselves at intervals. Humming sawmills fill the air with life, and wild, romantic views, greet one at every turn. The appointments of the resort are most complete in every detail. There are about fifty boiling and cold springs on the lake shore. They are well kept and cared for. Excellent bathing facilities have recently been erected, where cold and hot sulphur baths, tub and plunge, can be taken. There are also steam baths, and the resort has become very popular. The baths are used with success by the rheumatic and gouty. The waters are also drunk for liver and kidney diseases, chronic constipation and cutaneous affections.

TAHOE CITY

The waters are sulphurous and saline, and a few are carbonated. They contain:

        Sodium Chloride.
        Calcium Sulphate.
        Magnesium Sulphate.
        Silica.
        Organic Matter.
        Free Sulphureted Hydrogen Gas.

The elevation is 6,250 feet. Bronchitis, asthma and consumption do well among the pines at this place. There are splendid facilities for camping, hunting and fishing.

KELLOGG'S SPRINGS

These mineral springs are located near Calistoga, in Napa County. The waters are saline and sulphureted. They are the private property of Mr. Foulkers. No development.

LANE'S MINERAL SPRINGS

Some thirty-five miles east of Stockton, in Calaveras County, lie these springs. They are about 1,000 feet above sea level and surrounded by hills and vales and forests of pine. The main spring flows fifty to seventy-five gallons per hour and the water is alkalo-sulphurous and chalybeate. The following analysis is supposed to have been made by the San Francisco Refining and Analytical Association and sent to me by the owner of the springs. The analysis is probably not correctly printed on the report furnished the writer:

LANE SPRINGS

S. F. REFINING AND ANALYTICAL ASSOCIATION, Analysts

Mineral Ingredients	U. S. gal. contains Grains	Mineral Ingredients	U. S. gal. contains Grains
Carbonate of Iron............	122.000 (?)	Lime Carbonate........	18.012
Magnesia Carbonate.........	38.512	Free Sulphuric Acid?	15.237
Epsom Carbonate (?)........	29.764	Silica......................	15.196
Alumina......................	2.009	Organic Matter.........	2.723
Soda Carbonate...............	8.524		

Total Solids, 251.977

Free Gases	Cubic Inches
Sulphureted Hydrogen......................	105.

The water has been in use for several years and is said to be beneficial in constipation, dyspepsia, chronic malarial poisoning, liver and kidney complaints. For bathing the waters are artificially heated.

LAS CRUCES HOT SPRINGS

These hot sulphur springs are located in Santa Barbara County, forty-two miles from the city of the same name. The waters are saline and sulphureted. The principal spring flows five hundred gallons per hour and has a temperature of 90° F. The waters are much used locally for skin diseases.

LICK SPRINGS

These are described under the head of Tuscan springs, of which they form the first two or three. The Lick springs were discovered in 1856, and soon afterwards the waters were subjected to chemical analysis with the result of obtaining large crystals of borax—the first borax discovered in the State. These crystals are still preserved in the Academy of Sciences.

LITTLE GEYSER SPRINGS

These consist of several small jets of hot steam issuing through the earth's crust at a temperature of 190° F. to 200° F. They are located three or four miles below the Geysers, in Sonoma County.

LITTLE YOSEMITE SODA SPRINGS

They are located on the north fork of Kern River, in Tulare County. The waters are palatable, alkalo-carbonated, impregnated with ferruginous salts. Used locally.

LITTLE YOSEMITE SODA SPRINGS

Oscar Loew, Analyst, 1876

Mineral Ingredients	U. S. Gal. contains Grains	Mineral Ingredients	U. S. Gal. contains Grains
Sodium Carbonate	20.97	Sodium Sulphate	trace
Magnesium Carbonate... } Calcium Carbonate........ }	16.02	Sodium Chloride	4.68
		Silica	7.31
Iron Carbonate	.92		

Total Solids, 49.90

Gases

Carbonic Acid....................excess

LITTON SELTZER SPRINGS

These excellent seltzer and soda springs are located about four miles north of the city of Healdsburg, in Sonoma County, on the line of the San Francisco and North Pacific Railroad.

LITTON SPRINGS

The springs and adjoining property—about 1,000 acres —have been incorporated, and extensive buildings, hotels, cottages and dwellings, as well as the improvement of the springs and grounds are contemplated. The Litton Springs have gained in reputation, and much of the water is used locally and commercially. The water is slightly acid when freshly drawn, but by exposure it soon becomes alkaline on account of the evaporation of the carbonic anhydride. It is much used as an antacid in dyspepsia, and in uric and lithic acid conditions of the urine. It has also aperient and diuretic properties. From the largest spring the flow is twenty gallons per hour. During the wet season it increases.

LITTON SELTZER SPRINGS
ALKALO-CARBONATED AND CHALYBEATE
Dr. Winslow Anderson, Analyst, 1888
Temperature 62° F.

Mineral Ingredients	U. S. gal. contains Grains	Mineral Ingredients	U. S. gal. contains Grains
Sodium Chloride	79.34	Ferrous Carbonate	2.14
Sodium Bicarbonate	6.26	Alumina	0.81
Sodium Carbonate	72.73	Borates	4.43
Potassium Carbonate	3.60	Lithium	trace
Magnesium Bicarbonate	13.90	Ammonia	.33
Magnesium Sulphate	6.75	Silica	8.09
Calcium Bicarbonate	14.05	Organic Matter	trace
Calcium Sulphate	5.03		

Total Solids, 223.46

Free Gases   Grains
Free Carbonic Acid Gas 375.60

Several years ago the following analysis was made by Prof. Hanks:

LITTON SPRING
SELTZER
Prof. Hanks, Analyst

Mineral Ingredients	U. S. Gal. contains Grains	Mineral Ingredients	U. S. Gal. contains Grains
Carbonic acid gas (combined)	42.96	Chlorine	78.38
Sulphuric Acid	2.36	Silicic Acid	2.92
Oxide of Iron	2.85	Lime	4.41
Magnesia	5.24	Soda	62.19
Alumina	27.38	Ammonia	27.38
Potash	27.38	Lithia	27.38
Boracic Acid	27.38	Organic Matter	27.38

Total Solids, 228.69.

Gases   Grains
Free Carbonic Acid Gas .... 383.75.

LOWER SODA SPRINGS

Opposite the mouth of Castle Creek in the Sacramento Valley, and on the Shasta Scenic Route in Shasta County, are two important soda springs. The upper one is about three and one-half miles farther up the canon, and about eight miles from Strawberry Flat, at the base of Mt. Shasta. The lower soda spring has an elevation of about 2,100 feet, and the upper spring that of 2,363 feet. The springs have gained considerable reputation among and are resorted to by many people suffering from uric or lithic acid, gravel, cystitis, nephritis, and albuminurea. The waters are alkaline and carbonated, and contain considerable quantities of iron salts. The temperature of the water is 52° F. The surrounding country is wild and picturesque, and a public resort has been established for the comfort of travelers from Mt. Shasta.

MADRONE MINERAL SPRINGS

These springs are situated some twenty-five miles southeast of San Jose, and about five miles north of Gilroy Hot Springs. They are at an elevation of about 2,200 feet, and beautifully located at the foot of "Pine Ridge." The mountain roads and drives are in good condition, and the scenery along the route is as fine as any in the State. At the springs we find ample accommodations, good bathing, hot or cold, and pure, bracing mountain air. The waters are "soda" impregnated with iron, and surcharged with carbonic acid gas. There is also an iron spring, and an alkalo-chalybeate spring containing arsenic, and another called white sulphur. The waters are used in the treatment of syphilis, rheumatism, skin diseases, etc., etc.

Route of travel is by the Southern Pacific Railroad to Madrone sixty-nine miles, and thence by stage twelve miles to the springs.

" MAGNETIC " MINERAL SPRINGS

These alkalo-chalybeate springs are found in Santa Cruz County near Watsonville. The waters are sold as a remedy for a great many diseases. No analysis.

MARK WEST SPRINGS

This mineral water resort is situated eight miles from Santa Rosa, near the famous "Petrified Forest," on Mark West Creek, in Sonoma county. It is reached by rail to Calistoga or Santa Rosa, and thence by easy carriage or stage to the springs over one of the most picturesque drives in that section of the country. During my recent visit, I observed that the mountains along the road were being cultivated, and beautiful villas and private mountain resorts were springing up in all directions. Extensive orchards of prunes and other fruits have been planted, and the whole country is active.

The springs are beautifully located at an elevation of 800 feet, in a small valley formed by the junction of four canons. The hotel and grounds are at the bases of three venerable mountains, called "Mt. Washington," "Mt. Lincoln" and "Mt. Grant." The temperature of the air ranges from 80° to 90° F., with pleasant, cooling and bracing sea breezes. The atmosphere is clear and dry.

There are excellent hotel accommodations and several cottages for family use. Hot sulphur and hot mud baths have been constructed with every facility for comfort and benefit. On the place are several springs. One large sulphur spring flows about 200 gallons per hour, and has a temperature of 82° F. The water is clear and not disagreeable to the taste. Its composition is:

> Sulphate of Sodium.
> Sulphate of Magnesium.
> Salts of Potassium—trace.
> Chloride of Sodium.

Carbonates of Sodium, Potassium and Lime, Silica and Alumina. It has also gases of carbonic anhydride and sulphureted hydrogen.

There is also an iron spring containing carbonate of iron, soda, magnesia and lime, with free carbonic acid gas. This is a highly chalybeate water, and has successfully treated many conditions requiring ferruginous tonics. The flow of this spring is 600 gallons per hour, and the water has a temperature of 65° F.

The largest spring has a flow of 5,000 gallons per hour; this is a sparkling carbonated water, very palatable, and gently aperient in its action. It is much used in dyspepsia arising from too free alcoholic stimulation, with the concomitant liver and kidney disorders. It is said to have vastly benefited patients suffering from chronic Bright's disease. The iron spring is used as a tonic, and the sulphur spring for cutaneous diseases, rheumatism, etc. The baths are sulphurous.

Analyses of these waters can not be made in time for publication.

MATILIJA HOT SPRINGS

They are located six miles from Nordhoff and fifteen miles from San Buenaventura in Ventura County. There are twenty-eight springs in all. They vary in temperature from 35° F. to 160° F. The average flow is 5,000 gallons per hour. Most of the hot springs are sulphureted and much used for syphilitic contaminations, strumous and skin diseases, rheumatism, etc. There is a comfortable hotel and resort at the springs.

MINERAL SPRINGS

Several springs by this name are found in Grizzly Cañon. The waters are salino-chalybeate, and charged with carbonic anhydride. No improvements.

McCARTHY'S HOT SPRINGS

Near Day's ranch, northeast of Fort Crook in Shasta County are located these mineral springs. Some of the water is reported sulphurous in character and the other ferruginous and carbonated. There is a local resort.

MILLS' MINERAL SPRINGS

About one mile above Anderson's resort in Lake County we find these springs. They are four in number. The hottest has a temperature of 170° F. The waters are principally sulphureted and saline, and the resort is growing every year. Good accommodations and splendid hot sulphur bathing can be found here. The surrounding country also affords excellent sport with the gun and rod.

MINERAL SPRINGS

Several springs, as yet unnamed, are known as mineral springs. Many of them are used locally.

Some of these are located twelve miles north of Wigginsville, in Siskiyou County.

Others are found on the east slope of Mt. Shasta, in Siskiyou County.

West of Butteville, in Siskiyou County, are found some more.

In Alpine County, on the mountain near Silver Lake, are several cold soda springs.

In Calaveras County are quite a number of mineral waters, especially in Salt Spring Valley. These waters are alkaline and rich in chlorides and carbonates.

On the west shore of Mono Lake in Mono County, lie several large calcic springs.

In Los Angeles County on the Encino ranch are a number of warm alkaline and carbonated springs having a temperature of 83° to 90° F. The waters are in local use.

In San Bernardino County, three miles above the mouth of Little Creek cañon are some warm springs, temperature 92° F. to 95° F.

MINERAL SPRINGS

ENCINO RANCH--LOS ANGELES COUNTY

OSCAR LOEW, Analyst

Mineral Ingredients	Parts in 1,000	Mineral Ingredients	Parts in 1,000
Sodium Carbonate	24.31	Silica	11.50
Magnesium Carbonate	——	Phosphoric Acid	trace
Calcium Carbonate	32.17	Sulphydric Acid	trace
Sodium Sulphate	54.46	Potassium	trace
Sodium Chloride	2.93	Lithium	trace

Total Solids, 125.37

Gases

Carbonic Acid Gas..................In excess

MISSION SAN JOSE HOT SPRINGS

About two miles southeast of the Mission San Jose, in Alameda County, are some notable springs. They were well known to the early Mexican and Spanish Fathers. There are four of these springs in use to-day, having a temperature of 80° F. The waters are alkalo-saline, having small quantities of carbonic anhydride and sulphureted hydrogen. Considerable local demand has been found for the waters.

MONO BASIN WARM SPRINGS

These waters are chlorinated and alkaline, and are located on the northeast shore of Mono Lake, in Mono County. The temperature varies from 85° F. to 90° F. Unimproved.

MONO BASIN WARM SPRINGS

F. M. CHATARD, Analyst

Mineral Ingredients	Grammes per Litre	Mineral Ingredients	Grammes per Litre
Sodium Carbonate	0.5072	Sodium Chloride	.2799
Magnesium Bicarbonate	.2114	Potassium Chloride	.1203
Calcium Carbonate	.1475	Alumina	.0018
Sodium Sulphate	.4631	Loss	.0158
Sodium Silicates	.2480		

Total Solids, 2.0850

A. 13.

MONO LAKE

This remarkable body of water is located near the center of Mono County, about ten miles south of the town of Bodie. The altitude is 6,730 feet. The length of the lake is, from east to west, about fourteen miles and its greatest breadth nine miles. The lake has been likened by Prof. W. F. McNutt (in his article on the mineral and thermal springs of California, read before the Ninth International Medical Congress) to the Dead Sea of the Holy Land. The same may be said of Owen's Lake (Hank's). At one time Mono Lake must have been much larger than it is at present, which is shown by the large terraces on all sides. The lake receives much of its water and its chemical salts from the rivers and creeks which flow through volcanic soil and empty into it. By evaporation of the water and the concentration of the salts deposited here for many centuries the mineral ingredients will undoubtedly prove valuable just as soon as man can separate and utilize them. (State Mineralogist.)

NEVADA FALLS

Numerous springs are found all over the Lake. The most curious of these are some of the fresh water springs holding in solution small quantities of calcium carbonate, which precipitate and deposit around the openings of the

springs, forming irregular tubes, clustered together in col-
umns. These vase-shaped structures are ten to forty feet
long, rising from the bottom of the Lake upward and above
the surface. In the center of these columnar pillars are
small holes, through which flows this sweet water. These
overflowing fountains have very aptly been likened to the
sponges found in the South Seas and known as "Neptune's
cups." In Mono Lake we find several islands, some two
or three miles long. Their composition is of volcanic

GEMS OF THE SIERRAS

material, and all over the surface are hot springs and jets
of hot steam, making the surrounding water quite warm.
On one or two of these little islands are small craters fifty
or more feet in diameter. They are now filled with water.

All around Mono Lake are unmistakable evidences of
great volcanic activity during the tertiary and post-tertiary
periods, and undoubtedly Mono Lake itself is a large
extinct crater.

The water, being likened to the Dead Sea, was supposed to be destitute of life. This, however, has been proved to be an error. There are found small, curious, wormlike, minute organisms, plainly visible to the naked eye, in the water near the surface. They seem to swim on their backs, and resemble the oars of a Venetian gondola or that of the Argo, noted in ancient mythology (Hanks). It is extraordinary that a water so constituted has vivifying power enough to sustain even these minute organisms, as there is found to be nearly 3,000 grains of solids in each gallon. The larvæ of these animals are thrown upon the shores of the lake by the waves, and there accumulate in large quantities. Here the Indian gathers them, and when dried they form one of the delicacies of the red man, who is said to delight in them, as did the good people delight in the locusts and honey in the days of yore.. The scenery in and around Mono Lake is grand, and well worth the trip. Situated as it is at so high an elevation, and surrounded on all sides by snow-capped mountains, a picture is presented to which only an artist could do justice.

The water itself is more like a bitter brine to the taste than mineral water. Its action is excessively diuretic, even in small quantities.

On analysis this " Dead Sea" water is found to contain .

MONO LAKE
CHLORINATED, ETC.
DR. WINSLOW ANDERSON, Analyst, 1887
Temperature 63° to 80.5° F.

Mineral Ingredients	U. S. gal. contains Grains	Mineral Ingredients	U. S. gal. contains Grains
Sodium Chloride	795.24	Calcium Chloride	1075.55
Sodium Carbonate	20.40	Calcium Carbonate	52.76
Sodium Sulphate	17.10	Calcium Sulphide	trace
Sodium Phosphate	5.93	Calcium Sulphate	57.07
Potassium Chloride	281.17	Ferrous Carbonate	7.14
Potassium Carbonate	10.60	Alumina	26.63
Potassium Phosphate	3 05	Borates	19.75
Magnesium Chloride	365.00	Silicates	9.62
Magnesium Carbonate	9.45	Organic Matter	24.00
Magnesium Sulphate	127.50		

Total Solids, 2915.16

Gases	Cubic Inches
Free Carbonic Acid Gas	17.16
Free Sulphureted Hydrogen	.62

The composition will probably vary in different localities, being influenced by the proximity of the different springs.

MONO LAKE—ANALYSIS

T. M. CHATARD, Analyst

Mineral Ingredients	Grammes per Litre	Mineral Ingredients	Grammes per Litre
Sodium Carbonate	19.49	Sodium Chloride	18.22
Magnesium Carbonate	.36	Potassium Chloride	2.23
Calcium Carbonate	.08	Silica	.28
Sodium Sulphate	10.07	Loss	.32
Sodium Biborate	.20		

Total Solids, 51.85

MONO LAKE—ANALYSIS

I. R. MURPHY, Analyst

Mineral Ingredients	Per Cent	Mineral Ingredients	Per Cent
Boracic Acid	large traces	Sodium Chloride	5.854
Carbonic Acid	abundant	Potassium Chloride	1.581
(free?)		Calcium Chloride	2.630
Hydrosulphuric Acid	abundant	Magnesium Chloride	8.206
(free?)		Calcium Sulphate	.402
Phosphoric Acid	traces	Calcium Sulphide	traces
Silica	traces	Magnesium Sulphide	traces

Total Solids.............. 18.673

Pure Water.............. 81.327

Total.............. 100.000

Compare Mono Lake with the waters of the Dead Sea and Great Salt Lake found elsewhere.

MONTECITO HOT SPRINGS

A LETTER FROM THE ABLE PEN OF REV. A. H. CARRIER.

Everyone in Santa Barbara knows something of the hot springs, Montecito. Not every one has learned the charm of the place by personal observation and experience. At an elevation of 1,460 feet above the sea in the heart of the most picturesque ravine with mountain walls rising almost perpendicularly around, with an opening toward the ocean and its outlying islands so that these seemed framed into a picture of extraordinary beauty, the place itself is unparalleled in its attractions by any spot along the line of our coast.

Winding around the spurs of the mountain a walk from the hotel, so well graded at present that an invalid would find no difficulty on it, leads to the famous Lookout Point from which the long-reaching valley and the Pacific beyond are seen stretching at one's feet. Santa Barbara seems so near that you feel that you could signal to your friends.

To one who cares to climb, the peak, 1,500 feet above, as I can testify, is exceedingly grand in its combination of mountains, of deep ravines, of distant peaks, of the San Rafael range, of the coast line from Hueneme to Gaviota, together with the boundless expanse of the ocean. The scene suggests the famous view from the Righi and from Mount Pilatus in Switzerland, with the added sublimity in this case of the vast Pacific.

As a sanitarium the Hot Springs afford what one might travel far to discover. The water issuing from the rocks at 120° Fahrenheit, charged with sulphur and other minerals, is Nature's own healing remedy, efficacious to a high degree in complaints of a rheumatic nature. Almost instant benefit is experienced by many persons from the combined external and internal use of these waters. The sense of rest after fatigue from these baths is something marvelous.

These hot springs are located five miles from Santa Barbara City in the same county. The waters are sulphurous and nearly all boiling hot. A resort is being erected for the treatment of invalids. Also suitable bathing facilities are being provided.

MOUNTAIN GLEN HOT SPRINGS

Some twenty-five miles north of Santa Barbara are found these springs. They are mostly sulphurous, and have a temperature from 60° to 100° F. There is a local resort.

MUD SPRINGS

Extensive hot mud springs are situated fifteen miles northeast of Honey Lake, in Lassen County. The property is unimproved.

Also on Antelope Creek, about ten miles east of Red Bluff, in Tehama County, is another region of hot mud springs. No analysis and no improvements.

NAPA SODA SPRINGS

These celebrated mineral springs are charmingly located on the southwestern slope of the Coast Range, about fifty miles from San Francisco and six miles from Napa City. The elevation is about 1,000 feet above the sea.

They are reached by ferry and rail to Napa City and thence by easy carriage to the springs. This drive from Napa to the springs is exceedingly pleasant. You pass neat and cozy farmhouses and homes, green pastures and

NAPA SODA SPRINGS

well-tilled fields, orchards, vineyards and groves. The air is fragrant with the perfumes of wild and cultivated flowers and resonant with the harmonious songs of a thousand birds. One feels envious of the quiet and peaceful rural life when thus contrasted to the busy whirl of the western metropolis.

As you speed along, " Napa Resort" is seen in the distance, looming up like an ancient fortress along the Rhine. At the end of a short hour you arrive at the Rotunda Hotel. Here the scenery is charming; a thousand feet above the valley and at the head of the cañon, you have full command of the country for miles around. Looking southward over the beautiful valley of Napa County, one sees a landscape which has probably never been surpassed for beauty, one which forever remains fresh in his memory. The green fields, cultivated farms, orchards and vineyards, gardens and houses, checkered here and there in an irregular manner, with their straight and winding lanes, creeks and rivers, with groves of stately oaks, and in the distance the San Francisco Bay, glistening and rippling in the sun's rays, blend to make a harmonious whole, to which only the trained pencil or brush can do justice. To the westward may be seen the great Pacific, guarded by its sentinel, Mt. Tamalpais, and the many ranges of mountains and hills. To the eastward Mt. Diablo looms up in the distance, half veiled in violet mists. To the north we see Mt. St. Helena and the Coast Ranges with their rich, alluvial valleys.

The local picture of Napa Soda Springs is scarcely less interesting. We find groves of oaks gracefully festooned with immortal mistletoe, the tall and stately pine and the eucalyptus globulus. We also find the Italian cypress, the palm, the olive, the fig and the orange tree, the odorous California buckeye and the fragrant laurel, the maple and the madrona, and tangled copses of flowering shrubbery everywhere.

Lawns and flower-beds, cultivated and natural, with the many shady nooks and cozy outlets—combined nature and art—produce as lovely a spot as the tired business man with his family, or the invalid with his many ailments, could possibly find. The climate is warm, dry and salubrious, and the resort has the mountain air and the sea breezes as well.

The mineral springs are among the most noted in the State. They number twenty-seven in all, with an average daily flow of about 4,000 gallons. The temperature of the water ranges about 65° F. to 68° F. The main spring, the Pagoda, from which most of the commercial Napa soda is obtained, had a temperature in 1888 of 67.7° F. This is an alkalo-chalybeate water strongly charged with carbonic anhydride, delightful, clear and sparkling, and has an agreeably pungent taste.

Over the Pagoda spring, engraved on a marble tablet, is the following invocation, a *fac simile* of one inscribed by Imperial decree above the springs at the famous Carlsbad, in Bohemia:

> " To suffering man from Nature's genial breast
>   A boon transcendent ever mayst thou flow ;
>   Blest holy fount; still bid old age to know
> Reviving vigor, and if health repressed
> Fade in the virgin's cheek, renew its glow
> For love and joy ; and they that in thy wave
> Confiding trust and thankful lave,
> Propitious aid, and speed the stranger band,
> With health and life renewed, unto their native land."

NAPA SODA—PAGODA SPRING

ALKALO-CHALYBEATE

DR. WINSLOW ANDERSON, Analyst, 1888

Temperature 67.7' F.

Mineral Ingredients	U. S. Gal. contains Grains	Mineral Ingredients	U. S. Gal. contains Grains
Sodium Chloride	7.14	Calcium Bicarbonate	.78
Sodium Bicarbonate	12.95	Calcium Carbonate	9.55
Sodium Carbonate	1.10	Ferrous Carbonate	7.90
Sodium Sulphate	1.62	Silica	.74
Potassium Bicarbonate	trace	Alumina	.57
Magnesium Bicarbonate	3.04	Organic Matter	trace
Magnesium Carbonate	21.76		

Total Solids, 67.15

Gases	Cubic Inches
Free Carbonic Acid	143.62

Over this spring is built a beautiful pagoda, supported by solid stone pillars and resting upon a tesselated marble floor. A natural stone basin has been artistically arranged, through which the sparkling soda bubbles in all its freshness.

NAPA SODA—"IRON SPRING"

ALKALO-CHALYBEATE

Prof. Lanzwert, Analyst. 1870

Temperature 68° F.

Mineral Ingredients	U. S. gal. contains Grains	Mineral Ingredients	U. S. gal. contains Grains
Sodium Chloride	5.20	Calcium Carbonate	10.83
Sodium Bicarbonate	13.12	Ferrous Carbonate	7.84
Sodium Sulphate	1.84	Silica	.62
Maguesium Carbonate	26.12	Alumina	.60

Total Solids, 66.17

Gases

Free Carbonic Anhydride......undetermined

NAPA SODA

The "Lemon Spring," or the natural Napa soda lemonade, flows considerably less than the Pagoda Spring. The water, however, is even more valuable as a tonic, containing more ferruginous salts. The lithium makes it beneficial in kidney diseases. Otherwise the water is very similar in its aperient and diuretic properties, as may be seen from the following analysis:

NAPA SODA SPRING—"LEMON SPRING"

ALKALO-CHALYBEATE WATER

Dr. Winslow Anderson, Analyst, 1889

Temperature 66.9° F.

Mineral Ingredients	U. S. gal. contains Grains	Mineral Ingredients	U. S. gal. contains Grains
Sodium Chloride	4.72	Calcium Carbonate	8.97
Sodium Bicarbonate	15.24	Ferrous Carbonate	8.11
Sodium Carbonate	4.65	Lithium	trace
Sodium Sulphate	.76	Boracic Acid	trace
Potassium Salts	traces	Alumina	.74
Magnesium Carbonate	25.19	Silicates	.83
Maguesium Sulphate	trace	Organic Matter	trace

Total Solids, 69.21

Gases	Cubic Inches
Free Carbonic Acid Gas	95.79

NAPA SPRINGS

The many other mineral springs at Napa Soda resort are very similar in composition. The waters are all alkalo-chalybeate, clear, cool and sparkling.

Napa Soda is highly esteemed as a beverage. It is sold in every city and town on the coast, and is one of the pleasantest summer drinks we have.

The water is an efficient aid to digestion, being antacid and tonic. When taken in the morning before breakfast its

action is gently aperient. The ferruginous salts held in solution by the carbonic acid gas are valuable in anæmia and chlorotic conditions, malarial toxæmia and many disorders requiring iron for the constructive metamorphosis of red-blood corpuscles. Much benefit is derived from a course at the springs in

PAGODA SPRING

Bright's disease of the kidneys and chronic cystitis, in acid conditions of the blood and urine, dyspepsia and indigestion, etc., etc. The Napa Soda Springs have also proved beneficial in the treatment of chronic and subacute metritis and ovaritis, and this water is better borne by the stomach in these and the many allied uterine complications than almost any other chalybeate tonic.

In the many cystic and nephritic disorders found on this coast these alkalo-carbonated and chalybeate waters have been found of great value.

The resort is open all the year round. The excellent climate, the high and dry location and the elegant accommodations add greatly to the comforts of the health and pleasure seeking public.

The Rotunda Hotel is a magnificent structure. It is built of solid stone masonry, quarried in one of the adjacent mountains on the extensive grounds. The rock is white and soft when first exposed to the atmosphere, but it rapidly parts with its moisture and becomes harder and harder the longer it remains in the air. The rotunda is a circular building, towering up seventy-five feet into the air and surmounted by a huge glass cupola which reflects the rays of the sun for miles around.

The structure is one hundred and twenty feet in diameter, and its interior is a fine work of mechanical art. The court, or grand central parlor, is about one hundred feet in diameter, handsomely furnished and lighted by a large gas chandelier of forty lights. Surrounding the parlor is a promenade, and exterior to this again are arranged apartments for guests, single and in suits. From this building the entire extensive grounds and landscape may be surveyed.

Picturesquely arranged on different portions and elevations of the premises are located the many handsome edifices belonging to Napa Springs, the most of which are built of stone, and have gas and running water in every room. There is the "Club House," in which are found all the various amusements, billiard tables, bowling-alleys, bagatelle tables, etc., for the use of the guests. The "Tower House," "Ivy House," The "Bellevue," "Garden House," "Music Hall," "Bottling House," and cottages are all at the disposal of the guests, as also lawn tennis and croquet grounds beautifully situated.

The waters are bottled fresh from nature's subterranean laboratories at the springs, and only natural mineral waters and gases are sent from the Soda Springs.

The dining hall deserves a passing notice, not only on account of its external architectural beauty, but for its excellent interior contents. The *cuisine* is in charge of an experienced *chef* and the *table d'hote* is superior, consisting of pure fresh milk, butter and eggs of country production, fresh vegetables and fruit from the gardens and orchard on the place, and the most nourishing and appetizing foods with all the delicacies of the season.

The extensive grounds cover over a thousand acres of hills and valley. The place is also well supplied with springs of fresh water, rippling over rocks and rills forming cascades and mountain streams which play over the pebbles or gently glide along the moss-covered banks. There are also splendid facilities for hot and cold Napa Soda baths in tub or plunge, and a swimming-bath measuring 150 feet in length by 50 feet in width, with water varying from 4 to 10 feet in depth.

Our sojourn at this resort during 1888, although necessarily brief, was, nevertheless, exceedingly pleasant, and we do not hesitate in pronouncing Napa Soda Springs one of the most delightful and salubrious watering-places on the Pacific Coast.

Newsom's Arroyo Grande Springs

About 14 miles south of San Luis Obispo lie these springs. They are reached by rail to Arroyo Grande and thence by easy stage or by drive from Nipomo. The situation is a pleasant one at an altitude of about 400 feet. The grounds and springs are well kept. The ocean beach road affords one of the finest drives in that section of the country. At the beach, swimming, fishing, and clamming are always in order. The hotel and cottages are pleasantly situated and afford good accommodations for guests. The climate

is one of almost perpetual sunshine with occasional spring
and fall rains. On the place are three principal springs
whose waters range in temperature from 40° F. to 100° F.
and flow the enormous amount of 49,000 gallons per hour.
The waters are salino-sulphureted and have gained considerable reputation in the treatment of old chronic rheumatism and gout, catarrhal affections of the bladder and
bowels, skin diseases, etc. For uterine troubles the hot
sulphurous douche has been of great benefit.

Warm and hot plunge and tub bathing facilities have
been constructed for the use of guests.

NEWSOM'S ARROYO GRANDE SPRINGS
LIGHT SALINO-SULPHURETED
Dr. Winslow Anderson

Mineral Constituents	Analyst, 1888 *Temperature 100.5° F.* U. S. gal. contains Grains	Unknown Analyst *Temperature 100° F.* U. S. gal. contains Grains
Sodium Chloride	4.10	4.16
Sodium Carbonate	1.75	—
Sodium Sulphate	3.92	4.06
Potassium Carbonate	.15	—
Potassium Sulphate	2.90	2.99
Magnesium Carbonate	6.41	6.61
Magnesium Sulphate	2.47	—
Calcium Carbonate	8.25	10.62
Calcium Sulphate	.76	.64
Ferrous Carbonate	3.98	4.15
Alumina	.33	.03
Silica	2.03	2.30
Organic Matter	.27	.52
Total Solids	37.32	36.08
Gases	Cubic Inches	Cubic Inches
Free Carbonic Anhydride	14.90	12.13
Free Sulphureted Hydrogen	3.56	3.72

NEW ALMADEN VICHY SPRINGS.

These springs are situated in the Coast Range of mountains, about 60 miles south of San Francisco. They are
near the New Almaden Mines in Santa Clara County. The

climate is lovely and mild during the whole year. At the springs has been erected a pretty little resort, which is growing in favor. The water is a heavy alkalo-chalybeate strongly charged with carbonic acid gas.

NEW ALMADEN VICHY SPRINGS
VICHY—ALKALO—CHALYBEATE
Unknown Analyst
Temperature 63° F.

Mineral Ingredients	U. S. Gal. contains Grains
Sodium Chloride	32.16
Sodium Carbonate	200.12
Magnesium Sulphate	12.00
Calcium Carbonate	32.00
Calcium Sulphate	40.20
Iron	4.08
Carbonic Acid	112.08
Silica	traces
Total	432.64

Recently the springs have ceased to flow, owing to the deep workings of the Almaden quicksilver mines.

On analysis this water is found to contain—

NICHOLAS SPRINGS
SALINO-CHALYBEATE

	Dr. Winslow Anderson Analyst, 1888	Baumgarten Analyst.
	Temperature 63.5° F.	
Mineral Ingredients	U. S. Gal. contains Grains	U. S. Gal. contains Grains
Sodium Chloride	1.14	.10
Sodium Sulphate	11.90	12.08
Magnesium Sulphate	103.62	105.09
Calcium Sulphate	43.07	49.34
Calcium Carbonate	7.55	—
Ferrous Sulphate	7.96	—
Ferric Sulphate	—	10.91
Ferrous Carbonate	2.43	—
Silica	6.09	6.41
Borates	.81	—
Organic Matter	.24	—
Total Solids	184.81	183.93
Gases	Cubic Inches	Cubic Inches
Free Sulphureted Hydrogen	17.90	undetermined

NICHOLAS SPRINGS

They are located in Santa Cruz County, on Mr. B. C. Nicholas' Ranch.

The water contains large quantities of Epsom salts and iron salts.

OJAI HOT SULPHUR SPRINGS

These springs are beautifully situated in Waterfall Canon, about five miles from the prosperous village of Nordhoff and fifteen miles from Ventura, in Ventura County. The route is to Ventura by Southern Pacific Railroad and thence by stage. The altitude at the springs is about 1,000 feet. Good accommodations are afforded at the growing resort and the vicinity boasts of fine fishing, hunting and scenery.

The springs flow about 50,000 gallons per hour and have a temperature ranging from 60° F., to 74 to 104° F. Several of the springs are carbonated and others are sulphureted.

The "Fountain of Life" spring is a cool soda; "St. Jacob's Well" is also cool and carbonated. One large spring was discovered by a man named Adam and the most natural thought for an Adam to have was of his tempter "Eve," so he named this water the "Mother of Eve." It is soft and heavily charged with sulphates and sulphureted hydrogen, and although the water tastes well enough, its smell is anything but agreeable. The water has a reputation for whitening and softening the skin and improving the complexion.

These Ojai waters contain: sodium, potassium and magnesium, carbonates and sulphates, calcium and ferrous carbonates, silicates, carbonic anhydride and sulphureted hydrogen gases.

Many people go there who are stiff-jointed, rheumatic and gouty, or affected with skin diseases, etc. They are all reported as receiving great benefit.

OWEN'S LAKE

This second "Dead Sea" in California is located at the southern end of Owen's Valley in Inyo County. It is eighteen miles long and ten miles wide and its waters are highly chlorinated and alkaline.

On analysis the lake water yields, according to Chemist Philips of London:

OWEN'S LAKE.

PROF. PHILIPS, London, Analyst

Temperature Not Given

Mineral Ingredients	Imperial Gallon Grains
Chloride of Sodium	2942.15
Sulphate of Soda	956.80
Carbonate of Soda	2914.43
Sulphate of Potash	35.74
Silicate of Potash	139.54
Organic Matter	16.94
Total Solids	7005.60

The most important of the auxiliary attractions of San Jose is the Lick Observatory on the summit of Mount Hamilton. A few years ago James Lick, a wealthy citizen of San Jose, gave his entire property, consisting of nearly five millions of dollars, to philanthropic institutions and and works of public improvement in the State. The most important of these bequests was that of $750,000 for the establishment of an astronomical observatory on Mount Hamilton, which was to be equipped with the most powerful telescope in the world. Mount Hamilton is located in the range of mountains east of the valley, and is twenty-six miles distant from San Jose. It stands 4,443 feet above the level of the sea, in an atmosphere cloudless during the entire year. From its summit there is an unbroken horizon, while its latitude is favorable for the most important observations. The county of Santa Clara has constructed, at an expense of about $100,000, a magnificent road to the top of the mountain. This road is of easy grade, finely constructed, and furnishes a beautiful drive. The scenery along the route is unsurpassed for beauty and grandeur. The work on the observatory and adjacent buildings has been completed and the placing of the crown disc for the great thirty-six-inch telescope (the largest in the world) has been accomplished. The buildings and instruments now completed

and in position are the observer's house, and the thirty-six-inch telescope, the transit house, the photo-heliograph and photograph house, the north dome and the fifteen-inch equatorial refractor, the meridian circle house and the six and one-half inch meridian circle; many auxiliary instruments, such as chronometers, sidereal clocks, etc., and a number of portable telescopes. The dome which covers the great telescope is made of steel plates; it is seventy-five feet in diameter, and weighs about one hundred and twenty-two tons.

Pacific Congress Springs and Sanitarium

These famous mineral springs are located in the Coast Range of mountains, about twelve miles southwest of San Jose, in Santa Clara County. They are so named from the similarity which exists between the waters of these springs and those of the noted Congress Springs at Saratoga, New York.

Santa Clara Valley is celebrated for its excellent climate and dry, pure and invigorating atmosphere, a place admirably suited for a health and pleasure resort where the cares of a busy life may be forgotten for a while, and where one can bask in the sunny smiles and breathe the perfumed air, and admire the picturesqueness of the place.

A large and commodious hotel and several cottages have been established at an elevation of seven hundred and thirty feet above the sea level. Excellent bathing facilities for hot and cold mineral baths have also been constructed. Some one hundred feet farther up the mountain side are the springs—purposely so arranged in order to give the guests a little walk to and from the springs.

The drives in and about Congress Springs are among the finest in the State, everything is first class, entertaining and pleasing, and thousands of people go there yearly for their health and recreation.

Route of travel—the Southern Pacific Railroad to Los Gatos, and thence by stage or carriage to the springs.

There are several springs on the premises, which flow in great profusion. The waters belong to the alkalo-chalybeate class, so valuable for table purposes. Their action is mildly aperient (from the presence of the Glauber's and Epsom salts), diuretic from the large amounts of carbonates, and antacid from carbonic acid gas, which forms alkaline carbonates with metallic bases. The waters are also largely tonic and ferruginous from the large quantity of iron salts.

PACIFIC CONGRESS SPRINGS
ALKALO-CHALYBEATE
Temperature 50° F.

Mineral Ingredients	Dr. Winslow Anderson Analyst, 1888 U. S. Gal. Contains Grains	Bauer or Thayer Analyst U. S. Gal. Contains Grains
Sodium Chloride	115.76	119.15
Sodium Carbonate	120.42	123.35
Sodium Sulphate	12.95	12.14
Potassium Carbonate	2.06	....
Magnesium Carbonate	26.34	....
Magnesium Sulphate	14.17	....
Calcium Carbonate	16.03	17.29
Calcium Sulphate	14.19	....
Ferrous Carbonate	13.87	14.03
Alumina	4.50	....
Silica, Alumina and Magnesia	....	49.93
Silica	3.98	....
Organic Matter	trace	....
Total Solids	334.27	335.94

Gases	Cubic Inches	Cubic Inches
Free Carbonic Acid Gas	44.17	Not Determined

This water has gained considerable celebrity in the treatment of anæmia, dyspepsia, liver and kidney troubles, irritability of the bladder, rheumatism, gout and cutaneous affections. The waters are shipped to all parts of the coast and are extensively used.

THE VALLEY OF PALMS
NO SUCH CLIMATE OR SCENERY ELSEWHERE IN THE UNITED STATES

Hundreds of lofty palms, with slender trunks towering seventy-five to one hundred feet in the clear atmosphere, crowned with magnificent clusters of fruit from ten to twelve

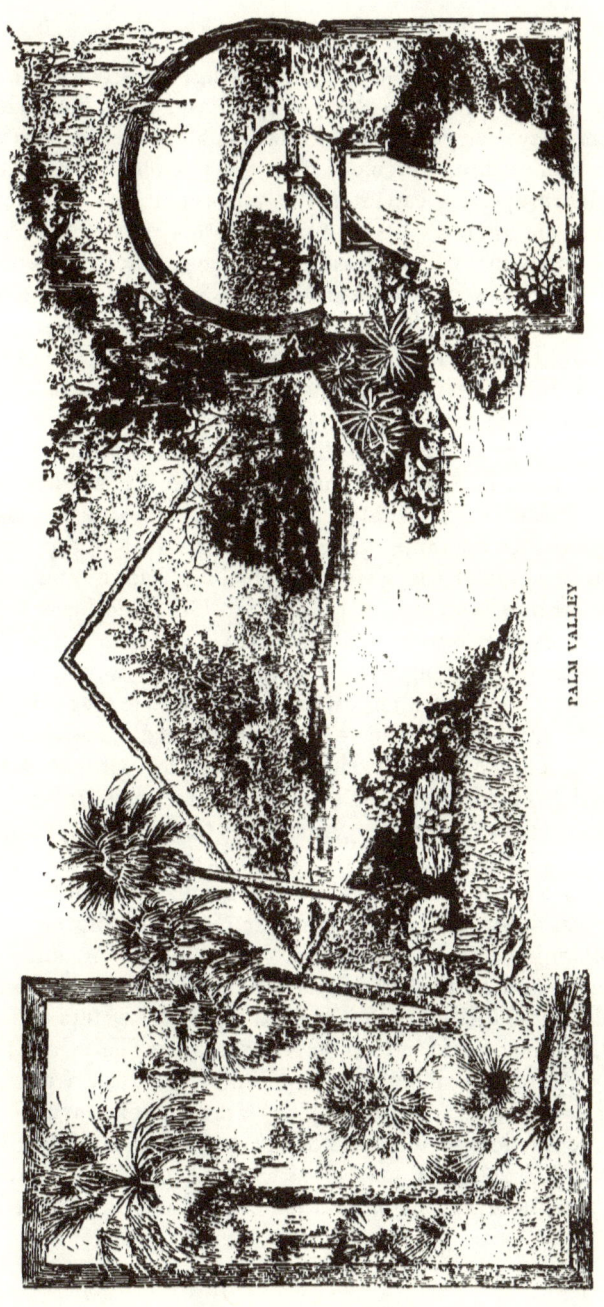

PALM VALLEY

feet in length. A hot mineral spring, fed from a natural well reaching far into the bowels of the earth, and whose waters have for years been known as a specific for rheumatism and all kinds of blood diseases. A fertile soil, whose genial properties cause fruits and vegetables to ripen a month and more in advance of any other part of the State. A balmy climate where frost and fog are practically unknown and where the most delicate invalid finds a canvas shelter comfortable the year round. Beautiful mountain streams pouring their wealth of water from the melting snows into the valley. In the background a lofty mountain range, towering over two miles into the blue ether. All this, and more, too, go to make up the principal natural advantages which the visitor finds at Palm Valley, in the northeastern part of San Diego County. This remarkable, and in many respects incomparable, valley lies at the foot of the southeastern slope of the grand San Jacinto Range, and a few miles from the valley, called the San Gorgonio Pass, which separates the range mentioned from the San Bernardino Mountains. For ages this valley, with its wonderful hot springs, or Aguas Calientes, has been known to the aboriginal inhabitants, and they have been accustomed to resort hither for the cure of their various ailments by bathing in the health-giving waters. Their legends of this region are numerous and interesting, including that of Tah-Quish, the demon of the mountains and the beautiful White Spirit, who is the guardian angel of the spring. From the very earliest occupation of the white settlers in California these springs have been well and favorably known. People from every direction flocked hither for the certain cure of manifold diseases which followed bathing in the waters. Gradually, a few white settlers have made homes here, and they learned by experiment the remarkable fact that fruits and vegetables would mature here at least six weeks earlier than in the earliest regions of other parts of the State. Taking the fertile soil, the marvelous climate and the wonderful springs, here was a combination of advantages which could not fail to be of the greatest value. A couple of years since, some capitalists secured possession of several thousand acres of land, constructed a stone-paved canal, ten miles long by which the water of Whitewater River was diverted upon the Palm Valley lands, and then established a settlement here which is manifestly destined to take a front rank among the health resorts of the world. They have also planted a tract of one hundred and forty acres with choice oranges and made many other improvements. Consumptives, rheumatics and other sufferers find almost immediate relief in the pure, dry air of Palm Valley, and the list of cures that have been effected here is, indeed, marvelous.

PAERT'S HOT SPRINGS

Near Benton, in Mono County, lie several hot springs. The waters are salino-sulphurous and used locally. No analysis.

PARAISO HOT SPRINGS AND SANITARIUM

These famous mineral springs are picturesquely situated in their mountainous retreat in the Coast Range, about one hundred and fifty miles from San Francisco and seven miles south of Soledad, Monterey County. They are of easy access by the Southern Pacific Railroad to Soledad and thence by stage or carriage over a charming mountainous drive to the springs.

The Paraiso mineral springs have gained considerable celebrity, having been located by the Franciscan fathers in 1790. The resort is charmingly located in a grotto guarded by three high mountains on as many sides, covered with groves of trees and mountain shrubbery, forming an excellent background to our beautiful landscape. See illustration.

Below the resort, and for miles beyond, is the fertile valley, traversed by the grand Salinas River and Arroyo Seco, and the far-away Gabilan Mountains —altogether forming a picture which only a Bierstadt could delineate.

The climate belongs to that smiling sunny south, whose atmosphere is redolent with the perfumes from the sweet-scented woods and the pine-laden forests, where the ozone and gentle sea breezes are wafted across the mountains to invigorate the fortunate dwellers.

At the springs are the cultivated grounds and gardens, orchards and flowers so pleasing at a mountainous resort.

PARAISO HOT SPRINGS

Here we find the many romantic nooks and commanding outlooks, the winding paths and sequestered retreats leading up and down the mountain sides. "Mussel Peak" and the shaded "Lovers' Walk," with the bright silvered streams below, gliding noiselessly on to the briny deep, afford ample food for the imagination and excellent exercise for the body.

The commodious hotel and cottages are of recent construction, and combine all the luxury and comfort with

convenience and wholesomeless that can be found anywhere.   The elevation is about fourteen hundred feet above
the sea level.   The temperature is equable and the air dry,
pure and balmy.   Many consumptives and asthmatics do
well at these springs.

There is also abundant fishing and hunting in the
immediate vicinity.

During the early days of California the friars at the
"Old Mission of Soledad," near the Salinas River, used to
go up to the springs and receive the sick, who bathed and
drank the water and carried much of it with them for
medicinal purposes.   They named it the Water of Paradise.

On the premises are several valuable springs, flowing
about 2,000 gallons per hour, consisting of "sulphur,"
"soda," and "iron waters."

The Hot Sulphur spring has a temperature of 100° F.
Others range in temperature from 105° F. to 118° F.

The following analysis is from the principal sulphur
spring at Paraiso.

PARAISO HOT SULPHUR SPRINGS

Dr. Winslow Anderson, Analyst, 1889

Temperature, 114° F.

Mineral Ingredients	U. S. Gal. contains Grains	Mineral Ingredients	U. S. Gal. contains Grains
Sodium Chloride	2.76	Calcium Carbonate	.89
Sodium Carbonate	1.15	Calcium Sulphate	4.40
Sodium Sulphate	37.10	Ferrous Oxide	.73
Potassium Sulphate	.83	Silica	2.55
Magnesium Carbonate	6.09	Organic Matter	7.35
Magnesium Sulphate	2.19		

Total Solids, 66.04

Gases	Cubic Inches
Carbonic Acid Gas	2.04
Sulphureted Hydrogen	9.25

This water forms one of the best bathing mediums
found on the coast.

The Great Paraiso Hot Soda or "Carslbad of America" is found upon careful chemical analysis to yield—

PARAISO SODA SPRINGS

Dr. Winslow Anderson, Analyst, 1889

Temperature, 118° F.

Mineral Ingredients	U. S. Gal, contains Grains	Mineral Ingredients	U. S. Gal, contains Grains
Sodium Chloride	3.37	Calcium Carbonate	1.30
Sodium Carbonate	5.06	Calcium Sulphate	6.45
Sodium Sulphate	34.60	Ferrous Carbonate	.89
Potassium Chloride	.82	Alumina	.56
Potassium Sulphate	trace	Silica	2.90
Magnesium Carbonate	.75	Organic Matter	4.15
Magnesium Sulphate	1.10		

Total Solids, 61.45

Gases	Cubic Inches
Free Carbonic Acid Gas	2.95

This water is found to be very similar to the noted Carlsbad of Austria, and of great value in rheumatism, gout, liver and kidney affections and chronic skin diseases.

The waters at Paraiso Springs have been found of great service in chronic rheumatism and arthritic affections, joint diseases, syphilitic and scrofulous contaminations and chronic skin diseases.

The soda and sulphur waters are tonic, antacid, laxative, diuretic and detergent and much prized in dyspepsia, torpidity of liver and intestines, glandular swellings, and for kidney and bladder diseases.

Thousands of visitors, invalids and pleasure-seekers, visit Paraiso Springs yearly and the superiority of the mineral springs, the excellence of the climate and the picturesqueness of the location bid fair to make Paraiso resort one of the most prominent mineral watering-places on the Coast.

PASO ROBLES SPRINGS

See El Paso Robles.

PEARSON'S SPRINGS

These are situated one and a half miles from Blue Lakes and fourteen miles from Lakeport in Lake County. They are reached by railroad to Calistoga and thence by stage. The springs lie in an elevated valley about six hundred feet wide with large mountains on each side. There are five important springs at Pearson's. One is known as the "Gas Spring" on account of the large amount of carbonic acid gas which constantly bubbles up. The water is a cool salino-chalybeate, having gently cathartic and diuretic properties combined with antacid and tonic. Then there is a "Sulphur and Soda," and a plain "Soda" spring, and the old "Bartlett."

The waters are used for liver and kidney diseases, malarial toxæmia, catarrhal affections, etc.

The water is artificially heated for bathing purposes.

PETROLEUM SPRINGS

Throughout the State a large number of valuable petroleum springs have been discovered, several of which are worked to good advantage. In Alameda, the first one was discovered in 1868, at the time of the great earthquake, on Mr. Brown's ranch, about four miles east of the town of Livermore. After one of the shocks, a large subterranean explosion was heard which displaced large masses of conglomerate rock and coarse sandstone. Simultaneously, a spring of water commenced to flow near the point of the explosion. As the water issued from the crevice it was observed to be covered with traces of petroleum. Inflammable gas also bubbled up through the water. This suggested the idea of prospecting for oil and gas in the vicinity. Accordingly, a drill hole was sunk about ten feet near the center of the spring. Immediately a dark tarry looking oil escaped. Later on (1875) a well was bored near the spring to a depth of forty-five feet, and water and petroleum commenced to flow. In 1886 several other wells were sunk, one to a depth of one hundred and sixty-five feet, and considerable oil and water continues to flow with bubbles of inflammable gas.

A large natural petroleum well is located in the ocean about one and one-half miles from the shore and about ten miles west of Santa Barbara. Its productiveness must be large, as the ocean water for miles around is covered with the floating oil. Ventura County is known as the "oil county of California." From this natural petroleum county, in 1888, were shipped 226,050 barrels of oil. The wells are from a few feet in depth to several hundred, and in one case 1,400 feet. The crude oils are refined at Santa Paula, yielding—

Illuminating oil	Inflammable gas
Domestic fuel	Distillates
Wood oils	Neutral oils
Lubricating oils	Malta (Bitumen)

Petroleum is found in Santa Cruz, Humboldt, Santa Clara, Los Angeles, San Mateo, Mendocino, Santa Barbara, San Benito, Monterey, San Luis Obispo and other counties in the State, and is forming one of our many valuable industries.

PIEDMONT WHITE SULPHUR SPRINGS

These springs are located in Alameda County, some three miles from Oakland, and have gained considerable local reputation in the treatment of rheumatism, jaundice, liver and kidney and stomach troubles.

The nearness of the resort to the city makes it especially valuable to business men, who can stay at the springs at night and return to San Francisco for business during the day. The resort and grounds are well kept. The hotel is convenient and commodious. The atmosphere is pure and refreshing, with the tonic sea breezes from the bay. The situation, on the western slopes of the Berkeley hills, commands one of the most picturesque views over the San Francisco Bay and the Golden Gate that can be found anywhere on the the coast.

PIEDMONT SPRINGS
CHALYBEATE AND SULPHUR WATERS
DR. WINSLOW ANDERSON, Analyst, 1889

Mineral Ingredients	*Temperature 58° F.* IRON SPRING U. S. gal. contains Grains	*Temperature 60° F.* WHITE SULPHUR U. S. gal. contains Grains
Sodium Chloride	5.10	7.91
Sodium Bicarbonate	11.70	9.40
Sodium Carbonate	0.52	6.20
Potassium Carbonate	3.15	.76
Potassium Iodide	trace	trace
Magnesium Carbonate	6.37	3.17
Magnesium Sulphate	1.03	17.80
Calcium Carbonate	2.13	3.32
Calcium Sulphate	1.60	7.09
Ferrous Carbonate	1.73	trace
Alumina	.45	trace
Borates	5.23	1.90
Silicates	4.19	5.06
Organic Matter	trace	trace
Total Solids	43.20	62.61
Gases	Cubic Inches	Cubic Inches
Carbonic Acid Gas	7.25	4.60
Sulphureted Hydrogen	trace	9.25

These analyses show that the waters are valuable as tonics, antacids, diuretics and aperients, and of value in dyspepsia, constipation, anæmia, rheumatism, liver and kidney troubles.

PIRU MINERAL SPRINGS

Located in Ventura County are a number of undeveloped mineral springs. The Piru is one of these.

RUBICON SODA SPRINGS

These excellent mineral soda springs are romantically situated in the beautiful Garden Valley, on the Rubicon River, some eleven miles west of Lake Tahoe. Everything surrounding them partakes of the picturesque—the tall mountains covered with groves of pine and spruce and capped by old century cedars. Here and there are traces of the slow yet persistent march of huge glaciers of bygone days; here and there are seen the volcanic sentinels in the form of huge granite pillars silently watching the Rubicon as its bright, silvered stream silently glides along the moss-covered banks. The hillsides are covered with sweet-scented shrubbery, and the valley with flowers, imparting their fragrant aromas to the ozonized mountain atmosphere—a most valuable combination for consumptives, asthmatics, persons suffering with chronic bronchitis, catarrh, etc., etc.

The owner of this beautiful mountainous resort is erecting commodious accommodations for guests and visitors.

The mountains afford ample opportunity for exercise with the gun, as the river does with the rod.

The atmosphere is bright, clear, pure and invigorating, imparting new life to the overworked brain and underworked body of busy city life.

The mineral springs themselves belong to the alkalo-carbonated class of waters, so valuable in the treatment of the many diseases noted under that chapter (*quod vide*), such as dyspepsia and gastric catarrh, torpidity of the liver and constipation of the bowels, Bright's disease of the kidneys, inflammation of the bowels and bladder, etc., etc. For a tonic the waters are excellent. Their action is also diuretic, detergent, aperient and antacid.

They are located at an elevation of 6,200 feet above the sea level, and are pure, clear and sparkling, containing, besides the mineral ingredients, large quantities of carbonic acid gas, so useful in the treatment of stomachic disorders.

New and excellent roads have been built, and the trip to Rubicon Soda Springs is full of picturesqueness and romance as the waters are full of health-giving and restorative qualities.

SALT LAKE

There is quite a body of water known as Salt Lake in Mono County, east of the geysers and located in Long Valley. The water is slightly charged with the chlorides of sodium, magnesium and calcium.

SALT SPRINGS

Unnamed and undeveloped. Situated:

On the south side of Mokelumne River, some six miles south of Silver Lake, in Calaveras County.

In Inyo County, north of Inyo Range and east of Black Mountain.

In Trinity County, eighty miles from Red Bluff, on a branch of Strong Creek.

On the east side of Panamint Valley, in Inyo County.

In Tehama County, on Salt Creek.

On the east side of Death's Valley, in Inyo County, eight miles south of the bend of Furnace Creek.

Near the Armagosa Mines, in San Bernardino County.

In Alameda County, northeast of Patterson's Pass.

SALT WELLS

In San Bernardino County there are a number of salt wells, located between Borax Flats and Indian Wells, in Salt Wells Valley. The waters are heavy, chlorinated and saline. A few are reported to be carbonated.

Salt deposits and salt mountains are numerous on this coast.

SAN BERNARDINO HOT SPRINGS

These springs are located in San Bernardino mountains and county. Some confusion has arisen about the identity of these springs and the Arrowhead Hot Springs,

FALLS NEAR SAN BERNARDINO

in the same county. The Arrowhead Springs are situated some fourteen miles farther inland and at a greater altitude, over 2,000 feet, and near the mountain, with the space denoted "Arrowhead."

The San Bernardino Springs (altitude 1,600 feet) are hot, having a temperature of 100° F. and 175° F., and the waters are largely calcic and earthy. Like most springs they have acquired some local repute, and are used for drinking and bathing purposes.

SAN BERNARDINO HOT SPRINGS
CALCIC AND SALINE

	No. 1	No. 2
Mineral Ingredients	Parts in 100,000	Parts in 100,000
Sodium Chloride	12.80	13.40
Sodium Sulphate	81.70	80.20
Potassium Sulphate	2.30	trace
Magnesium Carbonate	trace	trace
Calcium Carbonate	10.70	11.00
Ferrous Carbonate	trace	trace
Silica	20.50	22.40
Total Solids	128.00	127.00

No. 1 is the large spring in front of the hotel, and No. 2 is the spring about two hundreds west of the hotel. The analyses were made by Oscar Loew.

SAN JUAN CAPISTRANO SPRINGS

These springs are light carbonated and much used in the southern portion of the State. They lie in San Bernardino County, near Capistrano.

SAN JUAN CAPISTRANO SPRINGS

Mineral Ingredients	Parts in 100,000	Mineral Ingredients	Parts in 100,00
Sodium Chloride	10.53	Calcium Carbonate	trace
Sodium Carbonate	11.10	Magnesium Carbonate	trace
Sodium Sulphate	trace	Lithia	trace
Potassium Carbonate	trace	Silica	7.66

Total Solids, 29.29

A. 15

For cystic and renal troubles this water has been found beneficial. The above analysis was made by Oscar Loew in 1876.

SAN MARCOS SULPHUR SPRINGS

These sulphur waters are found seven miles northwest of Santa Barbara, in the same county. They have a temperature of 120° F., and are used locally for skin diseases, etc.

SAN JUAN HOT SPRINGS

These springs, like the San Marcos, have attained some celebrity in the treatment of syphilis and cutaneous diseases. No analysis.

SAN RAFAEL SPRINGS

The water is slightly saline and carbonated, and used locally to a limited extent. The springs are situated near the town of San Rafael, in Marin County.

SANTA BARBARA HOT SPRINGS

These famous hot sulphurous and soda springs are situated in the beautiful Santa Ynes Mountains, six and a half miles northeast of Santa Barbara city. The springs are picturesquely located amid the forest-covered mountains at an elevation of 1,450 feet above the sea level.

Excellent accommodations have been provided at the springs, and the resort is rapidly becoming celebrated.

On the premises we find some thirty mineral springs, some of which are sulphurous, others saline and chalybeate, ranging in temperature from 99° F. to 122° F. Seven of the principal springs are used for drinking and bathing purposes.

SAN MARCOS HOTEL AND GROUNDS AT SANTA BARBARA

On careful chemical analysis No. 1 and No. 2 and the Sulphur Spring yield:

SANTA BARBARA "SULPHUR SPRINGS"
CARBONATED AND SULPHUR SPRINGS

	OSCAR LOEW, Analyst, 1876		DR. WINSLOW ANDERSON Analyst, 1888
Mineral Ingredients	No. 1 Parts in 100,000	No. 2	U. S. gal. contains Grains
Sodium Chloride................ 8.7		7.6	1.74
Sodium Carbonate.............29.6		24.8	2.17
Sodium Sulphate 5.0		trace	14.92
Potassa...........................trace		trace	——
Magnesium Sulphate..........——		——	7.75
Calcium Sulphate..............trace		trace	6.03
Aluminium Sulphate...........——		——	2.90
Arsenic ....——		——	trace
Silica.............................. 4.2		6.0	1.18
Sulphuric Acid...................——		—·——	trace
Organic Matter.................——		——	trace
Total Solids.........47.5		38.4	35.95
Gases			Cubic Inches
Carbonic Anhydride...........trace		trace	19.14
Sulphureted Hydrogen.......trace		trace	9.16

These waters are of great value in the treatment of rheumatism, gout, joint affections, Bright's disease, liver trouble and bladder irritation. Being antacid, considerable benefit may be derived from the waters in dyspepsia and acid conditions of the blood and urine.

Perhaps the greatest benefit accrues from bathing in the sulphurous and saline waters, especially in syphilitic and scrofulous contaminations, glandular enlargements and chronic skin diseases.

At the time the country was under Spanish control a commission was sent out to report on these hot springs. The waters were highly recommended by them for many diseases, particularly skin diseases. Since that time thousands of visitors and invalids have used the waters with decided benefit.

Recently a large and commodious hotel and a spacious Pagoda bath-house, with stained glass and every modern facility, have been constructed.

It will be observed that the waters resemble much the famous Hot Springs in Arkansas. The resort is a growing one and deserves success.

SANTA ROSA WHITE SULPHUR SPRINGS AND RESORT

The Santa Rosa Springs are pleasantly situated about two miles from the town of Santa Rosa in Sonoma County. The surrounding country is delightful and the climate is beautiful. At the springs we find a growing resort; good accommodation and a well-kept and thriving place.

The springs flow in abundance, having waters of the light salino-sulphurous class. The waters are mostly sulphureted and cold, having temperatures from 59° F. to 62° F.

The principal spring is found to contain on analysis:

SANTA ROSA SPRINGS
LIGHT-SALINO-SULPHUROUS
Dr. WINSLOW ANDERSON, Analyst, 1886
Temperature 60.4° F.

Mineral Ingredients	U. S. gal. contains Grains	Mineral Ingredients	U. S. gal. contains Grains
Sodium Chloride	5.72	Calcium Sulphate	1.40
Sodium Carbonate	2.19	Ferrous Carbonate	trace
Sodium Sulphate	6.90	Alumina	.93
Potassium Carbonate	.63	Borates	trace
Magnesium Carbonate	.75	Silica	1.16
Magnesium Sulphate	9.07	Organic Matter	trace
Calcium Carbonate	trace		

Total Solids, 28.75

Gases	Cubic Inches
Free Carbonic Acid Gas	4.16
Free Sulphureted Hydrogen	6.47

The action of this water is slightly aperient and diuretic, acting on the stomach, liver and intestinal tract. It is useful in congestion of the liver due to malarial poisoning and in rheumatism, kidney and bladder troubles, and skin diseases.

Excellent bathing facilities have recently been constructed, the water being artificially heated.

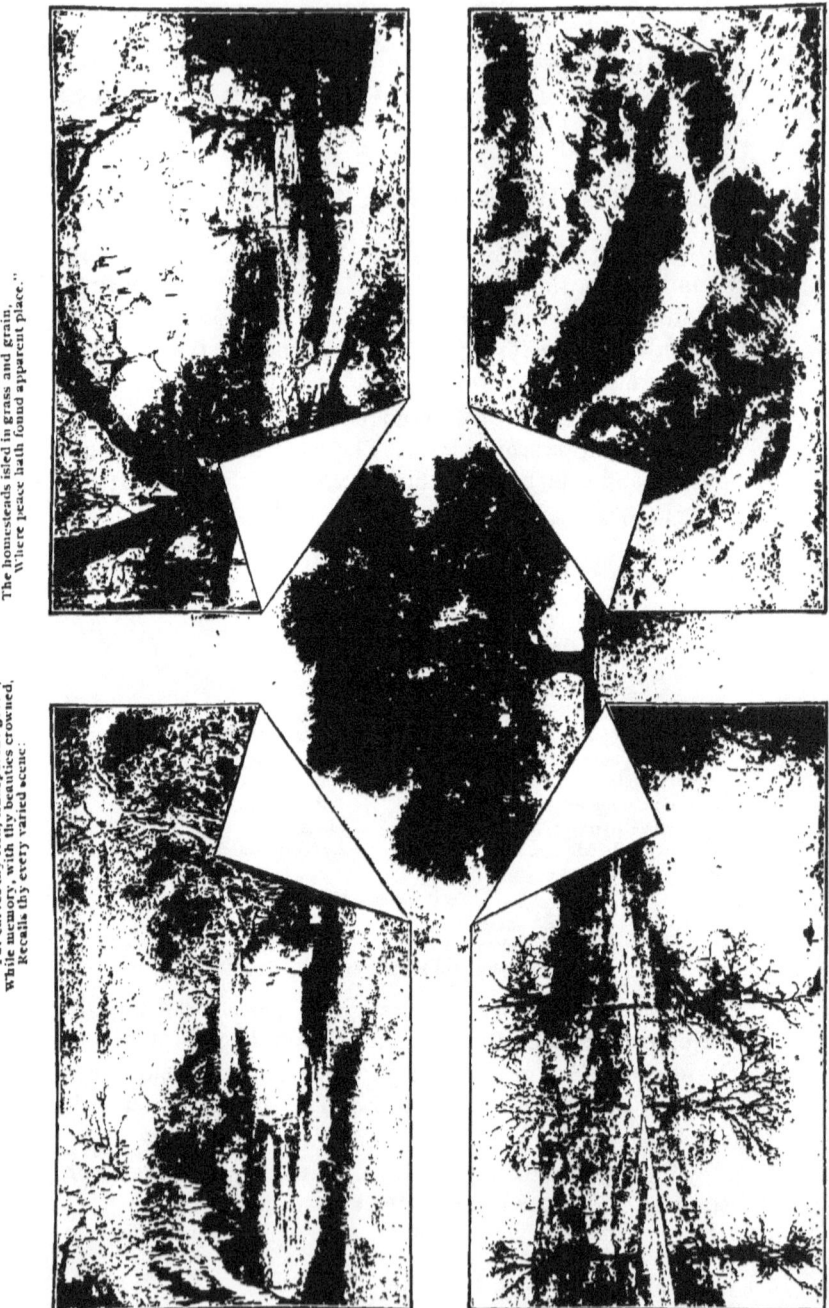

"The hills that wave in graceful chain—
The shores of Nature's loveliest trace;
The homesteads isled in grass and grain,
Where peace hath found apparent place."

"Clear mirror of the region round!
Far curves thy rich, transparent green;
While memory, with thy beauties crowned,
Recalls thy every varied scene:"

SANTA YSABEL COLD AND HOT SULPHUR SPRINGS

Several of the most valuable mineral springs in the State are located two and a half miles southeast of Paso Robles on the line of the Southern Pacific Railroad, and are known as the "Santa Ysabel Springs."

They are picturesquely situated in a small cañon about one mile east of the Salinas River. Surrounded on all sides are the rolling hills covered with groves of gigantic oaks, towering pines and clustering manzanitas, which shade the many cozy nooks and commanding outlooks on the premises. The hillsides are clad in luxuriant foliage, sweet scented shrubbery and a profusion of flowers of many hues, which are all pleasing to the eye and render the bright, pure and invigorating mountain air redolent with fragrance. As you sit at these yet undeveloped fountains, viewing the charming scenery and breathing the tonic ozonized mountain atmosphere, mixed with the sweet and fragrant aromas of the flora, the mountain stream glides along its silvered path amid fern laden, moss covered banks with here and there a rippling miniature cascade, and as the birds are chirping and singing their happy notes, a feeling of luxurious contentment fills your very soul and you regret you cannot remain forever in this paradise.

> " Not a cloud in all the sky,
> Save a few light fleeces,
> Which here and there, half mist, half air,
> Like foam on the ocean go floating by."

The climate belongs distinctively to that smiling sunny south where the air is balmy and the thermometer ranges from about 60° F. to 75° F. all the year around.

The springs themselves are located in the center of a large tract of land, at an elevation of 1,000 feet above the sea, and distant from the coast about thirty miles. The soil is unusually rich and fertile, producing every known variety of fruit as ascertained from the U. S. experimental station close by.

ADOBE BUILDINGS AT SANTA ISABEL AND VICINITY

The main warm sulphur spring, "No. 1" is situated near the side of the road in this beautiful little cañon. It is six feet long and four feet wide and flows the enormous amount of 20,000 gallons per hour. The waters are clear and sparkling, lightly sulphureted and freely carbonated, having a temperature of 96.3° F. Subjecting this spring to a careful chemical analysis, it is found to contain:

SANTA YSABEL WARM SULPHUR SPRING No. 1.
SALINO-SULPHURETED
Dr. WINSLOW ANDERSON, Analyst, 1886

Temperature 96.3° F.

Flows 20,000 gallons per hour

Mineral Ingredients	U. S. gal. contains Grains	Mineral Ingredients	U. S. gal. contains Grains
Sodium Chloride	18.10	Magnesium Sulphate	4.85
Sodium Bicarbonate	29.04	Calcium Carbonate	2.45
Sodium Carbonate	6.91	Calcium Sulphate	2.32
Sodium Sulphate	7.25	Manganese Carbonate	.13
Sodium Iodide	trace	Ferrous Carbonate	.98
Potassium Bromide	trace	Borates	trace
Potassium Iodide	trace	Alumina	.73
Potassium Chloride	trace	Barium Salts	trace
Potassium Carbonate	.83	Silica	1.63
Magnesium Carbonate	6.16	Organic Matter	trace

Total Solids, 81.43

Gases	Cubic Inches
Free Sulphureted Hydrogen	4.65
Free Carbonic Acid Gas	11.75

From this analysis it will be observed that the water is very similar to the famous Arkansas Springs. For centuries this and the other springs have been used by the Indians and early Mexicans and Spanish settlers and Franciscan Fathers, who both drank and bathed in the water. Tradition tells us that they traveled hundreds of miles to reach the springs where marvelous cures were made; facts substantiated through the personal experience of the present inhabitants.

The waters are tonic, antacid, diuretic, aperient and alterative, acting on the organs of secretion and excretion, stimulating the process of eliminating the morbific and deleterious agencies of tissue metamorphosis, thereby purifying the blood and establishing healthy normal action of all the organs.

SANTA YSABEL RANCH HOUSE AND ADOBE RUINS

VIEW FROM SUMMIT OF HILL BACK OF RANCH HOUSE

No. 2. Warm Sulphur Spring. This spring lies a few feet east of No. 1 and a little nearer the road. On analysis it is found to be very similar in composition.

No. 2. SANTA YSABEL

SALINO-SULPHUROUS

Dr. Winslow Anderson Analyst, 1886

Temperature 96.2° F.

Mineral Ingredients	U. S. Gal. contains Grains	Mineral Ingredients	U. S. Gal. contains Grains
Sodium Chloride	18.07	Magnesium Sulphate	4.76
Sodium Bicarbonate	29.02	Calcium Sulphate	2.31
Sodium Carbonate	6.83	Calcium Carbonate	2.50
Sodium Sulphate	7.30	Manganese Carbonate	.12
Sodium Iodide	trace	Ferrous Carbonate	.95
Potassium Iodide	trace	Alumina	.71
Potassium Bromide	trace	Borates	trace
Potassium Chloride	trace	Barium Salts	trace
Potassium Carbonate	.81	Silica	1.05
Magnesium Carbonate	6.15	Organic Matter	trace

Total Solids, 81.18

Gases	Cubic Inches
Free Sulphureted Hydrogen	4.60
Free Carbonic Acid Gas	11.08

No. 3 is a warm sulphur mud spring situated a few feet west of No. 1.

No. 3. WARM SULPHUR MUD SPRING

SALINO-SULPHUROUS MUD

Dr. Winslow Anderson, Analyst, 1886

Temperature, 95° F.

Mineral Ingredients	U. S. gal. contains Grains	Mineral Ingredients	U. S. gal. contains Grains
Sodium Chloride	17.10	Magnesium Sulphate	3.94
Sodium Bicarbonate	27.04	Calcium Carbonate	2.45
Sodium Carbonate	7.06	Calcium Sulphate	2.35
Sodium Sulphate	7.25	Manganese Carbonate	.36
Sodium Iodide	trace	Ferrous Carbonate	.63
Potassium Iodide	trace	Alumina	.65
Potassium Bromide	trace	Borates	trace
Potassium Chloride	trace	Barium Carbonate	trace
Potassium Carbonate	.43	Silica	6.32
Magnesium Carbonate	5.73	Organic Matter	.76

Total Solids, 82.07

Gases	Cubic Inches
Free Sulphureted Hydrogen	4.71
Free Carbonic Acid Gas	7.10

DRIVE ON BANK OF YSABEL LAKE

The hot sulphurous mud is excellent for bathing purposes, as indeed are the other warm sulphur springs. Extensive facilities for this purpose will be constructed in the near future and many cases of rheumatism, gout, glandular enlargements, chronic joint diseases and cutaneous affections may hope for much relief by prolonged bathing in these sulphurous water and mud baths.

About a quarter of a mile farther up the little cañon are located the cold or white sulphur springs. They bubble up in many places over an area of some several hundred feet. The temperature varies from 56° F. to 60° F. and the flow is not nearly so extensive as it is in the warm springs. The cold or white sulphur waters are also tonic, antacid, and alterative, and in a less marked degree laxative and diuretic. In other respects they resemble the warm sulphurous water, excepting that they are much lighter. The following analyses are of the two principal (Nos. 1 and 2) springs located near the road.

SANTA YSABEL SPRINGS
(Nos. 1 and 2 Cold or White Sulphur Springs)
LIGHT ALKANO-SULPHURETED

	Dr. Winslow Anderson, Analyst, 1889 *Temperature 59° F.*	Dr. Winslow Anderson, Analyst, 1889 *Temperature 59.2° F.*
Mineral Ingredients	U. S. Gal. contains Grains	U. S. Gal. contains Grains
Sodium Chloride	11.47	11.50
Sodium Carbonate	13.16	13.09
Sodium Sulphate	5.10	5.07
Sodium Iodide	trace	trace
Potassium Iodide	trace	trace
Potassium Bromide	trace	trace
Magnesium Carbonate	7.41	7.37
Magnesium Sulphate	4.05	4.00
Calcium Carbonate	1.09	1.06
Calcium Sulphate	2.90	2.95
Manganese Carbonate	.34	.35
Ferrous Carbonate	.25	.26
Alumina	.83	.84
Silica	1.17	1.20
Organic Matter	trace	trace
Total Solids	47.78	47.69
Gases	Cubic Inches	Cubic Inches
Free Sulphureted Hydrogen	3.24	3.25
Free Carbonic Acid Gas	11.41	11.30

STREAM ABOVE YSABEL LAKE

From the mineral ingredients these hot and cold sulphurous waters exhibit on analysis, we pronounce them of great therapeutic value, especially in chronic rheumatism, chronic arthritis, scrofula and glandular enlargements and chronic cutaneous diseases. For torpidity of the liver and bowels, dyspepsia, and catarrhal affections of the kidneys and bladder, experience teaches us that this class of water promises much relief and assists materially the internal medication in effecting a cure.

Persons suffering with consumption, chronic bronchitis, asthma, catarrhal affections of the naso-pharynx, etc., may expect to do well in a climate so mild and exhilarating and by the use of the sulphurous steam and waters.

The mineral springs and surrounding country are owned by a San Francisco syndicate. Extensive improvements have already begun, good roads and building sites for hotels and cottages are laid out and a depot landing selected. A large mountain lake is in course of construction, which will be from 800 to 1,000 feet long by several hundred feet broad. On its waters will be several pleasure boats. About one hundred feet above it on a pleasant plateau, having a commanding view over the entire Salinas Valley, will be reared a large and commodious hotel, surrounding it will be built several cozy cottages for private and family use. Excellent facilities for hot sulphurous steam, water and mud bathing will be arranged at the principal springs. Within a short distance of the hotel will be convenient railroad facilities.

With the natural advantages of climate, soil and picturesque surroundings and the excellent mineral waters and pure mountain streams, Santa Ysabel Resort promises to be one of the pleasantest inland watering places in that section of the country.

The Santa Ysabel Resort will be under the patronage of the Presbyterian Church, a sufficient guarantee that it will be a well-kept and properly conducted place, where families

may be sent unattended with perfect safety.   There will be
no saloons or whisky-shops and the surroundings will be
eminently proper.

SARATOGA SPRINGS

In Inyo County at the south end of Funeral Range and
a little south of Death's Valley are located these pleasant
springs.   The immediate neighborhood of Funeral Range

REMAINS OF PREHISTORIC DAM WITH CROSS-SECTION

and Death's Valley need not detract from the resort which
is in every way a good one and constantly growing in popularity.

SARATOGA MINERAL SPRINGS

These Saratoga Springs are located in Lake County,
about fourteen miles from Lakeport.   The waters are cold

and contain sulphur, magnesia, soda and iron. There is a growing resort on the place, where visitors may enjoy the beautiful mountain scenery in the vicinity, as well as the water.

SEIGLER'S SPRINGS

These noted springs are located at the foot of Seigler Mountain at an elevation of 2,372 feet above the sea, in Lake County. They are near Adam's and Bonanza Springs. Seigler Springs lie in Seigler Valley, which is about one and a half miles long by half a mile in width. The surrounding country with the excellent drives afford magnificent views and recreation compared with the narrow limits of the ordinary city life. There are found twenty or more springs containing soda, magnesia, iron and arsenic. The flow approximates 3,000 gallons per hour.

The "Arsenic" Spring has a temperature of 96° F. and is much used for syphilis, scrofula and cutaneous diseases.

The Soda Spring is alkaline and carbonated and is a delicious drinking water. This has been used with much success in Bright's disease, bladder troubles, etc.

The Magnesia Spring is strongly charged with Epsom salt and carbonic acid gas. A glassful before breakfast insures an easy and painless evacuation.

The Sulphur Spring is mostly used for bathing and for lung, liver and rheumatic troubles.

Accommodations are good and one's time can be very pleasantly spent in this mountainous resort, where one feels freed from all the toils and cares of the world.

SHAFER'S HOT SPRINGS

These springs are located in Lassen County at the north end of Henry Lake. The waters are thermal, having a temperature of 210° F. and contain salines and sulphates. There is a local resort.

A 16.

SHAFER'S HOT SPRINGS

F. W. CLARKE, Analyst, 1883

Temperature 210° F.

Mineral Ingredients	Grammes per Litre	Mineral Ingredients	Grammes per Litre
Sodium Sulphate	0.4715	Sodium Chloride	0.3266
Calcium Sulphate	.0409	Potassium Chloride	.0180
Magnesium Sulphate	.0020	Silica	.1008
Sodium Silicate	.0613		

Total Solids (50.18 grains to gallon)..........1.0211

SHASTA SODA

These soda springs are located on Shasta scenic route in Siskiyou County. They are carbonated and ferruginous and much prized by travelers.

SIMMON'S HOT SULPHUR SPRINGS

These sulphurous waters have gained more than a local reputation in the alleviation of chronic rheumatic troubles. They are located in Sulphur Cañon, near Wilbur Springs in Colusa County. The waters have a temperature of 170° F. and are highly charged with sulphureted hydrogen. Extensive improvements are reported.

SKAGGS' HOT SPRINGS

These excellent springs are located in Sonoma County, in the Coast Range, eight miles west of Clairville, twenty miles east of the coast and fourteen miles northwest of Healdsburg. The locality is picturesque and salubrious, surrounded by the many huge mountains covered with rich California verdure. The resort is of easy access by the S. F. & N. P. Railroad to Clairville and thence by stage eight miles. The comfort of the guests at the hotel is well looked after and everything is first class.

There are four principal springs at Skaggs', flowing about 1,000 gallons per hour. The waters are thermal, alkalo-chalybeate having a temperature from 120° F. to 140° F. The main spring is located in the dry bed of Dry Creek, a tributary of Russian River. The water is agreeably pungent to the taste and clear and sparkling as it issues forth from mother earth.

SKAGGS' SPRINGS

ALKALO-CARBONATED (HEAVY)

Dr. Winslow Anderson Analyst, 1888		Prof. Hilgard Analyst,
Temperature 128.5° F.		

Mineral Ingredients	U. S. Gal. contains Grains	U. S. Gal. contains Grains
Sodium Chloride.........	5.54	5.900
Sodium Bicarbonate.....................	159.03	161.270
Sodium Biborate..................	24.19	26.470
Sodium Iodide...............	.13	trace
Potassium Chloride................	.34	.200
Potassium Sulphate.................	.94	.260
Potassium Iodide.................	trace	———
Magnesium Carbonate.................	11.46	11.113
Magnesium Sulphate........	1.27	———
Calcium Carbonate.................	3.75	2.197
Ferrous Carbonate.................	.62	.054
Barium Carbonate.................	.25	.240
Strontium Carbonate.................	trace	.024
Lithium Carbonate.................	trace	.060
Alumina.................	trace	.004
Silica........	8.83	7.023
Organic Matter.................	trace	———
Total Solids.................	216.35	214.815

Gases	Cubic Inches	
Free Carbonic Anhydride.................	124.25	Not Determined

SODA BAY

This natural curiosity is situated on the west shore of Clear Lake and consists of a large spring, several feet in diameter, from which a large quantity of water rises. It is so heavily charged with natural carbonic acid gas as to raise the waters as it bubbles up nearly a foot from the surface of the water, giving the spring the appearance of active ebullition. The water is alkaline and stained with ferruginous salts. It also contains soda, lime and magnesia, etc.

SODA LAKE

On the Mojave River and in the Saline Flats in San Bernardino County is located this saline and soda lake.

SODA LAKE
(Saline Flats on Mojave River)

OSCAR LOEW, Analyst, 1876

Mineral Ingredients	Parts in 100,000	Mineral Ingredients	Parts in 100,000
Sodium Sulphate	63.1	Phosphoric acid	trace
Calcium Sulphate	21.2	Potassium	trace
Magnesium Sulphate	8.5	Lithium	trace
Sodium Chloride	170.8	Organic Matter	19.0
Silica	trace		

Total Solids, 282.6

SODA POND

In Mono County, just north of the Salt Lake, in Long Valley, is situated quite a large soda pond. The water is said to consist largely of carbonates of soda in solution.

SODA SPRINGS

Unclassified and undeveloped. Situated *in Tuolumne County*, nine miles west of Tuolumne River, west of Mono Pass.

Three miles northwest of little Shasta in Siskiyou County.

Near Shasta County line on the Sacramento River, in Siskiyou County.

On a branch of McCloud River in Shasta County, east of Lower Soda Springs.

At the bifurcation of McCloud's River in Shasta County.

East of Volcano Springs in San Diego County.

At Soda Bar, two miles from the Oregon line in Siskiyou County.

In San Diego County southwest of Volcano Springs.

CLEAR LAKE

On the Linkville Yreka Road, in Siskiyou County.

In Lake County, eight miles east of Clear Lake.

In Inyo County, east side of Death's Valley and eight miles below Salt Springs.

All the soda springs are cold and the waters are alkaline carbonated. No analysis.

SPRINGS OF DOS PALMAS

OSCAR LOEW, Analyst

Mineral Ingredients	Parts in 100,000	Mineral Ingredients	Parts in 100,000
Calcium Carbonate..............trace		Silica...........................trace	
Calcium Sulphate................. 32.6		Phosphoric Acid.............trace	
Magnesium Sulphate............ 31.0		Manganese...... ....trace	
Sodium Chloride..................230.8			

Total Solids, 294.4

The Dos Palmas Springs are located in Coahuila Valley in San Diego County. The waters are chlorinated, having temperatures from 82° F. to 92° F. The waters are used locally for kidney and bladder troubles.

STEAMBOAT SPRINGS

In Plumas County, southeast of Lassen's Peak, are located a number of boiling springs, which spout and puff as they issue from the earth's crust. No analysis.

STEWART'S HOT SPRINGS

These are located in Warm Spring Valley in Modoc County and are attracting considerable attention. No analysis in time for this article. An analysis of all the springs will be made as soon as possible.

SULPHUR SPRINGS

Unclassified. Located *in Tehama County*, four miles southwest of Tom's Head Mountain.

West of San Fernando Peak in Ventura County.

Santa Cruz County has several hot sulphurous springs, seven miles east of Watsonville.

On Brown's Creek in Shasta County and southeast of Douglas City.

West fork of south branch of the Sacramento River, Shasta County.

Above mouth of Castle Creek in Shasta County.

In Modoc County, three miles north of Canby in Black Cañon.

One mile northeast of Buena Vista Lake and thirty miles south of Tulare Lake in Kern County.

In Kern County ten miles west of the southern shore of Tulare Lake.

On the south side of San Fernando Mountain in Los Angeles Co. (Analysis.)

In Siskiyou County, eight miles north of Blake Butte, in the southern part of Shasta Valley.

Twenty miles from San Miguel Mission, seven miles north of the county line, in Monterey County.

In Mohawk Valley in Plumas County.

In San Bernardino County, near Dry Lake.

Northeast of San Luis Mountains is San Luis Obispo County.

Ten miles northeast of San Miguel Mission is San Luis Obispo County.

In Inyo County, six miles south of McComrich's well, in Desert Valley.

South of Resting Spring in Inyo County.

SULPHUR SPRING

(South side of San Fernando Mt.)

OSCAR LOEW, Analyst

Mineral Ingredients	Parts in 100,000	Mineral Ingredients	Parts in 100,000
Sodium Carbonate	6.21	Phosphoric Acid	trace
Calcium Carbonate	50.60	Sulphohydric Acid	5.00
Sodium Sulphate	23.87	Potassium	trace
Sodium Chloride	trace	Lithium	trace
Alumina	trace	Iron	trace
Silica	trace	Manganese	trace
Organic Matter	trace		

Total Solids, 85.68

Gases

Carbonic Acid Gas.........In Excess

Summit Soda Springs

Near the summit of the Sierra Nevada Mountains are located these famous soda springs. They are of easy access by the Central Pacific Railway to Summit Station and thence by stage or carriage some twelve miles to the springs in Placer County.

The drive is a beautiful one, winding along through scenes of mighty grandeur, over mountains and down valleys, surrounded by lofty mountains covered with evergreen groves of pines and spruce and cedars and perpetually donned with snowy caps. Here and there are the deep ravines, covered with picturesque foliage, then mountainous peaks which seem to reach into the skies. Now we gain the summit and the magnificent view of the high Sierras is unobstructed for miles around. Here the imposing majesty of the Creator is felt in all His sublimity.

The springs themselves (see illustration) are located in an expansion at the head of the deep cañon along which winds one of the forks of the American River. The surroundings are exceedingly picturesque. The air is pure, dry and invigorating, and cool and pleasant during the heated Summer season. The altitude is 6,009 feet above the level of the sea—an excellent place for persons suffering with bronchial, catarrhal and asthmatic affections.

At the springs the accommodations at the hotel and cottages are superior—bathing facilities have been added, and everything is convenient and pleasant.

The hills are well stocked with wild game and the rivers are filled with mountain trout, affording all the sport with the gun and rod that may be desired.

For a man worn out with the mental strain of business cares who seeks rest for his brain and invigorating exercises for his body, no more delightful place than Summit Soda Springs and health resort can be found.

On analysis the Summit Soda yields:

SUMMIT SODA SPRING
ALKALO-CHALYBEATE WATER

Mineral Ingredients	DR. WINSLOW ANDERSON Analyst, 1888 U. S. gal. contains Grains	J. F. RODOLPH Analyst, 1878 U. S. gal. contains Grains
Sodium Chloride	26.18	26.22
Sodium Bicarbonate	4.11	——
Sodium Carbonate	5.75	9.50
Potassium Carbonate	.82	trace
Magnesium Carbonate	4.05	4.20
Calcium Bicarbonate	38.93	43.20
Calcium Carbonate	6.55	——
Ferrous Oxide	——	1.75
Ferrous Carbonate	2.70	——
Borates	trace	——
Alumina	1.13	1.75
Silica	1.94	2.06
Organic Matter	trace	——
Total Solids	92.16	88.68
Gases	Cubic Inches	Cubic Inches
Free Carbonic Acid Gas	{ 187.25 Saturated	186.35

The water is antacid, diuretic, aperient and tonic; most excellent in the treatment of dyspepsia, torpidity of liver and bowels, Bright's disease, irritation and stone in bladder, etc.

Comparative Table of Analyses of the different drinking waters used in some of the larger cities in America, including Lake Tahoe's waters:

ANALYSES DRINKING WATERS

Total Solid Ingredients	U. S. gal. contains Grains	Total Solid Ingredients	U. S. gal. contains Grains
Lake Tahoe	3.00	Detroit River (Detroit)	5.72
Lake Cochituate (Boston)	3.37	Ohio River (Cincinnati)	6.74
Mill River (New Haven)	4.00	Hudson River (Albany)	7.24
Lake Ontario, (Rochester)	4.16	Lake Michigan (Chicago)	8.01
Jamaica Pond { Brookline. Boston	4.40	Croton River (N. Y. City)	10.60
		Spring Valley Water (S. F.)	11.20
Schuylkill River (Phila.)	5.50		

This shows that Lake Tahoe is the purest and best water available in America for drinking purposes and that Spring Valley water is the worst in use in any large city. Let us have water from Lake Tahoe by all means.

GENERAL VIEW OF LAKE TAHOE—BY THOMAS MORAN

LAKE TAHOE

My soul bowed down in wondering humble awe,
When first thy peaks and waterfalls I saw ;
And every hour but shows how vain 'twould be
For my frail mind to hope to picture thee.
Thy spell shall live and those who view thee now
Have passed with ages 'neath thy mighty brow,
And like thy mists, in gorgeous gleamings curled,
Our names have melted from this changing world.
—Mrs. Jean Bruce Washburn

TAHOE SPRINGS ON LAKE TAHOE

These are located near the State line. They are described under the head of Lake Tahoe or Carnelian Springs.

Lake Tahoe itself is a magnificent sheet of water located most picturesquely among the snow-capped Sierras at an elevation of 6,250 feet. It is about 20 miles long and 12 miles wide and has an average depth of 1,500 feet. Lake Tahoe's water is exceptionally pure. On analysis it is found that one gallon does not yield more than three grains of solids, whereas Spring Valley in San Francisco shows over nine grains of foreign matter to the gallon. It is hoped that the day may come when we shall enjoy "Tahoe's" pure water for drinking purposes in San Francisco.

TEMESCAL HOT SPRINGS

Located in San Diego County. Used locally.

TASSAJARA HOT SPRINGS

At the head of Arroyo Seco, in Monterey County, are located these hot saline and sulphurous waters. The Spanish and the aborigines in the vicinity frequented these springs for many years and were apparently much benefited. No analysis; used locally.

THERMAL ACID SPRINGS

These remarkable springs are found in the Caso Range, twelve miles east of Little Owen's Lake and sixteen miles southeast of Olamoha, in Inyo County.

The country for miles around the springs is rich in pure crystallized sulphur, having no doubt been ejected by the sulphurous laden steam in the form of sulphurous anhydride (SO_2). On being exposed to the atmosphere and surrounding products of sulphureted hydrogen (H_2S), the sulphur was deposited pure and water liberated.

$$SO_2 + 2H_2S = 2H_2O + 3S.$$

This is probably the explanation of the formation of these large sulphur banks.

The water now flows through the small crevices and fissures accompanied by sulphurous steam and vapors in rather limited quantities.

On analysis the waters are found to contain:

THERMAL ACID SPRINGS

Unknown Analyst

Mineral Ingredients	Parts per 1,000	Mineral Ingredients	Parts per 1,000
Sodium Sulphate	2.5	Sulphuric Acid	78.4
Potassium Sulphate	15.1	Nitric Acid	trace
Magnesium Sulphate	15.3	Chlorine	trace
Calcium Sulphate	1.2	Ammonia	trace
Aluminium Sulphate	127.0	Lithium	trace
Ferric Sulphate	33.2		

	Parts
Total Solids	272.7
Water pure	727.3
Total	1,000.0

This water is not much used as far as the writer can learn, nor does he know to whom to give credit for the above analysis. Well diluted and properly administered this acid sulphate water ought to be valuable in many conditions requiring tonic and astringent remedies.

The sulphur banks will also prove of commercial value in time.

THERMAL SPRINGS

Unnamed and unimproved. Located *on Battle Creek* some five miles above Morgan's Ranch in Plumas County.

In Inyo County, opposite Black Rock, on Owen's River.

Near the mines of Darwin in Inyo County.

Ten miles east of Telescope Peak in Inyo County.

TOLENAS SPRINGS

These noted springs are located about five miles north of the town of Suisun in Solano County, adjoining the famous Tolenas onyx quarries on the Tolenas or Armijo's Rancho. They are easily reached by rail from San Francisco or Sacramento to Suisun and then by easy stage over a good level road.

The resort is at an elevation of 1,235 feet and is pleasantly located. The view from the springs is quite extensive. On a clear day the State capital, Suisun Bay and Valley, Gordon, Wooden, Elmira, etc., may easily be seen. There are nineteen springs in all at Tolenas, flowing between six hundred and seven hundred gallons per hour. The temperature varies from 60° F. to 65° F.

TOLENAS
ALKALO-SALINE AND CHLORINATED

	Dr. Winslow Anderson Analyst, 1888 *Temperature 61.5° F.*	J. Hawston, Jr. Analyst
Mineral Ingredients	U. S. gal. contains Grains	U. S. gal. contains Grains
Sodium Chloride	194.16	215.92
Sodium Carbonate	46.93	53.36
Sodium Bicarbonate	6.45	—
Sodium Biborate	19.13	20.56
Potassium Chloride	6.47	5.68
Potassium Iodide	1.75	2.08
Magnesium Carbonate	11.58	10.88
Calcium Carbonate	49.80	48.32
Ferrous Carbonate	.89	.64
Alumina	1.10	.96
Silicates	1.92	1.00
Organic Matter	trace	—
Total Solids	340.18	360.00
Gases	Cubic Inches	Cubic Inches
Free Carbonic Acid Gas	31.27	33.73

These springs have had a local reputation for over thirty years and of late the water has been bottled and sold extensively all over the State. The resort is also in a flourishing condition, which indicates public appreciation.

The water is indorsed by many who have used it. In chronic skin affections, eczema, scrofula, and syphilitic contaminations the water seems to do well. Chronic gastric disturbances, kidney and bladder diseases improve under the use of the Tolenas Soda. The water is gently aperient and strongly diuretic.

TULE RIVER SODA SPRINGS

On the south fork of the Tule River a little east of Porterville in Tulare County lie a number of cold soda springs. The waters are much used locally and a resort is contemplated. No analysis at present.

TUSCAN OR LICK SPRINGS

These springs are located about nine miles northwest of Red Bluff on the Sacramento River in Tehama County. They are reached by stage from Red Bluff.

The springs lie in the center of a rough and rugged country showing signs of extinct volcanic action, at an elevation of about six hundred feet. In this volcanic region of Tuscan are upwards of one hundred springs. Three only are in active use and are known as the " Red" Spring, the " White" Spring and the " Black" Spring. The " Red" Spring was analyzed by Dr. F. W. Hatch several years ago, and contains:

TUSCAN RED SPRINGS
Temperature 78° F. to 80° F.

Sulphuric Acid	Carbonic Acid
Hydrochloric Acid	Bicarbonate of Iron
Lime	Potassium Chloride
Sodium Chloride	Magnesia
Lithia	Alumina

Iodine

The " White" and the " Black" have not been analyzed. The waters are saline and sulphurous and have proved efficacious in rheumatism, constitutional syphilis, glandular disorders, etc. The waters resemble somewhat the famous Blue Lick Springs of Kentucky.

They act as a diuretic in small quantities and laxative in larger ones. Excellent bathing facilities have been arranged for hot and cold baths and many people make pilgrimages yearly to this volcanic resort.

The waters cannot be analyzed in time for issuance in this work.

Doolan's Ukiah Vichy Springs and Health Resort

About thirty-two miles from Cloverdale and three short miles from Ukiah, county seat of Mendocino, are located the Doolan Vichy Springs. They lie nestled among the enchanting hills which fringe the boundary line of Lake and Mendocino counties. They were formerly reached by a drive from Cloverdale or Calistoga, but now the springs are of much more easy access by the picturesque and interesting route of the new San Francisco and North Pacific Railroad which runs to Ukiah.

Nature could not have done more for this natural sanitarium than it has. From April to'November the climate is delightfully balmy and the atmosphere is pure, clear and invigorating. In the immediate vicinity are excellent fishing and gunning. The resort is rapidly growing and commodious accommodations can be found. Bathing facilities are claimed to be superior. The waters are gaining in celebrity in cases of gout, rheumatism, scrofula and chronic kidney and bladder troubles and cutaneous diseases.

Bathing in the Vichy renders the skin soft and clear and very soon heals up any skin irritation.

The waters belong to the alkalo-carbonated class and are clear and sparkling and of an agreeably pungent taste.

DOOLAN'S UKIAH VICHY SPRINGS

Their action is almost identical, as indeed is their chemical composition, with the noted Ems on the Lahn; Fachingen of Nassau, Germany; and Vichy of Grande Grille, France.

From the following chemical analysis, made in 1888, it will be observed that the waters from the Doolan Vichy are heavily charged with carbonic acid gas and carbonates and that they contain some iron and potassium salts.

Solid Ingredients in One Gallon of 231 inches in Grains	Doolan's Ukiah VICHY of California analyzed by Dr. ANDERSON Temp. 93° F.	VICHY France Grande Grille analyzed by BOQUET Temp. 105.8° F.	FACHINGEN Nassau Germany analyzed by FRESENIUS Temp. not given	EMS ON THE LAHN Germany analyzed by FRESENIUS Temp. 115° F.
Sodium Chloride................	28.60	32.80	36.48	62.16
Sodium Carbonate..............	195.52	208.00	155.84	84.24
Sodium Sulphate...............	.36	18.32	1.12	trace
Sodium Phosphate..............	......	6.24	.41	......
Potassium Chloride	.09	......	......	......
Potassium Carbonate..........	trace	16.32	......	......
Potassium Sulphate...........	trace	......	......	3.03
Magnesium Carbonate........	19.75	11.04	10.85	6.80
Calcium Carbonate............	18.14	18.48	16.09	10.00
Ferrous Carbonate.............	.07	.16	.64	.16
Strontium Carbonate..........	......	.08	trace	trace
Barium Carbonate.............	......	......	......	trace
Lithium Carbonate.............	......	......	trace	......
Borates........	trace	......	......	......
Arseniates........	......	.08	......	......
Aluminates........	trace	......	trace	trace
Silica..........................	5.92	.40	2.09	2.88
Total......................	268.43	311.88	223.52	169.27
Gases, cubic inches Carbonic Acid Gas.............	224.75	14.74	263.76	54.24

For an antacid, tonic, aperient, diuretic and alterative mineral water the Ukiah Vichy ranks among the finest on the Coast.   They have proved highly beneficial in Bright's disease, torpidity of the bowels and liver.   For dyspepsia and acid conditions of the urine and the blood they are excellent.

The waters are soon to be sold commercially.

Owing to recent developments the flow has increased enormously, flowing now about 20,000 gallons per hour.

On the premises are numerous springs which will soon be developed and analyzed.

A. 17

UPPER SODA SPRINGS

These excellent mineral springs are situated at an elevation of 2,363 feet, in Siskiyou County on the Shasta scenic route of the Southern Pacific Railroad. They are beautifully surrounded by the almost precipitous walls of the Sacramento Cañon, mountain streams and immense forests of pine, fir, spruce, cedar, etc., and some of the grandest scenery in the Sierras. Ever watching is Mt. Shasta, with its snow-capped apex and bountifully fertile base. Here and there are the enormous granite shafts, rising hundreds of feet into the atmosphere. The projecting rocks and huge boulders seemingly almost ready to fall and dash headlong down the cañon.

At the springs is a very quiet, commodious, comfortable, good, old-fashioned hotel with large airy verandas. Plenty of room for everybody both inside and outside.

The mineral water belongs to the Alkalo-carbonated or *soda* class, sparkling and effervescing, exceedingly palatable and wholesome.

It contains chlorides of soda and potassa, carbonates and bicarbonates of soda, magnesia, potassa, iron, lime, manganese, sulphates of soda and magnesia (Glauber's and Epsom salts) and a large quantity of free carbonic acid gas.

These springs have become famous in the treatment of uric acid and lithic acid diatheses, gravel and calculi, inflammation and irritation of the bladder and kidney, etc.

The water acts as an aperient, diuretic, tonic and antacid, and is of great value in acid conditions of the stomach, blood or urinary secretions.

VALLEJO SULPHUR SPRINGS

Near Vallejo in Solano County are located several sulphur springs, which are used considerably, locally. The temperature ranges from 80° F. to 90° F. The waters act well on torpid portal circulation.

Volcanic Mineral Springs

In Death's Valley, Inyo County, are located several remarkable springs. One of these was analyzed by Prof. Price several years ago and found to contain over 4,000 grains of solids in a gallon. The water is ?chlorinated and alkaline, containing, presumably, both sulphureted hydrogen and carbonic acid gas.

VOLCANIC MINERAL SPRINGS

Prof. Price, Analyst

Mineral Ingredients	U. S. gal. contains Grains	Mineral Ingredients	U. S. gal. contains Grains
Sodium Chloride	1840.72	Organic Matter	13.48
Sodium Carbonate	1724.11	Iodine	traces
Sodium Sulphate	651.02	Bromine	traces
Sodium Sulphide	46.34	Iron	traces
Potassium Chloride	132.30	Boracic Acid	traces
Magnesia and Lime	traces	Phosphoric Acid	traces
Silica	14.28		

Total Solids, 4422.25.
Gases not determined

The water is not used to any extent.

Volcanic Springs

Several other volcanic springs are located near Volcanic Station on the line of the S. P. R. R. in San Diego County. The waters are reported to be sulphurous.

Warm Springs

Unnamed, and not, or little, improved. Located *in Kern County* near the head of Walker's Basin.

In Modoc County, ten miles west of Alturas, in Warm Spring Valley.

On the east side of Pitt River on Hot Creek and north of Round Valley in Modoc County.

Twelve miles southwest of Camp Cody in San Bernardino County.

Near Little Owen's Lake.

WARM SPRING, NEAR LITTLE OWEN'S LAKE

Oscar Loew, Analyst, 1876

Mineral Ingredients	Parts in 100,000	Mineral Ingredients	Parts in 100,000
Sodium Chloride	26.9	Calcium Carbonate	12.0
Sodium Carbonate	45.2	Magnesium Carbonate	trace
Sodium Sulphate	8.0	Silica	trace
Potassa	trace	Organic Matter	trace

Total Solids, parts 92.1

In Inyo County, nine miles from Amargosa mines.

In Lassen County, southwest of Pittville.

These springs, and many others of which I cannot obtain any reliable information, are warm and sulphurous in character. A few are reported calcic and alkaline. Their temperature varies from 85° to 132° F.

WARM SULPHUR SPRINGS

In Kern County on Posa Creek, near Simmis Valley, are found a number of warm springs, with temperatures from 74° to 90° F. The waters are used locally for rheumatism and cutaneous affections.

WARNER'S RANCH SPRINGS

These are situated some thirty miles from San Diego in San Diego County. These springs are also spoken of as Aguas Calientes by the Spanish, although not identical with the Aguas Calientess described under that head.

The flow of Warner's Springs is about 1,500 gallons per hour. The temperature is from 74° to 142° F. The waters are sulphurous and saline and much resorted to by the inhabitants of that section of the country. Their great reputation is the treatment of syphilis and chronic skin diseases. A pleasant little resort has been established on the place and a great many people go there to bathe and drink the waters.

WATERMAN'S SPRINGS

These mineral springs are located about a mile west of Arrowhead in San Bernardino County. They are the private property of Mr. Waterman, who prizes them highly. A description for publication is not obtainable.

WHITE SULPHUR SPRINGS

These excellent springs and resort are located about two and a half miles south of St. Helena in Napa County. They are of easy access by ferry and rail via Napa City to St. Helena and thence by carriage. The resort is well-kept, commodious and pleasant. The grounds are handsomely laid out and ornamented with shrubbery and evergreens, orchards and flowers.

The White Sulphur comprise nine springs with temperatures from 69° F. to 142° F. The waters are light, sulphureted and alkaline and are much extolled by a great many who have used them. They seem very well adapted to the treatment of rheumatism and joint complications both by way of bathing and for internal use; also for congestion and inaction of the chylo-poetic viscera, glandular swellings and cutaneous affections.

ANALYSES WHITE SULPHUR SPRINGS.

MINERAL INGREDIENTS	No. 2 PROF. LE COSTE'S Analysis, 1871 Temp. 83.5° F. U. S. Gal. contains Grains	No. 5 DR. W. ANDERSON'S Analysis, 1888 Temp. 77.5° F. U. S. Gal. contains Grains	No. 6 PROF. LE COSTE'S Analysis, 1871 Temp. 86° F. U. S. Gal. contains Grains	No. 7 PROF. LE COSTE'S Analysis, 1871 Temp. 69.5° F. U. S. Gal. contains Grains	No. 9 DR. W. ANDERSON'S Analysis, 1888 Temp. 69° F. U. S. Gal. contains Grains
Sodium Chloride......................	21.72	22.36	23.41	14.23	11.91
Sodium Carbonate.........	......	.09	......	......	2.14
Sodium Sulphate....................	8.26	10.60	11.33	12.84	7.15
Magnesium Chloride...............	.87	1.41	2.22	.65	.45
Magnesium Carbonate............	.62	.75	.56	4.36	2.70
Calcium Chloride....................	1.32	.93	.86	.78	.35
Calcium Carbonate.................	1.25	1.87	2.45	5.56	5.82
Calcium Sulphide..................	......	.53	......	......	trace
Sodium Sulphide....................	2.65	.76	1.85	1.62	trace
Alumina............................	......	.23	......	......	.62
Silica...............................	......	.02	......	......	1.43
Organic Matter.....................	......	trace	......	......	trace
Total Solids..........................	36.69	40.15	42.68	40.04	32.57
SPECIFIC GRAVITY	1.00026	1.00038	1.00040	1.00038	1.00023
Gases	Cubic In.	Cubic In.	Cubic In.	Cubic In.	Cubic In.
Sulphureted Hydrogen............	6.15	5.19	4.25	trace	trace

WHITE SULPHUR SPRINGS.

Located *in Amador County*, two miles north of Plymouth.

In Inyo County, at the edge of Panamint Range, 12 miles north of Panamint.

In the town of Santa Rosa, in Sonoma County, used locally.

In Tehama County, southwest of Red Bluff, in Bear Gulch.

These waters are heavy and light, salino-sulphurous and sulphureted. Some are reported to have large excess of sulphureted hydrogen and others both carbonic acid gas and sulphureted hydrogen.

In Santa Rosa the water is used by most of the inhabitants for bathing, facilities having been constructed for hot steam, hot tub and plunge baths. It is observed that these hot sulphur baths are excellent for incipent colds and rheumatism and in many cases of chronic rheumatic troubles.

WILBUR SPRINGS.

These mineral springs are located thirty miles from Colusa in Colusa County. They are pleasantly situated and have acquired considerable reputation from their therapeutic properties. At the springs are good accommodations in the hotel and cottages and excellent camping facilities. The resort is reached by railroad to Williams and thence by stage. The waters are hot and sulphureted, containing:

WILBUR SPRINGS
THERMAL SALINO-SULPHURETED WATER
DR. WINSLOW ANDERSON, Analyst

Mineral Ingredients	U. S. gal. contains Grains	Mineral Ingredients	U. S. gal. contains Grains
Sodium Chloride	19.75	Calcium Carbonate	8.44
Sodium Carbonate	3.40	Calcium Sulphate	20.62
Sodium Sulphate	26.19	Ferrous Sulphate	4.16
Potassium Chloride	.46	Alumina	3.93
Potassium Iodide	.75	Silicates	6.95
Magnesium Carbonate	5.10	Organic Matter	1.74
Magnesium Sulphate	22.90		

Total Solids, 124.39

Gases	Cubic Inches
Sulphureted Hydrogen	43.97

WITTER'S MINERAL SPRINGS.

These mineral springs are pleasantly located in Lake County, about one mile east of Pearson's Springs, five miles from Upper Lake and three miles from Blue Lake.

The resort—a growing one—is picturesquely located, having good views of the lakes, valleys and mountains in the vicinity.

The resort comprises a good commodious hotel, several cottages and excellent bathing facilities for hot and cold mineral baths.

The springs are all cold and flow about sixty gallons per hour. They are at an elevation of 1,800 feet. There are cold soda and iron springs and cold sulphur springs. The principal water is known by the very emphatic if not euphonious name of "Dead Shot," having reference to the action of the water on the diseases for which it is recommended. These are : liver and kidney diseases and bowel disorders. The water contains:

WITTER'S MINERAL SPRINGS
"DEAD SHOT" ALKALO SULPHUROUS
Dr Winslow Anderson, Analyst

Temperature 59.3° F.

Mineral Ingredients	U. S. Gal. contains Grains	Mineral Ingredients	U. S. Gal. contains Grains
Sodium Chloride	17.42	Ferrous Carbonate	1.17
Sodium Carbonate	5.96	Manganese Carbonate	.86
Sodium Sulphate	11.50	Alumina	1.65
Potassium Carbonate	3.15	Borates	.42
Magnesium Carbonate	7.10	Silica	6.33
Magnesium Sulphate	20.62	Organic Matter	.76

Total Solids, 76.94

Gases	Cubic Inches
Carbonic Acid Gas	7.65
Sulphureted Hydrogen	5.25

Young's Natural Gas Well and Mineral Springs

These natural wonders are on the property of Mr W. G. Young and are located on the eastern edge of Kelseyville, on a little elevated ground about three miles south of Clear Lake. The surroundings are picturesque, lying, as they do, just within the lower extremity of Big Valley and near the base of "Uncle Sam" Mountain. The country is fertile and the land valuable, being among the best in Lake County. The climate of Lake County is noted the world over for its salubriousness, the air being mild, dry and balmy.

The elevation at the gas well is about 1,500 feet, giving a commanding view to the surrounding country; and well may Lake County be called the "Switzerland of America,"

for a more picturesque view could not be found than that of
Clear Lake, lying in the embrace of the surrounding mountains peacefully smiling on the outstretched and prolific
valley with its gigantic oaks, the largest in the State, and
old Uncle Sam, like an ancient guardian, watching the
beautiful landscape.

GAS WELL AT KELSEYVILLE ON THE PROPERTY OF W. G. YOUNG
From a Photograph by G. E. Moore, Lakeport

In 1888 Mr Young bored a well for gas. When down
about one hundred and fifty-eight feet a large volume of
water and gas rushed out with considerable force. The well
is now ejecting, and has been so continuing from the time

it was bored, a large stream of mineral water and gas, which rises into the air to a height of about forty feet, from seventy to eighty times every minute. For a moment it stops and then comes another violent ejection in a true Geyser style. The flow is about 6,000 gallons per hour and the water has a temperature of 76° F.

Within a year it is estimated that over 5,000 people visited this natural wonder, the only one in the State of its kind. The water has been extensively used by the inhabitants of Kelseyville and surroundings, who pronounce it excellent for the liver, kidney and bowels.

YOUNG'S GAS WELL
ALKALO-SALINE AND FERRUGINOUS WATER
Dr. Winslow Anderson, Analyst, 1889
Temperature 76° F.

Mineral Ingredients	U. S. Gal. contains Grains	Mineral Ingredients	U. S. Gal. contains Grains
Sodium Chloride	15.76	Manganese Carbonate	.18
Sodium Carbonate	36.52	Ferrous Carbonate	4.95
Sodium Sulphate	19.16	Barium Carbonate	trace
Potassium Carbonate	3.40	Lithium Carbonate	trace
Potassium Iodide	.78	Borates	3.12
Magnesium Carbonate	7.14	Alumina	5.13
Magnesium Sulphate	21.90	Silicates	6.45
Calcium Carbonate	6.36	Organic Matter	trace
Calcium Sulphate	9.72		

Total Solids, 140.62

Gases	Cubic Inches
Free Carbonic Acid Gas	9.60
Petroleum and Carburetted Hydrogen (inflammable gas)	traces

This water contains all the elements to make it valuable therapeutically. Its action is tonic and anticid, of great value in dyspepsia; it is aperient or laxative according to the amount taken, acting on the liver and bowels; it is also diuretic from the carbonates and would be of value in Bright's disease of the kidneys, inflammation of the bladder, in acid conditions of the urine, etc., etc. We understand that the owner contemplates erecting a first-class health and pleasure resort on the premises. Bathing facilities would also be of considerable importance, as the water, heated, would be very useful for rheumatism, chronic joint diseases, white swellings, scrofula and chronic cutaneous diseases, and glandular enlargements.

Several inflammable gas wells are also found on the grounds—(see article in book, "Inflammable Natural Gas"). One of these is about fifty feet west of the spring, and during our visit in 1888 the gas was ignited and burned with a pale blue flame and yellow tips, giving forth empyreumatic odors, probably due to the incomplete oxidation of the carbon products. This can easily be remedied by using suitable burners. The gas is largely light carburetted hydrogen (CH_4) and of considerable value in an economic point of view as the whole of Kelseyville and a large resort besides could easily be lighted and heated by the natural product from Nature's chemical laboratory.

Several other minor gas wells are also found on the premises and it is contemplated to utilize this valuable product.

ZEM ZEM SPRINGS

(MEANING "HOLY WELL IN MECCA")

These mineral springs are located on the southeastern side of Clear Lake, in Lake County. The waters have a temperature of 64° F., and contain:

Soda, alumina, magnesia, silica, etc. The waters are highly carbonated.

There is a small resort at the springs.

For dyspepsia and kidney diseases the waters seem to be beneficial. For rheumatism and diseases of the liver, the springs have some notoriety. Analysis said to have been made by Dr. Boon.

Sulphur	50 parts in 1,000
Iron	27 parts in 1,000
Magnesia	28 parts in 1,000
Solid Matter	105 parts in 1,000

" Tired of its own bright charms, the golden day
Rests in the arms of evening; all is still;
Nor leaf, nor flower moves, lest the spell might break
Which holds the Earth bound fast in twilight chains.
From yonder hawthorn tree some leaf-hid bird
Breathes to the dying day a soft farewell,
That, mingling with the stillness, seems to weave
Into the silence threads of melody.
Wild roses, since the dawn, have deeply blushed
Beneath the sun's warm kisses; now at Eve
Faint odors, passing sweet, possess the air—
Rich incense offered to the Queen of Night !
For lo! a silvery light falls all around,
As up the violet heavens a pale young moon
Climbs high and higher still.
        A low-voiced breeze,
Rising with balmy sigh amid the hills,
Comes ling'ringly adown the rocky glen,
Floats o'er the uplands, kisses every flower,
And whispers that the fair, sweet Day is dead !
Now restful thoughts and calm enter the heart,
And soothe the tired brain; as from on High
A blessing falls on everything below:
Cool shades to Evening—rest and peace to Man.''

The following analytical tables of all the important mineral waters in the world are arranged alphabetically, commencing with those of Oregon, Western States, Southern and Southwestern States, Virginia, Pennsylvania, New York, New England and lastly the European mineral springs, numbering in all about two hundred.

OREGON MINERAL SPRINGS

BEER SPRINGS, ORE.
PURGATIVE
Analyst unknown

Mineral Ingredients	U. S. gal. contains Grains	Mineral Ingredients	U. S. gal. contains Grains
Sodium Chloride	8.96	Calcium Chloride	5.36
Magnesium Chloride	4.48	Calcium Carbonate	15.44
Magnesium Carbonate	12.88	Calcium Sulphate	8.48
Magnesium Sulphate	48.40	Vegetable Ex. Matter	3.36

Total Solids, 107.36

DES CHUTES HOT SPRINGS, WASCO COUNTY, ORE.
THERMAL
L. M. DORNBACH and PROF. E. N. HORSFORD, Analysts
Temperature 143° and 145° F.

Mineral Ingredients	U. S. gal. contains Grains	Mineral Ingredients	U. S. gal. contains Grains
Sodium Chloride	20.416	Potassium Chloride	2.000
Sodium Carbonate	34.496	Magnesium Chloride	1.216
Sodium Sulphate	9.464	Calcium Sulphate	1.824
Sodium Silicate	8.200	Iron	trace

Total Solids, 77.616

Gas	Cubic Inches
Carbonic Acid	22.56

WILHOITS SODA SPRINGS, CLACKAMAS COUNTY, ORE.
ALKALINE AND SALINE
J. H. VEACH, M. D., Analyst

Mineral Ingredients	U. S. gal. contains Grains	Mineral Ingredients	U. S. gal. contains Grains
Sodium Chloride	201.000	Magnesium Sulphate	6.480
Sodium Carbonate	87.568	Calcium Carbonate	32.224
Sodium Sulphate	3.400	Ferrous Carbonate	6.000
Magnesium Carbonate	85.320	Iodine	trace

Total Solids, 421.992

Gas	Cubic Inches
Carbonic Acid	336.00

Western States Mineral Springs

ALPENA WELL, ALPENA CO., MICH.

SULPHURETED

Prof. S. P. Duffield, Analyst

Mineral Ingredients	U. S. gal. contains Grains	Mineral Ingredients	U. S. gal. contains Grains
Sodium Chloride	68.256	Calcium carbonate	38.296
Sodium Carbonate	10.912	Calcium Sulphate	30.056
Potassium Carbonate	trace	Ferrous carbonate	1.360
Magnesium carbonate	37.288	Alumina and silica	3.083

Total Solids, 189.256

Gases	Cubic Inches
Carbonic Acid	8.40
Sulphureted Hydrogen	35.36

BETHESDA SPRINGS, WAUKESHA CO., WIS.

ALKALINE AND CALCAREOUS

C. F. Chandler, Analyst

Mineral Ingredients	U. S. gal. contains Grains	Mineral Ingredients	U. S. gal. contains Grains
Sodium Chloride	1.160	Calcium Carbonate	11.824
Sodium Carbonate	.872	Ferrous Carbonate	.032
Sodium Sulphate	.544	Alumina	.120
Sodium Phosphate	trace	Silica	.736
Potassium Sulphate	.456	Organic Matter	1.984
Magnesium Carbonate	7.344		

Total Solids, 25.072

BUTTERWORTH SPRINGS, GRAND RAPIDS, MICH.

CALCAREOUS

S. P. Duffield, Analyst

Mineral Ingredients	U. S. gal. contains Grains	Mineral Ingredients	U. S. gal. contains Grains
Sodium Chloride	12.728	Calcium Carbonate	5.792
Sodium Carbonate	3.472	Calcium Sulphate	75.136
Potassium Chloride	9.816	Ferrous Carbonate	.704
Magnesium Chloride	41.856	Alumina	.408
Magnesium Carbonate	3.456	Silica	.512
Calcium Chloride	6.101	Organic Matter and Loss	.664

Total Solids, 160.648

EATON RAPIDS, EATON CO. MICH.

CALCAREOUS

Mineral Ingredients	Frost Well Prof. Duffield Analyst U. S. gal. contains Grains	Shaw Well Prof. Kedzie Analyst U. S. gal. contains Grains	Mosher Well Prof. Kedzie Analyst U. S. gal. contains Grains
Sodium Chloride	7.672	.896	.896
Sodium Carbonate	......	11.568	5.376
Sodium Sulphate	......	......	......
Potassium Carbonate	......	1.272	1.152
Magnesium Carbonate	7.592	3.840	4.520
Magnesium Sulphate	......	......	......
Calcium Carbonate	38.528	20.736	19.432
Calcium Sulphate	3.864	48 128	45.160
Ferrous Carbonate	1.984	1.232	1.000
Ammonium Nitrate	......	trace	trace
Silicic Acid	......	1.400	2.336
Silica	13.112	......	......
Organic matter and loss	.752	.896	.848
Total Solids	73.504	89.968	80.920

Gases	Cubic Inches	Cubic Inches	Cubic Inches
Carbonic Acid	18.36	16.00	15.36
Sulphureted Hydrogen	......	trace	trace

EATON RAPIDS, EATON CO., MICH.

CALCAREOUS

Mineral Ingredients	Stirling Well C. T. Jackson, M. D. Analyst U. S. gal. contains Grains	Bordine Well Prof. Kedzie Analyst U. S. gal. contains Grains
Sodium Chloride	......	1.496
Sodium Carbonate	4.336	3.776
Sodium Sulphate	10.488	......
Potassium Carbonate	......	2.272
Magnesium Carbonate	......	4.976
Magnesium Sulphate	7.824	......
Calcium Carbonate	......	28.104
Calcium Sulphate	45.984	57.496
Ferrous Carbonate	2.336	1.024
Ammonium Nitrate	......	......
Silicic Acid	......	......
Silica	......	2.000
Organic Matter and Loss	......	......
Total Solids	70.908	101.744

Gases	Cubic Inches	Cubic Inches
Carbonic Acid	16.00	16.00

FRENCH LICK SPRINGS, ORANGE CO., IND.
SULPHURETED

Mineral Ingredients	Pluto's Well J. G. Rogers, M. D. Analyst U. S. gal. contains Grains	Pro-erpine J. G. Rogers, M. D. Analyst U. S. gal. contains Grains
Sodium Chloride.....	110.536	90.920
Sodium Carbonate.................................	....	10.528
Sodium Sulphate.....	22.368	36.720
Potassium Chloride................................	....	5.008
Magnesium Chloride........	....	8.048
Magnesium Carbonate.............................	1.584	4.496
Magnesium Sulphate..........................	18.112	29.328
Calcium Chloride.................................	5.344	......
Calcium Carbonate................................	6.944	20.288
Calcium Sulphate................................	60.584	141.000
Alumininm and Iron Carbonates...................	trace	2.496
Silica	....	1.696
Total Solids	255.472	350.528
Gases	Cubic Inches	Cubic Inches
Carbonic Acid...................................	14.96	10.216
Sulphureted Hydrogen...........................	25.44	17.000

FRUIT PORT WELL, OTTAWA CO., MICH.
SALINE
C. G. WHEELER, Analyst

Mineral Ingredients	U. S. gal. contains Grains	Mineral Ingredients	U. S. gal. contains Grains
Sodium Chloride............	464.024	Calcium Chloride.......	111.104
Sodium Carbonate..........	4.520	Calcium Carbonate......	3.544
Sodium Sulphate...........	45.992	Ferrous Carbonate......	5.440
Potassium Chloride........	.432	Manganese Carbonate....	.080
Magnesium Chloride..... .	46.808	Alumina................	trace
Magnesium Carbonate.......	2.464	Silica and Silicates......	10.600
Magnesium Bromide........	.760		

Total Solids, 695.768

GREEN SPRINGS, SANDUSKY CO., O.
PURGATIVE
O. N. STODDARD, Analyst

Mineral Ingredients	U. S. gal. contains Grains	Mineral Ingredients	U. S. gal. contains Grains
Potassium Chloride..........	2.480	Ferrous Carbonate......	19.696
Potassium Bromide.........	16.760	Ferrous Sulphate........	6.528
Magnesium Carbonate.......	22.384	Alumina................	.976
Magnesium Sulphate........	36.136	Silica	6.096
Calcium Sulphate...........	105.408		

Total Solids, 216.464

Gas		Cubic Inches
Carbonic Acid		96.48

GREENCASTLE SPRINGS, PUTNAM CO., IND.

CHALYBEATE

Mineral Ingredients	North, or Daggy, Spring U. S. gal. contains Grains	Middle, or Dewdrop, Spring U. S. gal. contains Grains
Sodium Chloride.............................	.792	.696
Sodium Carbonate.................................	.096	.064
Sodium Sulphate..................................	.136	.069
Potassium Carbonate.............................	.088	.072
Magnesium Carbonate............................	4.704	5.336
Magnesium Sulphate............................	1.048	1.032
Calcium Carbonate...............................	14.552	11.880
Ferrous Carbonate.....	.408	2.384
Silicic Acid.....................................	.088	.008
Alumina......	.160	.072
Loss and Undetermined...........................	.096	.224
Total Solids....................	22.168	21.864

HUBBARDSTON WELL, IONIA CO., MICH.

CALCAREOUS

PROF. P. H. DOUGLASS, Analyst

Mineral Ingredients	U. S. gal. contains Grains	Mineral Ingredients	U. S. gal. contains Grains
Magnesium Carbonate......	6.352	Ferrous Oxide..........	.152
Calcium Carbonate.........	16.536	Silica	.136

Total Solids, 23,176

IDAHO HOT SPRINGS, CLEAR CREEK CO., COL.

THERMAL

J. G. DOHLE, Analyst

Temperature, 87° to 115° F.

Mineral Ingredients	U. S. gal. contains Grains	Mineral Ingredients	U. S. gal. contains Grains
Sodium Chloride.............	4.16	Magnesium Sulphate.....	18.72
Sodium Carbonate..........	30.80	Calcium Chloride	trace
Sodium Sulphate.............	29.36	Calcium Carbonate.......	9.52
Sodium Silicate.............	4.08	Calcium Sulphate........	3.44
Magnesium Chloride.........	trace	Ferrous Carbonate.......	4.16
Magnesium Carbonate........	2.88		

Total Solids, 107.12

A. 18

INDIAN SPRINGS, MARTIN CO., IND.

SULPHURETED AND SALINE

E. T. Cox, Analyst

Mineral Ingredients	U. S. gal. contains Grains	Mineral Ingredients	U. S. gal. contains Grains
Sodium Chloride..	39.368	Magnesium Sulphate....	30.302
Sodium Carbonate	3.616	Calcium Carbonate......	33.104
Sodium Sulphate	11.824	Calcium Sulphate..	20.232
Potassium Carbonate.......	2.520	Ferric Oxide...........	trace
Potassium Sulphate........	2.400	Iodides and Bromides......	trace
Magnesium Chloride........	.056	Silicic Acid...........	.448
Magnesium Carbonate.......	18.914	Aluminum Sulphate......	.832

Total Solids, 163.736

Gases	Cubic Inches
Carbonic Acid.......................	9.52
Sulphureted Hydrogen.................	3.36
Oxygen	3.92
Nitrogen.............	.648

LAFAYETTE, TIPPECANOE CO., IND.

SALINE AND SULPHURETED

C. M. Wetherell, M. D., Analyst

Mineral Ingredients	U. S. gal. contains Grains	Mineral Ingredients	U. S. gal. contains Grains
Sodium Chloride............	324.720	Calcium Carbonate......	8.352
Magnesium Chloride........	29.656	Calcium Sulphate.......	56.336
Magnesium Carbonate.......	28.720	Ferric Oxide	.496
Magnesium Iodide..........	trace	Aluminium	trace
Calcium Chloride	3.720	Silica.................	.404

Total Solids, 452.464

Gases	Cubic Inches
Carbonic Acid.......................	12.16
Sulphureted Hydrogen.................	1.02
Nitrogen............................	4.88

LANSING WELL, INGHAM CO., MICH.

SALINE

Dr. Jennings, Analyst

Mineral Ingredients	U. S. gal. contains Grains	Mineral Ingredients	U. S. gal. contains Grains
Sodium Chloride	266.792	Magnesium Carbonate...	11.368
Sodium Carbonate..........	64.752	Calcium Carbonate......	62.256
Sodium Sulphate...........	25.048	Ferrous Carbonate.......	1.144
Potassium Sulphate........	12.432	Silica.................	3.304

Total Solids, 447.096

Gas	Cubic Inches
Carbonic Acid.......................	196.00

LESLIE WELL, INGHAM CO., MICH.

CALCAREOUS

Prof. R. C. Kedzie, Analyst

Mineral Ingredients	U. S. gal. contains Grains	Mineral Ingredients	U. S. gal. contains Grains
Sodium Chloride	3.040	Calcium Sulphate	5.864
Potassium Carbonate	2.372	Ferrous Carbonate	1.368
Magnesium Carbonate	5.200	Silica	1.728
Calcium Carbonate	17.712	Organic Matter	.536

Total Solids, 38.320

Gas	Cubic Inches
Carbonic Acid	13.44

LODI ARTESIAN WELL, WABASH CO., IND.

SULPHURETED

Dr. Pahle, Analyst

Mineral Ingredients	U. S. gal. contains Grains	Mineral Ingredients	U. S. gal. contains Grains
Sodium Chloride	502.464	Calcium Chloride	47.928
Sodium Sulphate	2.136	Calcium Carbonate	2.016
Potassium Sulphate	.800	Calcium Sulphate	55.552
Magnesium Chloride	53.536	Calcium Phosphate	1.200
Magnesium Carbonate	.656	Silicic Acid	.520
Magnesium Iodide	trace	Sulphur (suspended)	5.000
Magnesium Bromide	.880	Nitrogenous Or. Matter	.800
Magnesium Sulphate	3.256		

Total Solids, 676.744

Gases	Cubic Inches
Carbonic Acid	undetermined
Sulphureted Hydrogen	7.92
Nitrogen	undetermined

MANITOU SPRING, EL PASO CO., COL.

ALKALINE

T. M. Drown, Analyst

Mineral Ingredients	Percentage	Mineral Ingredients	Percentage
Sodium Chloride	36.69	Potassium Chloride	10.01
Sodium Bicarbonate	24.01	Magnesium Bicarbonate	8.89
Sodium Sulphate	4.78	Calcium Bicarbonate	15.62

Total Solids, 100.00

MIDLAND WELL, MIDLAND CO., MICH.
PURGATIVE
S. P. Duffield, M. D., Analyst

Mineral Ingredients	U. S. gal. contains Grains	Mineral Ingredients	U. S. gal. contains Grains
Sodium Chloride	27.240	Calcium Sulphate	3.712
Sodium Sulphate	18.384	Aluminium Phosphate	1.440
Potassium Sulphate	68.472	Silica	2.464
Magnesium Chloride	1.824	Organic Matter	2.056
Calcium Chloride	5.176	Loss	2.672

Total Solids, 133.440

OWOSSO SPRING, SHIAWASSEE CO., MICH.
CHALYBEATE

Mineral Ingredients	U. S. gal. contains Grains	Mineral Ingredients	U. S. gal. contains Grains
Sodium Chloride	2.096	Ferrous Carbonate	11.544
Magnesium Carbonate	11.304	Alumina }	
Calcium Carbonate	17.824	Silica }	.616

Total Solids, 43.384

PERRY SPRINGS, PIKE CO., ILL.
ALKALINE

	No. 1 Middle Spring H. Engelmann, M. D. Analyst U. S. gal. contains Grains	No. 2 Upper Spring H. Engelmann, M. D. Analyst U. S. gal. contains Grains	No. 3 Lower Spring H. Engelmann, M. D. Analyst U. S. gal. contains Grains
Mineral Ingredients			
Sodium Sulphate	.440	1.096	1.384
Sodium Silicate	.120	.384	.576
Sodium & Potassium Silicates	2.640	2.280	3.448
Potassium Carbonate	1.592	1.448	1.256
Magnesium Carbonate	10.080	8.776	6.216
Calcium Carbonate	11.040	13.720	13.664
Ferrous Carbonate	.408	.320	.200
Aluminium Silicate			.272
Total Solids	26.320	28.024	27.016

SALT LAKE HOT SPRINGS, UTAH.
THERMAL
C. T. Jackson, Analyst

Mineral Ingredients	U. S. gal. contains Grains	Mineral Ingredients	U. S. gal. contains Grains
Sodium Chloride	19.544	Magnesium } Calcium } Carbonates	3.576
Sodium Sulphate	5.536		
Magnesium Chloride	.528	Calcium Chloride	4.528
Ferric Oxide	.168		

Total Solids, 33.880

SALT LAKE MINERAL SPRINGS

SULPHURETED

Unknown Analyst

Mineral Ingredients	Beck's Hot Springs Per cent	Warm Springs Per cent
Chloride of Sodium.......	.95506	.77248
Chloride of Magnesium...........................	.4334	.01588
Sulphate of Magnesium............................	......	......
Carbonate of Magnesium..........................	......	.03412
Chloride of Calcium	.06957	......
Sulphate of Calcium........	.01907	·13668
Silicate of Calcium..............................	.....	......
Carbonate of Calcium............	.03001	.03321
Chloride of Potassium............................	.03761	.03388
Sulphate of Potassium...........................	......	......
Alumina...	......	......
Silica...	.00315	.00212
Organic Matter..................................	trace	......
Iron..	trace	......
Iodine..	......	......
Bromine..	......	......
Water..	......	......
Volatile..	......	......
Other matter....................................	......	......
Total...	1.25871	1.02845

Gases	Cubic Inches
Free Carbonic Acid...........	undetermined
Sulphureted Hydrogen........	undetermined

SPARTA ARTESIAN WELL, MONROE CO., WIS.

CHALYBEATE

J. M. Hinson, Analyst

Mineral Ingredients	U. S. gal. contains Grains	Mineral Ingredients	U. S. gal. contains Grains
Sodium Chloride............	.112	Ferrous Carbonate......	8.664
Sodium Carbonate..........	.120	Manganese Carbonate...	trace
Sodium Iodide..............	trace	Barium Carbonate.......	trace
Sodium Sulphate............	1.840	Lithium Carbonate......	.016
Sodium Phosphate..........	.056	Strontium Carbonate....	.008
Potassium Sulphate.........	.528	Ammonium Carbonate...	trace
Magnesium Carbonate.......	1.992	Aluminium Phosphate...	.048
Calcium Chloride...........	.504	Silica	.232
Calcium Carbonate..........	.232	Hydrogen Sulphide.......	trace
Calcium Sulphate...........	.144		

Total Solids, 14.496

SCHUYLER SPRING, SCHUYLER CO., ILL.

CHALYBEATE

Dr. BLANEY, Analyst

Mineral Ingredients	U. S. gal. contains Grains	Mineral Ingredients	U. S. gal. contains Grains
Magnesium Sulphate	2.984	Alkaline Sulphates	7.832
Calcium Sulphate	73.936	Silica	1.312
Ferrous Sulphate	89.960		

Total Solids, 156.024

SPRING LAKE WELL, OTTAWA CO., MICH.

SALINE

PROF. C. G. WHEELER, Analyst

Mineral Ingredients	U. S. gal contains Grains	Mineral Ingredients	U. S. gal. contains Grains
Sodium Chloride	405.528	Calcium Carbonate	.096
Sodium Carbonate	.040	Ferrous Carbonate	.736
Sodium Sulphate	46.696	Manganese Carbonate	.048
Potassium Chloride	4.288	Lithia	trace
Magnesium Chloride	36.200	Ammonia	.016
Magnesium Carbonate	trace	Alumina	trace
Magnesium Bromide	2.168	Silica	.504
Calcium Chloride	113.416	Organic Matter	18.288

Total Solids, 628.024

ST. LOUIS SPRINGS, GRATIOT CO., MICH.

ALKALINE

S. P. DUFFIELD, M. D., Analyst

Mineral Ingredients	U. S. gal. contains Grains	Mineral Ingredients	U. S. gal. contains Grains
Sodium Carbonate	61.472	Calcium Silicate	5.600
Magnesium Carbonate	8.640	Ferrous Carbonate	.728
Calcium Chloride	trace	Silica	2.392
Calcium Carbonate	40.152	Organic Matter	1.664
Calcium Sulphate	55.400		

Total Solids, 176.048

Gases	Cubic Inches
Carbonic Acid	10.88
Sulphureted Hydrogen	trace

VERSAILLES SPRINGS, BROWN CO., ILL.
ALKALINE

Mineral Ingredients	Magnesia Spring G. A. Marriner Analyst U. S. gal. contains Grains	Ourry Spring J. V. Blaney, M. D. Analyst U. S. gal. contains Grains	Monitor Spring J. V. Blaney, M. D. Analyst U. S. gal. contains Grains
Sodium Chloride.................	trace	trace	trace
Sodium Carbonate................	....	7.624	7.624
Sodium and Potassium Carbonates..	1.320	trace	trace
Magnesium Carbonate............	8.952	7.464	6.984
Calcium Carbonate..............	14.600	12.112	16.136
Calcium Sulphate...............	trace	2.088	......
Ferrous Carbonate....	.064	......	2.136
Alumina and trace of Iron........	.....	.728	......
Silica	1.400	.816	1.704
Organic Matter.....	.....	trace	trace
Total Solids...........	26.336	30.832	34.584

Gas   Cubic Inches
Carbonic........................ ... .24.00

WEST BADEN SPRINGS, ORANGE CO., IND.
SULPHURETED

E. T. Cox, Analyst

Mineral Ingredients	U. S. gal. contains Grains	Mineral Ingredients	U. S. gal. contains Grains
Sodium Chloride............	77.984	Calcium Chloride	7.280
Sodium Carbonate	1.112	Calcium Carbonate.......	41.376
Sodium Sulphate	3.104	Calcium Sulphate.......	11.184
Potassium Carbonate........	.624	Ferric Oxide............	.088
Potassium Sulphate........	1.368	Iodide..................	trace
Magnesium Chloride........	11.400	Bromide	trace
Magnesium Carbonate.......	39.160	Silicic Acid.............	.440
Magnesium Sulphate........	36.152	Aluminium Sulphate.....	4.552

Total Solids, 235.824

Gases	Cubic Inches
Carbonic Acid........................	5.12
Sulphureted Hydrogen.................	4.88
Oxygen	1.68
Nitrogen	5.44

YELLOW SPRINGS, GREENE CO., OHIO
CALCAREOUS

WAYNE and LOCK, Analysts

Mineral Ingredients	U. S. gal. contains Grains	Mineral Ingredients	U. S. gal. contains Grains
Sodium Chloride............	.152	Calcium Carbonate......	19.568
Magnesium Chloride........	.168	Calcium Sulphate	1.352
Calcium Chloride...........	1.544	Ferric Oxide............	.392

Total Solids, 23.176

SOUTHERN AND SOUTHWESTERN MINERAL SPRINGS

ARKANSAS HOT SPRINGS

Mineral Ingredients	Parts in 10,000	Mineral Ingredients	Parts in 10,000
Sodium Chloride	.0003	Alumina	.0137
Sodium Sulphate	.0115	Iron	.0030
Potassium Sulphate	.0070	Iodine	trace
Magnesium Chloride	.0010	Bromine	trace
Calcium Sulphate	.0033	Water	.0043
Calcium Silicate	.0139	Silica	.0567
Calcium Carbonate	.1203	Organic Matter	.0420

Total Solids, .2800

Gases

Free Sulphureted Hydrogen........... excess

Free Carbonic Acid................... excess

HOT SALINO-SULPHUROUS

DRS. OWEN and CONE, Analysts

Temperature, 100° to 148° F

Qualitative

Sodium Chloride	Magnesia Sulphate
Sodium Sulphate	Calcium Bicarbonate
Magnesia	Iron
Magnesia Sub-carbonate	

CALCIC-THERMAL

PROF. E. H. LARKIN, Analyst

Temperature 95° to 180° F.

Mineral Ingredients	U. S. gal. contains Grains	Mineral Ingredients	U. S. gal. contains Grains
Sodium Chloride	.008	Ferric Oxide	.104
Sodium Sulphate	.376	Iodine	trace
Potassium Sulphate	.232	Bromine	trace
Magnesium Carbonate	.128	Alumina	.448
Calcium Carbonate	3.968	Silica	1.864
Calcium Sulphate	.112	Organic Matter	.704
Calcium Silicate	.464	Water	.144

Total Solids, 8.552

BLADEN SPRINGS, CHOCTAW CO., ALA.

ALKALINE

Mineral Ingredients	Vichy Spring J. L. & W. P. Riddell Analysts U. S. gal. contains Grains	Branch Spring J. L. & W. P. Riddell Analysts U. S. gal. contains Grains
Sodium Carbonate	46.328	41.208
Magnesium Carbonate	.288	.608
Calcium Carbonate	.872	2.136
Calcium Sulphate	2.256	2.792
Ferrous Carbonate	.496	.232
Manganese Sulphate	trace	.....
Organic Matter	2.256	1.896
Total Solids,	52.496	48.872

Gases	Cubic Inches	Cubic Inches
Carbonic Acid	65.44	59.20
Sulphureted Hydrogen	trace	trace
Chlorine	1.84	1.84

ALKALINE

Mineral Ingredients	Old Spring Prof. R. T. Brumby Analyst U. S. gal. contains Grains	Sulphur Spring J. L. & W. P. Riddle Analyst U. S. gal. contains Grains
Sodium Chloride	7.696	.....
Sodium Carbonate	32.888	34.936
Magnesium Carbonate	1.360	.648
Calcium Carbonate	2.752	2.416
Calcium Sulphate	.016	2.960
Ferrous Carbonate	.....	.760
Ferrous Sulphate	.240	.....
Manganese Sulphate	.....	trace
Crenic Acid	.728	.....
Hypocrenic Acid	.600	.....
Silica and Alumina	2.104	.....
Organic Matter	.....	1.248
Loss	.320	.....
Total Solids	48.704	42.968

Gases	Cubic Inches	Cubic Inches
Carbonic Acid	32.56	52.88
Sulphureted Hydrogen	undetermined	.56
Chlorine	.....	1.84

BLOUNT SPRINGS, BLOUNT CO., ALA.

SULPHURETED

Mineral Ingredients	Red Sulphur Prof. R. Brumby Analyst U. S. gal. contains Grains	Sweet Sulphur Prof. R. Brumby Analyst U. S. gal. contains Grains
Sodium Chloride...................................	32.32	30.88
Magnesium Chloride..............................	6.00	.....
Magnesium Carbonate............................	4.40	3.60
Magnesium Sulphate..............................	1.60	2.40
Calcium Carbonate................................	6.80	4.48
Ferrous Carbonate................................	1.92	1.12
Total Solids.....	53.04	42.48

Gases	Cubic Inches	Cubic Inches
Carbonic Acid.....................................	6.00	6.00
Sulphureted Hydrogen............................	14.96	12.56

BLUE LICK SPRINGS, UPPER AND LOWER,
NICHOLAS, CO., KY.

SULPHURETED

Mineral Ingredients	Upper J. F. Judge and A. Fennel Analysts U. S. gal. contains Grains	Lower Robert Peter, M. D. Analyst U. S. gal. contains Grains
Sodium Chloride.....................................	516.536	512.856
Potassium Chloride	1.800	1.392
Potassium Sulphate................................	12.976	8.936
Magnesium Chloride..	37.728	32.392
Magnesium Carbonate............................	.144	.136
Magnesium Bromide..............................	3.808	.240
Magnesium Iodide................................	.152	.048
Calcium Carbonate................................	25.064	23.656
Calcium Sulphate................................	44.136	33.992
Alumina (Calcium Phosphate and Ferric Oxide)........	1.968	.360
Silicic Acid......................................	1.000	1.104
Loss..	14.880	17.728
Total Solids.....	660.192	632.840

Gases	Cubic Inches	Cubic Inches
Carbonic Acid.....................................	48.16	98.80
Sulphureted Hydrogen..	8.16	18.24

CHARLESTON ARTESIAN WELL, S. C.

THERMAL

Prof. C. U. Shephard, Jr., Analyst

Temperature 87° F.

Mineral Ingredients	U. S. gal. contains Grains	Mineral Ingredients	U. S. gal. contains Grains
Sodium Chloride	75.672	Calcium Phosphate	
Sodium Carbonate	58.824	Ferrous Phosphate	.008
Magnesium Carbonate	.008	Aluminium Phosphate	
Calcium Carbonate	1.120	Silica	.016
		Organic Matter	.024

Total Solids, 135.672

Gas	Cubic Inches
Carbonic Acid	2.24

CATOOSA SPRINGS, CATOOSA CO., GA.

PURGATIVE

Mineral Ingredients	All-Healing Wm. J. Land Analyst U. S. gal. contains Grains	Red Sweet Wm. J. Land Analyst U. S. gal. contains Grains
Sodium Chloride	.128	.144
Sodium Carbonate	.248	.288
Sodium Sulphate	1.496	1.696
Potassium Carbonate	.104	.112
Potassium Sulphate	2.200	2.488
Magnesium Carbonate	7.024	7.944
Magnesium Bromide	.296	.328
Magnesium Sulphate	26.536	29.976
Calcium Carbonate	3.520	3.976
Calcium Bromide	1.208	1.368
Calcium Sulphate	38.840	43.864
Calcium Nitrate	.416	.472
Calcium Fluoride	.016	.016
Ferrous Carbonate	.128	.144
Manganese Carbonate	.008	.016
Lithium Carbonate	trace	trace
Strontium Carbonate	.040	.048
Strontium Sulphate	.200	.232
Ammonium Nitrate	.120	.136
Crenic Acid	.024	.024
Apocrenic Acid		
Aluminium Sulphate	.504	.664
Total Solids	83.056	93.936

Gases	Cubic Inches	Cubic Inches
Carbonic Acid	9.36	9.28

CATOOSA SPRINGS, CATOOSA CO., GA.

PURGATIVE

Mineral Ingredients	White Sulphur Wm. J. Land Analyst U. S. gal. contains Grains	Buffalo Wm. J. Land Analyst U. S gal. contains Grains
Sodium Chloride	.136	.112
Sodium Carbonate	.256	.024
Sodium Sulphate	1.672	1.672
Potassium Carbonate	.112	.016
Potassium Sulphate	2.320	2.312
Magnesium Carbonate	8.400	8.696
Magnesium Bromide	.304	.328
Magnesium Sulphate	32.008	33.016
Calcium Carbonate	3.848	3.856
Calcium Bromide	.144	.152
Calcium Sulphate	44.808	45.000
Calcium Nitrate	.320	.032
Calcium Fluoride	.016	.008
Ferrous Carbonate	.280	.280
Manganese Carbonate	.024	.016
Lithium Carbonate	trace	trace
Strontium Carbonate	.040	.010
Strontium Sulphate	.208	.288
Ammonium Nitrate	.096	.912
Crenic Acid } Apocrenic Acid }	.008	.008
Aluminium Sulphate	2.472	2.384
Total Solids	97.472	99.152

Gases	Cubic Inches	Cubic Inches
Carbonic Acid	9.52	9.76
Sulphureted Hydrogen	.08	trace

COOPER'S WELL, HINDS CO., MISS.

CHALYBEATE

PROF. J. L. SMITH, Analyst

Mineral Ingredients	U. S. gal. contains Grains	Mineral Ingredients	U. S. gal. contains Grains
Sodium Chloride	8.360	Calcium Sulphate	42.120
Sodium Sulphate	11.704	Calcium Crenate	.312
Potassium Sulphate	.608	Ferric Oxide	3.360
Magnesium Chloride	3.480	Aluminum Sulphate	6.120
Magnesium Sulphate	23.280	Silica	1.800
Calcium Chloride	4.320		

Total Solids, 105.464

Gases	Cubic Inches
Carbonic Acid	32.0
Oxygen	12.0
Nitrogen	36.0

CRAB ORCHARD SPRINGS, LINCOLN CO., KY.

PURGATIVE

Mineral Ingredients	Foley's Spring R. Peter, M. D., Analyst U. S. gal. contains Grains	Sowder's Spring R. Peter, M. D., Analyst U. S. gal. contains Grains	Crab Orchard Salt R. Peter, M. D., Analyst U. S. gal. contains Grains
Sodium Chloride....................	17.728	58.320	4.77
Sodium Sulphate....................	59.072	23.200	4.20
Potassium Sulphate................	9.912	17.376	1.80
Magnesium Carbonate.............	7.640	21.872	......
Magnesium Sulphate...............	205.280	174.312	63.19
Calcium Carbonate.................	53.184	29.512	......
Calcium Sulphate...................	10.792	91.328	2.54
Calcium, Magnesium, Ferrous Carbonates and Silica............	......	......	.89
Ferrous Carbonate.................	trace	trace	......
Bromine...........................		trace	trace
Silica.............................	3.264	1.224	......
Loss and Moisture..................	34.584	......	......
Water of Crystallization and Loss....	......	......	22.61
Total Solids..........	401.456	417.144	100.00
Gas	Cubic Inches	Cubic Inches	
Carbonic Acid.................	not estimated	not estimated	

ESTILL SPRINGS, ESTILL CO., KY.

Mineral Ingredients	Red Sulphur Sulphureted R. Peter, M. D. Analyst U. S. gal. contains Grains	Chalybeate R. Peter, M. D. Analyst U. S. gal. contains Grains	Irvine Spring Purgative R. Peter, M. D. Analyst U. S. gal. contains Grains
Sodium Chloride....................	4.896	.528	17.608
Sodium Carbonate................	1.344	......	......
Sodium Sulphate..................	10.032	.696	......
Potassium Sulphate...............	5.360	.640	2.504
Magnesium Carbonate.............	4.840	2.680	2.568
Magnesium Sulphate...............	.584	9.792	263.280
Calcium Chloride...................	......	......	1.688
Calcium Carbonate................	11.776	9.272	30.728
Calcium Sulphate.................		16.672	31.896
Ferrous Carbonate................		1.864	1.328
Aluminium Phosphate.............		trace	......
Silica............................	.352	1.864	4.024
Organic and Volatile Matters......	2.336	8.224	......
Loss..............................		......	85.888
Total Solids..........	41.520	52.232	441.512
Gases	Cubic Inches	Cubic Inches	
Carbonic Acid.....................	40.08	33.20	
Sulphureted Hydrogen.............	.56	......	

HARRODSBURG SPRINGS, MERCER CO., KY.
PURGATIVE.

Mineral Ingredients	Greenville Spring Raymond, Analyst U. S. gal. contains Grains	Saloon Spring Raymond, Analyst U. S. gal. contains Grains
Sodium Chloride....	trace	9.92
Magnesium Carbonate......	22.96	2.08
Magnesium Sulphate...........................	129.96	223.36
Calcium Carbonate............	4.80	23.92
Calcium Sulphate......	88.48	81.92
Ferrous Carbonate............................,,,,,,,,,	......	2.88
Total Solids......	245.52	344.08

MONTVALE SPRINGS, BLOUNT CO., TENN.
CHALYBEATE

Mineral Ingredients	Prof. J. B Mitchell Analyst U. S. gal. contains Grains	J. R. Chilton, M. D. Analyst U. S. gal. contains Grains
Sodium Chloride.................................	1.960	......
Sodium Sulphate...................................	4.512	8.816
Magnesium Chloride...........	......	.096
Magnesium Sulphate............................	12.000	17.072
Calcium Chloride................................	......	.144
Calcium Carbonate.............................	13.256	......
Calcium Sulphate...............................	74.208	81.944
Ferrous Carbonate.............................	2.400	......
Ferric Oxide.....................................	......	1.192
Alumina........................	.496	......
Silica...	......	trace
Organic Matter...., ...	......	.040
Total Solids.........................	108.832	109.304

OCEAN SPRINGS, JACKSON CO., MISS.
CHALYBEATE
J. L. SMITH, analyst

Mineral Ingredients	U. S. gal. contains Grains	Mineral Ingredients	U. S. gal. contains Grains
Sodium Chloride. 47.768		Ferrous Oxide..... ..... 4.712	
Potassium Chloride.......... trace		Iodine.................... trace	
Magnesium Chloride.......... 4.968		Alumina................ trace	
Calcium Chloride............ 3.880		Organic Matter.......... trace	

Total Solids, 61.328

Gases	Cubic Inches
Carbonic Acid..........................	9.76
Sulphureted Hydrogen,..................	1.28

OLYMPIAN SPRINGS, BATH CO., KY.
SULPHURETED
Dr. Peter, Analyst

Mineral Ingredients	U. S. gal. contains Grains	Mineral Ingredients	U. S. gal. contains Grains
Sodium Chloride	166.016	Ferrous Carbonate	trace
Potassium Chloride	10.672	Ferrous Bromide	trace
Magnesium Chloride	55.392	Alumina	trace
Magnesium Carbonate	7.232	Silica	1.048
Calcium Carbonate	13.936	Water and Loss	78.660
Calcium Sulphate	trace		

Total Solids, 332.896

Gases	Cubic Inches
Carbonic Acid	not estimated
Sulphureted hydrogen	not estimated

PAROQUET SPRINGS, BULLITT CO., KY.
SULPHURETED
Prof. P. L. Smith, Analyst

Mineral Ingredients	U. S. gal. contains Grains	Mineral Ingredients	U. S. gal. contains Grains
Sodium Chloride	309.600	Magnesium Bromide	.312
Sodium Carbonate	.376	Calcium Chloride	67.712
Sodium Iodide	.152	Calcium Carbonate	2.400
Sodium Bromide	.176	Calcium Sulphate	2.280
Sodium Sulphate	2.416	Ferrous Carbonate	.176
Potasium Chloride	.488	Aluminium Sulphate	.496
Magnesium Chloride	48.032	Silica	3.904
Magnesium Carbonate	1.504	Organic Matter	2.136
Magnesium Iodide	.248		

Total Solids, 442.408

Gases	Cubic Inches
Carbonic Acid	6.00
Sulphureted Hydrogen	30.00

ST. LOUIS ARTESIAN WELL, ST. LOUIS, MO.
SALINE
Dr. Litton, Analyst

Mineral Ingredients	U. S. gal. contains Grains	Mineral Ingredients	U. S. gal. contains Grains
Sodium Chloride	350.608	Calcium Carbonate	10.632
Potassium Chloride	9.008	Calcium Sulphate	45.672
Magnesium Chloride	38.336	Ferrous Carbonate	.528
Magnesium Carbonate	1.016	Silica	.136
Calcium Chloride	27.584		

Total Solids, 483.520

Gases	Cubic Inches
Carbonic Acid	6.56
Sulphureted Hydrogen	.24

WARM SPRINGS, MERRIWETHER CO., GA.

THERMAL

Prof. A. Means, Analyst

Temperature 90° F.

Mineral Ingredients	U. S. gal. contains Grains	Mineral Ingredients	U. S. gal. contains Grains
Magnesium Oxide	93.44	Ferrous Oxide	17.12
Calcium Oxide	37.12		

Total Solids, 147.68

Gases	Cubic Inches
Carbonic Acid	8.88
Sulphureted Hydrogen	trace

WARM SPRINGS, MADISON CO., N. C.

THERMAL

Mineral Ingredients	Bathing Springs E. Adelmarth, M. D. Analyst Temp. 102° F. U. S. gal. contains Grains	Drinking Springs E. Adelmarth, M. D. Analyst Temp. 97° F. U. S. gal. contains Grains
Sodium Chloride	.912	1.096
Sodium Sulphate	9.024	8.904
Potassium Chloride	.312	.504
Potassium Sulphate	.360	.472
Magnesium Chloride	.216	.369
Magnesium Sulphate	1.344	8.128
Calcium Chloride	10.104	8.944
Calcium Sulphate	40.880	40.536
Soluble Silicates	8.968	9.536
Total Solids	72.120	78.488

Gases	Cubic Inches	Cubic Inche
Carbonic Acid	10.96	10.72
Sulphureted Hydrogen	1.76	2.48

VIRGINIA MINERAL SPRINGS

ALLEGHANY SPRING, MONTGOMERY CO., VA.

CALCAREOUS

F. A. GENTH, Analyst

Mineral Ingredients	U. S. gal. contains Grains	Mineral Ingredients	U. S. gal. contains Grains
Sodium Chloride	.224	Manganese Carbonate ...	.048
Sodium Sulphate	1.424	Barium Carbonate	.016
Potassium Sulphate	3.080	Lithium Carbonate	trace
Magnesium Carbonate	.206	Strontium Carbonate	.048
Magnesium Sulphate	42.392	Aluminium Phosphate	.016
Magnesium Nitrate	2.680	Aluminium Silicate	.168
Calcium Carbonate	3.008	Ammonium Nitrate	.464
Calcium Sulphate	96.056	Silicic Acid	.728
Calcium Fluoride	.016	Organic Matter	1.664
Ferrous Carbonate	.128		

Total Solids, 152.456

Gases	Cubic Inches
Carbonic Acid	9.60
Sulphureted Hydrogen	trace

AUGUSTA SPRINGS (STRIBLING), AUGUSTA CO., VA.

	No. 1 Chalybeate D. K. Tuttle, M. D. Analyst	No. 2 Sulphureted D. K. Tuttle, M. D. Analyst	No. 3 Chalybeate D. K. Tuttle, M. D' Analyst
Mineral Ingredients	U. S. gal. contains Grains	U. S. gal. contains Grains	U. S. gal. contains Grains
Sodium Chloride		.040	
Sodium Carbonate	.760	6.240	.984
Sodium Sulphate			
Potassium Carbonate	.352	.744	.760
Potassium Sulphate			
Magnesium Carbonate	.976	2.008	1.104
Magnesium Sulphate			
Calcium Carbonate		9.632	.832
Calcium Sulphate	.224	1.248	3.088
Ferrous Carbonate	.072	.128	.112
Silicic Acid	1.320	.040	.912
Total Solids	3.704	21.280	7.792
Gases	Cubic Inches	Cubic Inches	Cubic Inches
Carbonic Acid	24.00	10.40	16.00
Sulphureted Hydrogen		.24	

A. 19

AUGUSTA SPRINGS (STRIBLING), AUGUSTA CO., VA.

ALUM

Mineral Ingredients	No. 4 Chalybeate D. K. Tuttle, M. D. Analyst U. S. gal. contains Grains	No. 5 Chalybeate D. K. Tuttle, M. D. Analyst U. S. gal. contains Grains	No. 6 Sulphureted D. K. Tuttle, M. D. Analyst U. S. gal. contains Grains
Sodium Chloride	......	......	......
Sodium Carbonate	......	......	......
Sodium Sulphate	.664	2.344	1.792
Potassium Carbonate	......	......	......
Potassium Sulphate	.536	8.904	1.008
Magnesium Carbonate	......	......	......
Magnesium Sulphate	.528	.344	6.576
Calcium Carbonate	......	......	......
Calcium Sulphate	14.656	16.944	19.112
Ferrous Carbonate	......	......	......
Ferrous Sulphate	9.536	13.144	12.920
Sulphuric Acid	5.048	9.816	6.536
Silicic Acid	1.952	2.112	2.112
Aluminium Sulphate	16.688	17.952	38.408
Organic Matter	3.752	......	......
Total Solids	53.360	71.560	88.464

BATH ALUM SPRING, BATH CO., VA.

CHALYBEATE

Mineral Ingredients	No. 1 A. A. Hayes, M. D. Analyst U. S. gal. contains Grains	No. 2 A. A. Hayes, M. D. Analyst U. S. gal. contains Grains
Sodium Chloride	.176	......
Sodium Silicate	2.024	3.152
Potassium Sulphate	......	.256
Magnesium Sulphate	2.816	1.280
Calcium Sulphate	3.808	2.536
Ferrous Oxide	14.512	21.776
Sulphuric Acid	5.808	7.880
Alumina	10.288	12.288
Ammonium Crenate	1.856	1.776
Total Solids	41.288	50.944
Gas	Cubic Inches	Cubic Inches
Carbonic Acid	1.12	8.00

BEDFORD ALUM SPRINGS, BEDFORD CO., VA.

CHALYBEATE

Prof. Gilliam, Analyst

Mineral Ingredients	U. S. gal. contains Grains	Mineral Ingredients	U. S. gal. contains Grains
Potassium Sulphate	10.160	Ferrous Sulphate	23.456
Magnesium Sulphate	12.664	Sulphuric Acid	19.976
Calcium Sulphate	18.672	Aluminium Sulphate	7.240

Total Solids, 92.168

BERKELEY SPRINGS, MORGAN CO., W. VA.

CALCAREOUS

A. A. Hayes, M. D., Analyst

Mineral Ingredients	U. S. gal. contains Grains	Mineral Ingredients	U. S. gal. contains Grains
Sodium Chloride	.896	Calcium Crenate	3.640
Magnesium Sulphate	.360	Ferrous Silicate	.640
Calcium Chloride	.208	Ferrous Crenate	.080
Calcium Carbonate	5.000	Loss	.064

Total Solids, 10.888

BLUE RIDGE SPRINGS, BOTETOURT CO., VA.

PURGATIVE

F. A. Genth, Analyst

Mineral Ingredients	U. S. gal. contains Grains	Mineral Ingredients	U. S. gal. contains Grains
Sodium Chloride	.248	Calcium Carbonate	3.776
Sodium Sulphate	.976	Calcium Sulphate	100.216
Potassium Sulphate	.400	Ferrous Carbonate	.296
Magnesium Carbonate	1.784	Silicic Acid	1.256
Magnesium Sulphate	47.552	Alumina	.144

Total Solids, 156.648

BUFFALO SPRINGS, MECKLENBURG CO., VA.

SULPHURETED

Mineral Ingredients	U. S. gal. contains Grains	Mineral Ingredients	U. S. gal. contains Grains
Sodium Chloride	trace	Magnesium Sulphate	8.000
Sodium Sulphate	1.304	Calcium Sulphate	3.496
Magnesium Chloride	trace	Ferrous Sulphate	2.600

Total Solids, 15.400

Gas	Cubic Inches
Sulphureted Hydrogen	1.20

CAPON SPRINGS, HAMPSHIRE CO., W. VA.

ALKALINE

Mineral Ingredients	No. 1. Main Spring J. W. Mallet Analyst Imp. gal. contains Grains	No. 2. Beauty Spring J. W. Mallet Analyst Imp. gal. contains Grains
Sodium Chloride	.056	.054
Sodium Carbonate	.591	.631
Potassium Sulphate	.170	.163
Magnesium Carbonate	1.441	1.269
Calcium Carbonate	8.325	8.355
Calcium Sulphate	.593	.408
Calcium Phosphate	.002	.002
Calcium Fluoride	trace	trace
Ferrous Carbonate	.041	.052
Manganous Carbonate	trace	trace
Lithium Carbonate	distinct trace	faint trace
Strontium Sulphate	trace	trace
Cupric Carbonate	......	trace
Alumina	.018	.015
Silica	.707	.672
Nitrates	trace	trace
Organic Matter	.204	.189
Total Solids	12.138	11.810

60° F. and 30 inches pressure

Dissolved Gases	No. 1. Cubic Inches	No. 2. Cubic Inches
Carbon Dioxide	8.57	7.81
Oxygen	1.76	1.69
Nitrogen	3.68	3.71
Free Gases	14.01	13.21

From No. 1 gas escapes in bubbles at frequent intervals to the extent of about 300 or 350 cubic inches per hour. This consists of:

	Cubic Inches
Nitrogen	78.74
Oxygen	9.02
Carbon Dioxide	4.38
Marsh-gas	7.87
	100.00

CHURCH HILL ALUM SPRINGS, VA.

CHALYBEATE

J. C. Booth, M. D., analyst

Mineral Ingredients	U. S. gal. contains Grains	Mineral Ingredients	U. S. gal. contains Grains
Sodium Chloride	4.624	Ferric Persulphate	51.264
Sodium Sulphate	1.944	Ferric Bisulphate	83.352
Potassium Sulphate	2.440	Ammonium Sulphate	.640
Magnesium Sulphate	86.064	Silica	10.424
Calcium Sulphate	88.832	Phosphoric Acid	trace
Ferrous Sulphate	24.184	Aluminium Persulphate	72.928

Total Solids, 426.696

GREENBRIER WHITE SULPHUR SPRINGS

GREENBRIER CO., W. VA.

SULPHURETED

Mineral Ingredients	Prof. A. A. Hayes Analyst U. S. gal. contains Grains	Prof. W. B. Rogers Analyst U. S. gal. contains Grains
Sodium Chloride		.520
Sodium Sulphate		9.352
Sodium Silicate		
Potassium Silicate	3.456	
Magnesium Silicate		
Magnesium Chloride	1.000	.160
Magnesium Carbonate		1.168
Magnesium Sulphate	35.416	19.032
Calcium Chloride		.024
Calcium Carbonate	7.072	3.598
Calcium Sulphate	78.352	73.184
Ferrous Sulphate		.152
Ferric Oxide	trace	
Aluminium Sulphate		.024
Iodine		undeterm.
Earthy Phosphates		trace
Organic Matter	4.360	.008
Total Solids	129.656	107.152

Gases	Cubic Inches	Cubic Inches
Carbonic Acid	11.28	8.48
Sulphureted Hydrogen	.24	2.96
Oxygen	.48	.40
Nitrogen	4.64	4.32

HEALING SPRINGS, BATH CO., VA.

THERMAL

Mineral Ingredients	Old Spring Prof. Wm. Aiken Analyst *Temp. 85° F.* U. S. gal. contains Grains	New Spring Prof. Wm. Aiken Analyst *Temp. 88° F.* U. S. gal. contains Grains
Sodium Chloride	.272	.288
Potassium Chloride	.232	.256
Potassium Sulphate	2.208	2.528
Magnesium Carbonate	1.248	1.968
Magnesium Sulphate	7.248	7.392
Calcium Carbonate	17.904	18.720
Calcium Sulphate	1.320	1.264
Ferrous Carbonate	.072	.272
Ferrous Sulphate	.176	.104
Ammonium Sulphate	.232	.232
Iodine	trace	trace
Bromine	trace	trace
Silicic Acid	1.896	1.824
Organic Matter	.856	.872
Total Solids	33.664	35.720

Gas	Cubic Inches	Cubic Inches
Carbonic Acid	4.64	4.80

HOT SPRINGS, BATH CO., VA.

THERMAL

Mineral Ingredients	Ladies' Boiler-Bath Col. Wm. Gilham Analyst *Temp. 110° F.* U. S. gal. contains Grains	Ladies' Sulphur-Bath Col. Wm. Gilham Analyst *Temp. 102° F.* U. S. gal. contains Grains	Gentlemen's Pleasure-Bath Col. Wm. Gilham Analyst *Temp. 78° F.* U. S. gal. contains Grains
Sodium Chloride	.120	.136	.128
Sodium Sulphate	1.024	1.008	.848
Potassium Chloride	1.600	.168	.160
Potassium Sulphate	1.344	1.824	.568
Magnesium Carbonate	2.680	2.800	2.016
Magnesium Sulphate	5.656	5.104	1.064
Calcium Carbonate	17.344	16.440	9.480
Calcium Sulphate	1.736	2.104	3.024
Ferrous Carbonate	.112	.064	.080
Silica	1.744	1.368	.688
Total Solids	33.360	31.016	18.056

HOLSTON SPRINGS, SCOTT CO., VA.

CALCAREOUS

PROF. HAYDEN, Analyst

Mineral Ingredients	U. S. gal. contains Grains	Mineral Ingredients	U. S. gal. contains Grains
Sodium Chloride..........)	1.52	Calcium Carbonate.......	6.40
Ammonium Chloride ...... }		Calcium Sulphate........	20.48
Sodium Sulphate............	trace	Aluminium Sulphate,.....	trace
Magnesium Sulphate........	12.72	Aluminium Phosphate....	trace

Total Solids, 41.12

JORDAN ALUM SPRINGS, ROCKBRIDGE CO., VA.

ALKALINE AND CHALYBEATE

Mineral Ingredients	Alum Spring Wm. E. Aiken Analyst U. S. gal. contains Grains	Chalybeate Spring J. W. Mallet Analyst U. S. gal. contains Grains
Sodium Chloride.............	.728	.112
Sodium Iodide...............	.704	......
Sodium Sulphate............	.176	.136
Sodium Silicate.............	2.512	......
Potassium Sulphate.........	1.312	.128
Magnesium Carbonate.......	......	.736
Magnesium Sulphate	5.176	......
Calcium Sulphate...........	4.440	3.712
Calcium Phosphate (tribasic)...	......	.016
Ferrous Carbonate..........	......	.704
Ferrous Sulphate...........	18.536	......
Ferrous Phosphate.........	.248	......
Ferrous Crenate............	.680	......
Manganese Carbonate.......	......	.040
Ammonium Crenate	.528	......
Sulphuric Acid.............	23.640	......
Alumina....................	......	.056
Aluminium Sulphate........	25.376	......
Silica	......	.720
Organic Matter.............	.584	.088
Total Solids	84.640	6.448

Gases	Cubic Inches	Cubic Inches
Carbonic Acid.............	6.16	5.60
Oxygen...................	......	1.60
Nitrogen	......	8.56

JORDAN'S WHITE SULPHUR SPRINGS, FREDERICK CO., VA.

SULPHURETED

T. Antisell, Analyst

Mineral Ingredients	U. S. gal. contains Grains	Mineral Ingredients	U. S. gal. contains Grains
Sodium Chloride	.760	Ferrous Carbonate	trace
Potassium Carbonate	9.704	Manganese Carbonate	.016
Potassium Sulphate	2.096	Silicic Acid	.256
Magnesium Carbonate	2.880	Alumina	.008
Calcium Sulphate	5.128		

Total Solids, 20.848

Gas	Cubic Inches
Sulphureted Hydrogen	2.00

KIMBERLING SPRINGS, BLAND CO., VA.

SULPHURETED

Dr. Tuttle, Analyst

Mineral Ingredients	Imp. gal. contains Grains	Mineral Ingredients	Imp. gal. contains Grains
Sodium Chloride	.4229	Calcium Sulphate	2.3169
Sodium Carbonate	6.2080	Silica	.0733
Potassium Carbonate	.7500	Iron	trace
Magnesium Carbonate	1.6200	Sulphureted Hydrogen	.1737
Calcium Carbonate	.7238	Organic Matter	2.160

Total Solids, 15.0486

NEW LONDON ALUM SPRINGS, CAMPBELL CO., VA.

CHALYBEATE

Prof. Gilham, Analyst

Mineral Ingredients	U. S. gal. contains Grains	Mineral Ingredients	U. S. gal. contains Grains
Potassium Sulphate	10.160	Ferrous Sulphate	23.456
Magnesium Sulphate	12.664	Aluminium	7.240
Calcium Sulphate	18.672	Sulphuric Acid, free	19.976

Total Solids, 92.168

OLD SWEET SPRINGS, MONROE CO., W. VA.

CARBONATED

PROF. W. B. ROGERS, Analyst

Mineral Ingredients	U. S. gal. contains Grains	Mineral Ingredients	U. S. gal. contains Grains
Sodium Chloride	.136	Calcium Carbonate	30.056
Sodium Sulphate	6.344	Calcium Sulphate	13.168
Magnesium Chloride	.312	Ferric Oxide	.144
Magnesium Carbonate	.824	Iodine	trace
Magnesium Sulphate	9.392	Silica	.168
Calcium Chloride	.144	Earthy Phosphates	trace

Total Solids, 60.688

Gas	Cubic Inches
Carbonic Acid	88.00

ORKNEY SPRINGS, SHENANDOAH CO., VA.

ALKALINE AND CHALYBEATE

Mineral Ingredients	Healing Spring J. W. Mallet Analyst U. S. gal. contains Grains	Powder Spring J. W. Mallet Analyst U. S. gal. contains Grains	Bear Wallow Spring J. W. Mallet Analyst U. S. gal. contains Grains
Sodium Chloride	.120	.352	.088
Sodium Carbonate	.016	3.248	......
Sodium Sulphide	......	.440	......
Potassium Chloride	.032	.024	.064
Potassium Sulphate	.184	.160	.208
Magnesium Carbonate	1.128	2.952	......
Magnesium Sulphate	......	......	2.440
Calcium Carbonate	8.264	3.816	......
Calcium Sulphate	1.144	1.752	.712
Calcium Phosphate (tribasic)	.016	trace	.008
Ferrous Carbonate	.464	.216	......
Ferrous Sulphate	......	......	4.536
Manganese Carbonate	.008	.016	......
Lithium Sulphate	......	......	.064
Sulphuric Acid	......	......	.352
Aluminium Sulphate	.032	.016	.056
Silica	.832	1.384	1.536
Organic Matter	......	trace	.064
Total Solids	12.240	14.376	10.128
Gases	**Cubic Inches**	**Cubic Inches**	**Cubic Inches**
Carbonic Acid	3.84	7.12	4.80
Sulphureted Hydrogen	......	4.88	......
Oxygen	1.36	......	.40
Nitrogen	2.48	2.32	1.20

RAWLEY SPRINGS, ROCKINGHAM CO., VA.,
CHALYBEATE
PROF. J. W. MALLET, Analyst

Mineral Ingredients	U. S. gal. contains Grains	Mineral Ingredients	U. S. gal. contains Grains
Sodium Chloride	.010	Manganese Carbonate	.016
Sodium Sulphate	.544	Lithium Carbonate	trace
Potassium Sulphate	.112	Ammonium Carbonate	trace
Magnesium Carbonate	.680	Alumina	.040
Calcium Carbonate	.440	Silica	.680
Calcium Sulphate	.104	Organic Matter	.288
Ferrous Carbonate	1.624	Loss	.584

Total Solids, 5.152

Gas	Cubic Inches
Carbonic Acid	6.16

RED SULPHUR SPRINGS, MONROE CO., W. VA.
SULPHURETED
A. A. HAYES, M. D., Analyst

Mineral Ingredients	U. S. gal. contains Grains	Mineral Ingredients	U. S. gal. contains Grains
Sodium Chloride	4.144	Calcium Sulphate	.552
Magnesium Carbonate	4.816	Silicious and earthy matter	.816
Calcium Carbonate	5.248	Organic Matter (Sulphur Compound)	8.392

Total Solids, 23.968

Gases	Cubic Inches
Carbonic Acid	8.00
Sulphureted Hydrogen	1.04

•

ROCK ENON SPRINGS, FREDERICK CO., VA.
COPPER SPRINGS
CHALYBEATE
GALE and MEW, Analysts

Mineral Ingredients	U. S. gal. contains Grains	Mineral Ingredients	U. S. gal. contains Grains
Sodium Carbonate	1.21	Ferrous Carbonate	14.25
Magnesium Chloride	1.12	Manganese Carbonate	1.05
Magnesium Sulphate	12.89	Alumina	.80
Calcium Carbonate	5.13	Silica	.42
Calcium Sulphate	3.56		

Total Solids, 40.43

By spectrum analysis lithia was also found in it.

ROCKBRIDGE ALUM SPRINGS, ROCKBRIDGE CO., VA.

CHALYBEATE

A. A. HAYES, M. D., Analyst

Mineral Ingredients	No. 1 U. S. gal. contains Grains	No. 2 U. S. gal. contains Grains,	No. 3 U. S. gal. contains Grains
Sodium Chloride	.424	1.008	.440
Sodium Silicate	2.544	......	......
Potassium Sulphate	......	1.768	......
Magnesium Sulphate	1.080	1.760	4.416
Calcium Sulphate	1.440	3.264	3.304
Ferrous Oxide	3.680	4.864	4.696
Ammonium Crenate	1.400	.704	1.224
Sulphuric Acid	18.776	15.224	5.512
Silicic Acid	......	2.840	1.704
Alumina	14.768	17.904	24.088
Organic Matter	......	......	1.016
Total Solids	**44.112**	**49.336**	**46.400**
Gas	Cubic Inches	Cubic Inches	Cubic Inches
Carbonic Acid	5.60	1.52	8.80

SALT SULPHUR SPRINGS, MONROE CO., W. VA.

SULPHURETED

Mineral Ingredients	Old Spring W. B. Rogers Analyst U. S. gal. contains Grains	Iodine Spring D. Stewart, M. D. Analyst U. S. gal. contains Grains
Sodium Chloride	1.576	1.504
Sodium Carbonate	......	10.800
Sodium Sulphate	22.360	24.000
Potassium Carbonate	......	2.328
Magnesium Chloride	.264	.280
Magnesium Carbonate	3.312	7.000
Magnesium Sulphate	18.208	20.000
Calcium Chloride	.056	.560
Calcium Carbonate	10.264	33.000
Calcium Sulphate	84.904	68.000
Ferrous Oxide	.096	1.064
Iodine	trace	.632
Bromine	......	.648
Silicic Acid	......	1.760
Alumina	......	.184
Earthy Phosphates (Soda and Lithia)	trace	.728
Organic Matter with sulphur	9.240	......
Total Solids	**150.280**	**172.488**
Gases	Cubic Inches	Cubic Inches
Carbonic Acid	13.28	34.56
Sulphureted Hdyrogen	3.44	19.12

SWEET CHALYBEATE SPRINGS, ALLEGHANY CO., VA.
CHALYBEATE
Prof. W. B. Rogers, Analyst

Mineral Ingredients	U. S. gal. contains Grains	Mineral Ingredients	U. S. gal. contains Grains
Sodium Chloride	.088	Calcium Chloride	.024
Sodium Sulphate	3.232	Calcium Carbonate	2.696
Magnesium Chloride	1.568	Calcium Sulphate	32.880
Magnesium Sulphate	7.176	Ferrous Oxide	.736

Total Solids, 48.400

Gas	Cubic Inches
Carbonic Acid	104.00

VARIETY SPRINGS, AUGUSTA CO., VA.
ALUM
Prof. Wm. Gilham, Analyst

Mineral Ingredients	U. S. gal. contains Grains	Mineral Ingredients	U. S. gal. contains Grains
Sodium Chloride	.296	Ferrous Sulphate	5.112
Potassium Sulphate	.288	Sulphuric Acid, free	1.368
Magnesium Sulphate	11.640	Aluminium Sulphate	34.408
Calcium Sulphate	13.328	Silica	1.136

Total Solids, 67.576

WARM SPRINGS, BATH CO., VA.
THERMAL
A. A. Hayes, M. D., Analyst
Temperature 96° to 98° F.

Mineral Ingredients	U. S. gal. contains Grains	Mineral Ingredients	U. S. gal. contains Grains
Potassium Sulphate	1.371	Ammonium Sulphate	.369
Calcium Carbonate	5.220	Magnesium and Alumin-	
Calcium Sulphate	14.531	ium Silicates	1.724
Ferrous Crenate	2.498	Carbonic Acid	6.919

Total Solids, 32.632

YELLOW SULPHUR SPRINGS, MONTGOMERY CO., VA.
SULPHURETED
Prof. W. M. Gilham, Analyst

Mineral Ingredients	U. S. gal. contains Grains	Mineral Ingredients	U. S. gal. contains Grains
Sodium Chloride	.072	Calcium Carbonate	8.640
Sodium Sulphate	.744	Calcium Sulphate	63.296
Potassium Chloride	.096	Calcium Phosphate	.016
Potassium Sulphate	.104	Ferrous Carbonate	.616
Magnesium Carbonate	1.384	Aluminium Sulphate	3.176
Magnesium Sulphate	21.096	Organic Matter	3.728
Magnesium Phosphate	.008		

Total Solids, 102.976

Gases	Cubic Inches
Carbonic Acid	10.00
Sulphureted Hydrogen	undetermined

Pennsylvania Mineral Springs

BEDFORD SPRINGS, BEDFORD CO., PA.

PURGATIVE

Dr. Church, Analyst

Mineral Ingredients	U. S. gal. contains Grains	Mineral Ingredients	U. S. gal. contains Grains
Sodium Chloride	10.000	Calcium Sulphate	15.000
Magnesium Sulphate	80.000	Ferrous Carbonate	5.000
Calcium Chloride	3.000	Loss	3.000
Calcium Carbonate	8.000		

Total Solids, 124.000

Gas	Cubic Inches
Carbonic Acid	74.00

CRESSON SPRINGS, CAMBRIA CO., PA.

SALINE

Mineral Ingredients	Iron Spring F. A. Genth Analyst U. S. gal. contains Grains	Alum Spring F. A. Genth Analyst U. S. gal. contains Grains	Magnesia Spring F. A. Genth Analyst U. S. gal. contains Grains
Sodium Chloride	.04063	.02336	1.22974
Sodium Bicarbonate	......	......	1.42582
Sodium Sulphate	1.64331	.70389	......
Potassium Bicarbonate	......	... ..	.20671
Potassium Sulphate	.32405	.42622	......
Magnesium Chloride	......	......	.55962
Magnesium Bicarbonate	......	......	.41434
Magnesium Sulphate	22.58007	27.69855	......
Calcium Chloride	......	......	1.30444
Calcium Bicarbonate	3.52946	......	.02252
Calcium Sulphate	48.91824	40.20179	.10912
Calcium Phosphate	.02914	trace	.00408
Ferrous Bicarbonate	5.03471	3.74756	.01753
Ferrous Sulphate	23.47923	16.25273	......
Manganese Bicarbonate	......	trace	trace
Ferric Sulphate	trace	33.38970	....
Lithium Sulphate	trace	.04693	......
Aluminium Sulphate	1.60466	21.20498	.. ...
Silicic Acid	1.20832	1.80794	.91455
Nitrous Acid	......	......	trace
Carbonic Acid, free	......	....	.66390
Alumina	......	......	.00876
Total Solids	108.39182	145.56374	6.88113

FAYETTE SPRINGS, FAYETTE CO., PA.

CHALYBEATE

F. A. Genth, Analyst

Mineral Ingredients	U. S. gal. contains Grains	Mineral Ingredients	U. S. gal. contains Grains
Sodium Chloride	.08522	Calcium Phosphate	.04822
Sodium Sulphate	.19965	Ferrous Bicarbonate	1.06709
Potassium Sulphate	.11525	Manganese Bicarbonate	.04795
Magnesium Bicarbonate	1.53414	Silicic Acid	1.19090
Magnesium Sulphate	.25472	Nitrous Acid	trace
Calcium Bicarbonate	9.33441	Carbonic Acid, free	.38284
Calcium Sulphate	.05542	Alumina	trace

Total Solids, 14.32181

GETTYSBURG, ADAMS CO., PA.

SALINE

Mineral Ingredients	Katalysine Spring F. A. Genth Analyst U. S. gal. contains Grains	Stremmel's Spring F. A. Genth Analyst U. S. gal. contains Grains
Sodium Chloride	.65790	.31836
Sodium Bicarbonate	.70457	3.37002
Sodium Sulphate	2.46776	.....
Potassium Sulphate	.20836	.15399
Magnesium Bicarbonate	.54260	5.82061
Magnesium Sulphate	6.77940	3.29559
Magnesium Borate	.03492	.....
Calcium Bicarbonate	16.40815	9.95838
Calcium Sulphate	.83145	.48243
Calcium Phosphate	.00679	.00963
Calcium Fluoride	.00954	.....
Ferrous Bicarbonate	.03585	.04203
Manganese Bicarbonate	.00669	.00483
Barium Sulphate	trace	.....
Lithium Chloride	trace	trace
Strontium Sulphate	.00427	....
Alumina	.00380	.02425
Silicic Acid	2.03076	1.75473
Nickel Bicarbonate	trace	.....
Cobalt Bicarbonate	trace	.....
Copper Bicarbonate	.00050	....
Organic Matter, with traces of Nitric Acid	.70870	....
Impurities suspended in water, like clays	1.10069	.....
Total Solids	32.54272	25.24987

MINNEQUA SPRING, BRADFORD CO., PA.

SALINE

F. A. Genth, Analyst

Mineral Ingredients	U. S. gal. contains Grains	Mineral Ingredients	U. S. gal. contains Grains
Sodium Chloride	.19209	Barium Bicarbonate	.01380
Sodium Bicarbonate	1.33046	Barium Sulphate	.00175
Potassium Bicarbonate	.13885	Lithium Chloride	trace
Magnesium Bicarbonate	1.58988	Zinc Bicarbonate	.01157
Magnesium Borate	.07980	Nitrite ⎫ of ammonia	
Calcium Bicarbonate	6.52477	Nitrate ⎭	.00025
Calcium Phosphate	.01231	Silicic Acid	.74194
Ferrous Bicarbonate	.04204	Alumina	.00253
Manganese Bicarbonate	.06299	Sulphureted Hydrogen	.01390

Total Solids, 10.75893

SALTILLO SPRINGS, HUNTINGDON CO., PA.

SALINE

Mineral Ingredients	McVitty's Spring F. A. Genth Analyst U. S. gal. contains Grains	McCarthy's Spring F. A. Genth Analyst U. S. gal. contains Grains
Sodium Chloride	.06329	.20571
Sodium Sulphate	1.00664	7.79412
Potassium Sulphate	.15624	.22291
Magnesium Bicarbonate	1.87476	.88262
Magnesium Sulphate	.00456	41.79795
Calcium Bicarbonate	9.84013	22.24300
Calcium Sulphate	......	72.19660
Calcium Phosphate	trace	trace
Ferrous Bicarbonate	.14022	.08108
Silicic Acid	.59007	1.16846
Sulphureted Hydrogen	.01490	.01589
Total Solids	13.69081	146.60834

NEW YORK MINERAL SPRINGS

ADIRONDACK SPRINGS, WHITEHALL, N. Y.

CARBONATED

Prof. C. Collier, Analyst

Mineral Ingredients	U. S. gal. contains Grains	Mineral Ingredients	U. S. gal. contains Grains
Sodium Chloride	14.340	Ferrous Carbonate	5.040
Sodium Carbonate	5.135	Manganese Carbonate	traces
Potassium Carbonate	5.317	Lithium Carbonate	.023
Magnesium Carbonate	16.818	Alumina	traces
Calcium Carbonate	18.543	Silica	.742
Calcium Sulphate	11.134		

Total Solids, 77.092

Gas	Cubic Inches
Free Carbonic Acid	67.275

ALBANY ARTESIAN WELL, ALBANY, N. Y.

SALINE

DR. MEADE, Analyst

Mineral Ingredients	U. S. gal. contains Grains	Mineral Ingredients	U. S. gal. contains Grains
Sodium Chloride	504.00	Calcium Carbonate	32.00
Sodium Carbonate	40.00	Ferrous Carbonate (with a	
Magnesium Carbonate	16.00	little Silica)	8.00

Total Solids, 600.00

Gas	Cubic Inches
Carbonic Acid	224.00

This well is five hundred feet deep.

AUBURN SPRINGS, near AUBURN, N. Y.

SULPHURETED

DR. CHILTON, Analyst

Mineral Ingredients	U. S. gal. contains Grains	Mineral Ingredients	U. S gal. contains Grains
Sodium Chloride	6.00	Magnesium Sulphate	25.60
Magnesium Chloride	2.00	Calcium Sulphate	120.00

Total Solids, 153.60

Gas	Cubic Inches
Sulphureted Hydrogen	12.00

AVON SPRINGS, LIVINGSTON CO., N. Y.

SULPHURETED

	Upper Spring	Lower Spring	New Bath Spring
	Prof. Hadley Analyst	Dr. J. R. Chilton Analyst	Prof. Beck Analyst
Mineral Ingredients	U. S. gal. contains Grains	U. S. gal. contains Grains	U. S. gal. contains Grains
Sodium Chloride	18.400		5.680
Sodium Sulphate	16.000	13.728	38.720
Sodium Iodide		trace	
Magnesium Sulphate	10.000	49.608	8.080
Calcium Chloride		8.408	
Calcium Carbonate	8.000	29.328	26.960
Calcium Sulphate	84.000	57.440	3.520
Total Solids	136.400	158.512	82.960
Gases	Cubic Inches	Cubic Inches	Cubic Inches
Carbonic Acid	5.60	3.92	
Sulphureted Hydrogen	12.00	10.00	.40

BALLSTON SPA, SARATOGA CO., N. Y.
SALINE

Mineral Ingredients	United States Geology of N. Y. U. S. gal. contains Grains	Ballston Artesian Lithian Well C. F. Chandler Analyst U. S. gal. contains Grains
Sodium Chloride	424.960	750.024
Sodium Carbonate	16.880	8.272
Sodium Bromide	......	3.640
Sodium Iodide	......	.120
Sodium Sulphate	1.76	......
Sodium Phosphate	......	.048
Sodium Biborate	......	trace
Potassium Chloride	......	33.272
Potassium Sulphate	......	.520
Magnesium Carbonate	5.760	107.024
Calcium Carbonate	29.200	165.200
Calcium Fluoride	......	trace
Ferrous Carbonate	trace	1.144
Barium Carbonate	......	3.176
Lithium Carbonate	......	5.608
Strontium Carbonate	......	.664
Alumina	......	.072
Silica	8.000	.760
Organic Matter	......	trace
Total Solids	486.560	1079.744

Gas	Cubic Inches	Cubic Inches
Carbonic Acid	244.00	426.08

Mineral Ingredients	Franklin Artesian Well C. F. Chandler Analyst U. S. gal. contains Grains	Condo Pentoucan Well C. F. Chandler Analyst U. S. gal. contains Grains
Sodium Chloride	639.344	645.480
Sodium Carbonate	65.600	23.856
Sodium Bromide	4.664	2.368
Sodium Iodide	.232	.224
Sodium Phosphate	.008	trace
Sodium Biborate	trace	trace
Potassium Chloride	33.928	9.232
Potassium Sulphate	.760	trace
Magnesium Carbonate	105.400	93.832
Calcium Carbonate	140.520	123.952
Calcium Fluoride	trace	trace
Ferrous Carbonate	1.168	1.664
Barium Carbonate	1.000	3.872
Lithium Carbonate	4.904	7.600
Strontium Carbonate	trace	.144
Alumina	.256	.392
Silica	.736	1.024
Organic Matter	trace	trace
Total Solids	1018.520	913.640

Gas	Cubic Inches	Cubic Inches
Carbonic Acid	460.08	358.32

A. 20

BALLSTON SPA, SARATOGA CO., N. Y.

SALINE

STEELE, Analyst

Mineral Ingredients	U. S. gal. contains Grains	Mineral Ingredients	U. S. gal contains Grains
Sodium Chloride	143.733	Calcium Carbonate	43.407
Sodium Bicarbonate	12.660	Ferrous Carbonate	5.950
Sodium Iodide	1.300	Silica	1.000
Magnesium Bicarbonate	39.100		

Total Solids, 247.150

CHERRY VALLEY, OTSEGO CO., N. Y.

Mineral Ingredients	Bath-House Spring Sulphureted J. R. Chilton Analyst U. S. gal. contains Grains	Spring north of Bath-House Sulphureted Prof. Perkins Analyst U. S. gal. contains Grains	Phosphate Spring Saline Prof. Perkins Analyst U. S. gal. contains Grains
Sodium Chloride	12.440	2.128	.472
Sodium Sulphate	11.080	......	.....
Sodium Sulphide	.600	......	.....
Potassium Chloride	......	2.488	.....
Magnesium Chloride	3.680	......	.....
Magnesium Carbonate	17.816	9.960	4.576
Magnesium Sulphate	24.560	......	.....
Calcium Chloride	2.800	.....	.....
Calcium Carbonate	9.416	14.752	2.864
Calcium Sulphate	57.680	149.464	5.272
Calcium Phosphate	......	......	13.768
Ferrous Carbonate	......	2.448	.624
Silex	......	3.640	.....
Silica	......	......	.624
Silica and Alumina	.360	......	.....
Organic Matter	.280	......	.....
Total Solids	140.712	184.880	28.200

COLUMBIA SPRINGS, HUDSON, COLUMBIA CO., N. Y.

SULPHURETED

Atwood, Analyst

Mineral Ingredients	U. S. gal. contains Grains	Mineral Ingredients	U. S. gal. contains Grains
Sodium Chloride	84.720	Calcium Carbonate	21.792
Sodium Sulphate	8.144	Calcium Sulphate	64.936
Sodium Phosphate	2.136	Ferric Chloride	3.416
Potassium Chloride	1.192	Loss	.816
Magnesium Chloride	31.432		

Total Solids, 218.584

Gas	Cubic Inches
Sulphureted Hydrogen	4.48

CHITTENANGO SPRINGS, MADISON CO., N. Y.

SULPHURETED

Mineral Ingredients	White Sulphur Prof. C. F. Chandler Analyst U. S. gal. contains Grains	Cave Spring Prof. C. F. Chandler Analyst U. S. gal. contains Grains	Magnesia Prof. C. F. Chandler Analyst U. S. gal. contains Grains
Sodium Chloride..................	1.032	1.568	1.832
Sodium Sulphate..................	.216	......	......
Sodium Sulphide..................	.112	.344	.752
Sodium Hyposulphite..............		.256	.016
Potassium Chloride...............	.152	.232	.328
Magnesium Carbonate.............	13.048	14.208	11.512
Magnesium Sulphate..............	1.952	7.584	12.712
Calcium Sulphate.................	81.416	26.120	115.080
Calcium Sulphide.................	......	1.120	.928
Ferrous Carbonate................	.056	.112	.232
Lithium Chloride.................	trace	trace	trace
Strontium Sulphate...............	trace	trace	trace
Alumina..........................	.080	.216	trace
Silica...........................	.280	.512	.576
Total Solids.............	**98.344**	**52.272**	**143.968**

Gases	Prof. Collier Analyst Cubic Inches	Prof. Collier Analyst Cubic Inches	Prof. Collier Analyst Cubic Inches
Carbonic Acid.....................	36.0	25.6	18.4
Sulphureted Hydrogen.............	.8	3.2	12.8

CLIFTON SPRINGS, ONTARIO CO., N. Y.

SULPHURETED

PROF. J. R. CHILTON, Analyst

Mineral Ingredients	U. S. gal. contains Grains	Mineral Ingredients	U. S. gal. contains Grains
Sodium Chloride.............	9.28	Calcium Chloride........	4.08
Sodium Sulphate.............	7.76	Calcium Carbonate.......	9.68
Magnesium Chloride..........	4.08	Calcium Sulphate........	69.20
Magnesium Carbonate........	13.12	Organic Matter.........	trace
Magnesium Sulphate.........	16.48		

Total Solids, 133.68

"Sulphureted hydrogen and carbonic acid abound, but the quantity having been materially lessened while conveyed to New York, the proper amount could not be ascertained."

FLORIDA, MONTGOMERY CO., N. Y.

SULPHURETED

Mineral Ingredients	U. S. gal. contains Grains	Mineral Ingredients	U. S. gal. contains Grains
Sodium Chloride	5.880	Magnesium Bicarbonate	6.972
Sodium Bicarbonate	22.143	Calcium Bicarbonate	8.317
Sodium Sulphide	2.008	Ferrous Sulphide	.176
Sodium Hyposulphite	.711	Alumina	trace
Potassium Sulphate	1.390	Silica	.793

Total Solids, 43.390

Gases	Cubic Inches
Carbonic Acid	32.169
Sulphureted Hydrogen	3.765

LEBANON SPRINGS, COLUMBIA CO., N. Y.

THERMAL

PROF. H. DUSSANCE, Analyst

Temperature, 73°

Mineral Ingredients	U. S. gal. contains Grains	Mineral Ingredients	U. S. gal. contains Grains
Sodium Chloride	.960	Calcium Carbonate	4.048
Sodium Carbonate	2.408	Ferric Oxide	.936
Sodium Sulphide	.016	Alumina	.448
Potassium Sulphate	1.040	Silicic Acid	3.248
Magnesium Sulphate	1.056	Organic Com- Glairine	.752
		pounds.... Barégine	9.464

Total Solids, 24.376

Gases	Cubic Inches
Carbonic Acid	.48
Nitrogen	3.52
Oxygen	2.00

LONGMUIR'S WELL, ROCHESTER, N. Y.

SULPHURETED

Mineral Ingredients	U. S. gal. contains Grains	Mineral Ingredients	U. S. gal. contains Grains
Sodium Chloride	52.16	Carbonates of Lime and Magnesia	11.84
Sodium Sulphate	55.92	Ferrous Oxide	trace

Total Solids, 119.92

Gas	Cubic Inches
Carbonic Acid	Small quantity
Sulphureted Hydrogen	17.28

MESSENA SPRINGS, ST. LAWRENCE CO., N. Y.

SULPHURETED

PROF. FRED F. MEYER, Analyst

Mineral Ingredients	U. S. gal. contains Grains	Mineral Ingredients	U. S. gal. contains Grains
Sodium Chloride	79.688	Magnesium Chloride	29.928
Sodium Sulphate	3.496	Magnesium Bromide	.672
Sodium Sulphide	1.408	Calcium Carbonate	3.376
Sodium Hyposulphite	4.208	Calcium Sulphate	60.928
Sodium Phosphate	1.320	Ferrous Carbonate	.360
Potassium Chloride	.504	Silicate of Soda	11.176

Total Solids, 197.064

Gases	Cubic Inches
Sulphureted Hydrogen	5.304

OAK ORCHARD SPRING, GENESEE CO., N. Y.

ACID

PROF. PORTER, Analyst

Mineral Ingredients	U. S. gal. contains Grains	Mineral Ingredients	U. S. gal. contains Grains
Sodium Chloride	1.432	Ferrous Sulphate	33.216
Sodium Sulphate	3.162	Aluminium Sulphate	6.413
Potassium Sulphate	2.479	Sulphuric Acid	133.312
Magnesium Sulphate	8.491	Silicic Acid	3.324
Calcium Sulphate	13.724	Organic Matter	6.654

Total Solids, 211.207

RICHFIELD SPRINGS, OTSEGO CO., N. Y.

SULPHURETED

PROF. REID, Analyst

Mineral Ingredients	U. S. gal. contains Grains	Mineral Ingredients	U. S. gal. contains Grains
Sodium Chloride	} 1.496	Magnesium Sulphide	} 2.000
Magnesium Chloride		Calcium Sulphide	
Magnesium Carbonate	11.840	Calcium Carbonate	6.900
Magnesium Sulphate	30.000	Calcium Sulphate	20.300
		Undetermined	153.496

Total Solids, 225.496

Gas	Cubic Inches
Sulphureted Hydrogen	2.64

SHARON SPRINGS, SCHOHARIE CO., N. Y.

SULPHURETED

Mineral Ingredients	White Sulphur Spring Dr. Chilton Analyst U. S. gal. contains Grains	Red Sulphur Prof. L. Reed Analyst U. S. gal. contains Grains
Sodium Chloride	2.240	.328
Sodium Carbonate	......	.344
Sodium Sulphate	......	......
Sodium Sulphide }	2.240	
Calcium Sulphide }		......
Magnesium Chloride	2.400	.728
Magnesium Carbonate	......	.408
Magnesium Sulphate	42.400	18.060
Magnesium Sulphide }		.888
Calcium Sulphide }		
Calcium Chloride	......	.064
Calcium Carbonate	......	8.976
Calcium Sulphate	111.600	96.640
Silicic Acid	......	.446
Total Solids	160.880	127.784
Gases	Cubic Inches	Cubic Inches
Carbonic Acid	......	4.56
Sulphureted Hydrogen	16.00	10.48
Atmospheric Air	......	4.00

Mineral Ingredients	Gardner Magnesia Prof. L. Reed Analyst U. S. gal. contains Grains	Chalybeate Prof. Maisch Analyst 1861 U. S. gal. contains Grains
Sodium Chloride	1.232	......
Sodium Carbonate	.336	......
Sodium Sulphate	......	3.736
Potassium Sulphate	......	trace
Magnesium Chloride	.432	......
Magnesium Carbonate	.800	8.960
Magnesium Sulphate	19.080	8.152
Magnesium Sulphide }	6.248	
Calcium Sulphide }		
Calcium Chloride	.160	......
Calcium Carbonate	6.736	......
Calcium Sulphate	93.496	63.800
Ferrous Sulphate	......	1.400
Silicic Acid	.400	......
Oranic Matter	......	28.480
Total Solids	129.520	114.528
Gases	Cubic Inches	Cubic Inches
Carbonic Acid	2.216	......
Sulphureted Hydrogen	6.000	......
Atmospheric Air	3.000	......

SARATOGA SPRINGS, SARATOGA CO., N. Y.

SALINE

Mineral Ingredients	High Rock Chandler, Analyst Temp. 52° F. U. S. gal. contains Grains	Red Appleton, Analyst U. S. gal. contains Grains	Congress Chandler, Analys U. S. gal. contains Grains
Sodium Chloride.................	390.127	83.530	400.444
Sodium Bicarbonate..............	34.888	15.327	10.775
Sodium Bromide.................	.731	......	8.559
Sodium Biborate................	......	......	trace
Sodium Iodide..................	.086	......	.138
Sodium Phosphate...............	......	......	.016
Potassium Chloride.............	8.497	6.857	8.049
Potassium Sulphate.............	1.608	......	.889
Magnesium Bicarbonate..........	54.924	42.413	121.757
Calcium Bicarbonate............	131.739	101.256	143.393
Calcium Phosphate..............	trace	......	......
Calcium Fluoride...............	trace	......	trace
Ferrous Bicarbonate............	1.478	......	.340
Barium Bicarbonate.............	trace	......	.928
Lithium Bicarbonate............	......	.942	4.761
Strontium Bicarbonate..........	trace	trace	trace
Alumina........................	1.223	......	trace
Alumina and Ferric Oxide.......	......	2.100	......
Phosphates.....................	......	trace	......
Silica.........................	2.260	3.255	.840
Organic matter.................	trace	......	......
Total Solids...................	628.039	254.719	700.895
Gas	Cubic Inches	Cubic Inches	Cubic Inches
Carbonic Acid..................	409.458	......	392.289

PART II

Mineral Ingredients	Columbian Chandler, Analyst U. S. gal. contains Grains	Hamilton Steele, Analyst Temp. 50° F. U. S. gal. contains Grains	Washington Chilton, Analyst Temp. 45° F. U. S. gal. contains Grains
Sodium Chloride.................	267.000	297.300	182.733
Sodium Bicarbonate..............	15.400	27.036	8.474
Sodium Iodide..................	2.560	3.000	2.243
Potassium Bromide..............	trace	trace	.474
Magnesium Chloride.............	......	......	.680
Magnesium Bicarbonate..........	46.710	35.200	65.973
Magnesium Sulphate.............	......	......	.051
Calcium Chloride...............	......	......	.203
Calcium Bicarbonate............	68.000	92.400	84.096
Ferrous Bicarbonate............	5.580	5.390	3.800
Silicic Acid...................	......	......	1.500
Alumina........................	......	......	trace
Silica.........................	2.050	......	......
Total Solids...................	407.300	460.326	350.227
Gas	Cubic Inches	Cubic Inches	Cubic Inches
Carbonic Acid	272.060	316.000	363.770

PART III

Mineral Ingredients	Putnam Chilton, Analyst Temp. 51° F. U. S. gal. contains Grains	Star Chandler, Analyst Temp. 50° F U. S. gal. contains Grains	Pavilion Chandler, Analyst U. S. gal. contains Grains
Sodium Chloride	214.300	398.361	459.903
Sodium Bicarbonate	14.320	12.662	3.764
Sodium Bromide		.571	.987
Sodium Biborate		trace	trace
Sodium Iodide	2.000	.126	.071
Sodium Sulphate	1.680		
Sodium Phosphate		trace	.007
Potassium Chloride		9.695	7.660
Potassium Sulphate		5.400	2.032
Magnesium Bicarbonate	51.600	61.912	76.267
Calcium Bicarbonate	68.800	124.459	120.169
Calcium Phosphate	.210		
Calcium Fluoride		trace	trace
Ferrous Bicarbonate	7.000	1.213	2.570
Barium Bicarbonate		.996	.875
Lithium Bicarbonate		1.586	9.486
Strontium Bicarbonate		trace	trace
Alumina	.560	trace	.329
Silica	.840	1.283	3.155
Organic Matter		trace	trace
Total Solids	361.010	617.367	687.275
Gas	Cubic Inches	Cubic Inches	Cubic Inches
Carbonic Acid	348.880	407.650	332.458

PART IV

Mineral Ingredients	United States Chandler, Analyst U. S. gal. contains Grains	Empire Chandler, Analyst U. S. gal. contains Grains	Excelsior Allen, Analyst U. S. gal. contains Grains
Sodium Chloride	141.872	506.630	370.642
Sodium Bicarbonate	4.666	9.022	15.000
Sodium Bromide	.844	.266	
Sodium Biborate	trace	trace	
Sodium Iodide	.047	.006	4.235
Sodium Sulphate			1.321
Sodium Silicate			4.000
Sodium Phosphate	.016	.023	
Potassium Chloride	8.624	4.292	
Potassium Bromide			trace
Potassium Sulphate		2.769	
Potassium Silicate			7.000
Magnesium Bicarbonate	72.883	42.953	32.333
Calcium Bicarbonate	93.119	109.656	77.000
Calcium Fluoride	trace	trace	
Ferrous Bicarbonate	.714	.793	3.215
Barium Bicarbonate	.909	.070	
Lithium Bicarbonate	4.847	2.080	
Strontium Bicarbonate	.018	trace	
Strontium Sulphate			trace
Alumina	.094	.415	
Silica	3.184	1.458	
Organic Matter	trace	trace	
Total Solids	331.837	680.436	514.746
Gas	Cubic Inches	Cubic Inches	Cubic Inches
Carbonic Acid	245.734	344.667	250.000

PART V

Mineral Ingredients	Saratoga A Pohle, Analyst U. S. gal. contains Grains	Seltzer Chandler, Analyst Temp. 50° F. U. S. gal. contains Grains	Union Chandler, Analyst Temp. 48° F. U. S. gal. contains Grains
Sodium Chloride........	565.300	134.291	453.299
Sodium Bicarbonate................	6.752	29.428	17.010
Sodium Bromide....................		.030	1.307
Sodium Biborate....		trace	trace
Sodium Iodide....................		.031	.039
Sodium Sulphate..................	2.500	......	......
Sodium Phosphate.................		trace	.026
Potassium Chloride...............	.357	1.335	8.733
Potassium Sulphate..............	.370	.557	1.818
Magnesium Chloride............	trace	......	......
Magnesium Bicarbonate... ...	20.480	40.339	109.685
Magnesium Sulphate.............	.288	......	......
Calcium Chloride.............	trace	......	......
Calcium Bicarbonate..	56.852	89.869	96.730
Calcium Sulphate........	.448	......	......
Calcium Phosphate...........		trace	......
Calcium Fluoride............		trace	trace
Ferrous Bicarbonate..............	1.724	1.703	.269
Barium Bicarbonate...........		trace	1.703
Lithium Bicarbonate..............	1.724	.699	2.605
Strontium Bicarbonate............		trace	trace
Boracic Acid.................		trace	......
Silicic Acid..................	1.460	......	......
Alumina.....................	.380	.374	.324
Silica.......................		2.561	2.653
Organic Matter..................	trace	trace	trace
Total Solids................	656.911	302.017	701.174
Gas Carbonic Acid....................	Cubic Inches 212.000	Cubic Inches 324.080	Cubic Inches 384.909

PART VI

Mineral Ingredients	Hathorn Chandler, Analyst Temp. 47° F. U. S. gal. contains Grains	Eureka Allen, Analyst U. S. gal. contains Grains	Geyser Chandler, Analyst Temp. 46° F. U. S. gal. contains Grains
Sodium Chloride......	509.968	166.811	562.080
Sodium Bicarbonate...............	4.288	8.750	71.232
Sodium Bromide..................	1.534	......	2.212
Sodium Biborate..................	trace	......	trace
Sodium Iodide......	.198	4.666	.248
Sodium Phosphate.............	.006	......	trace
Potassium Chloride.............	9.597	......	24.634
Potassium Bromide.		1.566	......
Potassium Sulphate................		......	.318
Magnesium Bicarbonate............	170.463	29.340	149.343
Magnesium Sulphate..............		2.148	......
Calcium Bicarbonate..............	170.646	41.321	168.392
Calcium Fluoride...............	trace	......	trace
Ferrous Bicarbonate..............	1.128	3.000	.970
Barium Bicarbonate...............	1.737	......	2.014
Lithium Bicarbonate.............	11.447	......	9.004
Strontium Bicarbonate............	trace	......	.425
Alumina......................	.131	.231	trace
Silica.......................	1.260	.531	.065
Organic Matter.................	trace	......	trace
Total Solids.................	888.403	258.365	991.540
Gas Carbonic Acid...................	Cubic Inches 575.747	Cubic Inches 239.000	Cubic Inches 454.082

PART VII

Mineral Ingredients	Crystal Chandler, Analyst Temp. 50° F. U. S. gal. contains Grains	Champion Chandler, Analyst Temp. 45° F. U. S. gal. contains Grains	Vichy Chandler, Analyst Temp. 50° F. U. S. gal. contains Grains
Sodium Chloride...	328.468	702.239	128.689
Sodium Bicarbonate...............	10.064	17.624	82.873
Sodium Bromide...................	.414	3.579	.990
Sodium Biborate................	trace	......	trace
Sodium Iodide.	.066	2.321	trace
Sodium Phosphate...............	.009	.010	trace
Potassium Chloride...............	8.327	40.446	14.113
Potassium Sulphate...............	2.158	......	......
Magnesium Bicarbonate...........	75.161	193.912	41.503
Calcium Bicarbonate...............	101.881	227.070	95.522
Calcium Fluoride................	trace	trace	trace
Ferrous Bicarbonate...............	2.038	.647	.052
Barium Bicarbonate...............	.726	2.083	.593
Lithium Bicarbonate.............	4.326	6.247	1.760
Strontium Bicarbonate...........	trace	.082	trace
Alumina........................	.305	.458	.473
Silica........................	3.213	.699	.758
Organic Matter..................	trace	trace	trace
Total Solids...........	537.155	1,195.582	315.176
Gas	Cubic Inches	Cubic Inches	Cubic Inches
Carbonic Acid..................	317.452	465.458	383.071

PART VIII

Mineral Ingredients	Kissingen Sharpless, Analyst Temp. 40° F. U. S. gal. contains Grains	Triton Sharpless, Analyst U. S. gal. contains Grains
Sodium Chloride................	338.500	238.496
Sodium Bicarbonate...............	67.617	46.888
Sodium Bromide................	1.800	1.800
Sodium Iodide.....	.042	.040
Potassium Chloride...............	16.980	16.984
Potassium Sulphate	trace	trace
Magnesium Bicarbonate...........	70.470	41.768
Calcium Carbonate...............	140.260	91.256
Calcium Fluoride...............	trace	trace
Ferrous Bicarbonate...............	1.557	1.128
Barium Bicarbonate	.992	.816
Lithium Bicarbonate...............	5.129	3.224
Strontium Bicarbonate	trace	trace
Alumina........................	trace	trace
Silica........................	1.280	1.280
Total Solids..............	644.627	443.680
Gas	Cubic Inches	Cubic Inches
Carbonic Acid..................	361.500	360.800

New England Mineral Springs

ALBURGH SPRINGS, GRAND ISLE CO., VT.

SULPHURETED

C. T. Jackson, M. D., Analyst

Mineral Ingredients	U. S. gal. contains Grains	Mineral Ingredients	U. S. gal. contains Grains
Sodium Chloride...........	8.760	Calcium Chloride.....}	
Sodium Sulphate...........	7.096	Calcium Carbonate...}	4.808
Potassium Sulphate......}		Insoluble Matters.......	.800
Potassium Sulphide ......}	9.896	Organic soil acid and loss	2.000
Magnesium Chloride........	5.016		

Total Solids, 38.376

BIRCHDALE SPRINGS, CONCORD, N. H.

CALCAREOUS

C. F. Chandler, Analyst, 1873

Mineral Ingredients	U. S. gal. contains Grains	Mineral Ingredients	U. S. gal. contains Grains
Sodium Chloride..............	.376	Calcium Carbonate........	1.456
Sodium Carbonate...........	.128	Ferrous Carbonate.......	.272
Sodium Sulphate.............	.256	Alumina............	.112
Sodium Phosphate............	.008	Silica...................	.920
Potassium Sulphate...........	.064	Organic Matter..........	.672
Magnesium Carbonate....	.504		

Total Solids, 4.768

CLARENDON SPRINGS, RUTLAND CO., VT.

CALCAREOUS

A. A. Hayes, M. D., Analyst

Mineral Ingredients	U. S. gal. contains Grains
Sodium Sulphate.....}	
Magnesium Sulphate..}	2.72
Calcium Chloride.....}	
Calcium Carbonate...	3.04

Total Solids, 5.76

Gases	Cubic Inches
Carbonic Acid..................	46.16
Nitrogen......................	9.60

HIGHGATE SPRINGS, FRANKLIN CO., VT.

SULPHURETED

	Champlain Spring	
	A. A. Hayes, M. D. Analyst	T. Sterry Hunt Analyst, 1867
Mineral Ingredients	U. S. gal. contains Grains	U. S. gal. contains Grains
Sodium Chloride...........................	.108	23.440
Sodium Carbonate	1.224	13.704
Sodium Sulphate.........................	.....	2.448
Potassium Chloride......................	.744	.....
Potassium Carbonate....................	3.672	.....
Magnesium Carbonate...............	1.216	5.832
Calcium Carbonate.......................	1.016	1.400
Ferrous Oxide.............................	.032	.....
Ammonium Carbonate..................	trace	.....
Crenic Acid................................	.896	.....
Silicic Acid................................	.816	.....
Total Solids........	9.784	40.824

LUBEC SPRINGS, LUBEC BAY, MAINE

SALINE

Dr. C. T. Jackson, Analyst

Mineral Ingredients	Imp. gal. contains Grains	Mineral Ingredients	Imp. gal. contains Grains
Sodium Chloride...........	199.000	Calcium Carbonate......	6.250
Sodium Sulphate...........	27.985	Calcium Sulphate.......	11.210
Magnesium Chloride........	62.840	Ferrous Carbonate......	2.490
Calcium Chloride..........	trace	Loss...................	12.720

Total Solids, 322.500

NEWBURY, ORANGE CO., VT.

SULPHURETED

Prof. Hall, Analyst

Mineral Ingredients	U. S. gal. contains Grains	Mineral Ingredients	U. S. gal. contains Grains
Sodium Chloride..............	.32	Magnesium Sulphate.......	.40
Sodium Carbonate...........	4.00	Calcium Carbonate.......	17.60
Sodium Sulphate............	2.40	Ferrous Phosphate.......	.40
Sodium Sulphite.	.32	Ferrous Oxide..........	trace
Potassium Nitrate...........	.40	Silica and Suspended Clay	8.80
Magnesium Carbonate........	2.40	Or. Matter and Ammonia.	.24

Total Solids, 37.28

Gas	Cubic Inches
Sulphureted Hydrogen..........undetermined	

CANADIAN MINERAL SPRINGS

CALEDONIA SPRINGS, PRESCOTT CO., PROVINCE OF ONTARIO, DOMINION OF CANADA

Mineral Ingredients	Gas Spring T. S. Hunt, Analyst *Temp.* 44½°F. U. S. gal. contains Grains	Saline Springs T. S. Hunt, Analyst *Temp.* 45° F. U. S. gal contains Grains
Sodium Chloride	406.176	375.472
Sodium Carbonate	2.832	10.272
Sodium Iodide	.024	.080
Sodium Bromide	.872	.984
Potassium Chloride	1.800	1.752
Potassium Sulphate	.304	.280
Magnesium Carbonate	30.672	30.152
Calcium Carbonate	8.624	6.848
Ferrous Carbonate	......	trace
Manganese Carbonate	......	trace
Alumina	.256	trace
Silica	1.800	2.472
Total Solids	453.360	428.312
Gas	Cubic Inches	Cubic Inches
Carbonic Acid	40.00	32.00

PART II

Mineral Ingredients	Intermittent Spring Saline T. S. Hunt, Analyst *Temp.* 50° F. U. S. gal. contains Grains	Sulphureted T. S. Hunt, Analyst *Temp.* 46° F. U. S. gal. contains Grains
Sodium Chloride	714.120	224.032
Sodium Carbonate	......	26.568
Sodium Bromide	......	.584
Sodium Sulphate	......	1.064
Potassium Carbonate	1.776	1.336
Magnesium Chloride	60.264	......
Magnesium Carbonate	50.352	17.136
Magnesium Iodide	.120	......
Magnesium Bromide	1.384	......
Calcium Chloride	16.728	......
Calcium Carbonate	7.368	12.240
Ferrous Carbonate	trace	trace
Alumina	trace	.152
Silica	1.312	4.896
Total Solids	853.424	288.008
Gas	Cubic Inches	Cubic Inches
Carbonic Acid	......	16.00

CAXTON SPRINGS, THREE RIVERS, QUEBEC, CANADA
ALKALINE AND SALINE
T. STERRY HUNT, Analyst

Mineral Ingredients	U. S. gal. contains Grains	Mineral Ingredients	U. S. gal. contains Grains
Sodium Chloride	686.624	Calcium Carbonate	12.592
Potassium Chloride	4.664	Ferrous Carbonate	.312
Magnesium Chloride	21.288	Iodine	traces
Magnesium Carbonate	61.768	Alumina	.288
Magnesium Bromide	1.992	Silica	2.792
Calcium Chloride	2.928		

Total Solids, 795.248

Gas	Cubic Inches
Carbonic Acid	79.44

SANDWICH SPRINGS, ONTARIO, CANADA
SULPHURETED AND SALINE
PROF. S. P. DUFFIELD, Analyst

Mineral Ingredients	U. S. gal. contains Grains	Mineral Ingredients	U. S. gal. contains Grains
Sodium Chloride	.560	Calcium Chloride	.056
Sodium Carbonate	48.560	Calcium Carbonate	38.504
Potassium Carbonate	trace	Calcium Sulphate	123.832
Magnesium Chloride	153.760	Silica	.112
Magnesium Carbonate	12.944		

Total Solids, 378.328

Gases	Cubic Inches
Carbonic Acid	10.00
Sulphureted Hydrogen	37.76
Nitrogen	.72

ST. CATHERINE'S WELLS, ONTARIO, CANADA
SALINE

Mineral Ingredients	Stephenson House Well Prof. Croft Analyst U. S. gal. contains Grains	Welland House Well Prof. Croft Analyst U. S. gal. contains Grains
Sodium Chloride	1,737.872	2,206.944
Sodium Iodide		.080
Sodium Bromide		trace
Potassium Chloride	20.696	16.480
Magnesium Chloride	198.080	237.152
Magnesium Iodide	.240	....
Magnesium Bromide	.360	....
Calcium Chloride	866.168	1,017.616
Calcium Carbonate		.480
Calcium Sulphate	127.848	115.432
Ferrous Carbonate		3.040
Ammonium Chloride	.448	
Silicic Acid		
Total Solids	2,951.712	3,597.224

European Mineral Springs

AIX-LE-BAINS, SAVOY, FRANCE

SULPHUR

Bonjean, Analyst

Temperature, 108° to 110° F.

Mineral Ingredients	U. S. gal. contains Grains	Mineral Ingredients	U. S. gal. contains Grains
Sodium Chloride	.466	Ferrous Sulphate	traces
Sodium Sulphate	5.608	Strontium Carbonate	traces
Potassium Iodide	traces	Aluminium Sulphate	3.200
Magnesium Chloride	1.000	Aluminium Phosphate	
Magnesium Carbonate	1.504	Calcium Phosphate	.136
Magnesium Sulphate	2.056	Calcium Fluoride	
Calcium Carbonate	8.672	Silica	.288
Calcium Sulphate	.936	Loss	.696
Ferrous Carbonate	.512		

Total Solids, 25.074

Gases	Cubic Inches
Carbonic Acid	3.12
Sulphureted Hydrogen	6.56
Nitrogen	152.32

AIX-LA-CHAPELLE, RHENISH PRUSSIA

KAISERQUELLE

SULPHUR

Liebig, Analyst

Temp. 131° F.

Mineral Ingredients	U. S. gal. contains Grains	Mineral Ingredients	U. S. gal. contains Grains
Sodium Chloride	162.168	Magnesium Carbonate	3.160
Sodium Carbonate	39.960	Calcium Carbonate	9.736
Sodium Bromide	.224	Ferrous Carbonate	.584
Sodium Iodide	.082	Lithium Carbonate	.016
Sodium Sulphate	10.168	Strontium Carbonate	.016
Sodium Sulphide	.584	Silica	4.064
Potassium Sulphate	9.488	Organic Matter	4.616

Total Solids, 244.816

Gases	Per Cent
Carbonic Acid	30.39
Sulphureted Hydrogen	.31
Carburetted Hydrogen	1.82

APOLLINARIS WATER, NEUENAHAR, RHENISH PRUSSIA
ALKALINE
Prof. Bischof, Analyst

Mineral Ingredients	U. S. gal. contains Grains	Mineral Ingredients	U. S. gal. contains Grains
Sodium Chloride	28.56	Calcium Carbonate	3.60
Sodium Carbonate	77.20	Ferric Oxide	1.20
Sodium Sulphate	18.40	Alumina	1.20
Magnesium Carbonate	27.12	Silica	.48

Total Solids, 157.76

Gas	Cubic Inches
Free Carbonic Acid	376.32

Exported largely to United States.

BADEN-BADEN, BADEN, GERMANY—HAUPTQUELLE
CHLORINE-THERMAL
Bunsen, Analyst
Temperature 155° F.

Mineral Ingredients	U. S. gal. contains Grains	Mineral Ingredients	U. S. gal. contains Grains
Sodium Chloride	132.160	Calcium Phosphate	.168
Sodium Bromide	traces	Ferrous Arseniate	traces
Potassium Chloride	10.064	Ferrous Bicarbonate	.296
Potassium Sulphate	.136	Manganese Bicarbonate	traces
Magnesium Chloride	.776	Ammonium Bicarbonate	.408
Magnesium Bicarbonate	.336	Alumina	.064
Calcium Bicarbonate	10.184	Silica	7.312
Calcium Sulphate	12.448	Nitrates	traces

Total Solids, 174.352

Gas	Cubic Inches
Carbonic Acid	2.392

BAGNERES-DE-BIGORRE (LA REINE) HAUTES-PYRENEES FRANCE
EARTHY-SALINO THERMAL
Ganderax and Rosieru, Analysts
Temperature 115.7° F.

Mineral Ingredients	U. S. gal. contains Grains	Mineral Ingredients	U. S. gal. contains Grains
Sodium Chloride	3.624	Calcium Sulphate	98.112
Magnesium Chloride	7.592	Ferrous Carbonate	4.672
Magnesium Carbonate	2.568	Silica	2.114
Magnesium Sulphate ⎫	23.128	Residue and Fatty Matter	.400
Sodium Sulphate ⎭		Loss	3.152
Calcium Carbonate	15.536		

Total Solids, 160.898

Gas	Cubic Inches
Carbonic Acid	undetermined

BAGNÈRES-DE-LUCHON (LAREINE) AUTHE-GARONNE FRANCE

LIGHT SALINO-SULPHUM

FILHOL, Analyst

Temperature 131° F.

Mineral Ingredients	U. S. gal. contains Grains	Mineral Ingredients	U. S. gal. contains Grains
Sodium Chloride	3.936	Calcium Sulphate	1.888
Sodium Carbonate	trace	Calcium Silicate	.088
Sodium Iodide	trace	Manganese Sulphuret	.192
Sodium Sulphate	1.296	Magnesium Silicate	.480
Sodium Sulphide	3.208	Ferrous Sulphide	.160
Sodium Silicate	trace	Cupric Sulphide	trace
Sodium Hyposulphite	trace	Aluminium Silicate	1.440
Potassium Sulphate	.504	Aluminium	trace
Phosphates	trace	Silica	trace

Total Solids, 13.792

Gas	Cubic Inches
Sulphureted Hydrogen	traces

BAREGES (BOUCHERIES), HAUTES-PYRÉNÉES, FRANCE

LIGHT SALINE

LATOUR, Analyst

Mineral Ingredients	U. S. gal. contains Grains	Mineral Ingredients	U. S. gal. contains Grains
Sodium Chloride	1.872	Calcium Carbonate	.112
Sodium Iodide	.056	Calcium Silicate	.640
Sodium Sulphate	1.176	Ferrous Sulphate	.640
Sodium Sulphite	.928	Aluminium Silicate...)	
Sodium Silicate	1.188	Calcium Silicate......}	.680
Magnesium Chloride	2.336	Bituminous, Glairine, and	
		Loss	.696

Total Solids, 10.324

BATH, ENGLAND—KING'S WELL

EARTHY-SALINO THERMAL

MERCK and GALLOWAY, Analysts

Temperature 117° F

Mineral Ingredients	U. S. gal. contains Grains	Mineral Ingredients	U. S. gal. contains Grains
Sodium Chloride	12.642	Calcium Sulphate	80.052
Sodium Sulphate	19.229	Ferrous Carbonate	1.064
Potassium Sulphate	4.641	Silica	2.982
Magnesium Carbonate	.329	Iodine	traces
Magnesium Chloride	14.581	Manganese Oxide	trace
Calcium Carbonate	8.820		

Total Solids, 114.34

A 21

BILIN, BOHEMIA

JOSEPHQUELLE—ALKALINE

REDTENBACHER, Analyst

Mineral Ingredients	U. S. gal. contains Grains	Mineral Ingredients	U. S. gal. contains Grains
Sodium Chloride	23.480	Calcium Carbonate	24.712
Sodium Carbonate	184.848	Ferrous Carbonate	6.40
Sodium Sulphate	50.800	Lithium Carbonate	.880
Potassium Sulphate	7.880	Aluminium Phosphate	.520
Magnesium Carbonate	8.784	Silica	1.952

Total Solids, 304.496

Gases	Cubic Inches
Free Carbonic Acid	120.736
Carbonic Acid combined as Bicarbonate	137.976

BOURBONNE, HAUTE-MARNE, FRANCE

SALINE

CHEVALLIER, Analyst

Temperature 140° F.

Mineral Ingredients	U. S. gal. contains Grains	Mineral Ingredients	U. S. gal. contains Grains
Sodium Chloride	368.880	Calcium Carbonate	18.112
Potassium Bromide	3.072	Calcium Sulphate	47.944
Calcium Chloride	45.464		

Total Solids, 483.472

BRIGHTON, ENGLAND

CHALYBEATE

MARCET, Analyst

Mineral Ingredients	U. S. gal. contains Grains	Mineral Ingredients	U. S. gal. contains Grains
Sodium Chloride	12.24	Ferrous Sulphate	14.40
Magnesium Chloride	6.00	Silica	1.12
Calcium Sulphate	32.72	Loss	.152

Total Solids, 68.00

Gas	Cubic Inches
Carbonic Acid	20.00

CARLSBAD, BOHEMIA
HEAVY SALINE
Prof. Fowler, Analyst

Temperature 143° to 165° F.

Mineral Ingredients	Imp. gal. contains Grains	Mineral Ingredients	Imp. gal. contains Grains
Sodium Chloride...........	47.856	Ferrous Carbonate	.1
Sodium Carbonate.........	58.169	Manganese Carbonate....	.038
Sodium Sulphate...........	119.215	Lithium Carbonate......	.120
Magnesium Carbonate......	8.220	Strontium Carbonate....	.044
Calcium Carbonate.........	14.220	Aluminium Phosphate....	.015
Calcium Sub-phosphate......	.009	Silica	3.463
Calcium Fluoride..........	.147		

Total Solids, 251.682

Gases	Cubic Inches
Nitrogen.............................	none
Carbonic Acid Gas......................	58.

CARLSBAD (SPRUDEL) BOHEMIA
PURGATIVE
Gottl, Analyst

Temperature 162.5° F.

Mineral Ingredients	U. S. gal. contains Grains	Mineral Ingredients	U. S. gal. contains Grains
Sodium Chloride............	69.792	Calcium Carbonate......	16.020
Sodium Carbonate..........	72.496	Ferrous Carbonate......	.248
Sodium Sulphate............	159.680	Aluminium Phosphate...	1.720
Potassium Sulphate.........	2.960	Silica	8.416
Magnesium Carbonate.......	3.192		

Total Solids, 334.664

Gases	Cubic Inches
Carbonic Acid..........................	62.40
Nitrogen...............................	.24

ALKALINE
Prof. E. Ludwig and Prof. J. Mauthner, Analysts, 1886

Mineral Ingredients	U. S. gal. contains Grains	Mineral Ingredients	U. S. gal. contains Grains
Carbonate of Iron...........	0.030	Chloride of Sodium......	10.418
Carbonate of Manganese......	0.002	Fluoride of Sodium......	0.051
Carbonate of Magnesium. ...	1.665	Borate of Sodium........	0.040
Carbonate of Calcium........	3.214	Phosphate of Calcium....	0.007
Carbonate of Strontium......	0.004	Oxide of Aluminium.....	0.004
Carbonate of Lithium........	0.123	Silicic Acid.............	0.715
Carbonate of Sodium........	12.980	Carbonic Acid, partly com-	
Sulphate of Potassium........	1.862	bined..................	7.761
Sulphate of Sodium........	24.053	Carbonic Acid, free......	1.898
Cæsium, Rubidium, Thallium, Zinc, Arsenic, Antimony, Selenium, Formic Acid, Undeterminable Organic Matter........................... }			traces

Amount of Solids....................... 55.168

Specific Gravity....................... 1.00330

Temperature in C°.................... 73.8

SPRUDEL SALZ (POWDER)

Dr. Sipoecz, Analyst

Mineral Ingredients	U. S. gal. contains Grains	Mineral Ingredients	U. S. gal. contains Grains
Sodium Sulphate	43.25	Sodium Fluoride	0.09
Sodium Carbonate	36.29	Sodium Borate	0.07
Sodium Chloride	16.81	Silicic Acid Anhydride	0.03
Potassium Sulphate	3.06	Iron Oxide	0.01
Lithium Carbonate	0.39		

CHELTENHAM, ENGLAND

SALINE

Parkes and Brande, Analysts

Mineral Ingredients	U. S. gal. contains Grains	Mineral Ingredients	U. S. gal. contains Grains
Sodium Chloride	400.00	Magnesium Sulphate	88.00
Sodium Sulphate	120.00	Calcium Sulphate	36.00

Total Solids, 644.00

CHALYBEATE

Parkes and Brande, Analysts

Mineral Ingredients	U. S. gal. contains Grains	Mineral Ingredients	U. S. gal. contains Grains
Sodium Chloride	330.40	Magnesium Sulphate	48.00
Sodium Carbonate	4.00	Calcium Sulphate	20.00
Sodium Sulphate	181.60	Ferric Oxide	6.40

Total Solids, 590.40

Gas	Cubic Inches
Carbonic Acid	20.00

CONTREXVILLE (PAVILION), VOSGES, FRANCE

CALCAREOUS

Henry, Analyst

Mineral Ingredients	U. S. gal. contains Grains	Mineral Ingredients	U. S. gal. contains Grains
Sodium Carbonate	11.504	Calcium Carbonate	39.416
Sodium Sulphate	7.592	Calcium Sulphate	67.160
Sodium Chloride	8.176	Ferrous Carbonate	.528
Potassium Chloride		Strontium Carbonate	trace
Potassium Sulphate	trace	Calcium Phosphate	
Magnesium Chloride	2.336	Or. Matter and Arsenic	4.088
Magnesium Carbonate	12.848	Silica	7.008
Magnesium Sulphate	11.096		

Total Solids, 171.752

Gases	Cubic Inches
Oxygen	undetermined
Carbonic Acid	2.32

EMS ON THE LAHN, GERMANY
KESSELBRUNNEN—ALKALINE
Fresenius, Analyst
Temperature 115° F.

Mineral Ingredients	U. S. gal. contains Grains	Mineral Ingredients	U. S. gal. contains Grains
Sodium Chloride	62.1640	Ferrous Carbonate	.1616
Sodium Carbonate	80.3032	Manganese Carbonate	.0280
Sodium Sulphate	.0488	Strontium)	
Potassium Sulphate	3.1496	Barium Carbonate)	.0240
Magnesium Carbonate	6.8080	Aluminium Phosphate	.0768
Calcium Carbonate	10.0728	Silica	2.9184

Total Solids, 169.7552

Gas	Cubic Inches
Carbonic Acid	54.304

FACHINGEN, NASSAU, GERMANY
ALKALINE
Fresenius, Analyst

Mineral Ingredients	U. S. gal. contains Grains	Mineral Ingredients	U. S. gal. contains Grains
Sodium Chloride	36.4592	Calcium Fluoride	.0216
Sodium Carbonate	155.8104	Ferrous Carbonate	.6408
Sodium Sulphate	1.0976	Lithium Carbonate	.0032
Sodium Phosphate	.4048	Lithium Phosphate	.0016
Magnesium Carbonate	10.8640	Strontium Carbonate	.0056
Calcium Chloride	.0272	Aluminium Phosphate	.0024
Calcium Carbonate	16.0880	Silica Phosphate	2.0880
Calcium Phosphate	.0032		

Total Solids, 223.5176

Gases	Cubic Inches
Carbonic Acid	263.800
Nitrogen	.200

The water of this spring is chiefly exported.

FRIEDRICHSHALL, SAXE-MEININGEN, GERMANY
PURGATIVE
Bauer, Analyst

Mineral Ingredients	U. S. gal. contains Grains	Mineral Ingredients	U. S. gal. contains Grains
Sodium Chloride	538.96	Magnesium Sulphate	316.40
Sodium Sulphate	333.84	Calcium Carbonate	.88
Potassium Sulphate	.16	Calcium Sulphate	89.92
Magnesium Chloride	248.64	Ammonium Chloride	.48
Magnesium Carbonate	28.24	Aluminium Chloride	.56
Magnesium Bromide	.16	Silica	1.68

Total Solids, 1,559.92

Gas	Cubic Inches
Carbonic Acid	42.56

GASTEIN, SALZBURG, AUSTRIA
THERMAL
WOLF, Analyst
Temperature, 87° to 160° F.

Mineral Ingredients	U. S. gal. contains Grains	Mineral Ingredients	U. S. gal. contains Grains
Sodium Chloride	2.88	Ferrous Carbonate	.40
Sodium Carbonate	.32	Manganese Carbonate	.16
Sodium Sulphate	12.08	Strontia	trace
Potassium Sulphate	.08	Aluminium Phosphate	.32
Magnesium Carbonate	.16	Silica	1.92
Calcium Carbonate	2.88	Organic Matter	trace
Calcium Fluoride	trace		

Total Solids, 21.20

Gases	Percentage
Oxygen	30.89
Nitrogen	69.11

GEILNAU, HESSE, GERMANY
ALKALINE
FRESENIUS, Analyst

Mineral Ingredients	U. S. gal. contains Grains	Mineral Ingredients	U. S. gal. contains Grains
Sodium Chloride	2.224	Calcium Fluoride	trace
Sodium Bicarbonate	65.136	Ferrous Bicarbonate	2.352
Sodium Sulphate	.528	Manganese Bicarbonate	.280
Sodium Borate	trace	Barium Bicarbonate	.008
Sodium Nitrate	trace	Lithium Carbonate	trace
Sodium Phosphate	.024	Strontium Carbonate	trace
Potassium Sulphate	1.080	Alumina	trace
Magnesium Bicarbonate	22.304	Organic Matter	trace
Calcium Bicarbonate	30.336		

Total Solids, 124.072

Gases	Grains
Carbonic Acid, free	171.200
Ammonium Bicarbonate	.080
Nitrogen	.952
Hydrogen Sulphide	trace

The water of this spring is used exclusively for export.

GIESSHUEBEL (NEAR CARLSBAD), BOHEMIA
ALKALINE
GOTTL, Analyst

Mineral Ingredients	U. S. gal. contains Grains	Mineral Ingredients	U. S. gal. contains Grains
Sodium Carbonate	56.768	Calcium Carbonate	11.672
Potassium Chloride	3.008	Ferrous Carbonate	.003
Potassium Carbonate	5.248	Alumina	.136
Potassium Sulphate	1.776	Silica	5.248
Magnesium Carbonate	2.720		

Total Solids, 86.579

Gas	Cubic Inches
Carbonic Acid	305.664

HALL, AUSTRIA

HAUPTQUELLE—SALINE

NETWALD, Analyst

Mineral Ingredients	U. S. gal. contains Grains	Mineral Ingredients	U. S. gal. contains Grains
Sodium Chloride	896.320	Calcium Chloride	23.464
Sodium Iodide	.488	Calcium Carbonate	3.840
Potassium Chloride	.392	Calcium Phosphate	.208
Magnesium Chloride	20.976	Ferrous Carbonate	.704
Magnesium Carbonate	1.936	Ammonium Chloride	.264
Magnesium Iodide	2.280	Silica	.584
Magnesium Bromide	4.144		

Total Solids, 955.600

Gas	Grains
Carbonic Acid	10.96

This is ranked rather as a medicinal brine.

HARROWGATE, ENGLAND

SULPHURETED

Mineral Ingredients	Old Sulphur Well A. W. Hoffmann Analyst U. S. gal. contains Grains	Montpelier Strong A. W. Hoffmann Analyst U. S. gal. contains Grains
Sodium Chloride	688.144	642.472
Sodium Iodide	trace	......
Sodium Bromide	trace	......
Sodium Sulphide	12.384	11.528
Potassium Chloride	43.760	4.600
Magnesium Chloride	44.552	43.736
Calcium Chloride	65.392	49.528
Calcium Carbonate	9.896	19.344
Calcium Sulphate	.104	.472
Calcium Fluoride	trace	trace
Ferrous Carbonate	trace	......
Manganese Carbonate	trace	......
Ammonia	trace	trace
Silica	.200	1.472
Organic Matter	......	trate
Total Solids	864.432	773.152

Gases	Cubic Inches	Cubic Inches
Carbonic Acid	17.600	11.208
Sulphureted Hydrogen	4.248	......
Oxygen	......	.384
Nitrogen	2.328	3.856
Marsh-gas	4.672	.424

HOLYWELL, NORTH WALES

CARBONATED

Unknown Analyst

Temperature, 52° F.

Mineral Ingredients	Imp. gal. contains Grains	Mineral Ingredients	Imp. gal. contains Grains
Sodium Chloride	.821	Calcium Carbonate	.13.685
Sodium Carbonate	1.432	Calcium Chloride	3.094
Potassium Chloride	traces	Calcium Sulphate	5.202
Magnesium Carbonate	2.688	Ferrous Carbonate	traces
Magnesium Sulphate	traces	Silicic Acid	2.737

Total Solids.............................29.650

Gases	Cubic Inches
Free Carbonic Acid	10.338

HOMBURG, HESSE, GERMANY

ELIZABETHBRUNNEN—SALINE

LIEBIG, Analyst

Mineral Ingredients	U. S. gal. contains Grains	Mineral Ingredients	U. S. gal. contains Grains
Sodium Chloride	633.20	Calcium Chloride	62.16
Sodium Sulphate	3.04	Calcium Carbonate	87.92
Magnesium Chloride	62.32	Ferrous Carbonate	3.68
Magnesium Carbonate	16.08	Silica	2.56

Total Solids, 870.96

Gas	Cubic Inches
Carbonic Acid	387.68

Mineral Ingredients	Kaiserbrunnen Hoffman, Analyst U. S. gal. contains Grains	Ludwigsbrunnen Hoffman, Analyst U. S. gal. contains Grains	Stahlbrunnen Liebig, Analyst U. S. gal. contains Grains
Sodium Chloride	839.52	383.68	638.88
Potassium Chloride	2.24	13.68	1.44
Magnesium Chloride	68.16	24.48	41.84
Magnesium Carbonate		.80	....
Calcium Chloride	140.00	58.24	85.36
Calcium Carbonate	5.44	43.92	60.24
Calcium Sulphate	1.36	1.20	1.20
Ferrous Carbonate	4.24	3.36	7.52
Silica	.72	1.60	2.48
Total Solids	1,061.68	532.96	838.96

Gas	Cubic Inches	Cubic Inches	Cubic Inches
Carbonic Acid	873.28	348.72	375.28

KISSINGEN (RAKOCZI), BAVARIA
SALINE
Liebig, Analyst

Mineral Ingredients	U. S. gal. contains Grains	Mineral Ingredients	U. S. gal. contains Grains
Sodium Chloride	357.68	Calcium Carbonate	65.12
Sodium Iodide	Trace	Calcium Sulphate	23.92
Sodium Bromide	.48	Calcium Phosphate	.32
Sodium Nitrate	.56	Ferrous Carbonate	1.92
Potassium Chloride	17.60	Lithium Chloride	1.20
Magnesium Chloride	18.64	Silica	.72
Magnesium Sulphate	36.00		

Total Solids, 524.16

Gases	Cubic Inches
Carbonic Acid	334.160
Ammonia	.056

KREUZNACH, RHENISH, PRUSSIA
SALINE

Mineral Ingredients	Elisenquelle Löwig, Analyst U. S. gal. contains Grains	Oranienquelle Liebig, Analyst U. S. gal. contains Grains
Sodium Chloride	583.064	869.640
Potassium Chloride	4.992	3.680
Magnesium Chloride	32.568	......
Magnesium Carbonate	.848	1.040
Magnesium Iodide	.280	.096
Magnesium Bromide	2.224	14.240
Calcium Chloride	107.112	181.992
Calcium Carbonate	13.544	2.040
Ferrous Carbonate	......	2.848
Lithium Chloride	4.904	......
Aluminium Phosphate	.200	.760
Silica	1.032	7.992
Total Solids	750.768	1,084.328

This is ranked rather as a medicinal brine.

LEUK (LORENZQUELLE) VALAIS, SWITZERLAND
CALCAREOUS
Brunner, Analyst
Temperature 123° F.

Mineral Ingredients	U. S. gal. contains Grains	Mineral Ingredients	U. S. gal. contains Grains
Sodium Chloride	.440	Calcium Carbonate	2.856
Sodium Sulphate	4.072	Calcium Sulphate	101.696
Potassium Chloride	.160	Ferrous Carbonate	.192
Magnesium Chloride	.216	Strontium Sulphate	.248
Magnesium Carbonate	.016	Silica	.816
Magnesium Sulphate	15.928		

Total Solids, 126.640

Gases	Cubic Inches
Carbonic Acid	2.08
Oxygen	1.52
Nitrogen	2.80

LUHATSCHOWITZ, MORAVIA
ALKALINE

Mineral Ingredients	Vincenzbrunnen Ferstl, Analyst U. S. gal. contains Grains	Amandibrunnen Ferstl, Analyst U. S. gal. contains Grains
Sodium Chloride	188.216	206.024
Sodium Carbonate	186.104	288.304
Sodium Iodide	1.056	1.032
Sodium Bromide	2.040	.808
Potassium Chloride	14.360	12.760
Magnesium Carbonate	3.376	4.544
Calcium Carbonate	37.472	38.552
Ferrous Carbonate	.888	1.080
Barium Carbonate	.560	.512
Lithium Carbonate	.072	.112
Strontium Carbonate	.744	.920
Silica	3.160	.856
Total Solids	438.048	555.504

Gas	Cubic Inches	Cubic Inches
Carbonic Acid	400.00	232.00

MARIENBAD (KREUZBRUNNEN,) BOHEMIA
PURGATIVE
KERSTEN, Analyst

Mineral Ingredients	U. S. gal. contains Grains	Mineral Ingredients	U. S. gal. contains Grains
Sodium Chloride	89.328	Ferrous Carbonate	2.800
Sodium Carbonate	68.752	Manganese Carbonate	.312
Sodium Sulphate	290.152	Lithium Carbonate	.392
Potassium Sulphate	3.592	Strontium Carbonate	.112
Magnesium Carbonate	25.600	Aluminium Phosphate	.432
Calcium Carbonate	36.840	Silica	5.432
Calcium Phosphate	.144		

Total Solids, 523.888

Gas	Cubic Inches
Carbonic Acid	125.60

MEINBERG (SCHWEFELQUELLE), LIPPE-DETMOLD, GER.
SULPHURETED
BRANDES, Analyst

Mineral Ingredients	U. S. gal. contains Grains	Mineral Ingredients	U. S. gal. contains Grains
Sodium Sulphate	46.752	Calcium Carbonate	17.192
Sodium Sulphide	.536	Calcium Sulphate	66.680
Potassium Sulphate	.040	Ferrous Carbonate	.064
Magnesium Chloride	8.280	Strontium Sulphate	.064
Magnesium Carbonate	1.376	Aluminium Phosphate	.080
Magnesium Sulphate	13.864	Silica	.960

Total Solids, 155.888

Gases	Cubic Inches
Carbonic Acid	10.48
Sulphureted Hydrogen	4.88
Oxygen	.16
Nitrogen	3.20

NAUHEIM, HESSE-CASSEL, GERMANY
KURBRUNNEN—SALINE
BROMEIS, Analyst

Mineral Ingredients	U. S. gal. contains Grains	Mineral Ingredients	U. S. gal. contains Grains
Sodium Chloride	879.384	Calcium Carbonate	.64.224
Potassium Chloride	32.376	Calcium Sulphate	5.920
Magnesium Chloride	17.240	Ferrous Carbonate	.1.160
Magnesium Bromide	2.360	Manganese Carbonate	.168
Calcium Chloride	65.720	Silica	.920

Total Solids, 1,069.472

Gas	Cubic Inches
Carbonic Acid	249.60

This is ranked rather as a medicinal brine.

NENNDORF, HESSE, GERMANY
TRINKQUELLE—SULPHURETED
BUNSEN, Analyst

Mineral Ingredients	U. S. gal. contains Grains	Mineral Ingredients	U. S. gal. contains Grains
Sodium Sulphate	36.392	Calcium Carbonate	27.048
Potassium Sulphate	2.712	Calcium Sulphate	64.968
Magnesium Chloride	14.808	Calcium Sulphide	4.440
Magnesium Sulphate	18.544	Silica	1.296

Total Solids, 170.208

Gases	Cubic Inches
Carbonic Acid	42.00
Sulphureted Hydrogen	10.24
Carburetted Hydrogen	.40
Nitrogen	4.88

NEUENAHR, RHENISH, PRUSSIA
MARIENSPRUDEL—THERMAL
MOHR, Analyst

Mineral Ingredients	U. S. gal. contains Grains	Mineral Ingredients	U. S. gal. contains Grains
Sodium Chloride	5.52	Calcium Carbonate	12.88
Sodium Carbonate	44.50	Ferrous Carbonate	.48
Sodium Sulphate	6.08	Silica	1.52
Magnesium Carbonate	21.44		

Total Solids, 92.72

Gas	Cubic Inches
Carbonic Acid	180.16

OBERSALZBRUNN, SILESIA

ALKALINE

Mineral Ingredients	Oberbrunnen Fischer, Analyst U. S. gal. contains Grains	Mühlbrunnen Fischer, Analyst U. S. gal. contains Grains
Sodium Chloride	8.96	4.96
Sodium Carbonate	70.48	64.72
Sodium Sulphate	31.84	20.88
Magnesium Carbonate	8.00	15.04
Calcium Carbonate	16.16	16.96
Ferrous Carbonate	.56	.32
Silica	2.08	2.40
Total Solids	138.08	125.28

Gas	Cubic Inches	Cubic Inches
Carbonic Acid	300.00	26.40

PLOMBIÈRES (SOURCE DES DAMES), VOSGES, FRANCE

THERMAL

Sherrier, Analyst

Mineral Ingredients	U. S. gal. contains Grains	Mineral Ingredients	U. S. gal. contains Grains
Sodium Chloride	2.200	Magnesium Silicate	1.224
Sodium Sulphate	5.016	Calcium Silicate	
Sodium Arseniate	.040	Alumina	.608
Sodium Silicate	5.008	Silica	.712
Potassium Chloride	2.200	Organic Matter	1.224
Potassium Silicate	.064		

Total Solids, 18.296

PUELLNA, BOHEMIA

PURGATIVE

Struve, Analyst

Mineral Ingredients	U. S. gal. contains Grains	Mineral Ingredients	U. S. gal. contains Grains
Sodium Sulphate	990.400	Calcium Carbonate	6.160
Potassium Sulphate	38.400	Calcium Sulphate	20.800
Magnesium Chloride	157.328	Calcium Phosphate	.024
Magnesium Carbonate	51.248	Silica	1.408
Magnesium Sulphate	744.688		

Total Solids, 2,010.456

PYRMONT, WALDECK, GERMANY

TRINKBRUNNEN—CHALYBEATE

Wiggers, Analyst

Mineral Ingredients	U. S. gal. contains Grains	Mineral Ingredients	U. S. gal. contains Grains
Sodium Chloride	30.016	Ferrous Carbonate	2.480
Sodium Nitrate	traces	Manganese Carbonate	.192
Potassium Sulphate	1.360	Lithium Chloride	.152
Magnesium Chloride	4.004	Ammonium Carbonate	.016
Magnesium Carbonate	5.920	Alumina	.064
Magnesium Sulphate	22.704	Silica	.152
Calcium Carbonate	58.208	Organic Matter	trace
Calcium Sulphate	52.872		

Total Solids, 178.200

Gas	Cubic Inches
Carbonic Acid	376.80

SCHLANGERBAD, NASSAU, GERMANY

THERMAL

Fresenius, Analyst

Temperature 82.4° to 89.6° F.

Mineral Ingredients	U. S. gal. contains Grains	Mineral Ingredients	U. S. gal. contains Grains
Sodium Chloride	14.600	Potassium Sulphate	.728
Sodium Carbonate	.632	Magnesium Carbonate	.376
Sodium Phosphate	.032	Calcium Carbonate	2.000
Potassium Chloride	.032	Silica	2.064

Total Solids, 20.464

SCHWALBACH, NASSAU, GERMANY

STAHLBRUNNEN—CHALYBEATE

Fresenius, Analyst

Mineral Ingredients	U. S. gal. contains Grains	Mineral Ingredients	U. S. gal. contains Grains
Sodium Chloride	.416	Magnesium Carbonate	7.728
Sodium Carbonate	.880	Calcium Carbonate	9.448
Sodium Sulphate	.488	Ferrous Carbonate	3.736
Sodium Borate	trace	Manganese Carbonate	.824
Sodium Phosphate	trace	Silica	1.968
Potassium Sulphate	.232	Organic Matter	trace

Total Solids, 25.720

Gases	Cubic Inches
Carbonic Acid	402.160
Sulphureted Hydrogen	.024

SEIDLITZ, BOHEMIA

PURGATIVE

STEINMANN, Analyst

Mineral Ingredients	U. S. gal. contains Grains	Mineral Ingredients	U. S. gal. contains Grains
Sodium Sulphate	139.52	Calcium Carbonate	42.32
Potassium Sulphate	35.28	Calcium Sulphate	33.12
Magnesium Chloride	8.48	Ferrous Carbonate	} .40
Magnesium Carbonate	1.60	Manganese Carbonate	
Magnesium Sulphate	636.40	Strontium Carbonate	.072
Magnesium Bromide and Fluoride	trace	Silica	.40

Total Solids, 897.592

SELTERS, NASSAU, GERMANY

SALINE

HASTNER, Analyst

Mineral Ingredients	U. S. gal. contains Grains	Mineral Ingredients	U. S. gal. contains Grains
Sodium Chloride	137.824	Calcium Carbonate	14.816
Sodium Carbonate	54.224	Calcium Sulphate	2.088
Sodium Sulphate	2.088	Calcium Fluoride	.0128
Sodium Phosphate	.0016	Ferrous Carbonate	.632
Potassium Chloride	2.312	Manganese Carbonate	.016
Potassium Bromide	.0016	Aluminium Phosphate	.0032
Magnesium Carbonate	12.128	Silica	2.000

Total Solids, 228.1472

Gases	Cubic Inches
Carbonic Acid	240.0000
Oxygen	.0368
Nitrogen	.2280

Is exported only.

SPA (POUHON), LIEGE, BELGIUM

CHALYBEATE

MONHEIM, Analyst

Mineral Ingredients	U. S. gal. contains Grains	Mineral Ingredients	U. S. gal. contains Grains
Sodium Chloride	1.256	Ferrous Carbonate	5.416
Sodium Carbonate	5.600	Aluminium Carbonate	.192
Magnesium Carbonate	1.928	Silica	1.736
Calcium Carbonate	4.640	Loss	.096

Total Solids, 20.864

Gas	Cubic Inches
Carbonic Acid	572.80

ST. MORITZ (GRANDE SOURCE), GRISONS, SWITZERLAND
CHALYBEATE
Planta and Kekulé, Analysts

Mineral Ingredients	U. S. gal. contains Grains	Mineral Ingredients	U. S. gal. contains Grains
Sodium Chloride	2.256	Ferrous Carbonate	1.384
Sodium Carbonate	10.912	Manganese Carbonate	.240
Sodium Sulphate	15.736	Phosphoric Acid	.024
Potassium Sulphate	.952	Bromide, Iodine, Fluorine	traces
Magnesium Carbonate	6.616	Alumina	.016
Calcium Carbonate	42.424	Silica	2.224

Total Solids, 82.784

Gas	Cubic Inches
Carbonic Acid	314.32

TŒPLITZ (HAUPTQUELLE), BOHEMIA
THERMAL
Wolf, Analyst
Temperature, 120° F.

Mineral Ingredients	U. S. gal. contains Grains	Mineral Ingredients	U. S gal. contains Grains
Sodium Chloride	3.464	Ferrous Carbonate	.152
Sodium Carbonate	21.080	Manganese Carbonate	.168
Sodium Sulphate	2.320	Strontium Carbonate	.216
Sodium Phosphate	.112	Crenic Acid	.272
Potassium Sulphate	.784	Aluminium Phosphate	.160
Magnesium Carbonate	.704	Silicon Fluoride	2.808
Calcium Carbonate	2.640	Silica	3.544

Total Solids, 38.424

Gases	Percentage
Carbonic Acid	4.74
Oxygen	.66
Nitrogen	94.59

TUNBRIDGE WELLS, ENGLAND
CHALYBEATE
Scudamore, Analyst

Mineral Ingredients	U. S. gal. contains Grains	Mineral Ingredients	U. S. gal. contains Grains
Sodium Chloride	2.46	Ferric Oxide	2.22
Magnesium Chloride	.29	Manganese	
Calcium Chloride	.39	Organic Matter	.44
Calcium Carbonate	.27	Silica	
Calcium Sulphate	1.41	Loss	.13

Total Solids, 7.61

VALS. FRANCE

DÉSIRÉE SPRING—CARBONATED

LABORATORY ACADEMY OF MEDICINE, PARIS, Analyst

Mineral Ingredients	In 1.000 Grammes	Mineral Ingredients	In 1.000 Grammes
Sodium Chloride	} 1.100	Calcium Bicarbonate... .	.571
Potassium Chloride	}	Ferrous Peroxide	} .010
Sodium Sulphate	} 0.200	Manganese	}
Calcium Sulphate	}	Alkaline Iodide....	traces
Sodium Bicarbonate	6.040	Lith'm Bicarbonate..strong traces	
Sodium Arseniate	trace	Alumina	.058
Potassium Bicarbonate	.263	Organic Matter	traces
Magnes'am Bicarbonate	.900		

Total Solids in 1.000 grammes, 9.142

Total in grains per U. S. gallon, 535.88

Gas
Free Carbonic Acid Gas........2.145 grammes

VICHY, FRANCE

GRANDE GRILLE—ALKALINE

BOQUET, Analyst

Temperature, 105.8° F.

Mineral Ingredients	U. S. gal. contains Grains	Mineral Ingredients	U. S. gal. contains Grains
Sodium Chloride	32.80	Magnesium Carbonate	11.04
Sodium Carbonate	208.00	Calcium Carbonate	18.48
Sodium Borate	trace	Ferrous Carbonate	.16
Sodium Arseniate	.08	Manganese Carbonate	trace
Sodium Sulphate	18.32	Strontium Carbonate	.08
Sodium Phosphate	6.24	Silica	.40
Potassium Carbonate	16.32		

Total Solids, 311.92

Gas	Cubic Inches
Carbonic Acid,	117.92

VICTORIAQUELLE, NEUENAHR, RHENISH PRUSSIA

ALKALINE

Mineral Ingredients	U. S. gal. contains Grains	Mineral Ingredients	U. S. gal. contains Grains
Sodium Chloride	7.28	Calcium Bicarbonate	26.40
Sodium Bicarbonate	86.40	Ferrous Oxide	} .80
Sodium Sulphate	5.84	Alumina	}
Magnesium Bicarbonate	29.92	Silica	2.00

Total Solids, 158.64

Gas	Cubic Inches
Carbonic Acid	102.88

WILDBAD, WUERTEMBERG

THERMAL

Temperature, 94° F.

Mineral Ingredients	U. S. gal. contains Grains	Mineral Ingredients	U. S. gal. contains Grains
Sodium Chloride	14.56	Calcium Carbonate	2.72
Sodium Carbonate	4.24	Ferrous Carbonate	} 1.60
Sodium Sulphate	3.20	Manganese Carbonate	}
Potassium Sulphate	1.60	Silica	3.12
Magnesium Carbonate	5.60		

Total Solids, 36.04

Gases	Cubic Inches
Carbonic Acid	undetermined
Oxygen	undetermined
Nitrogen	undetermined

WEILBACH, HESSE, GERMANY

ALKALINE

FRESENIUS, Analyst

Mineral Ingredients	U. S. gal. contains Grains	Mineral Ingredients	U. S. gal. contains Grains
Sodium Chloride	77.5416	Magnesium Carbonate	4.4504
Sodium Carbonate	58.9984	Calcium Carbonate	6.0032
Sodium Iodide	.0080	Ferrous Carbonate	.1544
Sodium Bromide	.0448	Manganese Carbonate	.0312
Sodium Sulphate	13.7384	Lithium Carbonate	.3616
Potassium Sulphate	3.3864	Silica	.7544

Total Solids, 165.2728

Gases	Grains
Carbonic Acid	47.6424
Ammonium Carbonate	.6968
Sulphureted Hydrogen	.0208

WILDUNGEN (STADTBRUNNEN), WALDECK, GERMANY

CALCAREOUS

Mineral Ingredients	U. S. gal. contains Grains	Mineral Ingredients	U. S. gal. contains Grains
Sodium Chloride	.568	Calcium Carbonate	30.224
Sodium Carbonate	3.936	Ferrous Carbonate	1.112
Sodium Sulphate	7.352	Manganese Carbonate	.424
Magnesium Carbonate	19.224	Alumina	.064
Magnesium Sulphate	2.312	Silica	2.232

Total Solids, 67.448

Gas	Cubic Inches
Carbonic Acid	341.60

A. 22

WESBADEN (KOCHBRUNNEN) NASSAU, GERMANY

SALINE

Fresenius, Analyst

Temperature, 155.75° F.

Mineral Ingredients	U. S. gal. contains Grains	Mineral Ingredients	U. S. gal. contains Grains
Sodium Chloride	420.00	Calcium Arseniate	.008
Potassium Chloride	8.96	Calcium Phosphate	.024
Magnesium Chloride	12.56	Ferrous Carbonate	.32
Magnesium Carbonate	.64	Manganese Carbonate	.032
Magnesium Bromide	.24	Lithium Chloride	.008
Calcium Chloride	28.96	Ammonium Chloride	1.04
Calcium Carbonate	25.68	Aluminium Silicate	.032
Calcium Sulphate	5.52	Silica	3.68

Total Solids, 507.704

Gases	Cubic Inches
Carbonic Acid	133.60
Nitrogen	.80

BRINES OF MICHIGAN

Mineral Ingredients	East Saginaw Company's Well Per cent.	Bangor Company's Well Per cent.
Sodium Chloride	16.86	19.86
Magnesium Chloride	.96	1.26
Calcium Chloride	2.27	2.96
Calcium Sulphate	.15	.07
Total Saline Matter	20.24	24.15
Water	79.76	75.85
Total Solids	100.00	100.00

BRINES OF NEW YORK

Mineral Ingredients	Syracuse Per cent	Salina Per cent
Sodium Chloride	15.36	14.94
Magnesium Chloride	.14	.13
Calcium Chloride	.08	.08
Calcium Sulphate	.57	.59
Total Saline Matter	16.15	15.74
Water	83.85	84.25
Total Solids	100.00	100.00

BRINES OF PENNSYLVANIA

EAST CLARION SALT SPRING, ELK CO., PA.

M. H. Boye, Analyst

Mineral Ingredients	U. S. gal. contains Grains	Mineral Ingredients	U. S. gal. contains Grains
Sodium Chloride	336.80275	Ferrous Bicarbonate	.72444
Potassium Chloride	.89971	Barium Chloride	1.72573
Magnesium Chloride	15.34206	Barium Bicarbonate	.12791
Magnesium Bicarbonate	.57155	Lithium Chloride	trace
Magnesium Nitrate	.13623	Strontium Chloride	.06260
Calcium Chloride	51.85625	Strontium Bicarbonate	.00487
Calcium Bicarbonate	9.79502	Ammonium Nitrate	.19172
Calcium Phosphate	trace	Silicic Acid	.69523

Total Solids, 418.94407

BRINES AND SEA-WATER

Mineral Ingredients	Sea-Water Von Bibra, Analyst U. S. gal. contains Grains	Dead Sea Von Bibra, Analyst U. S. gal. contains Grains
Sodium Chloride	1,671.34	6,702.73
Sodium Iodide	trace	trace
Sodium Bromide	31.16	156.53
Sodium Phosphate	trace	......
Potassium Chloride	......	682.63
Potassium Sulphate	108.46	......
Magnesium Chloride	199.66	4,457.23
Magnesium Sulphate	34.99	......
Calcium Chloride	......	1,376.75
Calcium Sulphate	39.90	38.07
Calcium Carbonate	trace	trace
Ferric Chloride	trace	1.50
Manganese Chloride	......	3.35
Ammonium Chloride	......	3.35
Aluminium Chloride	......	31.37
Silver	trace	......
Copper	trace	......
Lead	trace	......
Arsenic	trace	......
Bitumen	......	trace
Silica	trace	trace
Organic Matter	trace	34.59
Total Solids	2,138.91	13,488.10

GREAT SALT LAKE, ETC.

Showing the comparative analyses of the Great Salt Lake, the Dead Sea and the Atlantic Ocean.

MINERAL INGREDIENTS	GREAT SALT LAKE			DEAD SEA	ATLANTIC OCEAN
	1849 Dr. Gale Analyst	1869 O. D. Allen Analyst	1879 J. T. Kingsbury Analyst		
Sodium Chloride................	20.196	11.8628	13.3765	12.110	2.6730
Sodium Sulphate..............	1.834	.0421	1.1213	......	......
Sodium Bromide...............	......	......	......	......	.0417
Magnesium Chloride..........	.252	1.4902	1.6908	7.822	.3229
Magnesium Sulphate..........	......	......	......	......	.1975
Magnesium Bromide..	......	......	......	.251	......
Calcium Chloride.............	......	......	......	2.455	......
Calcium Sulphate.............	......	.0858	.1485	.068	......
Potassium Chloride...........	......	......	......	1.217	.1290
Potassium Sulphate...........	......	.5363	.4107	......	.1629
Aluminum Compounds.........	......	......	......	.056	......
Lithium....................	......	trace	......	......	......
Boracic Acid................	......	trace	......	......	......
Chlorine, excess.............	......	.0862	.1250	......	......
Total	22.282	14.9634	16.8818	23.979	3.5271

CALIFORNIA

" Pious Portala, journeying by land,
Reared high across upon the heathen strand,
　　　Then far away
Dragged his slow caravan to Monterey.

The mountains whispered to the valleys, ' Good '
The sun, slow sinking in the western flood,
　　　Baptized in blood
The holy standard of the Brotherhood.

The timid fog crept in across the sea,
Drew near, embraced it and streamed far and free,
　　　Saying ' O ye
Gentiles and Heathen, this is truly He. '

All this the Heathen saw; and when once more
The holy Fathers touched the lovely shore—
　　　Then covered o'er
With shells and gifts the cross their witness bore."

Bret Harte.

ORIGIN OF THE NAME OF CALIFORNIA.

Many hypotheses have been advanced relative to the origin of the name of California.

Some writers favor the theory that the word is of aboriginal origin depending on some misunderstood words of the natives. Several writers among the Jesuit Missionaries point out the possibility of the word being derived from the Latin Calida fornax (hot furnace), as the southern part of Lower California was first touched by the discoverers during the hot season. Other less reasonable conjectures regarding the origin of the name have been found, until the noted antiquarian, Edward Everett Hale, promulgated, April 30, 1862, through the American Antiquarian Society the most authentic as well as the most probable account of the first use of the name California as follows:

There lived in Seville a favored Spanish novelist, Ordonez de Montalvo, who published a romance in 1510 entitled "Las Sergas del esforzado caballero Esplandian," in which the name appears twice as will be seen by the following translation. The romance was very popular and rapidly passed through several editions from 1510 to 1526. One of these issued from Madrid in 1521 is used for the translation.

TRANSLATION

The exploits of the very valiant Knight Esplandian, son of the excellent King Amadis of Gaul.—[Madrid, 1521.]

Furnished by Prof. Henry G. Hanks, State Mineralogist of California, in his sixth Annual Report, 1886.

Translated by Mr. Camilo Martin, Consul for Spain.

CHAPTER CLVII

The marvelous and not thought of succor with which the Queen Calafia came to the Port of Constantinople in favor of the Turks.

I wish you now to know a thing the most strange which ever either in writing or in people's memory could be found, by which the city was the following day on the point of being lost, and how from there where the danger came, salvation came to it. Know then that to the right hand of the Indies, there was an island called California, very near the part of the terrestrial Paradise, and which

was inhabited by black women, without there being among
them even one man, that their style of living was almost
like that of the Amazons. They were of robust bodies
and valiant and ardent hearts and of great strength; the
island itself was the strongest that could be found in the
world through its steep and wild rocks; their arms were all
of gold and also the harness of the wild beasts on which they
rode after taming them, as there was no other metal in the
whole island; they dwelled in well-finished caves; they
had many ships in which they went to other parts to obtain
booty, and the men whom they made prisoners they took
along, killing them in the way you shall hear further on.
And sometimes, when they were at peace with their adversa-
ries, they used to mingle with them with entire confidence;
if any of them gave birth to a son, he was put to death at
once. The reason for it, as it was known, was because in
their thoughts they were resolved to lessen the men to so
small a number that they would be able to master them
without much trouble, with all their lands, and preserve
those who would understand that it was convenient to do
so that the race might not perish.

In this island, called California, there were a great many
griffins, the like, on account of the ruggedness of the land
and the very many wild beasts therein contained, were not
found in any other part of the world; and when they had
little ones these women would go covered with thick skins
to catch them by tricks, and they would bring them to their
caves and there rear them; and when they were accustomed
to them, they would feed them with those men and with the
male children they bore, so often and with such cunning
that they very well learned to know them, and never did
them any harm. Any man who landed on the island was
at once killed and eaten by them; and though they might
be glutted, they would not the less take them and lift them
up, flying through the air, and when tired of carrying
them, they would let them fall, where they would be killed

at once. Well, at the time when those great men of the pagans departed with those large fleets, as history has already told you, there reigned in said Island California, a queen very tall of stature, very handsome for one of them, of blooming age, desiring in her thoughts to do great deeds, valiant in spirit, and in cunning of her fearless heart, more so than any of the others that before her reigned in that seigniory. And having heard how the greatest part of the world was moving in that expedition against the Christians, she, not knowing what beings were the Christians, nor having any knowledge of other countries except those which were next to hers, wishing to see the world and its different races, thinking that with her great valor and that of her adherents all that would be gained she would have, by force or by cunning, the largest share of, she spoke with all those that were skilful in war, telling them that it would be well that, going in their great fleets, they should follow the same road that those great princes and eminent men were taking, inciting and encouraging them by laying before them the very great honor and gain that might result to them from that undertaking; above all, the great fame that would resound in the whole world about them; that remaining in the island as they were, doing nothing but what their ancestors had done, would be only to be buried in life, like living dead, passing their days without fame and without glory, like wild animals.

So many things said to them by that very valiant Queen Calafia, that she not only moved her people to consent to the undertaking, but they, with their great desire that their fame should be published in many parts, hurried her to put to sea at once, so as to happen to be in the danger jointly with those great men. The Queen, who saw the determination of her people, ordered her great fleet to be supplied with provisions, and with arms all of gold and with all other necessaries; and she ordered the repairing of her largest vessel, made like a grate of thick timbers, and she had put into her up to five hundred griffins, which as you have been told, she had raised from tender age and fed with the flesh of men, and having therein also put the animals on which they rode and which were of different kinds ; also, the best chosen and best armed women which were in the fleet, and leaving such garrison in the island as to be secure, she put to sea with the others, and she hurried so much that she joined the fleets of the pagans the night of the combat, of which you have been told, which caused them all very great pleasure, and then she was visited by those great lords, who showed her great reverence. She wanted to know in what state was their enterprise, begging them to relate it to her minutely ; and having heard the report from them, she said : " You have fought this city with your many people and could not take it; well, I with mine, if it is agreeable to you, will on the following day, try the reach of my power, if you will accept my advice." All those great lords answered her, that whatever was by her indicated, they would order it executed. " Then notify at once all the other commanders that to-morrow, on no account, they nor theirs leave their quarters, until it is so ordered by me, and you shall see a fight the most strange never seen before this day, and of which you never have heard spoken." This was then made known to the great Sultan of Liquia and the Sultan of Halapa, who had charge of all the armies which were on land, and who thus ordered their people, wondering much what could be the thought and deed of that Queen.

Thus leaving very little if any doubt that the name " California" had its origin in the fertile brain of Señor Montalvo.

> " Then felt I like some watcher of the skies,
>   When a new planet swims into his ken;
> Or like stout Cortez, when with eagle eyes
>   He stared at the Pacific, and all his men
> Looked at each other with a wild surmise—
>   Silent upon a peak in Darien."

HISTORICAL SKETCH OF THE DISCOVERY AND EARLY OCCUPATION OF CALIFORNIA

It was in the year 1534, during one of these waves of popular enthusiasm which every now and again pass over large communities and inflame the minds of men, that California was discovered. These waves attacking the

OLD MISSION, LOS ANGELES

deepest interest of ambitious men frequently serve to impart an impetus to scientific research in astronomy, chemistry, physics and especially explorations and discoveries of new worlds. To-day as for centuries back explorations and excavations are constantly being pushed ahead. New expeditions are fitted out frequently for polar research and heroes thirsting for fame and the discovery of the open Polar Sea are pushing on with feverish excitement eager to outdo their predecessors. At the close of the fifteenth century the particular enthusiasm of Spain was the discovery of America. No time was lost in building fleets and sending them out, once Columbus had found the way, to fully explore the new continent and discover the western passage to the Indian seas.

Accordingly we find that Hernando Cortez, fully equipped set sail with his fleet and landed at Vera Cruz in April, 1519. Columbus believed in the Western passage until the day of his death. Cortez, while sailing along the Gulf of Mexico, thought he had found this coveted passage, and when he landed on the eastern coast of Mexico it was believed that Asia had been reached. Later on, however, when he had taken possession of the Aztec Capital, Cortez was convinced that the two continents were not identical, although Mexico was still supposed to be a part of the eastern continent, separated perhaps by a strait or a peninsula which the older explorers had not discovered. This problem the Spanish invader concluded to solve, and the easiest and surest way of accomplishing this was to go to the west seas and follow the western shores northward until the mouth of the strait or Asia itself should be found.

Reaching the western shores of Mexico amid great hardships and many privations, Cortez followed the coast northward until he came to a good harbor. Here he founded the city of Zacatula, about 175 miles north of Acapulco, and commenced building his fleet. Ship-building at best is a tedious undertaking, especially in a new country with hostile natives and the intoxication of conquest to divert one's attention. Still Cortez persevered and in the Spring of 1532 his first ships left Zacatula on their way northward. Hearing nothing from the first expedition, Cortez the next year (1533) sent out two more ships to ascertain the fate of the lost vessels and then push on to Asia. The voyage was supposed to take only a few months under favorable circumstances.

The expeditions of 1533 were under the command of a cousin of Cortez, Diego Becerra de Mendoza and Hernando Grijalva. This latter commandant soon became disheartened and losing faith in the undertaking, returned to Zacatula with his ship. Becerra de Mendoza, however, was made of different stuff and determined to push on with a chivalrous spirit—despite the fact that his crew became mutinous. Being of a haughty disposition he ruled his men with an iron hand, which only added fuel to the fire already kindled. The crew became more and more unmanageable and finally mutinied, with the pilot, Fortuna Jimenez at their head, killing commander Mendoza and putting the officers next in command on the wild shores of Colima to share the fate of their many comrades who had fallen while fighting the savages under Cortez.

Pilot Jimenez now took command of the ship and not caring to meet his fate at the hands of Cortez, pushed up the Mexican coast to find if possible the Asiatic continent and return to Europe. They sailed northward for many months, until one bright morning in the early part of the following year (1534) Jimenez discovered what he supposed to be an island on the western horizon. Bearing down upon it, a good, calm bay was found surrounded by green hills covered with shade trees. Here they decided to put ashore and explore the new country. The vessel was accordingly anchored at a safe distance from the shore and Jimenez with many of his crew took to the boats and landed on a fine sandy beach. No sooner had they landed than the beach swam with huge, dusky savages who overwhelmed the few dozen sailors like an avalanche with such deadly effect that Pilot Jimenez and a score of his faithful followers were slain before the ship could be reached and moved away from the deadly poisoned arrows so fatally wielded by the hostile aborigines.

Thus ingloriously died the discoverer of California, a few short moments after setting his foot upon the Golden

shore, for the supposed island was in reality Lower California and the place of landing was at what is now known as
La Paz in the little bay about seventy-five miles north of
Cape Palmo on the eastern side of the peninsula and on
the western side of the Gulf of California.

The few remaining sailors who succeeded at length in
getting their ship under way after several months reached
Cortez at Zacatula. After recounting to him the unlucky
passage of the vessel and how they had mutinied and
killed his cousin Mendoza and how in turn the large
coppery savages had killed their pilot and many of the men,
Cortez anxiously inquired what the Indians wore and if
there were any evidences of richness in their attire. To
this the men answered that the natives were well armed
with bows and arrows, stone and copper knives etc., and that
they wore strings of large pearls around their necks and
pieces of bright shining metal, presumably gold, on their
persons. This was enough for Cortez to judge of the
wealth of the supposed Island, and he at once set to work
to refit and get in readiness another expedition. Early in
the following year (1535) Cortez set out with a large fleet
for Jimenez Bay which he reached May 3rd of the same
year. This way was christened Santa Cruz. Here he
landed many of his colonists and then explored the coast
up and down the Californian and Mexican shores. The
Gulf of California was named the Sea of Cortez; it afterwards received the name of Mar Roxa (Red Sea) from the
peculiar red color of its waters, arising probably from the
discoloration of the Red Colorado (Red River), which
emptied into it large volumes of dark red water. Having
cruised around this red sea nearly a year, Cortez returned
to Santa Cruz to look after his colonists. Here he found
many of them killed and the rest suffering from great pri-
vation, heartily sick of their new home and begging to be
taken away from the hostile aborigines. Accordingly the

CHURCH AND STUDY NEAR DEL MONTE

fleet brought away every European from Santa Cruz in the early part of 1536 and he returned to Zacatula very much discouraged by the experiment.

After resting for a few years Cortez again fitted out a fleet, which started in 1539, commanded by Captain Francisco de Ulloa. This expedition rounded Cape St. Lucas and coasted up the western side of California as high as the Cedros Island off Cape San Eugenio, more than half way up the peninsula coast. It was during this voyage (1539-40) that the name California first appears to have been applied to the peninsula, having undoubtedly been taken from the romance of Montalvo which was published thirty years before.

Everything north of Cape St. Lucas was supposed to be an island or peninsula leading northward to Asia, and to this whole country was applied the name of California.

In 1542, another expedition was fitted out, this time from Navidad, in Mexico, under instructions from the Viceroy of Spain. The command was given to Juan Rodriguez Cabrillo one of the pilots of Cortez. To this man of undoubted courage belongs the honor of discovering Nueva California or Upper California proper. He sailed over the course of Ulloa and pushing on northward, anchored in San Diego Bay, naming it San Miguel.

October 3, 1842, Cabrillo left San Diego with a determination to reach Asia. He sailed northward, touching at the Santa Catalina Island which he found inhabited by natives. Anchoring off San Pedro, he took formal possession of a large Indian town named Xuca, on the coast of Ventura. As he sailed up the coast, dotted here and there with Indian towns, Cabrillo finally reached Monterey Bay, and remained there some time to view the country which pleased him so much. Proceeding northward again he passed Point Reyes, and reached as far north as Cape Mendocino which he named Mendoza, after the

Viceroy of Spain. He then turned southward, discovering the Farallones Islands which he named after his pilot Farallo.

From the records left by Cabrillo there is not the slightest mention made of San Francisco Bay, making it very certain that this daring navigator failed to enter the Golden Gate, for had he done so he would undoubtedly have left us some description of the finest harbor on the Coast.

At this time the Spanish claims in the new world—El Dorado or California, extended from Mexico to the Arctic circle. Colonization was encouraged and attempted from Mexico to San Francisco but not beyond it.

In the mean time England was watching America and especially the Golden West with a jealous eye. Several expeditions were sent out to the Atlantic shores.

In the year 1577 Sir Francis Drake fitted out a ship ostensibly for a buccaneering expedition along the Spanish Main, but Spanish commerce was the objective point of the Spanish Main or anywhere else. Having gathered considerable booty and sacked several newly settled towns along the Spanish coast, Sir Francis desired to head for England by way of the Cape of Good Hope. Destiny foiled this plan. It is just such accidents which play such an important part in the making of history. Drake's vessel got into coast currents and tradewinds which took him so far north that he got into a very cold region. As soon as it became practicable he headed south again and got into latitude 38 degrees, somewhere off the cliffs of Bodega or Drake's Bay. From the whiteness of the cliffs, Drake called the supposed new country New Albion from the resemblance to the coast of England. This was in the year 1578-9. Here Sir Francis landed. He found the Indians going about nearly nude. They were inclined to be peaceable and were desirous he should remain with his " wonder of the sea ". The natives offered the " White Chief " their whole country. Drake accepted in the name of Queen

Elizabeth and set up a post with an inscription thereon announcing the discovery and acceptance of this New Albion.   He then sailed away.

The exact place of Drake's landing has been a mooted question and caused considerable discussion.   Drake's Bay, Bodega Bay and San Francisco Bay, all claim the honor. Drake's Bay is in the same degree of latitude as noted by Sir Francis, and the coast even to-day greatly resembles, both in height and color, the white cliffs seen on the English Channel at Dover and Brighton.   Had Bodega been the landing place, surely some description of Tomales Bay would have been made; and had it been San Francisco Bay, which is considerably farther south than 38 degrees north latitude, this clever and daring explorer was not the man to have left without exploring the many arms of this great inland sea, one of the finest harbors in the world. Not one word about the Golden Gate reaches us from the accounts of Drake's expeditions, a fact, taken with others, which goes far to prove that Sir Francis Drake did not even dream of such a bay as that of San Francisco.

Many of the Spanish explorers and vessels both before and after Drake's voyage found Point Reyes, but not one of them say a word about San Francisco Bay.

In 1584 Francisco Gali, sailing a Philippine vessel from Macao and Japan to Acapulco, was taken by the great Oceanic current and tradewinds and carried as far north as Cape Mendocino.   Putting about, he succeeded in coasting down to Cape St. Lucas, but discovered nothing new.   A few years later, Carmenon, another Philippine commander was commissioned to explore the coast more minutely to find a safe harbor for Spanish vessels.   He also passed the Golden Gate without seeing it, although his vessel ran so closely ashore as to founder off Point Reyes.

Philip III of Spain, commissioned Sebastian Vizcaino in 1602 to explore the coast of California ; to find a suitable harbor for the Philippian ships, and to hunt for the western passage to Asia. He arrived at San Diego Bay the following year and changed the name from San Miguel to San Diego. He then proceeded on his voyage up the coast reaching as far north as Point Reyes and Mendocino. His chroniclers noted carefully many ports of the coast and described them in detail but not one word about San Francisco Bay—a further proof that it had never been discovered.

Histories and exaggerated accounts of the exploits of Cortez, Jimenez, Cabrillo, Drake, Carmenon and Vizcaino continued to attract attention and excite the adventurous spirits of another hundred years. Exploring expeditions were sent out under royal charter and under individual patronage to discover and explore this wonderful country whose shores were sands of gold and strewn with pearls of fabulous value. Adventurous spirits headed commands for this new world in 1615, 1633 and half a dozen more up to 1668. Most of them coasted up and down the Pacific shore without discovering anything new. None of them ever entered San Francisco Bay, or if they did so, left no record behind them which they would have been most likely to do, had they entered the Golden Gate.

The Early Mission Fathers

For over one hundred years from 1668 to 1779 slow progress was made in civilizing and colonizing California. Occasional expeditions followed in the track of their predecessors with similar results. Still the highly colored accounts of the rich El Dorado with mountains of gold and shores of pearl, continued to spread and enthuse the adventuresome souls of the age.

In 1677 the Spanish government decided that the Californian conquest and colonization should be undertaken again, this time with more vigor and with the additional aid of the Fathers of the church. Accordingly the Crown appointed Admiral Don Isidro Ontondo commandant of the expedition. The evangelizing missionaries were selected from the Jesuits, the most powerful spiritual organization in Mexico at that time. The Archbishop of Mexico con-

OLD MISSION CHURCH AT SANTA BARBARA

ferred the honors of leading the evangelizers, on Father Eusebio Francisco Kuhn—a much beloved German priest. Admiral Ontondo was to afford military protection while Father Kuhn and his priests converted the Indians. It was not, however, until 1683 that the expedition set sail up the Gulf of California and active operations commenced. For two years the brave expedition met with varying success in the Lower California. Many natives were christianized and much good was done.

The Spanish exchequer was not in a particularly flourishing condition at this time, and the court determined that such a heavy drain on its resources could not be maintained as nothing of much value was returned to Spain in exchange for her expensive conquest and evangelizing expedition, and the scheme was deemed impracticable. After a second effort by Ontondo and Kuhn the Spanish government withdrew the expedition and offered the entire control and large grants to the Jesuits if they would continue the projected undertaking. This proposal was not accepted by the Fathers and thus abruptly terminated for a short time the grand undertaking.

Father Kuhn, who had affectionately been called El Padre Kino, was bitterly disappointed at this unexpected turn of affairs, as he had fondly dreamed of the day when his missions would extend over the entire new country. While pondering over the subject Father Kuhn met with a priest as zealous as himself and these two courageous and uniting heroes, in their love and their great enthusiasm for the Catholic faith undertook themselves without means and without support to accomplish what the Spanish Crown had failed to bring to a successful issue. The second hero was Father Salvatierra. Later on Fathers Picolo and Ugarta joined Fathers Kuhn and Salvatierra and the four pioneers set to work with zeal and determination. Almost insurmountable obstacles were overcome and painful hardships endured, and it is pleasing to record that at length success crowned their efforts. The faithful servants established missions in various parts of Lower California.

In 1691 Kuhn explored the Gilda valley and noted the ruins of a once flourishing race. Between 1700 and 1709

Kuhn and his associates discovered that Lower California was not an island but part of the main land. The missions now extended from Cape St. Lucas to San Diego and from the City of Mexico to the Arizona line.

From 1725 to 1760 the Jesuits lost ground in their own dominion. Popular feeling ran high against them–although they had converted the desert and barren country into a veritable oasis. Miners and settlers began to pour into the land of wealth. Hatred was fomented against the priests and secularization assiduously advocated. So much pressure was brought to bear against the pioneer Fathers, that King Charles III of Spain issued an ordinance in 1766 making it imperative for all Jesuits to leave the Spanish dominions. The decree of banishment reached our peninsula in 1768 and they were forced to leave the field of their hardships and toils—the field of their early deprivations and painful though prosperous progress, and California was once again inhabited by aborigines alone.

THE FRANCISCAN FRIARS

During the latter half of the eighteenth century England, France and Spain were much interested in America and their respective colonial possessions. England had succeeded in obtaining the upper hand of France in several engagements which resulted in the great possessions of France in Asia (Hindoostan) and America (Canada) becoming English provinces. England, becoming bold, was looking after further conquests. Spain took warning and, although friendly with England, yet desired to look after her Californian possession.

Shortly after the Jesuit Fathers had been banished, Spain decreed that the Franciscan Friars should take charge of the Peninsula or Lower California missions and also establish missions in Upper or New California as

MISSION SAN MIGUEL—FOUNDED, 1772

rapidly as possible in order to occupy and be in possession
of the country should England or France direct attention to
the Golden West.

The chief establishment of the Franciscan Monks in
New Spain was located at San Fernando, and to it was
intrusted the labor of evangelizing the Indians and establishing missions up the coast. The head of this influential
convent honored Junipero Serra by selecting him director
and head of the California Missions.

The early history of California is inseparable from that
of Friar Serra—a man of superior intellect and fervid
religious zeal who had early been ordained and attracted considerable reputation as a preacher. He had spent many
years among the Indians of San Luis Potosi and was well
fitted to undertake the task. Friar Serra had renounced
the world and all its amusements. He found no attraction
in woman's society and less in the jovial companionship of
his own sex. He was ever serious and never indulged in
a smile or jocularity of any kind. His habits were austere
and he frequently practised personal chastisement, lashing
himself with wire ropes and stones and burning himself
with torches. He sought to be a simple, humble, obedient,
zealous Friar, without hypocrisy or pride. He made many
friends and few enemies and lived as pure a life and did as
many noble deeds as has fallen to the lot of any priest
before or since.

Early in the year 1769, several expeditions both by
land and by sea brought the Fathers of St. Francis to San
Miguel (now San Diego). They suffered much and several died from starvation on the trip from Mexico. Shortly
after the arrival of Friar Serra active work began, and on
July 11, 1769 the first Mission was founded—the Mission
of San Diego.

About the same time a small expedition with Portala
in command set out for Monterey. With this party were
Friars Crespi and Gomez. Onwards they marched and

finally reached the mouth of the Salinas River.   The coast by land looked different from what it had been described by sea and our party were not able to discover Monterey Bay. Thinking that perhaps it was still farther north the expedition resolved to push forward.   On the last day of October the company reached one of the heights on San Pedro and here halted for recuperation.   While camping here, a small expedition under sergeant Ortega set out to explore the coast for a few days.   Reaching the shore of the Pacific they tramped along the beach.   Arriving at the cliffs opposite Seal Rocks they were unable to go farther on the shore and took to the hills.   Ascending the cliffs, not by the well built road and beautiful grounds of Sutro's heights, but up the rough and rugged rocks they climbed.   Imagine the amazement with which Ortega gazed on the extensive inland sea and the Golden Gate.   This was the first time of which we have any record that San Francisco Bay was seen by European eyes.

During Ortega's absence, all remained quietly in camp excepting a few soldiers who were out hunting for game in the northeastern hills.   Having ascended several hundred feet above the surrounding country they too saw the large inland sea.   So San Francisco Bay was discovered by the two companies of Portala's expedition about the same time. On receiving the news Portala and Crespi broke camp on the 4th of November 1769 and determined to look at this large sheet of water themselves.   They could scarcely believe that it was correct as the many earlier explorers by sea had never even hinted at the existence of such a large body of water and surely it could hardly have escaped their experienced eye.   Reaching the San Bruno summits the whole expedition saw what Ortega and the soldiers had simultaneously discovered.   The company now retraced their steps to report the discovery of a harbor large enough to contain the whole Spanish fleet, and arrived at San Diego January 24, 1770.

April next, two more expeditions, one by sea and the other by land, were sent out to discover Monterey. The *San Antonio* with Father Serra on board sailed April 17, 1770 and reached the harbor of Monterey May 31st. They found the bay just as it had been described over a hundred and fifty years before. The land expedition reached the bay a week preceding. There was a grand jubilee and on the third of June the Mission of San Carlos was founded. The fort of Monterey was established and the whole country was formally occupied and taken possession of in the name of the King of Spain.

Immediately the news of these important discoveries and occupations were sent to Mexico and to Spain. High Masses, congratulations and receptions followed this important extension of the Spanish Crown.

Liberal and extensive provisions were made for the further establishment of missions. Expeditions were fitted out and missions established in rapid succession. The San Antonio Mission was located at the Santa Lucia Mountains July 14, 1771. Another one, that of San Gabriel was founded in August of the same year and located on the San Gabriel River. The San Luis Obispo Mission was founded the following year. In 1776 two missions were founded— one the San Juan Capistrano and the other the Mission Dolores at San Francisco.

From the time Portala's expedition discovered San Francisco Bay in 1769 several exploring companies had been sent out to report on this wonderful sea which had so completely escaped detection. Friar Crespi explored the eastern side of the bay as far north as the Carquinez Straits in 1772. Here he discovered the San Joaquin and the Sacramento Rivers. In 1774 another expedition explored the western shore of the bay as far as the Golden Gate, and in 1775 the ship *San Carlos*, with the *Saint Ayala* entered the Golden Gate—the first time its waters had been disturbed by anything excepting the Indian canoes. In 1776

MONTEREY BATHS

Friars Palou and Cambon with several married civilians and soldiers established the San Francisco Mission. This was the first occupation of San Francisco now 114 years ago. The military and the civilians occupied the presidio whilst the Fathers set to work building the old Mission Church. Many other missions were now being established in several parts of California. Evangelizing the Indians was pushed as rapidly as possible. The country becoming populated and the soil cultivated, herds of cattle and horses and sheep flourished and the golden shores of California were soon made to blossom like the rose. The Missions rapidly prospered and soon became very wealthy and influential, ruling and governing the country for many years.

Within about fifty years, the Franciscan Friars had established twenty-one missions, with large farms and extensive flocks. They were carrying on extensive trade in hides, tallow, wool and wine. They owned about twenty-five to thirty miles of the choicest land around each mission. These "golden days" continued from 1770 to 1822. About this time the Spanish power in Mexico had its downfall and with it the Missions and powers of the Franciscan Fathers commenced to decrease, until finally in 1845 they were formally abolished and their property confiscated.

For several years prior to this confiscation settlers had been constantly increasing. The Mexicans had been attracted by the richness of the soil and the healthfulness of the climate. Trappers and hunters and citizens in delicate health and with adventurous spirits crossed the high Sierras and flocked to California. Between 1840 and 1845 more than 5,000 people had crossed the long plains and scaled the high mountains to make their homes on the shores of the Pacific.

Before the close of 1846 there were 8,000 persons who had come by land and by sea to live in California. From 1822 to 1845 occasional skirmishes and petty wars occurred between settlers in the north and settlers in the south, and between California residents and Mexican troops. The country continued to prosper and immigration steadily increased. During the war between the United States and Mexico in 1846-8, over 12,000 persons arrived in the State. In 1850, September 9th, the State of California was

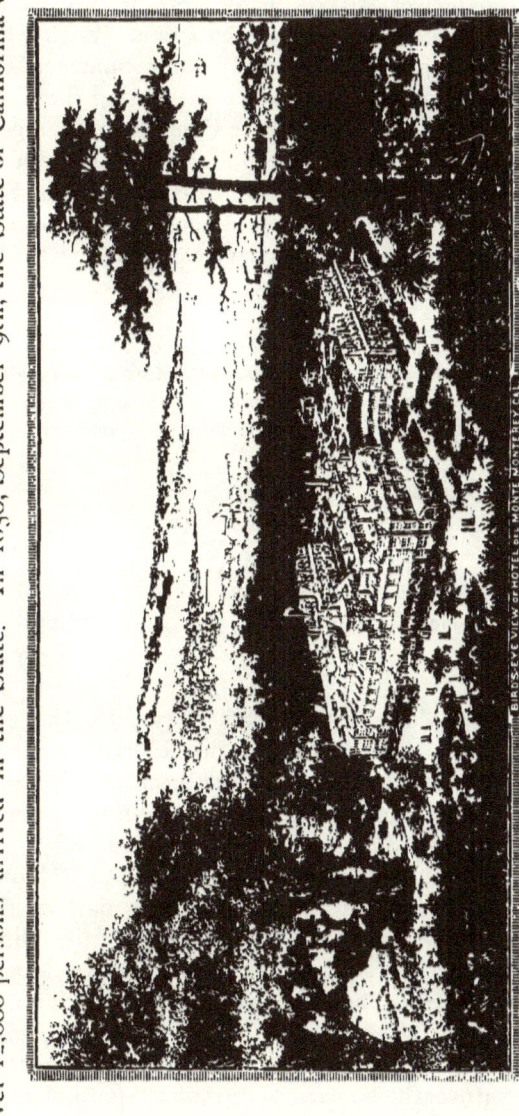

BIRD'S-EYE VIEW OF HOTEL DEL MONTE (MONTEREY, CAL.)

admitted into the Union. In February 1848 Marshall discovered the first nugget of gold on the estate of General Sutter in Sonoma County. This was the beginning of the golden era of California.

The news spread like wildfire. In less than four years from this date over 250,000 people were in the State and mining became the universal occupation. With such an enormous immigration, necessarily a large number of outlaws found their way here as well. It was during these stirring times that the noted "Vigilance Committee," composed of some of our best citizens, was obliged to administer justice and restore law and order. From this time on the State of California has increased in population, mineral and agricultural worth more rapidly than any other State in the Union.

> " Know'st thou the land where the lemon-trees bloom,
> Where the gold orange grows in the deep thicket's gloom,
> Where a wind ever soft from the blue heaven blows,
> And the groves are of laurel, and myrtle, and rose ? "

THE CLIMATE OF CALIFORNIA

> " The empire of climate is the most powerful of all empires."
> —*Montesquieu.*

So much has been written regarding the climatic advantages of the Pacific Coast, that I shall confine myself to giving a brief outline of this subject, merely touching upon the most salient points, and then, only as they bear upon the subject of health and health resorts.

The continuous tide of emigration to California is largely the outcome of an effort on the part of Eastern people to escape the rigor that characterizes the climate of the vast extent of country east of the Rocky Mountains. In California the changes from the oppressive heat of Summer to the intense cold of Winter are unknown nor do Californians suffer from the many atmospheric eccentricities that sweep over the Eastern country in the form of blizzards, cyclones and tornadoes. Even thunder storms are practically unknown here. The configuration of this State, which is nearly 800 miles long and traversed by two mountain ranges, would give rise to the greatest climatic variations were it not for certain modifying influences which do not exist anywhere else in the United States— influences which reduce the differences that would otherwise exist in a range of over sixteen degrees of latitude. Professor Whitney remarks, in his recent work on the United States:

" The causes of this condition of things in the Pacific Coast belt are as follows: The proximity of the great area of water from which the prevailing winds blow toward the land, as will be seen farther on ; the modification which the temperature of this ocean undergoes near the American Coast by the Asiatic Coast current and the northern or Arctic Coast current ; and the position of the mountain ranges near the coast. The fact that the prevailing winds blow from this great water area toward the land has a powerful influence in bringing about a uniformity of climate along the edges of the land, and this is still further aided by the peculiar nature of the currents along this coast. The influence of the warm Asiatic current, the Kuro-Siwo, is distinctly felt in raising the temperature as far south as the northern border of California; from here south, the cold Arctic current which apparently emerges from under the warm current, makes its presence felt in lowering the temperature along the coast nearly or quite as far south as the southern boundary of the country."

A little farther on he states that "on the California coast the winds are very strong and steady from the northwest in the Summer, but decidedly more to the southwest in Winter. In Summer the intensely heated plateau to the east draws the air from the Pacific, which blows with violence through every depression in the Coast Ranges towards the heated land-mass. There is no ' wind-gap' in the Coast

ORANGE GROVE
AND VINEYARD

VIEW AT
"SUNNY SLOPE"
SAN GABRIEL

PALM TREES
SAN GABRIEL VALLEY

BANANA GROVES AT WOLFSKILL'S

TYPICAL SOUTHERN CALIFORNIA

Ranges so deeply and widely cut as that of the Golden
Gate at San Francisco. At this point the cold winds from
the sea find entrance to the Great Valleys of Sacramento
and San Joaquin, and the mass of air thus set in motion
spreads itself out fan-like after passing through the Gate
so that the prevailing winds in those valleys during the
Summer are always from the Bay of San Francisco towards
the mountains. The hotter the weather in the interior the
more violent the wind at San Francisco. But this condition
is limited to the daytime. At night the rapid cooling of
the higher plateau checks or stops altogether the indraught
of air, and an almost entire calm prevails at San Francisco,
while the cool air flows in a gentle breeze down the slopes
of mountains, in a reverse direction from that which it had
during the daytime."

VELOCITY OF WINDS

Protected from the ocean by the Coast Ranges, the air
as a rule is dry, so that a degree of heat varying from 95°
to 100° F. can be borne with perfect comfort, whereas in
the humid atmosphere of the Atlantic Coast this temperature if kept up for any length of time would be insuffer-
able and in many cases fatal. Now this dryness and
lightness of atmosphere, relieved by cool dewy nights,
gives California a first place among sanitariums, as these
two attributes, accompanied by a uniform mean temperature
are of prime importance in all lung and throat affections.

A glance at the appended table will satisfy the reader
that California is unrivaled as far as uniformity of climate
goes, and that it will compare favorably with the most
celebrated resorts in the world, either in the United States
or abroad.

A. 21

These refreshing winds begin about the latter part of April, and continue through the Summer months. The velocity varies slightly from year to year. Commencing daily about

PACIFIC GROVE

one or two o'clock P. M. and lasting for two or three hours; the trade-winds blow in a south-easterly direction in the vicinity of San Francisco.

The following table, obtained from the records of the United States Signal Service office, gives the average monthly velocity of the wind in miles during the past three years.

	1886	1887	1888
March	13.5	15.2	13.3
April	15.5	17.6	16.7
May	16.9	18.7	17.1
June	22.5	21.5	19.6
July	21.7	20.0	19.6
August	21.2	21.4	19.5
September	18.1	17.2	17.4
October	14.0	13.6	13.3

Mean Temperature

	Jan.	Feb.	Mar.	April	May	June	July	Aug.	Sep.	Oct.	Nov.	Dec.
Coronado, California	55.9	58.5	55.0	57.2	60.4	63.1	67.0	70.5	66.6	59.7	56.0	56.0
Naples	46.5	48.5	52.0	57.0	66.5	71.0	75.0	76.5	72.5	65.0	54.5	50.5
Mentone	48.0	48.0	52.0	57.0	63.0	70.0	75.0	75.0	69.0	64.0	54.0	49.0
Rome	47.6	49.4	52.0	56.4	64.5	69.2	73.3	74.0	69.5	63.6	58.8	49.6
Nice	45.8	49.0	51.4	57.0	63.0	69.0	73.6	74.3	69.4	61.8	53.7	48.6
Florence	41.0	45.0	48.0	56.0	64.0	69.0	77.0	76.0	70.0	59.0	53.0	47.0
Mean Temp. at Coronado for 16 years	53.5	54.7	56.0	58.2	60.2	66.6	67.1	69.0	66.7	62.9	58.1	56.0

	Mean Temp. of Year	Mean Temp. of Summer	Mean Temp. of Winter
San Francisco	56.00°	60.0°	51.00°
Washington	56.07°	76.3°	36.05°

Difference in San Francisco............................. .9°

Difference in Washington............................. 36.25°

Rainy Season

While we have two seasons, the dry and the wet, a very general impression regarding the latter needs correcting. Eastern people suppose that when the rains once begin they are continuous for six months. Rains may begin in October or November and continue for several days. Then we enjoy a period of several weeks when the air is free from dust, the roadbeds are hardened, the vegetation takes a new start, and the sun beams over a land of balmy luxuriance.

The following figures, representing the mean temperature of January and July, and the average annual rainfall (in inches) in Mentone, St. Paul, St. Augustine (Florida), and also in San Diego, Santa Barbara, Los Angeles, and Monterey (California), afford a subject well worthy of consideration.

	TEMPERATURE		
	January Degrees	July Degrees	RAINFALL Inches
San Diego	57	65	10
Santa Barbara	56	66	15
St. Augustine	59	77	55
St. Paul	13	73	30
Mentone	30	69	23
Los Angeles	55	67	18
Monterey	50	65	14

RAINFALL

The very finest climate in California will be found near the coast between the 34th parallel and the 38th parallel, taking in Los Angeles, Santa Barbara, Monterey, Santa Cruz and San Francisco. Again taking the center of this region which will be in and around Monterey in latitude 36°, 37', the following table shows the maximum, minimum and mean temperatures and rainfall for each month during the eight years, as follows:

MONTHS	Temperature for the Month			RAINFALL
	Maximum	Minimum	Mean	
1884				
January............	64.00	31.00	49.51	2.60
February..........	74.00	28.00	50.60	5.34
March.............	70.00	40.00	54.51	6.08
April.............	71.00	45.00	56.95	3.75
May..............	78.00	50.00	59.68	.36
June	69.00	56.00	61.13	1.80
July..............	76.00	53.00	61.01	......
August......	77.00	50.00	61.11	.07
September........	77.00	44.00	57.52	.03
October	77.00	40.00	54.39	1.81
November	71.00	40.00	52.23	.30
December	68.00	30.00	52.01	5.33
1885				
January......	65.00	35.00	49.90	1.22
February.	68.00	35.00	52.46	.09
March..	81.00	41.00	55.95	.40
April...............	76.00	43.00	58.43	1.70
May...............	77.00	52.00	59.35	.20
June..............	69.00	52.00	59.40	.03
July..............	75.00	54.00	62.50	......
August.............	76.00	53.00	60.31	......
September........	72.00	44.00	59.10	......
October......	72.00	41.00	58.13	......
November..	74.00	38.00	56.52	6.65
December	73.00	35.00	54.29	1.73
1886				
January....	70.00	30.00	52.10	3.09
February...........	75.00	39.00	54.70	1.14
March...	72.00	33.00	52.10	2.52
April...............	70.00	42.00	56.10	3.39
May...............	72.00	50.00	59.90	.08
June...............	78.00	51.00	59.90	......
July..............	76.00	55.00	60.80	......
August.............	79.00	54.00	60.12	......
September........	79.00	47.00	58.90	......
October......	72.00	38.00	54.55	.70
November.	71.00	32.00	50.90	.78
December	70.00	36.00	51.70	.60
1887				
January	68.00	31.00	49.60	.35
February.	72.00	29.00	48.30	4.92
March.............	80.00	35.00	53.65	.60
April...............	78.00	43.00	53.30	1.16
May...............	85.00	50.00	56.51	......
June...............	80.00	55.00	62.00	.05
July..............	76.00	55.00	61.60	......
August.............	74.00	54.00	62.10	......
September........	83.00	50.00	62.60	.25
October..	90.00	48.00	61.40	......
November.	74.00	38.00	57.50	1.35
December	66.00	37.00	51.51	1.81

We have necessarily a great variety of climates in a state extending through ten parallels of latitude, and in some places nearly the same number of parallels of longitude—32° to 40° North Latitude and 114° to 124° West Longitude.

VIEW OF OAKLAND

COMPARATIVE ANNUAL METEOROLOGY OF SAN FRANCISCO AND NEIGHBORHOOD

For the years of 1877, 1878, 1879, 1880, 1881 and 1882.

TEMPERATURES	1877	1878	1879	1880	1881	1882
Mean Temperature of the year....	56.29	55.28	55.11	53.69	55.62	54.49
Mean Temp.of warmest day.......	76.00	69.33	75.33	70.66	70.00	69.33
Mean Temperature of coldest day	41.63	37.00	33.66	41.00	42.00	35.00
Maximum Temp. for the year.....	96.00	84.00	93.00	89.00	87.00	84.00
Minimum Temp. for the year......	30.00	27.00	27.00	29.00	31.00	30.00
Greatest daily variation of Temp.	38.00	33.00	46.00	36.00	35.00	31.00
Least daily variation of Temp....	1.00	2.00	......	1.00	1.00	1.00
Greatest monthly range of Temp	47.00	46.00	46.00	48.00	40.00	42.00
Rainfall in inches for the year....	11.09	31.71	28.91	28.07	26.07	18.87
No. of clear and fair days for year	301	255	266	258	276	276
No. of cloudy days for year........	64	110	99	108	89	89

SEASONS	1877	1878	1879	1880	1881	1882
Mean Temperature of Spring......	55.18	55.73	56.15	52.97	56.35	54.12
Mean Temperature of Summer....	61.17	59.36	60.07	58.95	60.27	60.06
Mean Temperature of Autumn....	57.67	56.92	56.73	55.86	54.78	56.44
Mean Temperature of Winter......	50.39	50.12	47.60	45.38	51.10	46.80

The above table may be considered a fair average of the meteorological phenomena obtaining in the yellow territory along the coast (52° to 60°), with this exception, that in going north the rainfall increases while the temperature slightly decreases, and in going south the opposite is the case.

COMPARATIVE TEMPERATURE

Points in California and points in a corresponding latitude on the Atlantic Coast.

From this comparative temperature table it will be seen that California Climate is much more equable.

Mean of Year	Mean of Winter	Mean of Summer	Latitude	POINTS IN CALIFORNIA	POINTS ON ATLANTIC COAST	Latitude	Mean of Summer	Mean of Winter	Mean of Year
DEG.	DEG.	DEG.	DEG.			DEG.	DEG.	DEG.	DEG.
...	...	...	42	................Yreka	Boston..................	42	69	28	48
63	45	88	41	.... Redding	New York	41	71	31	51
64	48	83	40	...................Chico	Philadelphia..	40	72	34	52
60	49	74	39	............Sacramento	Baltimore.............	39	73	33	53
56	51	60	38	.......San Francisco	Washington..........	38	76	36	56
57	52	64	37	...........Monterey	Richmond	37	75	37	56
63	50	85	36	...................Tulare	Norfolk..............	36	74	36	54
61	53	68	35	.......Santa Barbara	Raleigh..............	35	76	42	60
65	58	73	34	..........Los Angeles	Atlanta	34	80	48	64
61	54	68	32	............San Diego	Savannah	32	81	53	67

Looking over that State from east to west and north to south, the following schedule will show the mean annual and the maximum and minimum temperatures, with the latitude and altitude of most of the points of interest in California :

LOCATION	Latitude	Altitude	ANNUAL TEMPERATURE		
			Average Maximum	Average Minimum	Mean
Anaheim	33.51	133	92.00	50.00	67.00
Auburn	38.57	1,360	83.00	39.00	58.00
Caliente	35.17	1,290	83.00	45.00	64.00
Calistoga	38.38	363	86.00	36.00	59.00
Chico	39.44	193	88.42	46.08	65.00
Colton	34.02	965	89.42	41.66	62.08
Colfax	39.08	2,422	85.42	41.50	56.91
Dunnigan	38.51	69	90.00	45.00	63.00
Fresno	36.45	292	90.12	45.00	64.34
Galt	38.18	50	88.00	43.00	62.00
Geysers	38.49	......	....	. .....	....
Gilroy	36.59	193	87.00	38.00	58.00
Indio	33.46	20	100.00	50.00	73.00
Keene	35.12	2,705	81.00	32.00	54.00
Livermore	37.42	485	88.00	39.00	58.00
Los Angeles	34.03	293	89.67	51.00	64.75
Martinez	38.02	10	76.00	42.00	56.00
Marysville	39.10	66	88.17	42.75	63.58
Merced	37.20	171	89.00	41.00	63.00
Mojave	35.02	2,751	87.00	47.00	63.00
Monterey	36.37	5	78.50	42.83	57.40
Napa	38.21	20	87.58	37.50	59.19
Oakland	37.49	12	69.33	42.58	54.75
Paso Robles	35.38	....	. .....	....	56.00
Redding	40.37	557	86.33	43.16	61.58
Red Bluff	39.08	308	90.50	45.67	64.00
Reno	39.31	4,497	72.00	32.00	49.00
Salinas	36.41	44	75.00	42.00	56.00
Sacramento	38.36	30	80.58	44.92	60.33
San Diego	32.45	....	82.83	47.50	61.00
Santa Barbara	34.26	30	81.00	46.18	60.00
San Mateo	37.34	22	78.00	44.00	54.00
San Luis Obispo	35.18	....	....	....	56.96
San Francisco	37.48	....	76.25	42.33	55.25
San Jose	37.21	91	83.08	39.83	56.75
Santa Cruz	36.58	18	82.67	42.42	58.08
Spadra	34.03	705	93.00	45.00	64.00
Stockton	37.58	23	79.50	41.50	58.00
Sumner	35.24	415	89.00	43.00	64.00
Summit	39.20	7,017	58.17	21.00	40.66
Tehachapi	35.06	3,964	78.00	32.00	52.00
Truckee	39.20	5,819	68.83	21.25	43.00
Tulare	36.13	282	87.00	43.00	64.00
Woodland	38.41	63	86.00	49.00	61.00
Yosemite Valley	37.47	....	....	....	....
Yuma	32.44	140	93.00	58.00	74.00

LOCALITIES IN THE OLD WORLD CORRESPONDING IN TEMPERATURE WITH POINTS IN CALIFORNIA

The following interesting table gives the annual temperature and latitude of corresponding places in the old world.

FROM 44 TO 52 DEGREES

CITY	LOCALITY	Mean Annual Temperature DEGREES	Latitude DEGREES
Carlstad	South-western Sweden	44	59
Dover	South-eastern England	45	43
Dantzig	North-eastern Prussia	46	54
Stromness	Orkney Isles	46	58
Breslau	South-eastern Prussia	46	51
Copenhagen	Denmark	46	55
Dresden	Austria	46	51
Edinburgh	South-eastern Scotland	47	55
Hamburg	Northern Germany	47	53
Dublin	Ireland	49	53
Munich	Bavaria	49	48
Prague	Bohemia	49	50
Leyden	Holland	50	52
Geneva	Switzerland	50	46
Frankfort-on-Main	Germany	50	50

The territory included in 44° to 52° is the higher Coast Ranges and the lower Sierras, the atmosphere of which is dry, pure and invigorating.

The mean Summer temperature is from 50° to 62°.

FROM 52 TO 60 DEGREES

CITY	LOCALITY	Mean Annual Temperature DEGREES	Latitude DEGREES
Turin	Northern Italy	53	45
Milan	Northern Italy	54	45
Toulouse	Southern France	55	43
Venice	North-eastern Italy	57	45
Constantinople	Turkey	57	41
Marseilles	Southeast France	57	43
Bologna	Northern Italy	57	44
Madrid	Central Spain	57	40
Mentone	South-eastern France	57	43
Toulon	Southern France	59	43
Florence	Northern Italy	59	43
Rome	Western Italy	59	41

FROM 60 TO 68 DEGREES

CITY	LOCALITY	Mean Annual Temperature DEGREES	Latitude DEGREES
Nice.................. .....South-eastern France..............		(a)	43
Naples....................South-western Italy.................		61	40
Lisbon................Portugal........................		61	38
Barcelonia.............North-eastern Spain................		63	41
Algiers...................Northern Africa......................		64	36
Gibraltar.................Southern Spain......................		64	36
Smyrna..................Western Asia Minor..............		65	35
Messina......... ....Sicily...................................		66	38

This territory (60° to 68°), extends on the Coast from San Diego to San Pedro at an average width of twenty-five miles, narrowing at the latter point to a few miles and extending north to Point Concepcion, also the valleys of the Sacramento and San Joaquin jointly from Sumner (latitude 35° 24′) to Redding (latitude 40° 37′) varying from forty to fifty miles in width and four hundred and fifty miles in length.

The mean Summer temperature of this region is from 68° to 72°, the mean Winter temperature from 45° to 55°.

FROM 68 TO 72 DEGREES

CITY	LOCALITY	Mean Annual Temperature DEGREES	Latitude DEGREES
Tunis.....................Northern Africa....................		68	37
Canton......... ....China..........		69	23
Las Palmas.............Canaries....		70	28
San Croix...............of Teneriffe..........		71	28
Cairo.....................Egypt...........		71	30
Macao...................China...........		72	22

This territory (68° to 72°) extends from Yuma to San Gorgonio along the line of the Southern Pacific Railway, and includes the larger portion of the south-eastern part of the State.

The mean Summer temperature of this region is from 80° to 88° and the mean Winter temperature 55° to 60°.

The territory running from 30° to 44° embraces the high timber Sierras and a portion of the North Coast Range extending from near Clear Lake to Oregon.

The territory running from 52° to 60° extends in a narrow strip along the Coast from near Point Concepcion (latitude 34°) to the Oregon line (latitude 42°). From

CLIFF HOUSE SCENE. SAN FRANCISCO

Point Concepcion in a southerly direction this belt leaves the Coast and trends in a south-easterly direction until near Tehachapi, where it divides, one branch running south to State line, the other running northeast, diminishing at State line in latitude 37°. This region is also represented along the foothills bordering the great valleys of the State, particularly the Sacramento and San Joaquin.

The mean Summer temperature of this territory is from 56° to 68°, and embraces a large number of the health resorts of the State, including nearly all the hot spring regions. Mean Winter temperature, 40° to 52°.

It will be observed from the following extensive monthly schedule that California compares favorably with the most noted health resorts of the world.

San Francisco having 330,000 inhabitants, 16.72 per 1,000 die. In Los Angeles where there are 80,000 people only 8.26 per 1,000 die, and in San Diego with 30,000 population there are only 6 die per 1,000. For the general mortality of 79 towns in California, the average is only 14.88 per 1,000.

Compare the figures with the mortality of the East and Europe.

In Manchester (N. H.)..................the mortality is		26.00	per 1,000
" Boston............................	"	"	23.80	"
" Fitchburg (Mass.)...................	"	"	29.00	"
" Danburry (Ct.).....................	"	"	27.30	"
" Albany (N. Y.).....................	"	"	20.51	"
" Long Island City....................	"	"	33.71	"
" New York............................	"	"	23.11	"
" Cleveland (O.)......................	"	"	23.62	"
" New Orleans........................	"	"	24.14	"
" Pensacola (Fla.)...................	"	"	26.40	"
" Raleigh (N. C.)....................	"	"	26.80	"
" Charleston (S. C.).................	"	"	33.10	"

BRITISH AMERICA

" Galt...............................	"	"	32.00	"
" Hull...............................	"	"	48.00	"
" Montreal...........................	"	"	25.95	"
" London.............................	"	"	18.82	"
" Liverpool	"	"	20.54	"
" Manchester.........................	"	"	29.68	"
" Glasgow (Scotland).................	"	"	20.32	"
" Dublin (Ireland)...................	"	"	22.76	"

EUROPE

" Genoa	"	"	26.67	"
" Havre..............................	"	"	37.95	"
" Naples.............................	"	"	39.59	"

With perfect sanitation such as we hope will soon be inaugurated in San Francisco, we do not hesitate in saying that the mortality will be reduced to 10 per 1,000 inhabitants. In Los Angeles, San Diego, San Jose, etc., the yearly mortality ranges from 5 to 10 per 1,000. In San Francisco however, many sick and dying people arrive from all over the coast and from the East, making the death-rate greater. But with perfect sewerage and the excellent purifying trade-winds, San Francisco will be one of the healthiest cities in the world.

MONSTER GRAPEVINE AT SANTA BARBARA

To thoroughly appreciate California one should leave the East in January or February; cross the Mississippi Valley where everything is bleak and desolate, and where the northwest wind whistles mournfully around house corners; then cross the broad Western prairies where the only sign of life to be seen is the thin, blue smoke floating upward from the snow-covered housetops; then over grim mountain ranges, dark snowsheds, and over frozen streams,

until the summit of the Sierras is reached, when the promised land gladdens the eye. Here are sunny slopes,
budding trees, hills carpeted with wild flowers, throngs of
song birds, cloudless blue skies, and life and warmth everywhere. Twenty years ago Bayard Taylor enjoyed this
experience, and wrote :

" Then let me purchase a few acres on the lowest slope
of these mountains, overlooking the valley, and with a distant gleam of the bay : let me build a cottage embowered
in acacia and eucalyptus, and the tall spires of the Italian
cypress. Let me leave home when the Christmas holidays
are over, and enjoy the balmy Januarys and Februarys, the
heavenly Marches and Aprils, of my remaining years here,
returning only when May shall have brought beauty to the
Atlantic shores. There shall my roses outbloom those of
Paestum ; there shall my nightingale sing, my orange
blossoms sweeten the air, my children play and my best
poem be written. "

Thy tawney hills shall bleed their purple wine,
  Thy valleys yield their oil ;
And Music with her eloquence divine,
  Persuade thy sons to toil.

Till Hesper, as he trims his silver beam,
  No happier land shall see ;
And Earth shall find her old Arcadian dream
  Restored again in thee !

—Bayard Taylor.